"Hey!" Esk exclaimed.

"Hay yourself, moo-brain!" the blanket said, forming a mouth on its surface. The blanket writhed and wrapped itself around his feet. Then it squeezed his legs and inched up his torso, constricting as it did. It did not pause in its squeezing as it spoke. Esk's legs were getting uncomfortable . . .

He thrust his legs apart, the ogre strength coming to him. The blanket tore—but then it fogged up and rose as a flying thing, hovering before him.

"Listen dung-head," its mouth said, "now I'm *really* going to make you sorry!"

## TOR BOOKS BY PIERS ANTHONY

| | |
|---|---|
| Alien Plot | Letters to Jenny |
| Anthonology | Prostho Plus |
| But What of Earth? | Race Against Time |
| Demons Don't Dream | Roc and a Hard Place |
| Faun & Games | Shade of the Tree |
| Geis of the Gargoyle | Shame of Man |
| Ghost | Steppe |
| Thyme | Triple Detente |
| Hasan | Vale of the Vole |
| Hope of Earth | Xone of Contention |
| Isle of Woman | Yon Ill Wind |

Zombie Lover

WITH ROBERT E. MARGROFF

| | |
|---|---|
| Dragon's Gold | Orc's Opal |
| Serpent's Silver | The E.S.P. Worm |
| Chimaera's Copper | The Ring |

Mouvar's Magic

WITH FRANCES HALL
Pretender

EDITED WITH RICHARD GILLIAM
Tales from the Great Turtle (Anthology)

WITH ALFRED TELLA
The Willing Spirit

WITH CLIFFORD A. PICKOVER
Spider Legs

WITH JAMES GOOLSBY AND ALAN RIGGS
Quest for the Fallen Star

WITH JULIE BRADY
Dream a Little Dream

WITH JO ANNE TAEUSCH
The Secret of Spring

# PIERS ANTHONY

# VALE
## OF THE
# VOLE

**TOR**®
*fantasy*

A TOM DOHERTY ASSOCIATES BOOK
NEW YORK

This is a work of fiction. All the characters and events portrayed in this book are either products of the author's imagination or are used fictitiously.

VALE OF THE VOLE

A Tor Book
Published by Tom Doherty Associates, LLC
175 Fifth Avenue
New York, NY 10010

www.tor.com

Tor® a registered trademark of Tom Doherty Associates, LLC.

ISBN: 0-812-57496-6

First Tor edition: March 2000

Printed in the United States of America

0  9  8  7  6  5  4  3  2  1

This novel is dedicated
to the nieces and nephews
I neglected before:

Erin and Caroline
Jenifer and Paul
Leigh and David

# CONTENTS

# I

# METRIA

It wasn't always easy, being the son of an ogre and a nymph. Sometimes the ogre started smashing things just for the joy of it, or squeezing the juice from stones one-handed, making an awful mess. Sometimes the nymph was rather empty-minded, or threw a tantrum. That was why Esk had made this cosy hideout that no one else knew about. Whenever things became too difficult at home, he came here to relax and unwind. He loved his parents, but there was virtue in solitude too.

He paused to look about and listen carefully. He didn't want any creature of Xanth, tame or wild, seeing him enter, because then the location would be no secret, and sooner or later his folks would learn of it, and his privacy would be lost.

His hideout was in the hollow trunk of a dead beerbarrel tree. He had been lucky: he had been in the vicinity in the month of AwGhost, when barrel trees gave up the ghost if they were going to, and had seen the spirit departing.

"Aw, Ghost!" he had exclaimed in the classic ogre manner, and that had enchanted the tree so that he could take over the husk without creating a local commotion. He had cut a door in the fat trunk that sealed tightly so that it didn't show from outside, and made vents so that the steamy beer smell could dissipate; his mother, Tandy, would never understand if he came home reeking of beer! Then he had set straw in the bottom, and brought in pillows from a nearby pillow bush, and carved decorative scenes in the walls, and made it perfect. He was rather proud of himself; his only regret was that he could not afford to boast of his accomplishment, because of the necessity for secrecy.

All seemed clear. He hooked his nails into the crevice and pulled the door open. It was a small door, with an irregular outline, so that its contour was not obvious. He ducked down to step through, then drew it carefully closed behind. He stepped across the floor and dropped onto his nest of pillows.

"Ouch!"

Esk jumped. "Who said that?" he demanded.

"Get your fat mule off me!" The voice came from below.

He looked but saw only pillows. "My fat what?"

"Your fat donkey!" the voice snapped. "Pony, horse, jack-ass, whatever—off!"

Esk finally got a glimmer of the word that was being sought. He got quickly off the pillows. "Where are you?"

The pillow shifted outline. A mouth formed in its center. "Here, you oaf! What did you think you were doing, putting gross anatomy like that in my face?"

"Well, I—"

"Never mind. Just don't do it again, moron."

"But pillows are *supposed* to be—"

"Oh? Did you ever ask the pillows' opinion about that?"

"Well, actually, no, but—"

"So there, imbecile! Now get out and let me sleep."

Esk got out. Then, as he wended his way home, he pondered. How had he been able to talk to a pillow? He knew of only one person who could talk to an object, and that was the King of Xanth, Dor. Since it was generally understood that talents did not repeat, except in the case of the curse fiends, that meant that it wouldn't be Esk's talent. Beside that, he already had a talent: that of protesting. Sometimes his mother said he protested too much, but she did not deny it was magic. Since no one had two magic talents, that, too, eliminated the possibility of talking to inanimate things.

Finally he worked it out. He was not the smartest person, being quarter ogre, but he never let go of a problem, being half human, and usually was able to come to some kind of settlement, however crude. It wasn't his magic, but the pillow's magic. He must have picked a special pillow, without realizing: one that was alive. All he needed to do was take it back out to the pillow bush and exchange it for another, and his problem would be solved.

Reassured, he continued on toward home, having forgotten whatever problem had brought him to his hideout. As he neared it he smelled the delicious odor of purple bouillon. That meant that his father, Smash, had gone into his full ogre guise and foraged for the makings. Smash was actually only half ogre, for Esk's grandparents on that side had been Crunch Ogre and an actress from the curse fiends. But when Smash got ogreish, no one could tell him from a full ogre; he swelled up horrendously and burst out of his trousers. Tandy, however, being of nymphly stock, preferred Smash as a man, so usually that was what he seemed to be.

Esk could not voluntarily turn ogre, but when he got mad enough or desperate enough he did develop some ogre strength. It never lasted long, but of course it didn't need to; one strike by an ogreishly-powered fist could pulverize the trunk of a rock maple tree. Similarly, he was normally inept at acting, but when he really had to he could become temporarily proficient. That was his heritage from his curse fiend grandmother. Most of the time it was his human heritage that dominated, since he was part human through both of his parents. He was a pretty ordinary person, with gray eyes and nondescript brown hair. He often wished he were otherwise, but really had no choice; he was obviously not destined for any sort of greatness.

But there was no use worrying about that; there was purple bouillon to be eaten!

Two days later, being bored, Esk returned to his hideout. He entered and checked the pillows. They all looked normal. "Which one of you is the live one?" he inquired, but had no answer.

He shrugged. He picked up the whole mass of them and took them out to the pillow bush, unceremoniously dumping them beside it. Then he picked several new ones. He had to do this periodically anyway, so they didn't get dirty and stale. He carried these to his tree and plopped them down inside.

He hesitated, then eased himself down on them. Contrary to what the living pillow had said, his posterior was not fat; in retrospect he wished he had corrected the pillow about that matter. But he always thought up the smart responses way too late. That, again, was part of his heritage: neither ogres nor nymphs were known for their quickness of wit.

He was hungry, so he brought out a pie he had picked some time ago. It was a humble pie, and they were always best when properly seasoned. This one was decked with sodden raisins, and had a crust that was rocklike, while its main body seemed to be decomposing. It was definitely ready for consumption.

He brought it to his mouth and took an ogreish bite. His teeth came down, dug in—and the pie erupted in his face. Raisins popped out and flew at his eyes, and the crust writhed against his lips. "Get your ugly cat out of here!" the pie exclaimed.

"My ugly what?" Esk asked, startled.

"Your ugly kitten, feline, grimalkin, tabby—"

"Oh, you mean my ugly puss?" he inquired, catching on.

"Your ugly whatever," the pie agreed, forming a wide mouth. "Just what did you think you were doing, ogreface?"

"Ogreface?" Esp repeated, appreciating the compliment. Then he realized that the pie probably hadn't meant it that way. "I was trying to—"

"Oh you were, you! Well, don't do it again!"

"But—"

"You never asked the pie whether it wanted to be chewed on, did you?"

"But it's humble pie! It's meant to be eaten!"

"A likely story. Now get your dim-witted face out of here so I can rest."

"Listen, pieface, this is *my* hideout!" Esk said, developing a smidgeon of heat. "I just tossed out an obnoxious pillow, and I'll do the same with you! You sure aren't very humble!"

"You just try to toss this cookie, and you'll be sorry, bean-brain!"

That did it. Esk carried the pie to the door, pushed the door open, and skated the disk out into the forest. Then he plumped down on his bed of pillows for a snooze.

It was a moderately cool day, and while true ogres loved cold weather, Esk didn't. He cast about until he found the tattered old blanket he had salvaged for this purpose, and drew it over him.

The blanket writhed and wrapped itself around his feet. Then it squeezed his legs, and inched up his torso, constricting as it did.

"Hey!" Esk exclaimed.

"Hay yourself, moo-brain!" the blanket said, forming a mouth on its surface. But it did not pause in its squeezing; Esk's legs were getting uncomfortable.

Abruptly concerned, he thrust his legs apart, the ogre strength coming to him. The blanket tore—but then it fogged and rose up as a flying thing, hovering before him. "Listen, dung-head," its mouth said, "now I'm *really* going to make you sorry!"

But Esk's ogre dander was up. He grabbed the blanket with both hands. "We'll see about that, threadface!" Then he tore it asunder.

The pieces fogged again. The whole thing became vapor. This time it re-formed into the shape of a demoness. "You're stronger than you look, bug-wit. But how long do you think you can oppose me?"

"What wit?" Esk asked, confused again.

"Flea-wit, ant-wit, chigger-wit—"

"Oh, nitwit!"

"Whatever. Why don't you answer the question?"

Now at last Esk caught on. "The pillow—the pie—they were all you! You assumed their forms!"

"Of course I did, genius," she agreed. "I was trying to get rid of you gently. But now it's no more Miss Nice Gal. I'm going to twist you into a pretzel and feed you to a dragon." In her natural form she had arms and hands, which were now reaching for him.

"Dragons don't eat pretzels," he said, realizing he was in

trouble. Demons (or demonesses) were notorious; they had inhuman strength and no conscience, and they could pass right through solid walls. If he had realized what he was dealing with, he would have left her alone. Now it was too late.

"I'll jam you down its mouth anyway," she said grimly. "Maybe it will forgive me in a century or two." The hands closed on his neck and squeezed.

But this stimulated his ogre strength to full potency. Contrary to popular lore, ogres didn't really like getting twisted into pretzels, whatever they might do to others. Esk grabbed her wrists and wrenched them apart. "Who are you?" he demanded.

"I am the Demoness Metria," she replied, fogging again. Her arms and hands reappeared at his throat, leaving his own hands empty. "DeMetria for short. Who are you?"

Esk grabbed her wrists again, and wrenched them outward again. "I am Eskil Ogre, and I'm not going to let you choke me."

"That's what you think, mortal," she said. Her substance fogged yet again and re-formed, and this time her arms were linked by a length of thin rope. She hooked this over his head and looped it around his neck. "You can't get this off before you're done for."

"No!" Esk gasped.

Now she seemed startled. "No?" Her grip relaxed.

Esk balled a fist and smashed her in the face. The blow was solid, but her head simply folded back on the neck, as if hinged, then snapped back into place as he withdrew his arm. She looked slightly aggravated.

"No," he repeated. "I protest it."

She reconsidered. "Well, maybe not. I suppose it would be pointless to kill you; your body would only stink up the region, and I don't care to haul it far enough so the smell wouldn't carry." The cord dissolved into vapor and coalesced about her arms; it was evidently part of her substance.

"Well, I'm going to throw you out of here!" Esk said, his ogre aspect still in force.

"I'd like to see you try it, mundaneface."

Mundaneface! Her insults were getting more effective. That kept his ogre aspect in force. "I'll try it!"

He tried it. He grabbed her about the middle and hauled her off her feet. Then he paused. Her body was humanoid and naked and voluptuous, and was now tightly pressed against him. He had been distracted by her words and actions, but now was noticing her shape. This was a new experience.

"Well, now," she said, smiling. "I didn't realize that you wanted to be friendly. Just let me get your clothes off—"

He dropped her. "Just get out!" he exclaimed, disgruntled.

"Forget it, junior. I found this place and it's mine."

"I *made* it and it's mine!" he retorted.

She arched an eyebrow. "You made a beerbarrel tree?"

"Well, not that, but I adapted it after it gave up its spirit. That's close enough."

"Well, I like it, but I don't like you, so I'm going to get rid of you."

"No."

She paused, studying him. "Ah, that's your magic, isn't it! When you say 'no,' you stop a creature from doing what she intends. That's why I'm changing my mind, against my better judgment."

"Yes." His talent was not exactly magician class, but it served him in good stead when he needed it.

"So I'd better not make any more threats because you'll just say no to them," she continued. "But I'll bet it isn't all inclusive. You can't say 'no' to the whole category of what I might try to do to get you out, but you can say it to each individual thing as I try it."

"Yes." She was catching on with dismaying rapidity. Obviously there was no ogre blood in her lineage.

"So I'll just have to find a way to make you want to leave," she concluded. "I can't hurt you directly, but you can't hurt me either, so we're even, for now."

"Why are you here?" he asked plaintively.

"Because it's getting too annoying back where I come from," she said. "The hummers, you know."

"The what?"

"Never mind. Mortals can't hear them, generally. But they drive demons crazy. They've gotten really bad recently, there in the Vale of the Vole, despite all we've done to eradicate them. So I've had enough; I've moved to where I can be comfortable, after my fashion."

"But you're trying to take the place where *I* can be comfortable, after *my* fashion," he protested.

"So sue me."

"What?"

"It's a mundane term. It means 'What are you going to do about it, stink-nose?"

"I don't understand. Is Sue a girl?"

She laughed, her whole torso jiggling. "I suppose we're stuck here together, junior. Might as well make the best of it. Maybe we'll even get to like each other, though that may be stretching a point. Come, let me initiate you into the ways of demon sex." She advanced on him.

"No!" he exclaimed.

She stopped. "There's that magic of yours again! I really wasn't going to hurt you, you know, this time. I can be very affectionate, when I pretend to be. Let me demonstrate."

"No." He was afraid of her now, as he had not been before, and ashamed for his fear. It wasn't because he thought she would use a pretext to get close to him and then try to choke him again; it was because he was afraid she would do exactly what she threatened, and that he would like it. He didn't trust a demon-stration.

She eyed him speculatively. "How old are you, Esk?"

"Sixteen."

"And I'm a hundred and sixteen, but who's counting? You're old enough, in mortal terms, and I'm young enough, in immortal terms. Why don't you let me buy this den from you, and pay for it with experience? I can show you exactly what it's all about, so that you will never have to embarrass yourself by being clumsy with a mortal girl."

Esk barged by her, dived out the door, and headed for home. Only when he was well away from the hideout did he ask himself why. Was he afraid that she would somehow lead him into some much worse embarrassment than he could guess? Or that he thought that what she offered was simply wrong? But *was* it wrong? He wasn't sure.

He thought about asking his parents about the matter. But then he'd have to tell them about his hideout, which he didn't want to do. Also, he suspected that they just wouldn't understand. His mother had never said much about it, but he understood that a male demon had once approached her, and that she had been horrified. He could guess how she would react to news of a demoness's approach to her son. She might even throw one of her tantrums at him, and that would hurt. His father loved those tantrums, because they reminded him of ogre slaps, but an ogre slap could knock a grown tree askew or put a network of cracks in a rock.

So he kept silent. Maybe Metria would tire of his hideout and go away. Demons were known to be inconstant, after all.

Several days later he ventured again to the hideout. He entered cautiously. There was no sign of the demoness. But he knew that she could be concealed as anything; only time would tell whether she really was gone.

He sat on the pillows, and there was no outcry. He shook out his blanket, with no protest. He found a piece of redberry pie and ate it without event. He began to hope.

It was surprising how quickly boredom set in. One thing about his experience with Metria: it had been interesting, in more than one way. Now that it was too late, he wondered whether he had been mistaken in turning down her offer. She might have provided him with some phenomenal experience!

He dug out his game of pebbles. His collection of stones had served well in past times to wile away dull hours. They were of several different colors, and he had fashioned a game by drawing them out of the bag one at a time and setting them down on the floor in patterns. Each stone had to be set next to one of its own color to form a line or curve. The object was for one color to circle another. He might draw several red stones in succession, not looking at each until it was clear of the bag, and Red would make progress against White; then White would produce several and reverse the advantage. Blue and Green and Gray were also in there fighting. Sometimes the colors made alliances, ganging up against each other. The game could get quite exciting, as he animated the personalities of the colors in his mind. The patterns could become quite convoluted.

He brought out the first stone. It was glistening black. He set it down, starting the game.

"Hey, freak, what do you think you're doing?" the stone asked.

He snatched it up and thrust it back into the bag and twisted the opening tight, trying to seal it in. But smoke issued through the material and swirled before him, and soon Metria was there. "I thought you'd given up and left it to me," she remarked.

"I thought *you'd* given up," he retorted.

"Demons never give up unless they want to. Come on, I really want this place. Can't we deal?"

"No." But then his foolish curiosity overcame him. "Why are you so insistent on this place, instead of just becoming a bird and perching on a branch or something?"

"This place is secluded and comfortable, and other creatures don't know about it. We demons need to spend most of our time in solid state, and it's easiest to do it while sleeping, so a good private place is valuable."

"I thought demons didn't need to sleep."

"We don't *need* to sleep, mortal. But we *can* sleep if we choose, and often we do. This is a perfect sleeping place, so I mean to have it."

"Well, I don't mean to let you have it."

Her lips formed a pout. "I'm trying to be nice about it, Esk. It's an effort. Suppose I give you *two* great experiences?"

"Two?"

"Sex and death."

"You already tried to kill me!"

"I mean the other way around. You can kill me, after you enjoy me."

"Demons can't be killed." But he found himself guiltily intrigued.

"We can't die, but we can do extremely realistic emulations of dying. You can choke me, and I'll gag and turn purple and my eyeballs will bulge way out and I'll struggle with diminishing force until finally I sag down and stop breathing and my body turns cold. It will be just like throttling a living woman."

"Ugh," Esk said, revolted.

"Well, what do you want, then? Three great experiences? Name your stupid price."

He was tempted to ask about the third experience, but decided that he probably would not like it any better than the second. "No."

"I'll even throw in the first one free," she said. "Just so you can fully appreciate what I offer. I can assume any form you wish, just to make it interesting. Is there any particular mortal girl you've been wanting to—"

"No!" he cried.

"Look, there's no obligation! I just want to demonstrate my good faith! I really want this den, without getting bothered all the time. I know an awful lot that you could hardly learn in a year, let alone in a day, and—"

"No!"

"Don't be so stuffy." She inhaled, making her breasts stand out splendidly, and leaned toward him.

"I said no three times," Esk said querulously. "Why aren't you stopping?"

"Because I'm not doing, I'm persuading," she said. "And you want to be persuaded, don't you, Esk?"

He was afraid that anything he said at this point would be a lie. He lurched out of the hideout, ashamed of himself. He *had* to get rid of the demoness, before she succeeded in corrupting him.

He stayed away a full ten days this time. But he felt out of sorts without the use of his hideout, and realized that he was actually giving it up to her without a fight. He had to go there and pester her until she left, instead of allowing her to do it to him.

He braced himself and went to the beerbarrel tree. All was quiet, outside and in, but he knew this was no certain indication of her absence. He sat on the pillows, shook out the blanket, ate a scrap of cheese, dumped all the colored stones out on the floor, and poked everything he could think of. There was no response from any of it. Could she really be gone this time? Or was she merely lying low, waiting until he relaxed, before appearing with some new offer? How many such offers could he resist, before he succumbed to the tempation. How many did he *want* to resist?

Already she was corrupting him, and she wasn't even trying!

Still, if she never manifested, then the hideout was his, even if she was here. Except that if she should be watching and listening to everything he did here, how could he ever really relax? He had to be sure she was gone, and not just out doing some temporary mischief elsewhere.

He heard something, faint in the distance outside the tree. He held his breath, listening.

"Eskil! Eskil!"

That was his mother's voice! She was searching for him, calling his name, and if he didn't show up soon, she was apt to discover this hideout! He scrambled out and ran to her, not directly but in a roundabout way, so as not to give away the location of his secret place.

"What is it, Mother?" he called when the direction was suitable.

Tandy turned to face him. She had kept much of her nymphly shape, and was a pretty figure of a woman. There was the corruption of the demoness again: How could he presume to notice such a thing about his own mother?

"Oh, Eskil," she said. "You must come home right away! It's horrible!"

He was gripped by sudden alarm. "What's horrible?"

"Your father—some other ogre smashed him, I think, and—"

His alarm became horror. "He's hurt?"

"He may not survive the hour! We have to get some healing elixir before it's too late!"

"I know where there's a spring!" he cried. "I'll go get it!" He took the little bottle she carried, and charged off through the forest, his heart pounding from more than the exertion. His father, dying!

He reached the spring and swooped with the bottle dipping out the healing elixir. Then he ran back toward the house.

He charged in. "Where is he?" he cried, panting.

Tandy turned from the table, where she was preparing leftover soup. "Where is who, dear?" she inquired mildly.

"Father! Smash Ogre! I have the elixir!"

Smash emerged from another room. He was in his human mode. "You called me, son?"

Esk looked from one to the other. "You—you're not hurt!"

Tandy's brow furrowed. "Whatever gave you the idea your father was hurt, Esk?"

"But you were just telling me, out in the forest—"

"I have not left the house all afternoon, dear," she said reprovingly.

"But—" But obviously it was true. His mother never interrupted leftover soup for anything short of a dire emergency, and it seemed there had been not even a mild emergency. How could he have thought—?

Then he understood. Metria! She could emulate anything or anyone! She had pretended to be his mother, and he had been completely fooled.

"I—I guess I had a dream," he said awkwardly. "I thought Father was hurt, so I fetched some elixir—"

"That was nice of you, dear," Tandy said, and returned her attention to her soup.

"But save the elixir," Smash said. "Never can tell when that stuff'll be handy."

"Uh, sure," Esk said, looking for a stopper for the vial. But now the vial fuzzed into vapor, and the elixir spilled to the floor. What a fool he had been!

Next day he returned to the hideout. "Metria!" he bawled. "Show yourself, you damned demoness!"

She appeared. "Why, I do believe you are having a change of mind," she said. "You never complimented me like that before."

"You made me think my father was dying!" he accused her.

"Of course, Esk. If one thing doesn't work, I try another. How else am I to be left in peace here?"

"You mean you're going to keep on doing things like that? Making me think my folks are in trouble?"

"Why of course not, Esk! Obviously that didn't work either, because here you are again."

He didn't trust this. "Then what—"

"I'll just have to do something real to your folks, so you won't have time to bother me."

It took only a moment for him to grasp that, despite his quarter-ogre heritage. "No!"

"That's a category denial, Esk. You know you can't enforce that. I'll get your folks one way or another, in time. You can't watch them both all the time."

He leaped at her. She started to dematerialize, then reconsidered. Instead she met him, flinging her arms about him. "But I'm still willing to deal for the den, and even to give you the free sample, if—"

The force of his leap was carrying them on, and now they landed together on the pillows. Metria wrapped her legs about his body and her arms about his head, hauling him in to her for a kiss. "I'm really being more than reasonable, for my kind," she whispered against his cheek. "All I want is to be left alone in my den."

"*My* den!" he gasped.

"Which I am offering a generous price for," she said. "Most men would grasp most eagerly at the chance, not to mention the flesh. Now just let me get these clothes off you—"

He wrenched himself away from her. "No!"

She sighed. "Well, no one can say I didn't try. I really have nothing against your folks, because they don't even know about the den. But if that's what it takes to—"

"No! I'll—I'll leave you alone! You leave them alone!"

"Why how nice of you, Esk," she said. "You are becoming reasonable. I shall be glad to leave all of you alone, as long as you do not come here."

Esk got to his feet, turned around, and walked away from her. He knew he had lost, and it galled him, but there seemed to be no other way.

Could he trust her to leave his folks alone? The more he thought about it, as he walked, the more he distrusted it. The demoness might decide she liked the house better than the tree, and act against the family anyway. Demons had no conscience; that was their great strength and weakness.

He had to get rid of Metria. Only then could he be quite sure that his family was safe. But how? Every time he tried to make her move, she tried to seduce him, or worse, and she seemed a lot closer to victory than he. Where could he find the answer?

Then he realized where. He would go ask the Good Magician Humfrey! Humfrey knew everything, and for one year's service would answer any question. It was a steep price, but would be worth it to save his family from the possible malice of the demoness.

His decision made, Esk felt better. Tomorrow he would start his trip to the Good Magician's castle.

# 2

# CHEX

Tandy hadn't wanted to let him go, of course, and he had been unable to tell her that it was to protect her and Smash and their house that he was doing it. So he had told another aspect of the truth: that it was time for him to take his Ogreish Rite of Passage (obviously the word was "right," but ogres weren't much on spelling) and perform some mighty act of destruction to become an adult, and so he wanted to go to the Good Magician to get advice. Smash had endorsed that enthusiastically, so Tandy really couldn't prevent it. And, in a sense, it was true; it *was* time for him to assert himself, and he *did* need advice. But the great act of destruction he contemplated was reversed; he actually wanted to prevent it by getting rid of Metria before she hurt someone. He hoped that wasn't too great a stretch of the reality.

"But the Good Magician requires a year of service for each answer!" Tandy had protested. "I know, because I served that year, when—"

"When he put you together with me," Smash had reminded her. That had ended that; of course she wasn't going to claim that the Good Magician had served her ill. He had indeed solved her problem by providing her with a companion who could stand up to the demon who theatened her.

And what companion could enable Esk to stand up to Metria? he wondered. What he really needed was a spell to make her simply go away and stay away, no questions asked. He would ask for it at the outset, so that he could banish her immediately; then he would serve out his year, satisfied that there was no threat to his folks.

Now he hiked west through the brush, garbed in the gray shirt and trousers his mother had insisted he wear, which matched his gray eyes. Such things were important to mothers. He was seeking one of the magic paths that led to the Good Magician's castle. They were enchanted to protect all travelers, so the trip should be easy enough. Here near home he was familiar with the land, so readily avoided problems, but when he hit strange territory he wanted to be on a path. Even as minor a nuisance as the curse burrs could be bad, if one stumbled into a bed of them unaware. Major threats, such as large dragons—well, it was best just to avoid those.

He found a path, but distrusted it, because it was too convenient. Sure enough, it led directly to a tangle tree. A full ogre might tramp down it anyway, being too stupid to know the difference, and bash the tree, being too strong to care, but Esk was only a quarter ogre and had to exercise some discretion. So he shunned the path—and sure enough, he blundered into a patch of curse burrs.

"Confound you!" he exclaimed as one dug into his leg. That one hesitated, then dropped off; his curse had been pretty mild. Too bad he didn't have any harpy blood; a harpy could curse so villainously that the foliage around her dirty body smoked. Curse burrs never bothered harpies!

Three more burrs were pricking him. "Go jump in the lake!" he exclaimed, and one fell off, reluctantly. "Your parent is a weed!" and another loosened. "May a dragon roast you!" and the third let go.

His problem was that he had never learned to curse effectively. Tandy, being a gentle creature, had not been any suitable role model in this respect, and Smash was not all that verbal; when annoyed, he simply turned ogre and bashed whatever bothered him. Esk knew that his education had been

neglected in this respect, but it was rather late to do much
about it.

There were two more burrs pricking his ankles. They were
difficult to reach, because when he bent over his backpack
tended to shift, so he sat down. Unfortunately, there were
more burrs below, and what the demoness had termed his
mule landed solidly on them.

"#©£$¢%¶Ø¿!!" he bawled, sailing up. The burrs flew
from him like *zzapping* wiggles, leaving little vapor trails behind.

Esk stared after them. He hadn't realized that he knew language like that! Of course, he had been stung hard in an
indelicate place, so had reacted involuntarily. Still . . .

He tried to recall what he had said, but could not. Apparently this was like his ogre strength or his curse fiend acting
that came only in extreme need. Too bad.

He resumed his trek, and in due course encountered a
promising path. It did not lead to a tangle tree or a dragon's
lair, so seemed good. He wasn't sure how to tell whether it
was enchanted, but if no hostile creatures appeared on it, he
would assume that it was.

He stopped for lunch. Tandy had made him blueberry sandwiches, his favorite, and current pie. His teeth received a
pleasant little shock when he bit into the pie and caused the
current to flow. The sandwiches were delightfully cold, because the berries had been harvested when blue with cold, in
the month of FeBlueberry, and retained their frigid nature.
Tandy had a special touch with food, which she said she had
learned while serving the Good Magician.

Well, maybe he would pick up useful skills too, while serving his term. By all accounts, the service the Magician required was not arduous, and was often beneficial to the server
in unanticipated ways. The monsters that came with questions
served as guardians, and Tandy had served as a housekeeper.
Smash Ogre had performed a task in lieu of a year, traveling
with Tandy and guarding her from danger. Esk would be willing to perform alternate service, especially in the company of
some young woman resembling his mother in certain respects.

But that reminded him of Metria, who had offered him
entirely too much companionship. He still wondered why he

had so resolutely refused her offer. It wasn't because he really valued his hideout; he could have fashioned another in a different region of the forest. Probably it was because he simply wasn't ready for the type of experience she offered—at least, not with a creature who was totally cynical about it. A real girl, with real feelings and sensitivities and concerns—that would have been most interesting. But a century-old unhuman creature who did it purely as a matter of bargaining—that was frightening. She could have gotten him fairly into it, then changed into a harpy or something, and laughed her demoniac head off. He did not trust her at all.

There, maybe, was the real key: trust. Demons were absolutely untrustworthy, because they had no souls; everyone knew that. The only safe way to handle a demon was to stay away from it, because there was no telling what it might do next. Metria had first tried to kill him, then to seduce him; now she threatened his family, and that only confirmed the popular wisdom. He hoped he reached the Good Magician's castle soon, so that he could set that matter right.

He completed his lunch and resumed walking. He did not know how far distant the Good Magician's castle was, but doubted that it was far. He knew a little geography, of course: his folks lived in the heart of Xanth, and to the southeast was Lake Ogre-Chobee, and Lake Wails to the east, and the great Gap Chasm to the north. The only direction remaining was west, where there was the Good Magician, and beyond him Castle Roogna, where King Dor lived. The King was a friend of Smash Ogre, but they hadn't been in touch for a while. Apparently King Dor had a child or two, and a pet dragon; that was about the extent of what was known.

There was a noise ahead. Esk paused, listening. That sounded like a small dragon, but it couldn't be, because it was on the path. But what else could pound and hiss like that? Now he smelled smoke, and that too suggested dragon. Dragons came in a number of varieties, adapted for land, water, and air, some were fire-breathers, some steamers, and some smokers. Suddenly he wished he were armed, but all he had was a walking staff.

The thing came into sight—and it was a dragon, a small brown smoker with bright claws and dusky teeth, because of

staining by the smoke. This was not the worst variety of
dragon, but any variety was trouble, because all dragons were
tough and hungry. What was it doing on the enchanted path?

Esk had no time to ponder, because the dragon was charg-
ing him, mouth agape. He hefted his staff, but it seemed
feeble even in the face of this rather small dragon; one chomp
would break the staff in two. He thought to jump out of the
way, but here the path was lined with curse burrs and worse.

The dragon scrambled right up to him, puffing smoke. It
was about Esk's own mass, and however small that might be
for a dragon, it was big enough to be a real threat to the
tender flesh of a man. The jaws were big and the teeth like
little daggers.

Those jaws and those teeth snapped at him. "No!" Esk said.

The dragon's snout moved aside, and the teeth chomped
on air. The smoky eyes looked startled. It was wondering how
it could have missed so ready a target. It reset itself and aimed
another chomp.

"No."

Again the bite missed. An angry plume of smoke issued
from the monster's mouth, bathing Esk and making him
cough. He fanned the air with his hands, dissipating the
smoke, but it clung to his clothing. Now he would smell like
a smoker!

The dragon, slow to grasp the nature of the opposition,
made a third attempt. Its jaws opened wide.

"No," Esk repeated, poking at the mouth with his staff.

The jaws froze in their open mode. They could not bite
down on the staff, because of Esk's magic. Disgruntled, the
monster backed away, and then it was able to close its mouth.

The dragon pondered. Just as the thought that perhaps it
should try once more started to percolate through the somewhat dense substance of its head, Esk said "no" once more.

This time the thought itself was balked. Out of sorts, the
little dragon moved on down the path, giving up on this particular prey.

Esk resumed his hike, disturbed. If this path was enchanted
against predators, why had the dragon been on it? If it was
not, was it the right one? He didn't want to be on the wrong

one. Yet it was the only path he had found; if it was wrong, where did it lead?

He sighed. For now, he would continue along it. Possibly it was an unenchanted tributary, and in due course it would intersect the enchanted one. If not—well, then he would simply have to scout cross-country for the right one.

As the day waned, the path gave no sign of merging with any other. It curved along contours and around large trees and crossed small streams just as if it had every business doing so. It certainly extended too far to be justified as a false path!

Then another little dragon appeared. Naturally it charged him. "No," he told it firmly several times, and finally it gave up and smoked on down the path.

*Two* dragons! One might have been a fluke, but two of a similar type? The enchantment was definitely flawed!

Now there was a notion: the spell might indeed exist, but have a glitch in it so that a certain type of creature could slip through. That would mean that this was after all the right path.

But as evening drew nigh, he worried. Even if it was the right path, there *were* dragons on it. How could he lie down and sleep, if a dragon might come upon him? He could only tell them no while he was awake; if he got chomped in the night he could cry no and stop it, but the original damage would still have been done. If he got chomped badly enough before he woke, he could be dead. Even a little dragon was nothing to ignore.

He concluded that he could not afford to sleep. Not until he knew it was safe.

Then he heard a commotion ahead. "Go away! Shoo! Shoo! Away!" It sounded like a woman.

He ran toward it. Soon he discovered not a woman but a centaur—a filly, with helplessly flapping wings and an ineffectively wielded staff in her hands. Another little dragon was attacking her, being held off only by the staff. The dragon evidently knew it could get by the staff before long. Smoke was puffing from it, as its internal fires heated.

Esk readied his own staff. "Get out of here!" he yelled at the dragon. Startled, it whipped around to face him, its smoke cutting off for a moment as it held its breath. Then, deciding that this was a possible rival for the prey, it let out its smoke with a ferocious growl and leaped at him.

"No!" Esk cried. The jaws snapped in air as the dragon drew its snout aside. It landed, disgruntled, beyond him. It started to turn back. "No," he repeated, and it traveled on away from him, too stupid to realize that this had not been its own decision.

"Oh thank you, traveler!" the filly said. "I don't know what I would have done, if—"

"Uh, sure," he said, looking at her more carefully. She had gray eyes and a brown mane, and the wings were gray, matching the eyes. She wore a petite knapsack, across which a sturdy bow was hung. The points of several arrows projected beside the knapsack. Evidently the dragon had come upon her so suddenly that she had not had a chance to set up with her bow. Her head was somewhat higher than his; this was because the human aspect of a centaur began above the equine aspect. Her shoulders were actually narrower than his.

Now he did a double take. *Wings?*

"Don't stare at me as if I'm a freak!" she exclaimed.

"I, uh, just never saw—that is—"

"My father is a hippogryph," she said. "I inherit my wings from him."

"Uh, yes, of course," he said. "But why didn't you just fly away?"

She put her face in her hands and burst into tears.

Completely discomfited, Esk stood on one foot and then the other, uncertain what to do.

In a moment her mood shifted somewhat. "I *can't* fly!" she said despairingly. "These wings just don't have enough lift!"

"Uh, sorry," he said awkwardly.

"Anyway, thank you for rescuing me from the dragon. I didn't expect anything like that here; the path is supposed to be safe."

"That's what I thought," Esk said. "But that's the third little smoker I've seen on it."

She brushed back her mane, which was just like the tresses of a human woman, and took a deep breath, which accentuated a bosom that also resembled that of a human woman, only more so. Centaurs, of course, did not wear clothing; they considered it to be a human affectation. "Hello," she said brightly. "I'm Chex."

"I'm Esk."

"Did you notice that we match?"

"Hair and eyes," he agreed. *And wings*, he added mentally; they matched his suit in color and, to a moderate but reasonable extent, in texture.

"My father is Xap Hippogryph. My mother is Chem Centaur."

She was making the introduction easy enough! "My father is Smash Ogre. My mother is Tandy Nymph."

"So you're a crossbreed too!" she exclaimed happily.

"Quarter ogre, half human, quarter nymph," he agreed. "The human portion is half curse fiend, technically. I'm going to see the Good Magician."

"Why so am I! What a coincidence!"

"Well, we are on the same path."

"Only one of us must be going the wrong way."

"Well, I live east of his castle, so I'm going west," Esk said.

"And I live west of it, so I'm going east."

They stood there, considering. "Maybe there's a turnoff one of us missed?" Esk said after a pause.

"That must be so," Chex agreed. "I was traveling pretty fast; I could have trotted past one."

"I was traveling slowly; I don't think I did."

"Then let's go west," she said brightly. "And look to the sides."

"You are easy to get along with," he remarked. They walked west, with him parallel to her front section. This was a little crowded on the path, but there didn't seem to be any better way to do it.

"I'm just mostly tired of traveling alone," she confessed. "That dragon—how did you get rid of it so easily? I couldn't make it quit."

"I just told it no. That's my talent—to protest things. The effect doesn't last long, but dragons aren't very smart, so it works well enough."

"I wish I had a talent," she said. "It used to be that centaurs weren't supposed to have magic, but now it's acceptable for the younger ones. My female parent is a mapmaker; she can project a map of anything. She told me how to reach the Good Magician's castle; it's hard to imagine that she could have been mistaken."

"Geography changes," he said. "Tangle trees make new paths all the time when the old ones get too familiar, and streams change their courses when their old beds get too rocky. The path must have changed since your mother surveyed it."

"That must be it," she agreed.

"And you probably have a talent; it just hasn't manifested yet."

"You're pretty easy to get along with yourself," she remarked with a smile that became her marvelously.

"I suppose I'm tired of traveling alone too." They laughed together. Esk realized with a tinge of guilt that he was finding it much easier to relate to this filly than to a real girl. Perhaps this was because nothing much was expected of a relationship between a man and a centaur; it was strictly convenience and company.

Now night was closing. "Perhaps we should stop for supper and a place to sleep," Chex said. "Do you think there will be other dragons?"

Esk had been thinking the same thing; his legs were tired. "I had feared I couldn't afford to sleep; maybe now we can take turns watching."

"Yes!" she agreed gladly.

They foraged for fruit, then set their watches: Chex would stand guard until she got sleepy, then would wake him for a similar spell. She assured him that she would not fall asleep without knowing it; some centaurs slept on their feet, but her legs tended to buckle, waking her.

Esk retreated to some bushes for natural functions, which modesty Chex found amusing, then piled some leaves beside the path and lay down. But though he was tired, he was not yet sleepy. "Are you going to the Good Magician to ask what your talent is?" he inquired.

She swished her tail as if snapping off a fly. "No; I'm afraid I would have to serve a year for news that I have none. My concern is more—well, awkward."

"Oh. I didn't mean to pry."

"It's all right. I can talk to you. It isn't as if you're a centaur."

"I'm not a centaur," he agreed. How well her sentiment echoed his own!

"It's to find out how to fly."

Of course! He should have guessed. "You know, your wings don't seem as big as those of the big birds," he said. "I'm not sure they could support you in the air even if they worked perfectly. I mean, they might lift a smaller creature, but not a centaur."

"That's obvious," she said somewhat coldly. "I've been practicing flapping them for months, developing my pectoral muscles, and as you can see they have filled out, but I just don't have the lift I require."

Esk was too embarrassed to tell her that he had taken her front muscles for breasts, and rather well-formed ones too. Centaurs wore only occasional harnesses or protections against heat or cold, and never concealed their sexual attributes. The breasts of female centaurs tended to be impressive by human standards, perhaps because they were structured to provide enough milk for offspring whose mass was several times that of human babies. Chex appeared to be no older than he was, but her breasts would have been considered more than generous on any human woman. Obviously, he had let himself be deluded by a preconception.

"What I meant to say was," he said somewhat awkwardly, "could it be that your magic talent is flying? That your muscles and wingspan only provide a small part of it, and magic the main part?"

"If it is, then why can't I fly?"

"Well, if you were flapping your wings instead of doing your magic, then it wouldn't work."

"But how would I work my magic?" she asked plaintively. "I *have* thought of that and tried to will myself into flight, but nothing happens."

"I don't know. I think you're right: you must ask the Good Magician. Maybe he will be able to tell you some spell you can invoke that will make it work."

"That is my hope," she said. "Why are you going to see him?"

"I have to find out how to get rid of a demoness who threatens my family." He explained the rest of it, except for the business of Metria's amatory offerings. That matter was too embarrassing.

"I'm surprised she didn't try to tempt you sexually," Chex said. "Human males are known to be vulnerable to that kind of inducement, and demons are unscrupulous."

He felt himself blushing in the darkness. "Uh, well—"

"Oh, that's right—you humans are sensitive about that sort of thing, aren't you! How quaint!"

"Quaint," he agreed. Then, not wishing to discuss the matter further, he closed his eyes, and in a moment he slept.

She woke him in deep darkness. "Esk! Esk!" she whispered urgently.

It took him a moment to get oriented. "Oh, yes, my turn to guard."

"No, I think a dragon's coming."

Suddenly he was completely alert. "Where?"

"From ahead. I smell the smoke. After my prior experience, I am more sensitive to that signal."

Now Esk smelled it too. "That's dragon, all right! I wish I could see it so I could know when to tell it no."

"Use your staff," she suggested. "I'll use mine, too."

"But I can't hit the dragon if I can't see it!"

"I mean as a sensing device. Hold it out in front of you, and when—"

"Right." He hefted his staff and pointed it toward the smell of smoke.

Now they listened, as the dragon huffed closer. Was his staff pointed correctly? Suppose the dragon slid under it or climbed over it? The monster seemed very close! The odor of the smoke was strong. If he waited too long, and got chomped before he—

"No!" he cried.

The huffing paused. "It's still some distance away," Chex murmured reprovingly. "Does your protest work at a distance?"

"No," Esk said, chagrined.

The dragon seemed to have paused because of the sound of his voice. Now it had a good notion where he was. It growled and charged.

"No!" Esk cried again. "NoNoNoNoNoNo!"

The dragon made a disgusted noise and retreated. They heard the scrabble of its claws on the path. "One of those nos must have scored," Chex said.

"Um," he agreed, embarrassed. He knew he had panicked, and come reasonably close to making a fool of himself. Again.

"I'm glad you are here," she said. "I could not have diverted it in the dark, and perhaps not in the daytime either. I would have had to run—and that has its own hazards, in the dark."

"My turn to keep watch," he said, preferring to change the subject.

"As you wish." He heard a gentle thunk as she lowered her body to the path. He wondered how the forepart of a centaur slept; did it lie flat on the ground or remain vertical? But he didn't care to inquire.

It turned out that she had kept watch for most of the night. Before very long the sky to the east lightened, and dawn was on the way.

As the morning arrived, he saw that neither surmise was quite right. Chex's humanoid torso was neither upright nor flat as she slept, but half-leaning back on her equine torso, above her folded wings. Her arms were clasped below her breasts—her pectoral muscles, he corrected himself. Her brown hair merged prettily enough with her mane. She was right, he thought; the hue of her hair matched his exactly, as if they were brother and sister. Could there be siblings of different species? Perhaps not directly, but if they had been delivered at the same time, when the order was for brown hair and gray eyes . . . well, with magic, anything was possible. At any rate, she was a very pretty figure in this repose.

A beam of sunlight speared down through a gap in the foliage and touched her face. Chex woke, blinking. "Oh, it's morning!" she exclaimed, lifting first her upper section, then her remaining body. "Let me urinate, and we can get moving." She stood at the side of the path, spread her rear legs and did it, while Esk stood startled. He knew that such things were unimportant to centaurs, and that he should simply accept her ways without reaction, but he knew he was about to flush embarrassingly.

Then he had a bright notion. "Me too," he said, and quickly made his way to a concealing bush and did his own business. She would think it was because of his quaint human modesty, and that was true, but it was mainly to give himself a chance to clear his flush before rejoining her.

"You really ought to do something about that foible," she remarked innocently as she plucked a pie from an overhanging tree. Her greater height, in the front section, caused her breas—her pectoral muscles to lift to his eye level as she reached up.

Esk did not respond, because he wasn't sure to which foible she referred. But he suspected she was right, and he resolved to try to learn how to perform natural functions in her sight without blushing. After all, each culture had its own ways, and he wasn't among human beings now. Certainly he never wanted to be caught staring at what he wasn't supposed to notice anyway.

She handed him the pie and reached for another. "Thank you," he said, fixing his gaze on the pie. But he didn't even notice what kind it was; he just bit into it and chewed.

They resumed their walk, and after an hour came to an intersection. "There it is!" Chex exclaimed happily, seeming not at all dismayed at this proof of her prior oversight. "The path I missed!"

"But there are two," Esk pointed out. "Which should we take—the one going north or the one going south?"

"That depends on whether the path we're on passes north or south of the Good Magician's castle."

"I know the Gap Chasm is north, but I don't know how far," Esk said. "Maybe if the north path leads there—"

"Then the south one leads to the castle," she finished. "So let's try the south, and if it's wrong, why, we'll just go north. It can't be far now."

They turned south. The trees grew larger, putting the path

in the gloom of perpetual shade; then they grew smaller, letting the sun shine down hotly. "I hope we encounter water soon," Chex said. "I'm sweating."

Esk hadn't realized that females of any persuasion sweated, but certainly her brown coat was glistening. "Maybe if you fanned yourself with your wings—" he suggested.

"Why, I never thought of that," she said. "I need to exercise them anyway." She spread her wings and moved them, generating a draft whose fringe he could feel. "Yes, that's much better, thank you."

The way opened out further, and now they came to a small lake. The path crossed it, passing right along the surface of the water.

They exchanged a glance. "Can a path go on water?" Chex asked.

"If it's an enchanted path," Esk replied doubtfully.

"Well, we'll see." She stepped forward—and her front hooves passed through the visible path and sank into the water with splashes.

Immediately, there was a stir in the lake. A wake appeared behind something huge and dark that was speeding toward them. No part of it quite broke the surface, and its outline was obscured by the refraction of the water, but it seemed exceedingly sure of itself.

Chex quickly stepped back. "I think we should go around the lake," she said. "If it was enchanted to enable travelers to cross over the water, that magic has been lost."

"Good thought," Esk agreed.

They started around, but the reeds at the edge twisted and bent toward them, showing moist surfaces that looked somewhat toothy. Esk knocked several away with his staff, and they withdrew with faint ugly hisses—but those on the other side leaned closer.

"Esk, I think we had better move rather quickly through this section," Chex said. "The footing beneath seems fairly firm; I believe I could carry you, if you would not consider this to be an indiscretion on my part. Then I could gallop—"

"Another good thought!" he said quickly.

He gave her his staff to hold, then she put her right hand

back over her torso, and he took hold of it from her left and she helped draw him up onto her back. "Take good hold of my mane," she advised.

He got a double handhold, up between her wings. Then she moved out, quickly advancing from walk to trot to gallop, while he hung on somewhat desperately. Water splashed up from her hooves.

About halfway around the lake, Chex turned her head around to face him. Esk was startled by the elasticity of her torso; from what would have been the human waist, she was able to twist halfway, and her neck twisted the other half, so that she was abruptly facing him, with her chest in profile. "I wonder if you could take your staff?" she inquired.

Then he saw her concern. Several rather mean looking birds were winging toward them. Their necks were crooked and their beaks curved, and they looked hungry.

"If you go slowly, I'll try to fend them off," he said, as he unclenched his fingers from her mane and took back his staff.

She slowed to a walk, using her own staff to knock at the leaning reeds. He balanced himself and squinted at the ugly birds. He thought he could stop them, if they came down singly.

But about five of them folded their wings partway and dived at him together. Their beaks looked very sturdy and sharp.

"No!" he cried as they converged.

It was almost too late for them to change course. Two birds plummeted into the water. Two more swooped just overhead, striving desperately to rise. The fifth did a crazy wiggle in air, using its wings to brake, and barely managed to reverse course before colliding with Chex's shoulder.

The wake in deeper water was coming toward them again. Esk tucked the staff under one arm and grabbed new holds on the mane. "Resume speed!" he said.

Chex resumed, flapping her wings to assist her progress. They made it around the rest of the lake without further event, rejoining the path.

Esk slid down. "I think we make a fair team," he said. "You have the go, and I have the stop."

"That's a nice way to put it," she agreed. "I was terrified!"

"Well, you're a filly; you're supposed to be frightened of violence."

"And you aren't?"

"Yes, I'm not supposed to be." He smiled. "Just don't ask me how it really is."

"No questions," she agreed.

The more he got to know her, the better he liked her. Despite their differences of culture, she tended to understand the fundamentals well enough.

They walked again. Soon they encountered a mountain. The path went through it, forming a dark tunnel around itself.

They paused. "It's supposed to be safe," Esk said. "But after the dragons and the lake, I'm nervous."

"Suppose we went in—and it wasn't safe?"

"Let's not go in."

"I like your thinking."

"But how do we get around it? I see tangle trees on the slopes."

"And dozens more of those birds roosting on the upper slopes," she said. "You know, I am quite sure there was no such mountain or tunnel on the map my dam showed me."

"Your damn what?" he asked, disgruntled by her language.

"My dam. My—you would call it mother."

"I wouldn't call my mother a damn anything!"

She laughed. "I suspect we have a barrier of communication. I mean that my mother's map did not have this particular feature of geography on it, so this must be the wrong path."

"Oh. Yes. Then we shouldn't have to try to pass this damn—this mother of a mountain."

She looked at him somewhat curiously. Evidently the barrier was still in operation. But they were agreed. They would turn back and try the north fork. He did not relish the return trip around the lake, but at least that was a known hazard.

# 3

# VOLNEY

The lake wasn't fun, but this time they were prepared, and they made it around without damage. They celebrated by pausing for lunch and drink. Chex had a cup she produced from her pack, with which she dipped water from the fringe of the lake and drank delicately. Then they traveled at a more leisurely pace north. In due course they reached the intersection, and this time proceeded along the north extension.

Yet another little dragon appeared. "I'm fed up with this!" Esk exclaimed. He charged forward, wielding his staff, feeling his ogre strength manifesting unbidden. He struck the dragon on the head, then rammed the staff under its body, picked it up, and heaved it into the forest. The dragon was not actually hurt, but was so surprised that it scuttled for cover elsewhere.

Chex was amazed. "That dragon weighed as much as you!" she exclaimed. "Yet you tossed it like a toy!"

"I told you, I'm quarter ogre," he said, relaxing. "Every so often something triggers it, and I do something ogreish."

"Evidently so," she agreed. "I can't say I was ever partial

to ogres, but I must confess it was a pleasure watching that dragon fly!"

"It would be more of a pleasure if I could summon that power at will," he said. "But it's involuntary, like a sneeze, and it doesn't last long. My father is much more of an ogre than I am, and my grandfather Crunch—"

"I'm happy with you," she said quickly. "After all, an ogre's intellect is inversely proportional to his strength."

"And his strength is directly proportional to his ugliness," he added.

"And to his taste for violence," she agreed.

"Well, of course. A good ogre can make a medium dragon turn tail just by smiling at it."

"A good ogre would do the same for me!"

"While a good ogress can sour milk by looking at it."

"And turn it to petrified cheese by breathing on it," she concluded. "Enough of ogres; let's see if we can reach the Good Magician's castle before nightfall."

They resumed their trek. The path wound onward, finding its way into craggy country that hinted of the great Gap Chasm to come. "This isn't promising," Chex muttered.

Esk didn't comment, because he agreed. Since this was the fourth direction they were exploring, one way or another, and there were no more, it had to be the one.

There was a sound ahead. "Not yet another dragon!" Chex exclaimed impatiently. "Those little monsters are positively swarming!"

"It's not growling," Esk pointed out.

"True. But it's not walking like a man or a centaur."

They stopped, waiting for whatever it was to come into view. In a moment it did so, surprising them both.

It was a creature larger in mass than Esk, but smaller than Chex. It had a lemon-shaped gray body, a small snout in front, and tiny feet.

"Why, that's a huge mole," Esk said.

But Chex's mouth was striving to fall open. "I thought they were extinct!" she said.

"Oh, no, there are many moles underground," Esk assured her. "I've seen them—"

"That's no mole!" she said impatiently. "*That's a vole!*"

"A what?"

But now the creature had spied them. It lifted its head, showing tiny eyes just beneath its fur. The eyes were brown. "Eh?" it inquired.

"Where are you from?" Chex asked the creature. She did not seem to be afraid, so Esk judged it to be harmless.

"Eh? A ventaur," it said.

"That's *centaur,*" Chex said primly. "I am Chex Centaur. Who are you?"

It peered more closely at her. "I am Volney Vole. Pleav allow me to pavv."

"Don't you know you're supposed to be extinct?" she asked.

"Volev don't vtink," it retorted indignantly.

"It has trouble with esses," Esk said, catching on.

The snout turned toward him. "And who are you, vir?"

"I am Esk."

"Hello, Evk. Pleav allow me to pavv."

"We aren't trying to prevent you," Chex said. "Just to learn about you."

"I have important buvinevv with the Good Magician. Pleav let me pavv."

"But we're looking for the Good Magician too!" Esk exclaimed. "We thought he was up this path!"

"Not thiv path," the creature assured him. "Only the Gap Chavm."

"But then the Good Magician is nowhere!" Chex said despairingly. "We have looked along all the other paths!"

The vole studied them. "Brown and gray," it remarked. "Good colorv."

"That's right, we all match!" Chex said. "Only you're brown in the eyes, not the fur."

"Thiv iv vurfave vuit."

Chex paused, translating it. "This is your surface suit?"

"That'v what I vaid, Chekv. I reverve it below." And the vole performed a sudden convolution, becoming brown. The most surprising thing was that its eyes turned gray. Now the three of them aligned as perfectly as they were able.

"Volney, I think we should have a talk," Chex said. "I think we are all in trouble, because we can't find the Good Magician."

"But I *muvt* find the Magician!" the vole said, sounding desperate. "It iv movt important!"

"It's important to us too," Chex said. "I think we'll find him faster if we compare notes and make common cause."

Volney considered. "Common cauve," he agreed. Then he convoluted again, changing back to his surface outfit, eyes and all.

"You see, Esk came looking for the Good Magician from the east," Chex said. "I came looking from the west. We both followed a path to the south, but it wasn't there, so now we were trying the north path—"

"And I came from the north," the vole finished. "It iv not there."

"So we seem to have a problem," she concluded. "We all need to see the Good Magician, but none of us can find him. Have you any notion how we should proceed?"

"What did you find to the vouth?"

"A mountain with a tunnel. That wasn't on the map my dam showed me."

"Your damn what?" the vole asked.

"Never mind! I'm sure the map was accurate."

"But featurev change."

"Yes. Still—"

"We muvt go to the end of that path," the vole decided. "That iv where it hav to be."

Chex sighed. "I suppose you're right. But we really don't find the prospect of going through that tunnel appealing. There have been signs that the enchantment on the path has been impaired, so that it is no longer completely safe for travelers. If the tunnel were to collapse—"

"A vole hole never collapvev," Volney said with certainty.

"That's right—you were a burrowing species," she said. "You must know about tunnels."

"All about them," the vole agreed. "If that tunnel iv not vafe, I will vimply make another."

Chex glanced at Esk. "Do you concur?" she asked. "Shall we try the south path again?"

"I guevv we'd better," he said.

She shot him a marvelously dark look, and he realized that it really wasn't very funny. His efforts at humor, like his efforts at original thought, tended to fall flat.

They proceeded back south, Chex leading, then the vole, then Esk. But it was now late in the day, and they realized that it would be night by the time they reached the tunnel, and that did not appeal at all. So they paused at the cross paths and ate some more fruit. Fruit was new to Volney, because he was not a climbing or reaching creature, but he liked it. Then he sniffed out some edible roots that were new to Esk and Chex, but that were similarly palatable after being washed in the fluid from some water chestnuts Chex plucked.

While they ate, they conversed. Esk and Chex told of their backgrounds and missions to the Good Magician, and Volney told of his.

The civilized voles were not, he explained, extinct. They had merely departed for a greener pasture, some centuries ago. The larger family of voles comprised burrowing creatures ranging from the tiny, vicious wiggle larvae to the huge amiable diggles, with many varieties of squiggles between. Because the civilized voles avoided publicity, most other creatures hardly knew of them, and regarded the squiggles as the dominant representatives of the type. The region of Xanth between Castle Roogna and the Gap Chasm had been getting crowded, so the voles had in due course traveled into the wilderness to the east, where they had settled by the meandering shores of the friendly Kiss-Mee River.

"Yes, I saw that on Mother's map," Chex said. "The Kiss-Mee River connects Lake Kiss-Mee with Lake Ogre-Chobee. It is an almost unexplored region of Xanth, and little is known about the details of its geography."

"Which iv the way we like it," Volney responded. "For centuriev we have burrowed there in private comfort. But now—"

"Something happened?" Esk asked, getting interested. Geography was not his favorite subject, but happenings had greater appeal.

"Divavter," Volney agreed. "It iv that horror I have come here to ameliorate. I wav choven to make thiv divreputable journey becauve of my ekvellent command of the vtrange language of the vurfave folk."

"Yes, you speak it very well," Chex said quickly, forestalling the somewhat less sensitive remark Esk was about to make.

"However, I note you have vome difficulty with your evvev," the vole said discreetly.

"Some dif—" Esk started, but was cut off by a flick of Chex's tail that stung his mouth with uncanny accuracy. The strike was not hard, but made him feel strangely light-headed. Sometimes she understood him almost too well!

"We all must do the best we can," Chex said gently. "Even those of us who have difficulty with our esses. Just what is this disaster you have come to ameliorate?"

"The very devtrucvion of the Vale of the Vole," he pronounced with feeling.

"The Vale of the Vole!" Chex repeated. "What a marvelously evocative name!"

"But the foul demonv devavtated it," Volney said sadly.

Esk lifted his head. "I smell smoke," he said.

Sure enough, another little smoker was coming along the path from the west. It spied them and let out a hungry puff.

"Get on the south path!" Esk snapped. Chex and Volney scrambled for it, leaving the east-west path clear.

Esk stationed himself just south of the intersection and waited. As the dragon charged up, he murmured "no."

The dragon tried to stop, but Esk said "no" again. Therefore the creature's feet kept going, carrying it right on by the intersection. In a moment it was out of sight, still traveling east.

"Very nice," Chex said. "First you stopped its attack, then you stopped its reversal. It had to keep on going, by which time it had lost track of what it had been after."

She understood his effort almost better than he did!

"That iv uvful magic," Volney agreed. "I regret I have no vuch talent."

"Don't voles have magic?" Esk asked.

"Nothing vignificant. We merely dig."

"You were about to tell us what happened to the Vale of the Vole," Chex said.

"Ah, yev, and a vad vtory it iv," Volney said sadly. He

went on to describe how the foul demons, who had previously shared the Vale almost unnoticed, decided to destroy the friendly Kiss-Mee River. Apparently its meandering contours displeased them, so they invoked monstrous magic and pulled the river straight.

"No more curves?" Chex asked, shocked. She was, of course, a creature of many esthetic curves.

"Does it matter?" Esk asked, somewhat duller about the esthetics. He was a creature of irregular lines and bumps.

"Of course it matters!" Chex exclaimed, her eyes almost flashing. "Just how friendly do you suppose a straight-line river is?"

"It iv unfriendly to the land, too," Volney said. He explained how the water now coursed directly down the straight channel, not pausing to support the fish isolated by its loss of loops and eddies, and was leaving many water-loving plants dry. The lush vale was becoming a barren valley. The lovely moist soil that the voles had dug in was now turning to dry sand and dust, and their tunnels were eroding. Paradise was converting to wasteland. Indeed, the remnant of the waterway was now known as the Kill-Mee.

"But can't you dig out new curves for the river to kiss?" Chex asked. "Can't you restore it to its natural state?"

It turned out that the voles could not, because the demons maintained guard and harassed anyone who tried to tamper with their inimical design. The voles were diggers, not fighters, and were helpless before the violence of the demons. If they could not restore the river, they would have to leave— but they knew there was no other region of Xanth as good as the Vale of the Vole had been. So Volney was now coming to ask the Good Magician for the answer to their problem: how to stop the demons from interfering with the restoration of the Kiss-Mee River.

"That's funny," Esk said.

Chex stared at him. "I find nothing humorous about the situation," she said severely.

"I mean, I'm looking for the Good Magician to learn how to stop another demon," he explained. "She came to take my hideout because things weren't so nice back where she came from. If the demons live in the Vale of the Vole, and they have fixed it up to suit themselves, why did she have to leave?"

"Maybe she came from some other area," Chex said.

"No, she mentioned the Vale, or maybe the Kiss-Mee, I'm sure of that. I remember it clearly because she—" But he didn't want to talk about the kisses the demoness had offered him. Because it hadn't been exactly kisses proffered.

"Perhaps vhe iv an unlovely demonevv," Volney said. "Vo the otherv vent her away."

"No, she's a lovely creature," Esk said. "That is, I mean, she can assume any form she wants, and that includes luscious—I mean sexy—uh, that is—"

"We are getting a notion what that is," Chex remarked dryly. "She *did* vamp you, didn't she!"

"Well, she offered, but—but I—I am trying to get rid of her. Anyway, what would be ugly to a demon, who can assume any shape? I don't think she would have left for that reason. Actually, she said it was the hummers that drove her away."

"Hummingbirds?" Chex asked, perplexed.

"No, these are something that mortals can't hear, but that drive demons crazy. So she left. So maybe it's ironic, that they straightened out the river but still aren't satisfied."

"Hummerv," Volney repeated musingly. "We may have heard of them. One of us overheard a demon say it was to get rid of them that they straightened the river. But we don't know what they are."

"Well, it seems to me that if you could just find out what they are," Chex said, "you might use them to make all the demons move out. Then you could restore the river, and the Vale of the Vole would be friendly again."

"Yev. Maybe the Good Magivian will tell uv that."

They moved on south along the path, through the big trees. But they had used up time resting and talking, and darkness was looming up from the gloom below the forest. "We had better make a good camp for the night," Esk said. "Maybe we can set up some stakes to hinder the dragons."

There was a crack of thunder. "We'll need more than that to keep from getting soaked," Chex said.

Esk squinted at the looming clouds. "We won't get soaked. That's a color hailstorm!"

She looked more carefully. "Why so it is! We had better get under cover. There's no telling how large those hailstones will be. And of course we'll still get wet when they melt."

"A storm iv bad?" Volney asked.

"It can be bad," Chex agreed. "It is best to play safe, and find suitable cover. But there seems to be little loose wood here to fashion a shelter; we may have to lean against the lee side of trees."

"Why not go under?"

"Under what?" Esk asked.

"Underground. We never vtay up when it iv uncomfortable above. In fact, we veldom vtay long above anyway."

"I can't go underground!" Chex protested.

Indeed, it would take a giant tunnel to get her below! But the storm was looming closer, and a veil of pastel colors was drawing down. They were certainly in for it.

Esk spied a fallen trunk. Abruptly he strode over to it, his ogre strength surging. He picked it up and swung it against the trunk of a giant standing tree. It splintered. He picked up the largest fragment and broke it against the tree, then took several of the remaining pieces and wove them together, forming a crude platform. He jammed the stoutest fragments into the ground vertically, then heaved the platform onto them.

Then his strength receded, and he was normal again, and tired. "You'll have to finish it," he gasped. "That's just the frame."

"That is good enough!" Chex exclaimed. She swept up an armful of brush and heaved it onto the platform. "That should stop the hailstones," she said as she gathered more. "When they melt, it will drip though, but I can stand getting wet. Thank you, Esk."

Meanwhile, Volney was digging. Where he had been there was now a mound of dirt and a hole in the ground. He was fast, all right.

The storm struck. Yellow hailstones crashed down through the foliage and bounced on the ground, leaving little dents.

Chex got under her shelter. She had to duck her head and

finally lie down, because it wasn't high enough, but it did provide protection.

Volney's snout appeared in the hole. "Evk!" he squeaked. "Here! There iv room!"

Esk scrambled for the hole as the hailstones bounced around him. They were becoming blue, now, and he knew that those were colder and therefore harder than the yellow ones. They would hurt.

He half slid into the hole. It descended for a body length, then curved, descended some more, and curved again. Hailstones were following him, rolling down. Then it rose, and debouched into a larger section; he could tell by the widening of the walls, but could not see anything in the dark. He moved into this, and came up against warm fur.

"There iv room for both," Volney said. "The stonev and water vtay below."

This was a nice, cozy design. The vole had hollowed out a den that was bound to remain dry, unless there got to be so much melt that it filled the whole tunnel.

"But suppose a dragon comes?" he asked.

"Then I vtrike the vupport, and the tunnel collapvev," the vole replied confidently. "No predator ever caught a vole in a hole."

And of course the dragons would not be foraging far during the storm, Esk realized. They didn't like getting battered any more than other creatures did. That meant that Chex should be safe enough too.

After a brief time the storm passed on. Esk sought to return to the surface, but the tunnel was entirely blocked by hailstones.

"Have no concern," Volney said. "I will make a new ekvit." In moments he did so, tunneling down, then around and up. The excavated dirt piled into one side of the main chamber, evidently intended for such storage.

Esk followed the vole, amazed by the velocity of the digging. "How do you do it so fast?" he asked.

Volney paused in the darkness, turning within the tunnel though it was only his own body width in diameter. "My vilver talonv," he explained. "Feel."

Esk felt, cautiously, and found cold metal. It seemed that

the vole donned the talons as a man would gauntlets. "Where do you carry such things? I never saw them before."

"I have a pouch for nevevvary toolv," Volney explained. Then he turned again and resumed his digging. Esk had to crowd to the left to avoid the dirt flying on the right.

Soon they broke surface. A shower of melting hailstones came down. They scrambled up through them, and stood knee-deep on Esk, waist-deep on Volney, in the foaming, colored slush. Much had fallen in that brief span.

Chex was under her shelter, almost hidden, for the stones were mounded above and around it. "I was worried you would drown down there!" she called.

"No, Volney has a really cozy den below," Esk said. "He is a truly amazing digger."

"No, only average," the vole demurred. "It is merely my volivh nature."

Nevertheless, Esk was discovering Volney to be as interesting and useful a companion as Chex. This group of travelers was random, but seemed about as good as could have been chosen for such a journey.

They set up a three-way guard roster, with Esk taking the first watch and Chex the last, in deference to the amount of time she had spent the prior night. Esk doubted that any dragons would appear until the slush had subsided, but he didn't care to gamble, and neither did the others.

Volney disappeared into his hole, and Chex settled down on a nearby elevation she cleared of slush. The shelter was useless for the time being, because of the mass of dripping slush on top.

He walked up and down the path, keeping himself alert as long as he could. The stars came out and flickered at him through the waving foliage. It was pleasant, and he was not at all lonely. He knew he would have been, by himself. It was nice making new acquaintances who had a similar mission and dissimilar talents. Too bad they would soon find the Good Magician's castle and have to separate.

When sleep threatened to overtake him despite his efforts, he went to the vole hole and called down it. "Volney! Volney! Are you ready for your watch?"

There was a subterranean snort as the vole woke. "Ready, Evk." The snout poked into the starlight.

Esk crawled down and around and into the den and curled up in the warm spot left by the vole. The den was rounded in such a way that the earth tended to support a curled body, and was really quite comfortable. He had hardly completed that realization before he slept.

When he woke, there was a warm body next to him. Volney was back, and Esk realized that the vole had finished his shift and turned it over to the centaur.

He crawled out, and discovered it was dawn. Chex was picking fruits and setting them on the platform. "No dragons!" she said briskly as she saw him.

Esk had a call or two of nature to answer. He nerved himself to do it in her presence, knowing that the sooner he navigated this social hurdle the better it would be. He started to take down his trousers.

"Don't do it here," she said. "We don't want the smell in our breakfast."

Oh. Well, he had made the gesture, such as it was. With relief he retreated to a more distant site and did his business. He didn't have to actually do it in her presence; he just had to be able to if the need arose.

They ate, and drank some meltwater Chex had saved in a pair of cups. Then Volney emerged, bringing out some tubers he had found somewhere underground, and they traded some of the remaining fruit for these. It was surprising how good the tubers were; the vole evidently had a fine nose for such things.

They resumed their walk along the path. When they reached the lake, Volney was taken aback. "I can't crovv that water!" he protested.

Obviously he couldn't. Esk wasn't certain whether voles could swim, but it hardly mattered; the giant monster out there made swimming hazardous. If the vole tried to splash around the edge, the way Chex had, he would be half floating, because his little legs were too short to achieve good purchase beneath the water. The reeds would eat him alive. If he tried to tunnel under, he would simply encounter muck that filled in as fast as he dug. There was no question: water was a formidable barrier.

He looked at Chex. No, it didn't seem feasible for her to carry the vole. Volney was too big, and not constructed for riding. Also, how would he, Esk, get around the lake, if she carried someone else?

"I think we should construct a raft," Chex said. "There is driftwood at the shore, some fairly substantial pieces, and if we use vines to bind it together, and long poles to move it, it should serve."

"A raft?" Volney asked. "What iv thiv?"

"It's like a boat, only clumsier," Esk said.

"What iv a boat?"

Chex looked at Esk, then back to Volney. "Your folk aren't much for water, are they?"

"We have great revpect for water," the vole protested. "We drink it, we bathe in it, we guide it into our burrowv for the nourivhment of root farmv. The meandering Kivv-Mee River wav the life-vevvel of our Vale." His whiskers drooped. "But now, of courve, the Kill-Mee River poivonv uv."

"But you don't go *on* it?" she persisted. "You don't swim or sail?"

"Vail?"

"A boat is a craft that floats on the surface of the water, carrying folk across it. A raft does this too. A sailboat is propelled by a sheet stretched out against the wind. You do not know of these things?"

"It voundv like movt intriguing magic."

She smiled. "Well, we'll try to demonstrate this magic for you, so you can tell your folk when you return. It should facilitate your use of the river. But tell me, how do you cross the Kiss-Mee?"

"We have bridgev over it and tunnelv under it," Volney explained. "They were much labor to convtruct, but give good vervice. Unfortunately, when the demonv vtraightened it, these crovvingv were left vtranded by vacant channelv, and now are uvelevv. The volev on the far vide are unable to join thove on the near vide."

"Couldn't you make new bridges or tunnels?" Esk asked.

"Not while the demonv guard the channel. They permit no activity of that nature."

Chex sighed. "You need the Good Magician's counsel, certainly! Well, let's get to it. We must gather as much wood as we can, as large and dry as we can, and tie it together. We should be able to fashion a raft large enough to support us all."

"You wivh dry wood?" Volney asked. "Will it not get wet when it touchev the water?"

"Dry, so that it isn't waterlogged, and will float better." She found a piece and picked it up. "We can make a pile here beside the path."

"Now at lavt I comprehend," Volney said. He set off in search of wood.

There was more driftwood and fallen wood in the vicinity than had been at first apparent, and before long they had a huge pile. They found strong vines, some of which they used to make a harness so that Chex could haul the largest pieces. Then they used that vine to tie the wood together.

By noon they had a large, ungainly structure that most resembled a pile of refuse. But when they heaved it into the water and shoved it to the deep region, it floated. They climbed aboard, with Esk and Chex wielding long poles, and by dint of pushing at the nether muck caused it to travel out toward the center of the lake.

"An island!" Volney exclaimed. "A floating island!"

"So it seems," Chex agreed.

"Shouldn't that be 'ivland'?" Esk asked.

Both stared at him. "Whatever for?" Chex inquired.

"Uh, no reason," he said, embarrassed. What could he have been thinking of?

The monster of the lake coursed close. "Go fry in the sun!" Chex called to it impolitely. "You can't get near us!"

The monster, irritated, charged the raft. Its bulk loomed huge. But Chex simply poked at one of its eyestalks with her pole, and it retreated. "Bullies have no courage when they face anything as large as they are," she remarked with satisfaction.

"OoOoOo," Volney moaned.

"What's the matter?" Esk asked. "That monster can't touch us."

"I feel ill," the vole said. Indeed, his fur seemed to be developing a greenish tinge.

"You're seasick," Chex said. "Here, I have a pill for that." She produced a green tablet from her knapsack.

Volney swallowed the pill. In a moment his fur turned gray again. "Much better," he said. "I don't like being veavick."

They continued poling, and made steady, slow progress across the lake. They paused midway for a lunch break; Chex had thoughfully harvested some fruit and put it aboard. Then they completed the voyage, bumping up against the far shore. They splashed to land and hauled the raft as high as they could, so that it would not drift away. They knew that they might need it again.

They resumed travel along the path, heading for the mountain. But the building of the raft and the voyage across the lake had taken much time and strength, and they decided to spend another night on the road before tackling the mountain. They were now becoming seasoned travelers, and no storm approached, so they had no significant problems this time.

# 4
# MYSTERY

They arrived at the mountain. It loomed as massively as before, with its deep dark tunnel through.

Chex shuddered. "I dislike confessing this, but I am slightly claustrophobic. I don't think I can walk that passage even if it is guaranteed safe. I'm afraid the mountain will collapse on me."

Volney sniffed at the rising bank. "But there iv no mountain," he protested.

"You can't see the mountain?" Esk asked, surprised.

"I vee it, but it ivn't there."

"You're not making sense."

"I will vhow you." The vole moved forward, into the bank—literally. His body disappeared into it.

"What?" Esk and Chex said together.

Volney's snout poked out of the slope. "It iv illuvion," he explained.

"Illusion!" Chex exclaimed. She reached out with one hand, and the hand passed into the apparent substance of the mountain. "Why so it is!"

"We never touched it!" Esk said, chagrined. "We just assumed it was real!"

"That explains why it wasn't on my dam's map!"

"What type of map?" Volney asked, confused. "An evil one?"

"Never mind. I just knew there wasn't supposed to be a mountain here—and there wasn't! What a relief!"

"Does this mean we can walk right through it?" Esk asked.

"Evidently so," Chex said, walking into it. For a moment her equine forepart was hidden, while her human upper portion remained in view, and, disconnected, her equine rump. Then the rest of her disappeared, and the shaggy slope of the mountain was unbroken.

Esk reached out to touch the visible surface. His hand encountered nothing; it vanished in the rock.

This was one persistent illusion! They knew it for what it was, yet it remained as clearly as before.

"But it's dark in here," Chex's voice came.

"Darknevv divturbv you?" Volney asked. "I have no problem with it."

"Suppose there's a wall or something?" she demanded. "I'm not worried about a mountain of illusion falling on me, but I don't want to bang my face."

"I can lead you," Volney said. "Volev never go bump in the night."

They set up a column, with Volney leading and Esk at the rear. They marched along the approximate route of the path, but it didn't matter since there was no mountain. At times Esk saw the light that shone down the tunnel and highlighted the contour of the rock, with Chex's body passing in and out of it; the effect remained eerie. But as they penetrated more deeply, the light diminished, until all was dark.

"Vtop!" Volney exclaimed abruptly. "There iv a chavm!"

"A chasm!" Chex echoed. "Can we go around?"

"I will ekvplore." They waited while the vole moved along, first to one side, then the other. "No, it crovvev the full region."

"You're sure it's not an illusion?" Esk asked, half facetiously.

"Quite vure. I cannot tell how deep or wide it iv, but it iv definitely prevent."

"Perhaps I can fathom it," Chex said. "I can explore it with my staff." There was the sound of the staff tapping. "It is too deep; I can't find the bottom." Then, "But I can find the far side! It is not too far; I could hurdle it."

"I cannot jump," Volney said. "But I could tunnel under it, if there iv rock below."

"Maybe that's best," Chex agreed.

There was the sound of rapid digging. Then there was the noise of splashing. "Oopv! I cannot tunnel through water!"

"Well, we got you across the lake," she said. "We should be able to get you across the chasm. After all, it's not exactly of the scope of the Gap Chasm."

"Can't tell," Esk said. "The Gap Chasm has extensions that jag a long way north and south. This could be one of those."

"You are not much help," she said.

"Maybe we could help him cross," Esk said. "We have our staffs; if we made a temporary bridge—"

"No, they aren't long enough. I touched the far side only at full extension."

"Well, if we tied them together—"

"They would bend in the middle, and then the ends would slide off."

"But if we stood on either side and held on to them—"

She considered. "Perhaps. But we would have to be very sure of our hold."

"You truvted me to lead you," Volney said. "I will truvt you to hold me."

They used the length of vine Chex had thoughtfully saved to bind the ends of the two staffs together as securely as was feasible. Then she made a leap in the dark and landed on the far side of the chasm. Then Esk poked the lengthened pole across, and she caught hold of it.

Now Volney donned his gripping talons—it seemed he had several sets for different applications—and took hold of the staff. He was not, as he had said before, a climber, but he could cling to a small root, and this was similar in diameter. He moved carefully out over the chasm, while Esk clung tightly to the end.

The pole sagged, for the vole's weight was formidable. Then an end slid toward the brink as the staffs formed a *V* in the center. Esk now regretted his notion; he was afraid that something would break, and Volney would be dumped into the dark depth. Fortunately he felt his ogre strength coming into play; he would not let Volney fall.

Then the pull changed. Esk's staff angled further toward the horizontal. The vole's weight was now on Chex's staff.

"I tire!" Volney's voice came. "I cannot climb!"

"Esk, let go your end!" Chex called.

"But—"

"I'm going to haul him up! Let go!"

Hoping he was doing the right thing, Esk let go. His staff immediately slid over the brink and clattered down.

But now there was the sound of motion. Chex was using her centaur strength to pull her pole up, the vole along with it. There was a rasping and a clatter. How was it going?

Then Volney's voice came. "I am here!" It was from Esk's level; the vole had reached the far side!

"I'm glad," Chex gasped. By the sound of it, she had been tiring too; her human arms were weak compared to her equine legs.

The rest was routine. Chex made sure Volney was all right, then leaped back across the chasm. Esk got on her back and she made one more leap, carrying him across.

Then they proceeded on through the mountain, and finally emerged into daylight on the south side. Esk knew that his relief was no greater than that of his companions.

Before them stood the castle. It had a moat and a solid outer wall. The drawbridge was down, and on it was a big empty cage.

They stopped just before the moat. "The Good Magician's castle is always beset by challenges," Chex said. "That is because the Magician doesn't want to be bothered by querents who aren't serious. But I don't see what kind of a challenge an empty cage would be."

"I've heard that the challenges are always slanted toward the visitors," Esk said. "Does an empty cage mean something to one of us?"

They exchanged glances. None of them had a notion.

"I suppose we could just go on in," Chex said. "But I distrust this. It is never supposed to be easy to get in, and if it seems so, then that must be a false impression. I would much rather understand the situation before committing myself."

Esk could only agree. "But how are we to understand it, if we don't go farther?"

"Oh, we should be able to reason it out to some degree," she said. "The intellect is always superior to blind action."

"That's not the ogre view," Esk said.

"We have uved vome intellect and vome acvion," Volney said. "If one doev not work now, we can try the other. But I find it odd that we have encountered vo many challengev on the way to the cavtle, and none now that we're here."

"That is strange," Esk agreed. "It's almost as if the challenges were in the wrong place."

"Or *were* they?" Chex asked, her wings flapping in her excitement. "Could that be the way the Good Magician planned it?"

"But aren't they supposed to be at the castle?"

"We assumed so, but how do we know? The Good Magician makes his own rules! He could have put the challenges anywhere along the route."

"But if they are slanted for particular visitors, how would the right ones be there for the right visitors? There are three of us."

But her excellent centaur mind was operating now. "I think he knew we were coming, and from which directions we were coming, so he could have set things up for each of us that the others wouldn't encounter."

"But he didn't!" Esk pointed out. "We all encountered the little dragons."

She looked at the cage. "Look—there are dragon droppings in there, and the bars are soiled with soot. Those little smokers were in there, but they got out!"

"They were let out," Volney said. "That cage hav a clavp only a human paw could operate. Mine couldn't."

"Why would they be let out before they were used?" Esk asked.

Chex shook her head. "I don't have the answer to that, but let's see if we can work it out. We three arrived together, and we helped each other get here. Does that seem usual?"

"No," Esk said. "I thought it was supposed to be one at a time."

"Well, let's pattern it. If things hadn't gone wrong, who would have come here first?"

"You would. You overshot the intersection; otherwise you would have arrived first, and then me, and finally Volney."

"So it seems reasonable that the Good Magician was setting up for me first. Now what would have been good challenges for me?"

"The mountain!" Esk exclaimed. "You're claustrophobic, so you were afraid to go into the tunnel until you realized that it was all illusion."

"And that could have been my first challenge," she said. "To figure out the nature of the mountain, as I certainly should have done, because of my dam's map. But I failed that challenge and turned back."

"Then I failed it too, because I was with you."

"But if you had come alone, you would have gone on through the tunnel, because you aren't claustrophobic," she said. "So it wasn't a challenge for you; it didn't matter whether you caught onto its nature."

"But that chasm inside—*that* would have stopped me, if I didn't fall into it."

"Whereas I had no trouble with that," she said excitedly. "So maybe those were two challenges, one for each of us, set up together because we were likely to arrive so close together that there wasn't time to set up complete alternates. It is making sense!"

"The lake!" Volney said. "I could not crovv the water! That wav my challenge! And the chavm too, becauve there wav more water below it, ekvending down and down."

"Yes. Because we were with you, we got you across, just as you got us through the mountain. We helped each other past each other's challenges! I doubt we were supposed to."

"But what about the little smokers?" Esk asked. "We did not release them."

She contemplated the open cage. "I think that collection of dragons would have been a formidable challenge for any of us. How could we have gotten by that?"

"I might have," Esk said. "I could have climbed over the

cage, and said no to any that tried to grab me through the bars."

"True. So that wasn't your challenge after all. But it would have been much more difficult for me or for Volney, because we don't climb. Just hanging onto our staffs across the chasm was all he could do. I suppose I might have tied a line to the cage and hauled it out of the way, but he—"

"I fear I would have had to turn back," the vole said. "Unlevv I had thought of your idea to uve a raft, then uved the branchev to fill in the chavm vo I could crovv that too."

"But as it happened, someone released those dragons, and we encountered several along the paths," she said. "We really must fathom that mystery before we can make sense of the larger picture."

"Obviously, something is wrong," Esk said. "Those smokers weren't meant to be loose, they were meant to be caged, and only get loose if the challengee messed up. Someone cut off the challenge before it started."

"So it seems," she agreed. "Would the Good Magician himself have done it?"

"I don't see why. If he didn't want the dragons here, he would not have brought them."

"The Gorgon, then?"

"She wouldn't mess up what he set up!"

"I agree," she said. "Could someone else have done it?"

"It doesn't seem likely."

"So we are left with the inexplicable," she concluded. "Perhaps now it is time to enter the castle, expecting the unexpected."

Esk nodded consent, nervously. Volney did not look any more comfortable.

They stepped on the drawbridge. They hauled the empty cage off, then crossed on over.

Suddenly an ogre loomed up before them. The thing was monstrous and hairy and ugly, and both Chex and Volney retreated in alarm.

But Esk's reaction was opposite! "Grandpa!" he exclaimed.

But it was not Crunch Ogre. It was some other male, not quite as ugly, but still quite formidable. It blocked their way.

"We're only coming to talk to the Good Magician," Esk

said, strongly suspecting that this would not provoke any reasonable response. "Will you let us by?"

He was correct. The ogre ope'd his ponderous and marbled maw and made a bellow of rage that shook the castle.

How was he to get past with his companions? Esk realized that this was a challenge, and it was his to meet and solve. But almost nothing could make an ogre stand aside; he was in a position to know that. Nothing except—

Except another ogre. There was the key!

But Esk could not invoke his ogre self just because he wanted to. It came of its own accord, when triggered by erratic circumstances.

Still, sometimes it was possible to arrange the trigger. It was risky—but so was standing before an ogre as if ready to be eaten.

"Wish me luck," Esk muttered back to the others. Then he strode forward, directly into the ogre.

For a moment the ogre was startled by this temerity. Then it grabbed for him with a ham hand.

Esk saw that meat hook coming, and his ogre nature reacted. Suddenly he roared, his ogre strength surging. "Go 'way, me say!" he bellowed, and bit at the other's paw.

The other reacted astonishingly. It shrank away, literally; as it retreated, it became smaller, until it looked very much like a man, and Esk towered over it. But Esk, his ogre dander up, wasn't satisfied; he smashed at it with his own ham fist.

Something shattered. Fragments of glass flew out, and the other ogre was gone. Esk stood before a man-sized frame from which jags of glass projected.

"It was a mirror!" Chex exclaimed. "Except—"

Esk's ogre nature left him. As he returned to the human condition, his intelligence increased, and he understood. "A reverse mirror!" he said. "It showed only the other side of me—the side that I wasn't. So when I was a man, it was my ogre self, and when I turned ogre, it turned human. Only I was ogrishly stupid and agressive, and broke it when I didn't have to."

Chex approached. "I don't think it was just a mirror," she said. "Volney and I saw it too, and it looked and sounded like a real ogre. Your state may have governed it, but it was real enough in its fashion. Like the illusion of the mountain, it was enough to do the job. If you hadn't cowed it—"

Esk shrugged. "Maybe so. Certainly it was my challenge, not anybody else's. This one wasn't let out early!"

"It wasn't alive," she pointed out. "The inanimate challenges remain in place; only the dragons are loose, and maybe whatever other animals were supposed to be used."

"It wasn't alive, so it didn't leave," he agreed, understanding. "So we still don't know whether anyone is in charge of the challenges. I don't like this."

"Neither do I," she said.

"Unlevv thiv iv the challenge?" Volney suggested.

Chex paused thoughtfully. "This mystery? This is the true challenge? Meant for all three of us to solve, together?"

"I do not know, I only guevv," the vole said.

"It is a most interesting conjecture," she said. "We knew to expect the unexpected, and that's about as unexpected as anything could be. It seems reasonable to conjecture that a more sophisticated challenge would be required to handle three dissimilar querents simultaneously."

"But why should there be three at once?" Esk asked. "We would have come separately, if we hadn't met on the paths."

"True. It does seem largely coincidental." She quivered her wings, pondering. "Is it possible that our missions are linked? That we did not arrive coincidentally, but that the three of us are destined to cooperate in some greater endeavor so that a single answer will serve us all?"

"But you knew nothing of the Kivv-Mee River," Volney protested.

"Yet Esk did encounter the sultry demoness from that region," Chex pointed out. "So his mission may have a common motivation with yours. I confess, however, that my own mission does not seem to connect. I think this is too speculative to be taken as fact, at least at this stage."

"Maybe the Good Magician will tell us soon," Esk said.

"Maybe," she agreed, but she seemed dubious.

They proceeded on into the castle proper. It was silent; no more challenges manifested.

"Halooo!" Esk called. "Anybody home?"

There was no answer.

They passed into the residential section of the castle. This should be beyond the region for challenges, ordinarily, but no one met them. "Maybe they stepped out for a bite to eat?" Esk suggested facetiously, but the humor, if any existed, fell flat.

They walked through chamber after chamber. All were cluttered with artifacts of magic and household existence; none had living folk. In the kitchen was a table with a petrified cheese salad in the process of composition; evidently the Gorgon had been making it when she abruptly departed. The greens were hardly wilted; she could not have left more than a day before. In a bedroom were toys and bins of assorted fruits: evidently the work of the Magician's son Hugo, who Chex had heard could conjure fruits. But no sign of the boy. Upstairs, in a crowded cubby of a study, was a high stool by a table with a huge open book: the Magician's Book of Answers, over which he was said to pore constantly. But no sign of the Magician himself. There was even a marker, showing the particular bit of information he had been contemplating; it seemed to relate to the aerodynamic properties of the third left central tail feather of the midget roc bird.

"I didn't know there was a midget roc bird!" Esk remarked.

"You're not the Good Magician," Chex reminded him.

"Obviouvly he was juvt finding hiv plave," Volney said. "He wav about to revearch the propertiev of ventaur wingv."

Chex and Esk stared at him. "That must be right!" Esk said. "To Answer your Question!"

Chex looked stricken. "But why did he go, then? I need that answer!"

"That veemv to be our challenge to divcover."

It was the same situation throughout the castle: everywhere there were evidences of recent and normal activity, but nowhere did any person or creature remain. All servants, if there had been any, had departed; all creatures had been released, in the same manner as the little smokers at the moat. Indeed, they now realized that the moat itself was empty; the moat monsters were gone. That was almost unheard of for the castle. Yet there was no sign of violence; it was as if the Good Magician and his family had simply stepped out for a moment—and not returned. What could account for this?

One region remained to be checked: the dungeon. That was said to be the region of major activity for some castles. Could they have gone down to check something there, and somehow gotten trapped below?

But the stair down was not blocked, and no door was locked. It could not have been any simple entrapment.

"If something happened down there," Chex said nervously, "it could remain dangerous. If, for example, he had a demon there—"

That sent a chill down Esk's back. "A demon could account for it," he agreed. "Some of them are just nuisances, like the one I encountered, but I understand that some are truly terrible. If he meant to keep it confined, but it got out—"

"Then it could have rampaged through the castle and smashed everything and everyone in it," Chex finished.

"Exvept there wav no rampage," Volney pointed out. "No vign of violenve."

"Not all demons are violent," Chex said. "Some are merely mischievous. They assume other forms, and tempt mortal folk into trouble. If the demons became a damsel in distress, right outside the castle, they all might have hurried out to help, and—"

"The Good Magician should never have been fooled by a demon," Esk protested. "He's the Magician of Information. He knows everything!"

She sighed. "I agree; it's a weak hypothesis. Let's gird ourselves and see what's down there."

They descended the stone stair. There was no sign of disturbance on the nether level either, and no sign of anything intended to confine a demon. Small vials crowded the shelves of storage chambers, all of them carefully stoppered; any severe activity should have shaken some vials so that they fell to the floor. This level was the same as the others: normal for its nature.

Except for one small chamber behind a closed door. Chex peered through the tiny barred window. "Activity," she murmured tersely.

Esk felt that cold shiver again. "What is it?"

"It seems to be a—an experiment of some sort," she said. "It's hard to make it out properly. There's a container on a hearth, and it's boiling, and the vapors are overflowing across the floor."

"He must have been cooking up a potion," Esk said, "and forgot to turn it off when he left."

"Then we had better turn it off," she said. "There is no sense letting it boil away to nothing."

Volney sniffed the air. "Beware," he said. "That vmellv like . . ."

When he did not continue, Chex prompted him. "Like what?"

"What?" the vole asked in return.

"What does it smell like?"

"What doev *what* vmell like?"

"That potion!" she said impatiently.

"Povion?"

"The one you just smelled!" she said. "How could you have forgotten it already?"

"I—forget," Volney said, seeming confused. "What am I doing here?"

"What are you—!" she repeated indignantly. "Volney, this is no time for games!"

"For what?"

Suddenly Esk caught on. "An amnesia ambrosia!" he exclaimed. "Volney's nose is more sensitive than ours, and he's closer to the floor. Those fumes must be spreading out and leaking under the door, so he got the first dose!"

"Amnesia!" she cried, alarmed. "We must get away from here!"

"Come on, Volney," Esk said. "We're going back upstairs!"

"Where?" the vole asked.

"Up! Up! To get out of the fumes, before they get us all!"

The vole balked. "Who are you?" he asked.

"He's forgetting everything!" Chex said. "We've got to get him out!"

"We're friends!" Esk said. "We must talk—upstairs! come with us!"

The vole hesitated, but remembered nothing contrary, so followed them up. They slammed every door behind them, and wedged strips of cloth from the sewing room under the last, to halt the creep of the vapor.

"Now I think we know what happened to the Magician and his family," Chex said. "That concoction got out of hand, and they forgot what they were doing!"

"But the Magician was upstairs," Esk said. "Those vapors sink; how could they have reached him there? They haven't even left the dungeon yet, and would have been less extensive a day ago."

She nodded. "True, true. I was thinking carelessly. Those fumes are a consequence of his departure, not a cause, probably. But we had better turn that pot off!"

They were agreed on that. But how were they to do it?

"Maybe there's a counterpotion," Esk said. "Something we can mix up and pour into the dungeon that will neutralize it. The Book of Answers might list it."

They hurried up and checked the book. "What would it be listed under?" Esk asked, turning the ancient pages.

"*M* for memory, perhaps," Chex said.

He found the *M*s. "Magic," he read. "What a lot there is on that subject!" He turned more pages. "Ah, here: Memory." But he frowned as he tried to read the detail. "I can't understand this! It's so technical!"

"Technical?" Chex asked.

"Yes. What does 'mnemonic enhancement enchantment' mean?"

She pursed her lips. "It's technical, all right," she agreed. "Probably only the Good Magician can interpret it; that's why he is the magician."

"We don't have time," he said. "We need something we can understand right now."

"We need a sudden bright idea," she agreed.

"I know little about magic," Volney said, evidently recovering from his whiff of amnesia. "But ivn't there a kind of wood that changev the magic polev?"

"Magic poles?" Esk asked blankly.

"Vo that whatever it iv, it iv not, and vive verva."

"Whatever it is, it is not," Chex said, piecing it out.

"And vice versa," Esk concluded. "I don't know—"

"I think it'v called reverve wood."

"Reverse wood!" Esk and Chex exclaimed together. "That's it!" one or the other added.

They hurried downstairs, checking shelves. "Found it!" Esk called, as he opened a kitchen cupboard. "The Gorgon must have used it for cooking, so that everything she looked at wouldn't be stoned." He fetched down the chip of wood.

"But are you sure it's the right kind?" Chex asked.

"We can test it," he said. "Come toward me. If it reverses my magic—"

"I understand." She strode toward him.

He held up the chip. "No," he said as she drew close.

She leaped at him. Suddenly her rather soft front was pinning him against the wall.

"Oops," she said, backing off. "I didn't mean to do that."

"I told you 'no' on your advance," he gasped. "But you accelerated it."

"So it is reverse wood!" she said.

"I hope it's enough." He looked at the chip, thinking of the chamberful of amnesia fumes below.

"It will have to be," she said firmly.

They took it down to the sealed door, unsealed the door, and hesitated. "We need to get it in the pot, I think," she said. "But if we get close, we'll forget."

"Not vo," Volney said. "Who holdv the wood—"

"Will reverse the amnesia!" Esk exclaimed. "I'll do it!" He hurried down the steps, holding the chip ahead of him. When he reached the bottom, he strode to the closed chamber, wrenched open the door, waded through the pooling vapors, and dumped the chip of wood in the boiling pot.

The effect was dramatic. Not only did the amnesia reverse, as he could tell by his abruptly sharpened memory; the pot halted its boiling and froze.

He returned to the residential floor. "Mission accomplished," he announced.

"Except that we still don't know what happened to the Good Magician," Chex reminded him. "So we still don't have the Answers we came for."

"Maybe a magic mirror can tell us where he went," Esk suggested.

They located a mirror. But as they approached, it flickered.

"Castle Roogna calling Magician Humfrey," it said. "Come in, Humfrey. Over."

"He's not here," Esk said to the mirror.

"Castle Roogna calling Magician Humfrey," it repeated. "Come in, Humfrey. Over."

"How do I turn this thing on to answer?" Esk asked.

The mirror formed an eye and eyed him. "You can't, ogre-snoot," it said. "I respond only to authorized personnel. Tell the Good Magician to get his dinky posterior down here and answer the King."

"But the Good Magician's not here!" Chex exclaimed.

"I didn't ask for excuses, nymph-noodle," the mirror retorted. "Just get him here."

"Listen, glassface!" Esk said, raising a fist.

"Uh-uh, mundane-brain," it said. "I'm worth a lot more than you are. It's a capital offense to break a mirror."

"Just put the King through to us, and we'll tell him what's happening here," Chex said angrily.

"Sorry, you don't have proper clearance, ponytail."

And the mirror went blank.

"I can see why mirrors get broken," Esk muttered.

"It's just the perversity of the inanimate," Chex said. "I greatly fear we'll just have to go on to Castle Roogna ourselves, and tell them what we have found here, and see what they can do about it."

"Cavtle Roogna?" Volney asked.

"It may be the only way we can make any progress toward the solutions to our problems," she said.

So indeed it seemed.

# 5
# IVY

They spent the night in the Magician's castle, and headed out for Castle Roogna in the morning. They brought along a ladder they found in a storage shed; Chex hauled it along by holding one end under an arm and resting the other end on her rump. The ladder interfered somewhat with her tail, so that the biting flies were more of a nuisance than usual, but the distance was not far.

They forged into the mountain of illusion, Volney leading the way. When he announced the chasm, Chex unshipped the ladder and pushed it out over the void. Then she secured one end, while Esk walked across it on hands and feet. At the other end, he sat and held it while Volney crossed. Finally they hauled the ladder the rest of the way across, and Chex made a running leap and hurdled the chasm as before. The whole business was accomplished much more swiftly and comfortably than their prior crossing.

They walked on out the north side and resumed the path. "You know, I wonder how those little smokers got across," Esk remarked. "Could they hurdle that distance?"

"They're pretty active," Chex said. "I suspect they could. Perhaps they charged forward blindly, and some made it while some did not. We don't know how many were in that cage."

He nodded. Her surmise seemed reasonable enough. Perhaps they had been lucky that only a fraction of the dragons had surmounted the hurdle.

Then they came to the lake. "And how did they cross this?" Esk asked. "Do dragons swim, and if they do, does the water monster let them pass?"

Chex glanced at the open water, where the monster waited, then at the side, where the carnivorous reeds waited. "They must have had some other way."

Volney sniffed the end of the path at the waterline. "If the mountain wav illuvion, could thiv be illuvion too?" he asked. "Or could it be another avpect?"

"Another aspect of illusion?" Chex asked, puzzled.

The vole walked out across the water.

Esk and Chex stared. "It's real!" Esk cried.

Chex slapped her own flank resoundingly. "A one-way causeway!" she exclaimed.

"I think not," Volney said.

But they were already racing for the path. Both stepped on it—and both sank through it and into the muck.

Yet Volney remained above the water. "How—?" Esk demanded, somewhat miffed.

"I keep my eyev cloved," the vole explained.

"Eyes closed?" Chex asked blankly as she hauled herself out.

"If what we vee iv not volid," Volney said, "then vometimev what we do not vee *iv* volid."

"What we do not see is solid," Esk repeated thoughtfully.

Chex nodded. "Another reversal. The Good Magician seems very fond of that sort of thing."

"Very fond," Esk agreed, in no better mood than she. Had they realized this before, they could have saved themselves an enormous amount of difficulty.

"But if the lake monster should encroach—" she said.

"It iv an enchanted path, iv it not?" the vole asked, proceeding forward.

She nodded. "True—it should be secure. The dragons were on it because they were travelers; the Good Magician let them go home early, for a reason we do not yet grasp. Other monsters should still be barred—and indeed, we have encountered no others on it. So the water monster should be barred." She shivered. "Yet I begin to feel claustrophobic again. I am by no means eager to trust myself on that path blindly, though I hardly relish the mucky trip around the lake."

Esk pondered. "Suppose you carried me, as you did before—and I kept my eyes open? Would the path become illusory because of me, or remain solid because of you?"

She smiled. "Let's find out! I wouldn't do this with just anyone, but I trust you, Esk."

Esk found himself flustered by the compliment. Centaurs were notoriously distrustful of the judgment of others.

Chex closed her eyes while Esk mounted. Then he directed her toward the path. "Straight ahead—no, slightly to your right," he said.

"That's too clumsy," she said. "Just gesture with your knees."

"My knees?"

"Press with the one on the side you wish me to turn from. That's much more efficient."

"Oh." He tried it, and sure enough, she moved quickly in response. In a moment he was directing her wordlessly.

He guided her onto the path, and the path held. It was, indeed, the walker's vision that determined it; as long as she kept her eyes closed, her footing was firm. When she drifted toward one side or the other, he kneed her gently, and she moved immediately back to the center. The lake monster eyed them, but did not approach; the path was indeed enchanted. The trip across was surprisingly easy.

"Well," Chex said as they arrived at the far side. "That is indeed a relief."

Esk dismounted, and they walked on along the path, their spirits restored. Perhaps at Castle Roogna they would discover the answer to the Good Magician's strange disappearance.

But as they drew closer to the castle, Chex became increasingly nervous. "Is something wrong?" Esk finally inquired.

She sighed. "I'm not sure. It is a personal matter."

"Oh. Not my business, then."

"Perhaps it is your business, because it may affect your reception, and Volney's."

The vole's little ears perked up. "There iv trouble at Roogna?"

"In a way. I shall have to rehearse some history to make it clear."

Esk shrugged. "We'll listen." He was more curious than he cared to admit; what could bother a creature who was completely open about natural functions?

"I am, as you have noted, a crossbreed," she said.

"So am I," Esk reminded her. "We might even have a common human ancestor somewhere way back."

She smiled briefly. "We might. But the centaur species, whatever its origin, considers itself a pure stock, and does not look kindly on adulteration."

"Oho! So they may not like you much!"

"Some may not," she agreed wanly. "Unfortunately, the ones who may look least kindly on my mixed ancestry are my grandsire and grandam on the centaur side."

"Your grandparents don't know?" Esk asked, surprised.

"My dam, Chem Centaur, did not find a mate of her own species. Centaurs are not common beyond Centaur Isle, so this problem can arise. She—associated with a hippogryph. This is why I have wings. But because she was aware that such a liaison might not be approved, she did not inform her sire and dam of the matter. Only her brother, Chet, with whom she was closer. Thus, to the indiscretion of the liaison was added that of deceiving her sire and dam. Such things are not necessarily light matters, with centaurs."

"But it really was her own business, wasn't it?" Esk asked. "I mean, she wasn't under any obligation to report to her parents, was she?"

"That was Chem's conclusion," Chex agreed. "It is possible that other centaurs might disagree."

"And your—grandparents—are at Castle Roogna," Esk concluded, getting the picture.

"I believe that they are."

"And when they see you, with your wings—"

"I am uncertain of the nature of their reaction."

"Maybe you can wait in the forest, while Volney and I go on in."

She sighed. "No, thank you, Esk. I believe it is time to face the melody."

"If that is the way you want it."

"I believe it is the way it must be. I do not like deception, and to the extent that my very existence represents a deception, I owe it to myself to eliminate it."

"I suppose that makes sense," Esk said. Centaurs were known to have an impervious sense of ethics, which had both advantages and disadvantages for others who dealt with them.

They moved well, encountering no more dragons; it seemed that the little smokers had finally gotten wherever they were going and left the path. As night approached, they judged that they were near Castle Roogna.

They set up an overnight watch system as before, not quite trusting the safety of the path. Nothing happened, and in the morning they feasted on fruits and tubers and resumed walking.

There was the sound of hooves ahead. "That's a centaur!" Chex exclaimed. "Oh, I'm nervous!"

Esk could understand her feeling. He was nervous too, but for a different reason; he had never been to Castle Roogna, and wasn't certain how the King would feel about a human-ogre crossbreed. Of course he was only bringing a message, at this point, about the absence of the Good Magician; still, he worried. Volney Vole did not look any more comfortable.

They drew to the sides of the path, so as to let the centaur pass if it had a mind to. But now Volney was sniffing the low-lying air nervously. "Ventaur—and dragon," he announced.

Chex immediately unslung her bow and nocked an arrow, and Esk moved to stand before the vole, so that he could say no if the dragon attacked.

"And human," Volney added.

A party of three—centaur, dragon, and human? How strange! Then he realized that their own party of centaur, vole, and human (approximately) was equivalently strange.

The centaur came into sight. It was a stout male, with a little girl on his back. A truly formidable dragon whomped along behind. Esk's nervousness increased; this could be a great deal of trouble!

"Uncle Chet!" Chex exclaimed, delighted.

The centaur slowed, startled. "Graywing!" he exclaimed.

"He calls me that," she murmured, flushing slightly with pleasure. "He doesn't mind my—"

"Who?" the little girl asked, as Chet stopped before them, and the dragon whomped to a halt behind, puffing steam.

"I'll introduce ours, and you introduce yours," Chet said briskly. "I am Chet Centaur, foaled of Chester and Cherie Centaur; this is Ivy Human, daughter of King Dor and Queen Irene; and beyond is Stanley Steamer, formerly known as the Gap Dragon."

Esk almost swallowed his tongue. The daughter of the King, and the Gap Dragon?

But Chex was doing her side of the introduction. "I am Chex Centaur, filly of Chem Centaur and Xap Hippogryph; this is Esk Human, son of Smash Ogre and Tandy Nymph; and this is Volney Vole from the Kiss-Mee River Valley, otherwise known as the Vale of the Vole."

"The Kiss-Mee River!" Ivy exclaimed excitedly. "I'd love to visit that!" She seemed to be ten or eleven years old, pretty in an elfin way, with very light green hair and eyes to match. "Is it really true that anyone who touches its waters gets so affectionate she just has to kiss the first person she meets?"

"Not anymore," Volney said grimly. "It hav been ruined by the demonv. Now it iv called the Kill-Mee River, and anyone who touchev it feelv like killing hiv neighbor."

"Say, Volney, do you have trouble with your—" Ivy started.

"We three met on the way to the Good Magician's castle," Chex explained quickly. "We all have Questions, but the Magician wasn't there, so—"

"Why, we were just on our way to see Magician Humfrey ourselves," Chet said. "He hasn't been answering his mirror, so we decided to go and see if there was any problem."

"Perhaps we should find a place to settle more comfortably, so we can compare notes," Chex said. "We seem to have much to discuss."

"Evidently so, cute niece," Chet said. He eyed her up and down. "You have filled out nicely since I saw you last."

"I've been exercising to develop my pectoral muscles, but it hasn't enabled me to fly."

"I can fix that!" Ivy exclaimed. "Let me ride you instead of Chet, and—"

"Wait, Ivy," the male centaur said. "First let's get to a better place, as she suggested. Then we can discuss everything, and try everything, without blocking traffic."

Traffic! Esk almost laughed. There was no other traffic on this path.

"Tangleman's close by," Ivy said. "He has a nice glade."

"Who?" Chex asked.

"Tangleman. He's a tangle tree."

"A tangle tree!"

"But don't worry," the child continued brightly. "He's reformed since Grandpa Trent turned him into a jolly green giant."

They made their way to Tangleman's grove. They had to cut through the jungle, but the dragon whomped ahead; any potential predators vacated the region in a hurry. The two centaurs walked side by side, and Esk and Volney brought up the rear.

Tangleman's glade was indeed nice, maintained as only the tangle trees knew how. Tangleman himself was a huge green man with writhing tentacles for hair and barklike clothing. He looked formidable indeed, but grinned broadly when he saw Ivy and her party. Obviously they had maintained cordial relations for years.

There was another round of introductions. Then Stanley and Tangleman settled down to a game of Dumpings and Dragons, which looked more like a battle than a friendly contest, but since Ivy wasn't concerned, the others weren't.

They compared notes and details. "So nobody remains in the Good Magician's castle," Chet said, perplexed. "We wondered, when we couldn't get through. But sometimes those mirrors get perverse, so we decided to check. Ivy likes to visit Hugo and the Gorgon anyway, and Stanley has a thing with the moat monster, so—"

"The moat monster's gone too," Chex said. "All the creatures have been released."

"That is very strange," Chet said. "The Good Magician can

be taciturn, but he takes good care of his environs, and he almost never lets a creature go before its term of service is done. It's as though they have moved out permanently."

"Yes—but on very short notice," she said. "Things were interrupted in progress."

"We shall have to tell King Dor of this," Chet said. "But it will have to wait a few days, because he and Queen Irene are away on business, up at the Water Wing. We were going to take a few days for the trip, but there doesn't seem to be much point, now."

"Don't you want to verify what we have told you?" Esk asked.

"Verify a centaur's report? Whatever for?"

Chex smiled. "He has not had much contact with centaurs, Uncle."

"Oh." Chet turned to Esk. "A centaur's accuracy of observation is perfect, and a centaur's word is inviolate. It would be a waste of time to recheck my niece's findings; they represent the same information I would obtain."

"Oh. Then I guess we can go on to Castle Roogna," Esk said said, out of sorts. He had known about centaur accuracy, but as usual hadn't been thinking clearly. Sometimes he regretted his ogreish descent.

"That, too, is pointless, until the King returns," Chet said.

"You mean we should just wait here?" Esk asked.

"Of course not," Chet said. "That would be wasting time."

"Then—?"

Chex laughed. "We shall simply have to find something else to do for a few days," she said.

"Let's figure out where Magician Humfrey is," Ivy said brightly. "Then we can tell my father where to find him."

"You have a map that locates lost magicians?" Chet inquired wryly.

"Well, no, not exactly. But I know who does: Chem. She has maps for everything!"

"My dam!" Chex exclaimed. "I haven't seen her in a year!"

"And my sibling," Chet said. "It has been longer than that, for me. She doesn't come around Castle Roogna often, now."

"Because of me," Chex said, casting down her gaze.

"Because our dam is just a bit conservative," Chet said. "I believe it is time to face that issue directly."

"That was my conclusion," Chex said.

"Of course. That gives us two reasons to go to see Chem."

"But we need three."

"Three?" Ivy asked.

"Centaurs need three reasons for doing things," Esk told her. He felt a mild and foolish gratification at this chance to show that he did know a bit about the breed.

The child considered. "That's right; I'd forgotten. We were going to Magician Humfrey's castle because he didn't answer his mirror, and I wanted to share another punwheel cookie with the Gorgon, and Stanley wanted to wrestle the moat monster. Three reasons. Now we know Humfrey's gone, so we don't have three reasons anymore."

"Where iv the mapmaking ventaur?" Volney asked.

"Oh, she's doing a detail map of the Gap Chasm," Chet said. "It is very convoluted."

"Stanley needs to see the Gap Chasm!" Ivy exclaimed. "He's going to take it over again any year now, so he needs to keep updated."

Chet nodded. "That is true."

"And that's three!" she cried jubilantly. " 'Cause Chem's at the Gap Chasm!"

"She does have a point, Uncle," Chex said, smiling. "We need a map, and to fetch my dam, and to take the dragon to the Gap Chasm."

"So it seems," he agreed.

"And we can learn all 'bout each other on the way!" Ivy said. "Oh, this is fun!"

"Never become temporary guardian for a little Sorceress," Chet said with resignation.

"And now let me see if I can make Chex fly," Ivy continued with unabated enthusiasm. She ran to Chex. "Lift me up!"

Chex, bemused, assisted the little girl in mounting. "Now flap your wings," Ivy directed. "Real hard."

"*Really* hard," Chet and Chex said together.

"Oh, pooh, you centaurs are all alike! Just do it!"

Chex spread her wings and flapped them. There was indeed

muscle on her chest; Esk tried not to stare at the way her breasts rippled as she made the effort.

"That's it!" Ivy cried. "Harder!"

Chex flapped harder—and an expression of surprise crossed her face. "I have more lifting power!" she said.

"Sure you do, 'cause that's my talent. Enhancement. Now take off."

It almost seemed that it was going to happen. Chex's front legs lifted from the ground. But no matter how hard she flapped, she could not get the rest of her body up; she remained standing on her hind legs.

"That's enough!" she gasped, dropping back down. "I'm winded!"

"Awww," Ivy said, disappointed. "Maybe you need to exercise some more."

"Perhaps I do," Chex agreed, flushed with her effort. "But for the first time, I came close! It was a wonderful feeling."

"It does seem odd that you should have functioning wings that don't quite do the job," Chet said. "Perhaps they require magic enhancement."

"I thought the Good Magician would know," Chex said.

"Sure he does!" Ivy said.

"Surely," Chet and Chex said together.

Ivy didn't even bother to say pooh. She jumped down and skipped off to the gaming monsters. "Time to get moving, boys!" she cried, wading into the melee. "We're going to the Gap!"

That got Stanley's attention immediately. The engagement broke up and the two lined up for the trip.

The party proceeded north, again cutting its own trail. Once a sleeping flying dragon woke, belching fire. Tangleman leaned over it and opened his mouth. The dragon gazed at the huge wooden teeth and scooted away. Another time a small tangle tree—one in the vegetative state—menaced them as they passed. Stanley reared up and puffed steam at it, and the tree quickly wilted back.

"I could get to like this sort of travel," Esk murmured.

"Yeah, it's real fun with them," Ivy said.

"Yes, it's really," both centaurs called.

Ivy stuck out her tongue. Esk buried a smile. He liked the little girl, even if she was a princess.

By nightfall they were near the Gap. They camped by a spring and posted no guards; they needed none in the present company. Esk noted with private satisfaction that Ivy was just as secretive as he was about natural functions; the centaur way was not the only way. In fact, Ivy was a fine antidote to the centaur attitudes.

In the morning they reached the Gap. It was a monstrous crevice whose faces descended clifflike to a narrow base far, far below. Esk felt dizzy just peering into it.

"We shall have to travel along it until we find a way down," Chet said. "That may require some time. There are bridges across it, but my sibling should be down inside it."

Volney sniffed the ground. "No need to vearch," he said. "The old vole holev remain; a large one will take uv down."

"Voles are very good with tunnels," Esk explained to the others as Volney moved along.

"But he's going away from the chasm," Ivy protested.

Then Volney found what he was sniffing for: the cavelike entrance to a large tunnel. "You may wivh light," he said as he plunged on in.

"I saw some lightning rods close by," Ivy said. She dashed off to pick them. They glowed more brightly as she held them, enhanced by her magic. Soon everyone who wanted one had a glowing rod, even Tangleman. They trooped down after the vole.

The tunnel was long and dank, and branched many times, but they followed Volney with confidence, and eventually came out at the base of the Gap. The vole hole had saved them a good deal of trouble.

"Now to find Chem," Chet said. "Stay with us, Stanley; we don't want Stella to find us and take us for prey."

"Stacey," Ivy said smugly.

"What?"

"Her name is Stacey Steamer," Ivy said.

"But she's listed as Stella."

"But I named her, same as I named Stanley. I can't help it if the ass who made the Lexicon got it wrong."

"The ass *didn't* get it wrong; he listed both," Chex said. "There's an ambiguity, that's all."

"But when I'm here, my name is right," Ivy said.

Chet shrugged, unable to refute that. Again the little princess had gotten the best of the centaur. Esk enjoyed that, privately.

Again Volney's nose simplified things. "They went that way movt revently," he announced, pointing west.

They traveled west, and in due course came upon Stacey and Chem. They were exploring an offshoot of the chasm, one with jagged walls angling upward. Chem was projecting an image of it and comparing the details to the real one, so as to match them perfectly. She was a lovely brown-maned, brown-eyed creature with a family resemblance to Chex.

Chex embraced her dam. "My, how you've grown, dear!" Chem exclaimed.

"I exercised."

"But whatever brings you here? I thought you were trying to learn how to fly."

"That's why I finally went to the Good Magician." She proceeded to that story, and to their need for a suitable map.

"But I cannot show the Magician on a map!" Chem protested. "I don't know where he is!"

"We thought you might be able to show a detailed map of where he might be," Chex explained.

"I suppose I could do that. Certainly I can detail any of the geography of that region for anyone who wishes to search for him."

So Chem reluctantly agreed to accompany them back to Castle Roogna. Her sibling and her filly understood her reticence; she had no more desire to brace her sire and dam on the matter of mixed-breed offspring than did Chex. But they all agreed that the time had come to do it.

Stanley decided to stay in the Gap awhile and visit with Stacey. Ivy pouted but yielded to necessity; she could not keep the Gap Dragon out of the Gap forever. They were now near one of the enchanted crossings, so would need no protection once they got to the upper level.

There was no vole hole in this particular section, but Chem had mapped it and knew a good way out. It was along a side crevice on the north slope. They trooped up the jagged V of it, following only the branches Chem indicated, and made their way through the puzzlelike labyrinth to the surface. Then they took the invisible bridge across, which was a novel experience for Esk. He peered down beyond his seemingly unsupported feet, and felt dizzy. After that he followed Volney's example and closed his eyes.

Tangleman departed for his glade, leaving just the three centaurs, two human beings, and one vole. They camped for the night, and when it rained they moved under a large umbrella tree. Volney didn't need it, of course; he simply dug one of his cozy burrows. Ivy insisted on spending the night there, to Esk's annoyance, until Chem projected a map of this region that showed where a good pillow bush grew. Then Esk gathered a fine pile of pillows and settled down in comfort.

They did not hurry in the morning. Centaurs were creatures of integrity, but somehow none of these three found reason to rush on to the castle. Actually, there was no reason; King Dor and Queen Irene were not due to return for another day. Chester and Cherie were supervising the grounds during the royal absence, as it happened, and keeping an eye on Ivy's little brother, Prince Dolph. That, Chet remarked, was challenge enough, for little Dolph could change form instantly to anything, and tended to become a mouse and sneak out when he was supposed to be studying boring Xanth history.

But, being the centaurs they were, they did not dawdle unduly either. Thus at midday they arrived at Castle Roogna.

Esk was impressed. He had seen the Good Magician's castle, so knew the general nature of such structures, but this was on a grander scale. Its walls towered above the moat, and the moat had not one but several monstrous monsters. The grounds were girt about with an orchard containing every kind of exotic tree, and beyond were more aggressive trees that were able to move their branches to block unwanted trespassers. To one side was the zombie graveyard, whose occupants would rise up in all their sodden horror when required in defense of the estate. There were even, Chet assured him, several ghosts in the castle, though these were relatively harmless, merely waiting for their stories to be told.

A tiny man-shape stood at the drawbridge. "A horse rear

with *wings!*" the figure exclaimed. "Wait till the caretakers see that!"

"Go tell them, Grundy!" Ivy cried happily. She was not aware of the gravity of the situation.

The golem ran swiftly into the castle. In a moment a pair of older centaurs appeared, male and female. They spied Chex together.

"Great!" the male exclaimed.

"Appalling!" the female breathed.

"Sire, Dam, this is my issue," Chem said, gesturing to Chex, who stood as if expecting to be struck.

"And she can almost fly!" Ivy said.

Chex's granddam said no further word. She turned and went back into the castle.

Her grandsire hesitated. "This may take a little time," he said, then hurried after his mate.

The three centaurs turned with similar looks of pain and walked away from the castle.

Ivy looked at Esk. "Does this make any sense to you?"

"Not any I like," he replied.

"I thought Cherie would be glad to meet her granddaughter!"

"I gather that centaurs don't approve of crossbreeding."

"Oh, pooh! Everybody crossbreeds in Xanth!"

Esk shrugged. "I fear Cherie Centaur doesn't see it that way."

"She doesn't like magic much, for centaurs," Ivy said thoughtfully. "Chester's better about that; he's got a talent, and so does Chet."

Chet found a place for Chem and Chex to stay the night, and Esk and Volney joined them. None of the three said anything about what had happened, but the pall of gloom was almost tangible. Esk realized that they had really hoped that Cherie would accept the situation. But centaurs, as Esk was coming to understand, were the most stubborn of creatures.

The next day King Dor and Queen Irene arrived back, and in the afternoon they had an audience with the three travelers. It was evident that they had no prejudice against crossbreeds; indeed, they openly admired Chex's wings. Ivy was there, now dressed in robes like the little princess she was, and so was her little six-year-old brother, Prince Dolph.

They listened gravely to Esk's report of the Magician's mysterious absence. Then they listened to Volney's story of the Vale of the Vole. It was apparent that they had already learned something of both these matters, and had come to a decision before holding the audience.

"Ordinarily, we would do our best to help the voles," King Dor said. "But this matter, coming as it does at the time of the crisis with the Good Magician, must wait. Our first priority is to locate Magician Humfrey."

"Oh, Daddy!" Ivy exclaimed indignantly. "Aren't you going to help them just a little?"

"Not at this time, Ivy. When we recover the Good Magician, then he should be able to help the voles, as Volney has come to ask him to do."

"But the bad demons are hurting that friendly river right now!" Ivy protested. "At least let me go with them!"

"No," King Dor said.

"But Daddy!"

Queen Irene turned to her daughter. "No," she repeated, and the tone seemed mild, but the girl shrank back as if severely rebuked.

That was it. There was to be no help of any kind from Castle Roogna. Esk couldn't help but wonder whether Cherie Centaur had anything to do with this cruel decision.

They filed out. Now Volney was as dejected as Chex. What could they do? All their missions were balked until the Good Magician was found.

As they departed the castle, Ivy dashed after them. "But maybe someone else will help!" she cried. "The other centaurs, or maybe the ogres, or someone! Maybe you could ask them! Maybe you three could do something yourselves!"

Esk brightened. His own mission to the Good Magician seemed relatively minor, now; surely he had been rationalizing when he thought that the demoness would harm his family. All she wanted was to be left alone in his hideout. He had made this trip for himself, really, to try to make himself important, or at least worthwhile, in some way. "I am related to the ogres and the curse fiends and the nymphs and fauns," he said. "I don't think my own problem is nearly as important as the voles' problem. I could ask those other folk, and maybe they would help get rid of the demons in the Vale of the Vole."

"I am related to the centaurs and to the flying monsters," Chex said, brightening similarly. "I want to learn to fly, but until the Good Magician is found, I might as well do something to help others. I think the voles need more help than I do, and I could ask those folk. Certainly I don't have much to keep me *here*."

"And I am related to the creaturev of the greater family of volev," Volney said. "The digglev, the vquigglev—I could avk, and maybe they would help. Vertainly it iv pointlevv for me to wait for the Good Magivion while my folk vuffer."

"Let's do it!" Esk said. "Let's all go and ask our distant relatives, and see what help we can get! Maybe we don't *need* the Good Magician or Castle Roogna!"

"That's the way," Ivy said brightly.

Somehow, in her presence, it all made sense. They would solve the problem of the Kiss-Mee River themselves!

# 6

# CENTAUR

C hex trotted south along the trail that her dam's map had shown. She expected to reach Centaur Isle in two days, and to spend one day there, and return in two. That should be plenty of time to complete the rendezvous with Esk and Volney, who were questing in other directions. They had agreed to meet in seven days, hoping that at least one of them had obtained help for the Vale of the Vole and the distressed Kiss-Mee River. A two-day margin for error seemed sufficient; centaurs were efficient creatures who seldom if ever made errors, in contrast to the bumbling human beings.

The trail wended parallel to the west coast of Xanth. It was neither well marked nor well maintained, but the protective enchantment was on it, so there should be no trouble with predators. Also, there was Ivy.

"Gee, this is fun!" Ivy exclaimed. She was on Chex's back, and *everything* was fun to her. Ivy's magic was Enhancement, and it was of Magician caliber. Since she perceived Chex as a wonderful creature who could almost fly, Chex, was now moving at a trot that exceeded in velocity her normal full gallop. The child's magic buoyed her phenomenally; it was indeed like flying, because her strength was so great and her feet so light. Also, the girl was good company; she made no unreasonable demands, and was an excellent rider. Chex's granddam Cherie had been tutoring her in more than academic subjects, obviously.

The thought of Cherie Centaur sobered Chex, however. By all accounts Cherie was a fine centaur, but she was conservative. She had tutored King Dor and Queen Irene, and now was tutoring the next generation, but certain matters were beyond her acceptance, such as magic in centaurs. And crossbreeding. Chester Centaur, in contrast, had the reputation of a roughneck, always ready to fight rather than reason; but he was quite tolerant about magic and crossbreeding. Uncle, Chet had said this was because of Chester's uncle, Herman the Hermit, who had had the magic ability to commune with will-o'-the-wisps and had died bravely in the defense of Xanth from the wiggles. Also, Chester was unable to perceive evil in anything his offspring might do. But though Chester had the muscle, Cherie had the will, and that will was manifesting now. Chex was subtly not welcome in the region of Castle Roogna.

But little Ivy was another matter, and a power in her own right. When they had made their decision to get other help for the voles, Ivy had insisted on participating. She could help persuade the centaurs of the Isle to help, she said. Besides which, she needed more education, and visiting Centaur Isle was part of it. Even Cherie had not been able to deny that logic, so Ivy had her way: she was coming along, just for this one trip.

"But you seem awful quiet," Ivy said after a bit. "Is something wrong?"

"Not with you, dear," Chex reassured her. "I was just thinking."

"About Cherie," Ivy said wisely.

"True."

"Chester's working on her, but you know how centaurs are. Nothing's more stubborn, when—oops. No offense meant!"

"None taken," Chex said. "We prefer to call it steadfastness."

"Maybe if you do something great, like saving the Kiss-

Mee, then she'll change her mind. Say, is it true that just drinking from that river is like getting smooched?" The child had broached this matter before, but evidently remained intrigued by it.

"That vernacular is—"

"Nonstandard usage," Ivy finished. "You centaurs are too stuffy!"

"But it is supposed to be true that the river, historically, has been very affectionate. However, it seems that it has suffered a radical personality change recently. That is why we wish to restore it to its natural state."

"Yeah. So now it's the Kill-Mee. That's funny!"

Then, exactly in time with Chex's correction: "Yes!"

Then Ivy laughed, and Chex had to laugh with her.

They were well along, making even better time than Chex had projected, thanks to the enhancement. Would her hooves never tire? Apparently not, while she was carrying the little Sorceress.

"What's that stink?" Ivy asked. Then, as Chex opened her mouth: "Smell!" How the child loved to tease.

Chex sniffed the air. "Decay," she said. "Some small animal must have died recently. We will pass by this soon."

But as they proceeded south, the odor intensified. "Ooo, ugh!" Ivy said, holding her pert nose. "That must be a big animal!"

"So it seems," Chex agreed. "All living creatures eventually die."

"Not the Good Magician," Ivy said.

"Well, he is missing, and we cannot rule out the possibility that—"

"Oh, pooh! He just went somewhere, so's not to be bothered."

Chex wished they could be sure of that. She did not argue the case.

The smell intensified into truly awful scope. "A monster!" Ivy gasped.

It was all Chex could do to keep from gagging herself. She had never before encountered miasma like this. "A monster," she agreed. "We've got to get by it soon!"

But they did not. The stench became almost palpable. Ivy

was coughing now. "What a stink!" she cried. "I can't even see!"

Chex drew to a halt, too distracted to protest the naughty word this time. She was having trouble with her own vision. They seemed to be swimming in the putrid vapor. "We'll have to go around it," she said.

"Castle Zombie!" Ivy exclaimed. "It's near here!"

"That's the odor? Zombies?"

"No, they smell, but not like this. I mean we could go there, and they'll tell us how to get around, 'cause they know about death and all that rot."

Chex decided not to try to correct that usage either. Zombies were creatures of death and rot. She was not enthusiastic about visiting such a castle, but it was obvious that something had to be done. Chem's map had shown the castle; the girl was correct about its proximity.

She turned back and trotted toward an intersection she had noted some way back. This alternate path would lead them to Castle Zombie. As they proceeded along it, the awful odor diminished. That was a relief. She felt as if there were foul sludge coating her lungs.

Ivy was right: there was a smell about Castle Zombie, but it was quite bearable after what they had experienced. Perhaps the zombies conserved their rotting flesh better, not allowing much of it to escape as gas. There were a number of them working on the grounds, evidently tending the putrid vegetation.

The castle itself looked as if it were decomposing, but Chex knew this was mostly illusion; it was of comparatively recent construction. Its moat was filled with slime, and a zombie water monster stewed in it. "Hi, Sleaze!" Ivy called out cheerfully, and the moat monster actually nodded. Everybody liked Ivy!

The lady of the castle came out to greet them. She showed no sign at all of zombie-ism. "Hi, Millie!" Ivy called, exactly as before.

"Hello, Ivy," the woman replied. "Who is your friend?"

"This is Chex. Chem's her moth—her dam. She's got wings!"

"I had noticed." The woman smiled at Chex. "You are welcome here, Chex, if you care to come in."

Chex was in doubt about what the interior of the castle might be like, but Ivy was not. "We care!" she cried, clapping her hands.

Millie smiled again. "You are so like your mother at that age—and so unlike, too."

"I know," Ivy said. "She was more serious. And more— her—" She made a gesture with her hands to indicate voluptuousness.

"Be young while you can, dear," Millie said.

"But when will I get all plushy and be able to fascinate men the way you do?" the girl asked plaintively.

"By the time you find the one you want to fascinate you will be able," Millie assured her.

"And what about me?" Chex asked with a quirk of a smile. "I am one of a kind."

"So is Rapunzel," Millie replied, "but she's married now."

"To Grundy Golem," Ivy said. "Which reminds me, when is Snortimer coming back?"

This jump was too much for Chex. "Who is Snortimer, and what does he have to do with unique creatures finding mates?"

"He's my Monster Under the Bed," Ivy explained. "Grundy borrowed him, and never returned him, and now it's awful quiet under my bed." Then, after the briefest of pauses. "Awfully quiet."

"Oh." Chex was more confused than before.

"There's a zombie monster under Lacuna's bed," Millie said. "I think he's lonely, now that she's grown up."

"Oh, goody! I'll go play with him!" Ivy dashed off.

Millie turned to Chex. "I presume this is not purely a pleasure visit?"

"It's a coincidental visit," Chex confessed. "We were going to Centaur Isle to seek help for the voles, who have a serious problem, but there's such a horrendous smell on the path that—"

"Oops! That must be the sphinx! Jonathan said it looked ill."

"Jonathan?"

"My husband, the Zombie Master. Sphinxes live a very long time, but on occasion they do die."

"That would account for it," Chex said. "Can anything be done?"

"Oh, yes, of course. Jonathan wants to find that sphinx and make a zombie of it before it's too far gone. Now that we know where to look, he'll go with a contingent of zombies and convert it. The process will take a few days, because a sphinx is a very large creature, but I know he will be grateful to you for the information."

"But I have a limited time to reach Centaur Isle and return," Chex said. "I can't wait a few days. Ivy thought you might know a way around."

"There is a way, but it is difficult. You would need a guide."

"I would be happy to have a guide, if one is available."

"A zombie guide."

Chex paused. She had not had prior experience with zombies, and was not enthusiastic. "I would have to carry a zombie?"

"Oh, no, of course not! We can give you a centaur."

"A zombie centaur?" This did not appeal either.

"Ordinary folk do have some difficulty accepting zombies as legitimate creatures in their own right," Millie said.

Chex remembered the difficulty some folk had accepting crossbreeds, too. "A zombie guide will be fine," she said, making an abrupt decision.

"Very well. I'll ask Horace." Then Millie raised her voice. "Ivy! You must be on your way now!"

"Aww!" Ivy called back. "Zomonster's fun!"

Millie winked at Chex. "Unless you would like to stay and have a meal with the zombies, dear."

Suddenly Ivy was running downstairs. "I'm ready to go, now, thanks all the same, Millie."

"But we have such really rotten food!" Millie protested, smiling. "The very best mold, and even a few dead maggots. Are you sure—?"

"Quite sure, thank you," Ivy said with urgent politeness.

"Perhaps another time, then," Millie said with seeming regret. She had evidently had prior experience with children. She led the way out.

Horace turned out to be a not-too-far gone centaur. His body was patched where hair had fallen out, and his face was somewhat worm-eaten, but otherwise he was all right.

"Please show Chex the alternate route to Centaur Isle," Millie said to him. "And wait for her return. Do you understand?"

"Yesh, Millie Ghosht," Horace said, speaking as well as he could with a rotten lip and tongue.

Chex helped Ivy mount. "Thank you, Millie; I really appreciate this."

"Anything in a good cause," Millie said. "It was nice to meet you, Chex."

Then Horace was moving off, and Chex had to hurry to catch up with him. "Bye, Millie!" Ivy called, waving frantically. "Bye, zombies!" Millie and several zombies waved back.

"Millie certainly didn't look like a zombie," Chex remarked.

"Oh, no, she's a ghost!" Ivy said.

"A ghost!" Chex exclaimed. But then she remembered what Horace had called her: ghosht.

"Well, she isn't really a ghost anymore," Ivy explained. "But she was one for eight hundred years, so we still call her Millie the Ghost."

"Eight hundred years!"

"Yes, and then she won a prize or something and was made alive again, and she took care of Daddy when he was little, and then she married the Zombie Master and lived happily ever after. She's real nice." Ivy paused.

Then: "Really nice!" in time with Chex's correction. And a laugh.

Horace turned his head. "Watsch niche?"

"Millie the Ghosht," Ivy replied promptly, stifling a giggle.

"Yesh," the zombie agreed.

"They aren't too bright," Ivy confided. "But they really are nice, when you get to know them. They defend Castle Roogna, you know."

Chex had known, because of the zombie graveyard there.

Nevertheless, she was picking up a lot of interesting material from this child.

The path they were following was easy to discern. Chex wondered why Millie had considered it to be so difficult as to require a guide. Then Horace drew to a halt.

"Zragon nesht ahead," he announced, losing a discolored tooth.

That would make it difficult! Chex unslung her bow. "A big one?"

"Many bigh onze," he said. "Vwe go around."

"I thought we were already going around."

But he was leading the way into a thick tangle of vegetation. It seemed to consist of truly monstrous vines.

"They're growing in dragon dung," Ivy remarked. "That must be why they're so big! But you know, these look like——"

Abruptly they came up to the biggest gourd Chex had ever imagined. "But that's a——" she started, shocked.

"Hypnogourd," Ivy finished, as Horace leaped into the giant peephole.

"We can't——" Chex protested, appalled. "No one escapes on his own from a gourd! There isn't even supposed to be any physical entry—it's all in the spirit! But he just——"

"I guess that's why we need a guide," Ivy said.

Chex nodded. Maybe it did make sense. If she wanted to keep their guide in range, she had to act promptly.

She nerved herself and leaped into the peephole.

She landed in thick vegetation much like that she had just left. But this had one important difference: it was zombie vegetation. The leaves of the plants were rotting, and the stems were mottled. Nevertheless, vines were extending toward the depressions of what appeared to be sunken grave sites. The vines were trying to tunnel into the ground here, rather than springing from it in the normal fashion.

But she couldn't pause to figure out this anomaly; Horace was disappearing on the winding trail ahead. She galloped after him.

"Funny—they're growing the wrong way," Ivy said. "But you know, that's not scary, the way it was when I was in here before."

"You were in the gourd before?" Chex asked, amazed.

"Yes. There was a whole big lake of castor oil! Triple ugh! And a bug room! I hated it. But here it's only plants growing into zombie graves."

"It's a zombie horror!" Chex exclaimed, catching on. "Things that frighten zombies—like plants boring into their graves and sapping their vitality, or whatever it is they have."

"That must be it!" Ivy agreed happily. "Zombie haunts!"

There was a sharp hiss ahead. It was a venomous snake, striking at Horace's leg. But the centaur leaped clear, and the fangs closed instead on a sickly rose plant.

Immediately the plant changed color, becoming healthy and vigorous. Beautiful red roses formed.

"But what's so bad about that?" Ivy asked. "If it had bitten Horace, he would've been healthy again, wouldn't he?"

"Which might be the ultimate horror, for a zombie," Chex said. "Just as getting bitten and turning zombie would be a horror for us." But it certainly was strange.

Horace drew up at a new threat: a region of slashing knives. There seemed to be no creature wielding them; the knives merely cut of their own volition. This was as awkward for living creatures as for zombies; how were they to pass?

Horace drew a rusty knife from his backpack. He hurled it into the melee.

Immediately the other knives attacked it. Sparks flew as metal rasped against metal. Soon the magic knives, their blood frenzy aroused, were slashing each other. Not long thereafter, all the knives were broken, having destroyed each other. It seemed safe to proceed through this region now.

Whereupon Horace turned and proceeded back the way they had come. Startled, Chex followed. What kind of a maze was this?

The path behind had changed. Now the zombie vegetation was zombie mineral; decaying stones, rusting metal, and dissolving plastic. Horace threaded his way through it, touching nothing except the ground—until, abruptly, he brought a front hoof down on a sodden green rock.

The rock fragmented. The chips fell to the ground and burned their way into it, sinking from sight. The ground itself caught fire, burning with a sickly greenish flame. Zombie fire.

Gradually a wooden underpinning was revealed, as the

earth above it burned away. The wood, oddly, was untouched by the flame, which flickered out.

Horace set his front hoof against the near end of the wood, and it descended. The far side lifted; the panel was hinged in the center. Beneath was revealed a flight of wooden steps, leading to a lighted cellar.

"Gee," Ivy whispered, intrigued.

Horace turned and walked back the way he had come, ignoring the steps. Chex, bemused, followed.

Again the setting had changed. Now it consisted of zombie animals: ratlike things that scurried haphazardly around, shedding fragments of themselves.

Horace stepped among them, taking care that his hooves crushed none. Chex followed, taking equal care. She could guess what would happen next: the centaur would select one creature to crush, and then a new way would open, and he would ignore it. This was a strange place even in its predictability.

Horace kicked a rat. The creature squealed. Immediately the others rose up and squealed too. Then they changed into numbers and rose into the air. The ground became a grid on whose squares the shadows of the numbers danced.

Horace lay down, his body covering a number of the squares. The numbers above those squares keened angrily and attacked. They spun so that their ends formed cutting surfaces and plunged at his body.

Chex, doubtful and not a little worried, lay down too. "I hope that zombie knows what he is doing," she murmured.

"I hope so too," Ivy whispered. "I don't like those numbers!"

Indeed, the numbers were attacking the two of them now, as well. They buzzed down like aroused bees—and passed right through their flesh without impact.

Chex laughed. "They must be imaginary numbers!"

"What?" Ivy asked.

"Numbers used in mathematics that aren't real," Chex explained. "But sometimes it is necessary to use them anyway."

"That doesn't make much sense to me," Ivy grumbled.

"I'm sure it doesn't! But this must be the home of those

numbers. They are probably the bad dreams of mathematicians."

Horace leaned his humanoid torso back and went to sleep.

Chex hesitated. Did the zombie really know what he was doing or had he given up? If so, could she afford to follow his example? There were certainly dangers here, and this was the gourd; they could be in real trouble, if—

"I guess we don't have much choice," Ivy said, for once not enthusiastic.

"So it seems, dear," Chex agreed. They both settled back and closed their eyes. To their surprise, they slept immediately.

Chex opened her eyes. It was day, and she lay on a beach. Across the open water she saw the distant outline of a large island.

She blinked. "Could that be Centaur Isle?" she asked aloud.

"Yesh," Horace said from behind her.

Ivy woke. "We're here!" she exclaimed. "But how did we get here?"

"We went to sleep in the gourd," Chex said, hardly believing it herself. "I can only surmise that to sleep in the realm of dreams is to wake in the realm of ordinary consciousness."

"I guess maybe we did need a guide," the little girl said.

"I guess maybe we did," Chex agreed.

"Gotcha!" Ivy exclaimed. "You spoke my language!"

"After what we just experienced, your language seems easier." Chex hefted herself up. "Is this really Centaur Isle," she asked Horace, "or merely a dream of it?"

"It really ish," he assured her. "Shortch cut."

So it seemed. Chex decided to accept things as they seemed, and get on with her mission.

Ivy slid off her back. "I gotta feel solid sand under my feet," she said. Chex understood; the experience in the gourd had been unsettling, even for a little Sorceress.

Now she had to cross the water to the Isle. There should be a ferry where the trail arrived. "I'll scout around for the crossing," Chex announced.

"I'll rest here," Ivy said. "It'll be safe enough, with Horace. Anyway, Mom gave me a protective charm."

Chex made sure. "You will wait here for me?" she asked Horace.

"Yesh," he said.

She set off along the beach, trotting east, because the closest approach to the Isle seemed to be in that direction. Soon enough her judgment was confirmed; there was a raft with a sail at a landing.

She trotted up. "Halloo!" she called.

A centaur of middle age emerged from a shelter. "Someone for crossing?" he asked.

"Yes. I need to go to Centaur Isle, and then to return—" She broke off, because the other was staring at her wings.

"Oh, a crossbreed," he said, with deep disgust. "Forget it."

"But I have to talk to the centaur Elders about—"

"We don't talk to crossbreeds," he said curtly. "Now get away from here before someone sees you."

"But—"

He reached for his bow.

"Now look!" she protested. "I have a right to be heard!"

The bow was in his hands. "Crossbreeds have no right to exist, let alone be heard," he said. "No one will talk to you. You'd be executed without trial if you set foot on the Isle. Now fly away before I'm put to the trouble of burying your body."

Appalled, Chex realized that he was serious. Her granddam's attitude was merely the echo of the prejudice of the larger community of centaurs. They were unable to tolerate any deviance from their norm.

For a moment she was tempted to stand her ground and put him to that trouble of burying her. But she knew it would not accomplish anything; the position of the centaurs was sealed. As Ivy had said: centaurs were stubborn.

She turned and trotted away, frustrated and disgusted. Now she appreciated why her dam had raised her largely isolated from her own kind. Uncle Chet had been around often, showing her his magic with boulders and pebbles, and some of the hermitlike forest centaurs had visited on occasion, but never any centaurs from either the village north of the Gap or from Centaur Isle. Her education was coming hard. Centaurs were supposed to be the most brilliant and consistent creatures of

Xanth, but her belief in this had been shaken. How could a species that was an obvious crossbreed between humanoids and equinoids be so restrictive about further crossbreeding?

Yet, as she considered the matter, she knew. If centaurs accepted unrestricted crossbreeding, as the equines did, they would eventually be fragmented as a species, as the equines were. There were no longer any true horses in Xanth, only in Mundania, where they couldn't interbreed with other species. In Xanth there were night mares and pookas and were-horses and sea-horses and hippogryphs and centaurs and unicorns and flying horses, and the original stock had been crossbred out of existence. Now the centaurs were preserving their variant as a viable species, and were doing what they had to do in that effort.

Still, there were even more crossbreeds involving the human stock than there were of the equine stock, ranging from elves to ogres to multi-mergings like the sphinxes, yet the original stock remained viable. Humans did tend to discourage crossbreeding, but were reasonably tolerant of what did occur. Thus centaurs were welcome at Castle Roogna, and other variants such as the golem and an ogre or two. So the restriction did not have to be absolute.

But, she reminded herself in an effort to retain centaur objectivity, the human stock had a major source of replenishment: Mundania. There had been many Waves of colonization from Mundania, each one adding to the straight human population of Xanth. Centaurs could not be reinforced similarly, for they existed only in Xanth. So the situations were not precisely analogous.

All of which did not make her feel much better. She could understand the position of the centaurs, without appreciating it. What she really needed was a species of her own.

She laughed to herself, somewhat bitterly. She was, as far as she knew, the only one of her kind in Xanth. Some species!

She arrived back at the spot where Ivy and Horace waited. "Any luck?" the little girl asked brightly.

"No luck," Chex said heavily. "They will not even talk to me, because I am a crossbreed."

Ivy pursed her lips. "The way Cherie won't?"

"Yes."

"Maybe I could do it—"

Chex considered. Ivy was a child, but she was also the King's daughter, and a Sorceress. The centaurs might give her an audience. But she would have to go to the Isle alone, and that would violate Chex's commitment to guard her. Also, if the centaurs would not even talk to a variant of their own kind, would they help a completely different species, the voles? This was highly doubtful.

"I think we should write this off as a bad job, dear," she said. "I underestimated the resistance of the centaurs to our effort."

Ivy shrugged. "Okay. Maybe we can get help from your sire's folks, instead."

"The winged monsters?" Chex considered, finding this alternative more interesting now that her major hope had been dashed. "Well, certainly I could go to my sire and ask. But he lives closer to central Xanth; we shall have to return to Castle Roogna first, and I can compare notes with Esk and Volney. Perhaps one of them has already found help."

"Um," Ivy agreed, glancing at her expectantly.

Chex waited, and Ivy waited. Finally Chex surrendered and said "Yes," in correction, and Ivy said it with her, then laughed. The odd thing was that this made Chex feel better.

Horace led them into the jungle, following another trail that showed signs of disuse. Chex realized that other creatures tended to avoid the paths used by zombies. Prior to this experience, she would have avoided it too. But after her rebuff by the living centaurs, she found the zombie centaur better company. The zombies were providing what help they could, and indeed, had enabled her to cut many hours off her trip south.

When the trail passed through looser forest, she drew up abreast of him. "May I ask you a question, Horace?"

"Yesh."

"How did you come to be a zombie?"

"I zdied."

Evidently he wasn't much for detail! "How did you die?"

"Peopleschooz."

"I beg your pardon?"

"Parzon?"

Not much for social niceties, either. But these could hardly be expected of those whose brains were rotten. "How did you die?" she repeated.

"Zome call it horschschooz."

"I don't understand."

"I think he said horse—" Ivy started.

"Don't say that word!"

"Manure," Ivy finished contritely. "A princess doesn't even know the other word."

"Let's hope not! But how could anything like that account for his death."

"I'm sure he can explain it, if I ask him," Ivy said confidently. "Here, let me ride him."

"I really don't think—"

"Oh, he can hold my weight all right. I talked to him while we were waiting for you. He's nice enough, for a zombie." She leaned across, and Chex had to move close to facilitate the transfer, lest the girl fall between them.

Ivy scrambled across and settled on Horace's back. "Horace, you're pretty strong," she said, and indeed, the zombie seemed to be in better physical condition than before. "You can talk well, too, I just know it."

"Zthank you," Horace said, and his voice did sound better. It was the child's magic, enhancing him.

"How did you die?" Ivy asked.

"People zhooz."

"People shoes!" Ivy exclaimed. "What they call horseshoes in Mundania! Where you throw these metal shoes."

"Yez." The pronunciation was less slushy, but still not perfect. There was only so much Enhancement could do, when lips were decayed and teeth missing.

"But how did a game kill you, Horace?" Ivy asked.

"Hit by a boot."

"Oh, an accident!" Chex exclaimed. "One of those hard metal shoes hit you on the head!"

"Yez. A heavy people zboot, with hob nailz."

"And then the Zombie Master revived you as a zombie."

"Yez."

"How do you feel, being a zombie?"

"It'z not zbad. But my oldz friendz won't play with me."

"I'm afraid the living aren't too fond of the undead," Chex said. "They're prejudiced." She had just had a good lesson in prejudice.

"Yez."

"But Zora Zombie's nice," Ivy said, transferring back to Chex. "She's almost alive."

"Zora is a friend of yours?"

"Yes. She helped Mom learn about zombies. Then she married Xavier."

"Xavier!" Chex exclaimed. "I know him! He rides Xap!"

"Yes. Xap's great. He's a hippogryph."

"I know. He's my sire."

"Oh!" Ivy squealed with delight. "I didn't realize! That's how you got your wings!"

"That's how," Chex agreed. "I know Xavier because he's been with Xap, but I didn't know he was married. He never mentioned it."

"I guess that's less important to males than to females," Ivy said.

"Unless he was ashamed of having a zombie wife."

"I don't think so," Ivy said. "He always seemed real—really proud of her, when he was with her."

"Then perhaps he was afraid that others would have the wrong picture of her, if they learned she was a zombie without meeting her."

"Maybe. You'd hardly know she's a zombie. That's how I know zombies aren't bad, 'cause she's baby-sitted me and she's great."

Horace veered to the side. "Gourd," he announced.

There was another of the huge variety that grew in dragon dung. Horace plunged into its peephole, and Chex followed.

Inside it seemed exactly the same as it had been on their prior entry. Chex had thought they would be in the region of imaginary numbers that they had left, but they were in the first stage, with the zombie vegetation.

They negotiated the region of knives the same way as before. "I wonder what's beyond those knives?" Ivy asked.

"Perhaps nothing," Chex said. "It may be only a ritual, where a particular action is required to change the setting of the maze. An intruder not knowledgeable about this matter might take the wrong direction."

They came to the buried trap door. "I'd sure like to see what's down there!" Ivy said.

Chex was getting quite curious too; the steps seemed very inviting. But she was sure it was a trap: if she deviated from the route of their guide, she would perhaps be trapped within the gourd.

They reached the numbers, and again lay down and slept— and woke not far beyond Castle Zombie. There was no giant gourd here, just as there had not been at the southern beach; they had emerged by some other mechanism.

Now night was approaching. They had been to the verge of Centaur Isle and back in a single day, a journey that would otherwise have taken three. Chex faced the prospect of returning to Castle Roogna two days early. That would be fine if Esk and Volney were back early, but not good if they were not.

She considered as the castle came into view, then made her decision. "Ivy, if Millie and the Zombie Master are willing, how would it be if we stayed here for two days?"

"Ooo, goody!" Ivy exclaimed, clapping her hands. "I can play with Zomonster all I want!"

So it was decided that simply. Castle Zombie seemed positively attractive, now.

# 7

# GATEWAY

Esk brought out the pill somewhat doubtfully. Ivy had brought three of them from the Castle Roogna armory, telling him that there were plenty of them and that she used them all the time when she was in a hurry. He had hardly wanted to suggest that the child was not telling the truth, so he had accepted them. But now that Chex had trotted off south with Ivy, and Volney was tunneling to his mission, he was worried. Suppose they didn't work?

Well, in that case he would have to proceed the oldfashioned way, hoping he could make it in time. He had slogged by foot from home to Castle Roogna; he could slog down to Lake Ogre-Chobee. But he hoped the pills worked.

He put one in his mouth and swallowed it. Nothing changed. It was supposed to enable him to travel almost masslessly, so that he could cover a great distance without impediment or fatigue. But maybe its enhancement worked only on the child whose talent was Enhancement.

He took a step—and shot through a tree. He had paused on the path that started out toward the lake. It curved, so a tree was ahead of him some distance ahead. Now it was behind.

Could his step have taken him through the tree? He reached slowly back and touched the trunk and met only slight resistance. The tree seemed to have become an illusion.

Which was the way the pill was supposed to work. The tree was as solid as ever; it was Esk himself who had become very much like an illusion. His mass had been nulled out, though he looked and felt the same as before. Ivy had told him true.

If Chex had pills like these, she would be able to fly! But of course she wanted to fly regularly, not just during the span of one dose.

He faced southeast and started walking. His feet touched the ground and sank into it slightly, giving him necessary traction. His body zoomed along as if it weighed no more than a feather. Obviously that was the case, though he felt the same. His leg muscles, primed to propel his full mass, had only a tiny fraction of it to move now, so had a great deal of extra strength. He tended to leap when he intended only to push off, and to sail through the air far further than he could normally have jumped. He had trouble keeping his balance, because what he thought were trifling corrections became powerful shoves. He careened through trees with impromptu abandon, lunging through a seeming forest of phantoms.

Soon he got it under control, however, and concentrated on rapid forward progress. It hardly mattered whether he stayed on the path; he could pass through brush and other obstacles with almost equal ease. When he tried to go through a hill he slowed, though, because the resistance of the ground against his body was greater than that against his feet. He had to go into a swimming motion, and this was less efficient. So he stayed above, and avoided trees when he conveniently could, so that they would not drag against him.

He admired the whizzing scenery. The nearer trees were passing so rapidly that they blurred, while distant ones were slower, and far mountains hardly changed at all. He tended to plow into hills, then to sail when descending their far slopes. He saw wild creatures, who were unable to move out of the way before he was upon them, but he was beyond them before they decided what to do. He spied a snoozing griffin and kicked at its nose without effect; the creature shifted its head, startled, as he left it behind. This was fun!

He was traveling rapidly, but he did have a good distance to go, so it was near nightfall before he came to the broad shore of Lake Ogre-Chobee. At last the pill was wearing off, and his normal mass was returning. Now he wished he had been less wasteful in the expenditure of his energy; his foot and leg muscles were tired in unusual ways because he had not been walking in the normal manner. The more the pill wore off, the less comfortable he became; he was good and sore!

He set about eating and making camp for the night, not too close to the water, because he didn't like the look of the green reptilian creatures in it. He was lonely now; he had gotten used to company, and decided that he preferred it. He finally settled in a tree for sleep; it wasn't comfortable, but it was relatively safe. He could tell any creature no, but he had to be awake to do it. He should be able to hear anything that tried to climb the tree in the night, or anything that landed in its foliage.

In the morning, cramped, he took care of routine needs, then addressed the problem of entry into Gateway Castle. The problem was that it was under the water. The only surface entrance was via a great whirlpool, and he didn't trust that. He could take another pill and become less dense than the water, and walk down through it and the castle wall—but then he would be inside in no state to talk with the inhabitants, and when the pill wore off they might not appreciate the manner of his intrusion. It would be better to apply at the front gate and be admitted legitimately. But where was the front gate?

Well, there must be a route for supplies. The curse fiends were said to be insular, caring little for outsiders, but they had to go out for food, wood, and other necessities. He would locate that supply route, and intercept someone on it, and explain his mission. Since he was related to these people, it should be possible to get some attention.

He walked along the shore, looking carefully for signs of activity. But the lake was huge, and the walk was long. The chobees came out, scrambling toward him on fat green legs. Their teeth were plentiful, and he didn't trust them, so he retreated into the forest until they did not follow.

Eventually he did discover evidence of activity. There was a region with cultivated trees, and that meant that someone was cultivating them. There were blue trees, and red trees, and orange trees, their fruits ripening nicely; there were yellow, green, and blue berry bushes. There were many different kinds of pie trees, and blanket trees, and all the other agricultural staples that a community of human beings required. He was definitely in the right region!

Sure enough, before long he heard voices, and came across young women harvesting an assortment of slippers from a grove of shoe trees. They wore simple blouses and skirts, evidently harvested from other trees at other times, in an assortment of pastel colors. Matching kerchiefs bound their tresses fetchingly.

He approached them. "Excuse me," he called. "I am looking for Gateway Castle."

"Eeeek! A man!" they cried with flattering alarm. Then they began counting: "One, two—"

"No!" he exclaimed, realizing what they were up to. The curse fiends, unlike other creatures, shared a common talent: that of cursing. A massed curse could be devastating; even his mother's tantrums, which were related, were bad enough. He did not want to be hit by a several-girl curse.

His "no," of course, stifled that; they lost their count and did not try to curse him. Still, they backed away from him distrustfully. "Don't hurt us, sir, we are only working girls," they exclaimed.

"I am only a traveler looking for Gateway Castle," he repeated. "But I don't know how to get in."

"Are you sure you're harmless?" one asked him.

"Quite harmless," he assured her.

"Then we will take you in with us when we go," she said. "But you will have to check in with the authorities."

"I shall be glad to," he said. "Meanwhile, may I help you harvest?"

They giggled, and decided to let him help. So for the next two hours he helped them select ripe shoes. It was important that there be pairs that matched in size and type and color; many excellent ones had to be left because they had no mates. Thus, this was not as easy a job as it had seemed; indeed, in some cases it seemed that it would have been about as easy to make the matching shoes as to find them.

It was fun doing this work, not because Esk had any particular affinity for work, but because the girls were of his own age, and flirted with him constantly, making remarks about lady slippers without mates. Esk realized that there might be more for him at Gateway Castle than just his mission. After all, his grandmother had been a curse fiend.

Then the time came for them to reenter the castle. They trooped along with their baskets of shoes, and Esk went with them. He had been tired when he encountered them, but did not feel so now. In fact, he was feeling very positive.

They came to a pier that projected some distance into the lake. They walked out on this and waited, and soon a thing appeared, rising from the deep water. It resembled a boat, and seemed to be made of wood, but it managed to sail *under* the water rather than on it. This was decidedly strange to Esk, but the girls crowded toward it without hesitation.

The top opened, and there was a hole down into the boat. The girls stepped across in turn, clinging to the handholds set inside the hole and passing their baskets of shoes across. Then they called to Esk, and he crossed too, and found that there was a ladder. He descended it until he was well below the surface of the lake, his feet finally touching the floor. Then one of the girls climbed back up. He glanced up to see what she was doing, and had to look away before he embarrassed himself by blushing. He had seen right up her skirt.

"Get it tight, Doris!" a girl called.

Tight?

Then the light diminished, and he realized what she was doing: pulling closed the lid to the boat. In the abrupt darkness, someone hugged him and another kissed him on the cheek, giggling. Then a lantern came on, and all the girls were standing sedately around him, not one giving evidence of having done anything untoward.

It was a stern woman with the lamp, coming from another chamber in the boat. "Everybody aboard?" she asked briskly.

"Yesm'—plus one!" There was another giggle.

The woman brought the lamp about, and spied Esk. "A man!" she exclaimed disapprovingly.

"We found him in the shoe trees," Doris said. "May we keep him, Matriarch?"

"Certainly not. He's going right back where he—"

"No," Esk murmured.

The woman looked nonplussed. "Well, the authorities will have to decide. Put him in the hold for now."

So Esk was conducted to the hold, which was simply the cargo compartment of the boat. He settled down among the baskets of shoes, while the girls sneaked winks at him from the adjacent compartment.

The boat began to move. First it sank, so that he knew it was under the water, even the entrance hatch, and that was eerie. Then it slid forward, propelled by some unknown mechanism. He couldn't tell whether there were men in another chamber poling it along as he and Chex had poled their raft, or whether it was magic.

In due course the boat bumped to a stop. A girl climbed up to the hatch and opened it, and fresh light descended.

Now the girls picked up their baskets and hauled them out of the craft. "Bye, Esk," each murmured as she passed, in low tones that the matron was not supposed to hear.

When all were gone, the matron strode up. "Come on, intruder," she snapped. "You'll be seeing the Magistrate."

He went where directed, climbing up and out of the hatch. He found himself inside a room whose floor was water. The boat was sitting in this, its hatch beside another pier. This time Esk could see down around it, as the water was illuminated and clear. Now the mechanism for the craft's travel was apparent: there was a winch and a rope attached to it! The boat had simply been hauled in to the underwater city, as it had probably been hauled out to the edge of the lake. Obviously, there would be no people sneaking in by night; the boat would not be sent out for strangers. He was lucky he had cultivated the girls. Not that he had minded that particular diversion; he had not realized before how pleasant such an association could be!

The matron marched him upstairs to a grim office. Here

the Magistrate frowned from his desk. "What do you mean by intruding where you aren't welcome?" the man demanded.

Esk was tempted to say that the girls had made him welcome, but suspected that would not be smart. "My grandmother was a curse fiend," he said. "I came to ask a favor from my relatives."

"A favor? A favor?" the man demanded, reddening. "We don't do favors for anyone; we curse!"

"Not even for relatives?"

The Magistrate huffed indignantly, but evidently felt obliged by his office to investigate this matter. "Who was your grandmother?"

"Well, I don't know what she was called here, because she gave up that name when she married my grandfather. But maybe you know of the case. She was an excellent actress—"

"*All* of us are excellent thespians," he said stuffily. "The theater is our vocation."

"Who impersonated an ogress," Esk finished. "My grandfather is an ogre."

"An ogre?" the man demanded, outraged. "None of our citizens would touch so brutish a beast!"

"I understand he abducted her from a set. But she married him from choice."

The man turned to a shelf behind him and pulled down a massive tome. He set it on the desk, opened it, and turned the pages, running his forefinger down the margins. "Ogre, ogre," he muttered as he searched.

"Crunch Ogre," Esk said helpfully.

The Magistrate grimaced. "Yes, here it is. Helpless damsel abducted by villainous ogre. We blasted him with a massive curse that killed all the trees of the region, but apparently the brute escaped."

"He became a vegetarian," Esk said. "The curse couldn't find him, because it was looking for a bone cruncher."

"A loophole!" the Magistrate said with withering disgust.

"They had a son named Smash, who married a nymph named Tandy, and I am their son," Esk said. "So I am related to the curse fiends, and now I come to ask a favor of my relatives."

"You may be related, barely, in a distasteful technical

sense, but that gives you the right only to visit, not to make demands on us. I will grant you a two-day visa; after that you will be banned."

"Oh, I don't intend to stay longer. All I'm asking is help for—"

"Don't tell me your business!" the man exclaimed. "You have no right even to ask, unless you earn it."

"Earn it? How do I earn it?"

"By providing something we need. What can you do?"

Esk considered. Obviously they would not be impressed by his ogre mode, even if he could invoke it, and he doubted that his sometime acting ability would be anything remarkable here. Then he remembered something his grandmother had mentioned that had seemed like a joke. "I can be an audience," he said.

"Someone must have told you," the Magistrate grumped.

"My curse fiend grandma," Esk agreed smugly, though he was surprised that this had worked. "You have everything you need except advance audiences, right? You need to try out your plays on ordinary folk, before your season commences, to be sure they register correctly. Well, I'm about as ordinary as they come."

"I'll grant you that, youngster. Very well, it is evident that you do have curse fiend lineage, even if you are a bad actor. Here is your visa; you have two days to be a good enough audience to warrant our consideration of your plea. Don't waste them."

"I won't," Esk promised. "If you will just tell me where to go to get to work—"

"First you must clean up. Did you expect to perform as an audience in that condition?" The Magistrate's nose wrinkled. He snapped his fingers, and a girl appeared.

Esk recognized her. She was Doris, the one he had seen on the ladder.

"Take this person to a guest room and clean and dress him appropriately," the Magistrate said.

"Yes, sir," the girl said meekly. She turned to Esk. "If you will follow me, person."

"His name is Esk," the Magistrate said. "He will be a sample audience for two days only."

"Yes, sir," Doris repeated. "Please follow me, Desk."

"Esk!" the Magistrate roared. "Can't you servants get anything straight?"

"No, sir," Doris said.

Esk followed her, intrigued. Doris knew his name; why was she pretending not to?

As soon as they were alone in the hall, he found out. "I subbed for the girl on duty," Doris confided. "If the Magistrate caught on, he'd have me flayed."

"But why? You've already put in a day's work harvesting shoes."

"I think you're cute. I thought if I showed you my legs, you'd like me. Now I get to wash you. That will be fun!"

"You—on the ladder—on purpose?" he asked, almost choking.

"Wasn't I naughty?" She giggled. "I knew you'd look."

But now the other part of this situation registered. "*You* are going to wash me?"

"It's part of the duty. We're servant girls, until we serve our apprenticeship. Then those with proper promise get to try out for parts, unless we manage to marry above our station. What's your station?"

Now it was clarifying. She was looking for a way to get a better position; her interest in him was little more than an act, taking advantage of an opportunity. He had been fascinated by what he had seen of her legs, but he found her motive less appealing. "My station is very low," he said. "I'm a crossbreed."

She gazed at him, appalled. "What a dirty word!"

"Yes. So you don't want anything more to do with me."

"That's true! You can wash yourself!" She pointed to an open door.

"Thank you," Esk said, entering the chamber. He was sure he had done what was best, but somehow he was disappointed. Her legs had been quite stunning.

By trial and error he figured out how to use the cleaning facility. It was a kind of miniature waterfall that came on when he turned a handle, and stopped when he turned the handle back. This was a new kind of magic!

When he emerged from the waterfall room he found new

clothing where he had left his old. His other belongings were neatly set beside; he had not lost his two remaining travel pills or his hand knife. That was a relief.

He donned the new clothing, which was evidently what a sample audience was supposed to wear. It was a light blue set of trousers and a matching long-sleeved shirt. Both fit him well enough. The curse fiends evidently knew how to entertain a guest, or an audience.

He stepped out of the chamber, looking around. Immediately a girl appeared. She was not Doris; this must be the regular one on duty. She was not as pretty or flirtatious, which was perhaps just as well; he didn't want to forget why he had come here. He really did want to help the voles, if he could.

"Now you must eat," the girl informed him.

She guided him to a cubby where a decent meal of fruits and cakes was waiting. Esk ate, going along with the local custom though not entirely comfortable with it. Then the girl wiped his face and combed his hair for him and took him to a quiet, darkened chamber. Was she going to show him her legs, he wondered? But she merely indicated the chair he was to sit in, which was wooden with a single brown cushion on it, and armrests. "The play will begin in a moment," she said, and departed.

Well, so far so good. He realized that he would have to watch and listen carefully, and form some kind of opinion so that he could make a competent audience report. What would happen if he didn't like the play? Would they throw him out? He hoped he liked the production.

Music sounded, coming from an adjacent chamber. There seemed to be a number of instruments, strings and winds and percussions, operating together harmoniously. Esk had never been much for music, but now he realized that he simply had not been exposed to competent music. This was very impressive, and it induced a positive mood.

There was a stage before him, mostly concealed by a large curtain suspended from the ceiling. Now that curtain brightened, seemingly lighted from below. It rose, showing the rest of the stage—and Esk leaned forward, interested, his interest heightened by the drama of the music.

The stage was a model of Castle Roogna! There was the

castle in miniature in the center, suggesting the full-sized castle at a distance. There was the front gate, and the moat, with a model of the serpentine monster to one side.

A young man of about Esk's own age walked to the center. He wore ordinary clothes, but also a small headband resembling a crown. There seemed to be plenty of room to stand despite the presence of the moat; Esk realized that the moat could be painted, so that there was no danger of the actors falling into the water. But it certainly looked real; this was a clever stage.

"How's things, moat?" the young man asked, speaking clearly and with good force, so that Esk heard him very well.

"The monster peed in me again, Dor," the moat complained.

Esk laughed; the joke had caught him completely by surprise. Suddenly he realized that the young man was supposed to be King Dor, who could talk to the inanimate and have it respond; that was the Magician-caliber magic that had qualified him for the office. Not the King as he was today, but as he was when young, before he assumed the throne.

"Well, that's what monsters do, when they're not biting people," Dor said reasonably.

"How do you expect me to keep clean?" the moat demanded. "I'm not a sewer!" And the music made a blah sound.

"I'm sure you can handle it." Dor walked around the stage, exchanging greetings with the other objects on it, including the door of the castle.

Just as the novelty was wearing off, a young woman walked onstage. She was rather pretty, with bright green hair, and wore her dress provocatively, though she looked a year or so younger than Dor. She was evidently a major character, because the music became excited as she entered, with little frills. "Hi, Dor!" she exclaimed, her voice well enunciated and carrying just as well as his did. Esk wished that real people spoke as clearly!

"Oh, hello, Irene," Dor said with obvious lack of enthusiasm. That was another thing: it was easy to read the feelings of the folk onstage.

"Let's go somewhere and kiss," Irene said, and the music

went into a naughty-sounding theme. Esk was reminded of
Doris, though this was a different girl. That started him on a
chain of thought: could Doris have been named after King
Dor? The curse fiends obviously had some interest in the folk
of Castle Roogna, since their play related.

"No, I've got to go talk to more things," Dor said.

"You care more about the inanimate than you do about
me!" Irene flared. There was a rumble of musical anger.

"Well, sure I do!" he retorted. "You're only a girl."

"I'm a *woman!*" she exclaimed.

"Ha," he said, with withering contempt. Esk found himself
trying to repeat the syllable himself, to get the exact inflec-
tion; what a way to cut someone down!

"I'll show *you!*" she exclaimed. She wrapped her arms
around him, heaved him up, and threw him into the moat.

There was a splash. Esk almost jumped out of his chair;
there was real water there after all, and Dor was in it, sopping
wet. What a surprise! He realized that the sound of the splash
had been enhanced by the music, contributing to his reaction.

"I'll get you for that!" Dor sputtered, climbing out.

"Ha!" Her use of the word was as effective as his. "You
can't touch me, 'cause I'm a girl." Indeed she was, and she
bared a bit of cleavage to prove it.

"Oh yeah?" Dor advanced on her threateningly

She stood her ground, the picture of feminine certainty.
"Yeah." More bosom showed, affecting Esk more than Dor.

Dor grabbed her and threw her into the moat. "Oooo!" Esk
found himself breathing, surprised again; he had thought Dor
was bluffing. Evidently the music had thought so too; it was
now a jangle of amazement.

"You—you—*man*, you!" Irene screamed. Her hair was
matted about her head and neck, and looked like seaweed
now. "I'll get you for that!"

"I was just getting even," Dor pointed out.

She climbed out. Her dress clung to her, enhancing contours that were more voluptuous than they had seemed before.
"That's no excuse!"

Dor, alarmed, started to walk offstage, but Irene ran after
him and caught him. She hauled him back toward the moat.

"No, you don't." Dor said, struggling to escape that fate. They got tangled together, and both fell in.

"You—you!" Irene cried, tearing at his clothes.

"That's what you say!" Dor retorted, attacking her clothes. Now they were fighting in the moat, their clothing coming apart. Flashes of Irene's body showed, and Esk gaped; that girl was supposed to be only fifteen years old?

Now they were locked in the struggle, chest deep in the water, while the mock moat monster watched. Suddenly Irene changed her tactics. She put her face up against Dor's and kissed him. The music made a naughty flourish.

"Oooo," Esk breathed as he saw Dor stiffen, then relax, then begin kissing back. It was easy to imagine himself in such a situation; he'd kiss back too, if a girl as lovely as that did that to him!

A new figure clomped onstage. This was a centaur, evidently mocked up by two human actors in a centaur suit. It was female, because of the two enormous breasts mounted on the front. The music became somber; this was a person not to be taken lightly. "Dor," she said, holding up a sheet of paper, "I have graded your essay. I want to comment on your spelling. Let me read this to you as you have it."

Dor and Irene continued kissing in the moat, oblivious of the centaur. Esk smiled; he understood how this could be.

The centaur cleared her throat and read, and as she did, the words appeared on a scroll that two arms held from offstage, showing the spelling. "Eye live inn the Land of Zanth, witch is disstinked from Mundania inn that their is magic inn Zanth and nun inn Mundania."

Then the centaur glanced into the moat and for the first time realized what was happening. "Dor! What are you doing with that girl?"

The kiss broke with a guilty start. The music abruptly ceased, leaving awkward silence. The two bedraggled youngsters stood in the moat, their tops half exposed. "Just, uh, quarreling," Dor said, shamefacedly.

"Quarreling! In that case I'd like to see what you consider being friendly!"

"We're getting to that, Cherie," Irene said with a marvelously obscure and unrepentant smile.

"Indeed you are not!" Cherie Centaur said severely. She reached down and took Dor by the ear. "You are coming to see the King, young man!"

As poor Dor was hauled out of the water, the curtain came down. The scene was finished.

Esk relaxed. He had expected to be somewhat bored by the curse fiends' art, but instead he had been fascinated. They were very good! He wondered whether this play was an accurate replication of history. Had Dor really torn off Irene's clothing in the moat? The King and Queen had seemed quite sedate when he had had audience with them, but perhaps they had been different when young and vital. Would little Ivy become conservative and dour when she grew up? Would Esk himself? What an awful prospect!

Soon the curtain rose on the second scene. This was the throne room of Castle Roogna. The King sat on the throne, and the Queen stood beside him. Both were every bit as dour as their generation seemed to be. The music was now grand and somber, as befitted royalty.

"Dear, we shall have to do something about our daughter, Irene," the Queen said.

"They don't call me King Trent for nothing," the King said grandly and somberly. "What's wrong with the girl?"

"She's lonely."

"She'll get used to it, Iris. We did, after all. Loneliness is good for royalty."

"I think we need to send her somewhere where there will be other girls her age. She has no one to play with, here."

"What about Dor? He's only a year older than she is."

"He pays no attention to her. He's too busy talking to things."

"He should be busy on his homework! He's supposed to be King after me, you know. He has to learn things."

"I know, dear. But—"

At this point the King launched into a lengthy and somewhat dull lecture on the responsibilities of kingship, and why a prospective King had to learn it all. Esk became impatient, then bored; he had no prospect of ever being a King, so had little interest in this subject.

Then Cherie Centaur trotted in, hauling Dor along by the

ear. "Do you know what I found this wretch doing, Your Majesty?" she demanded righteously.

"You will surely tell me at a length," King Trent muttered, and Esk smiled; he knew the feeling.

"He was stripping off your daughter's clothes!" Cherie said indignantly.

Esk frowned. That did not ring true. The centaurs hardly cared about exposure of bodies, as they did not wear clothing themselves. Even if Dor and Irene had done more than kiss, the centaur wouldn't have minded; centaurs regarded sexual interplay as another natural function. It was Dor's poor spelling that should have excited Cherie's ire.

"What?" the King demanded.

"In the moat," Cherie continued. "If I had not arrived when I did—"

The King fixed a steely glare on bedraggled Dor. "Well, what do you have to say for yourself, young man?"

"She started it!" Dor protested.

"And his spelling is atrocious," Cherie concluded.

"That does it!" King Trent exclaimed. "I hereby banish this wretch to Mundania!"

"No, please!" Dor wailed, sinking to the floor in wretched supplication.

"The King has Spoken," Queen Iris said with satisfaction. "I never did like the way that boy frittered away his time with objects."

"She shouldn't call her daughter an object," Dor muttered to himself, his voice nevertheless carrying clearly to the audience. The music made a snide laugh.

A guard came in and marched Dor out as the curtain dropped.

Esk concluded that he didn't like this scene as well as the first. After all, Irene *had* started it, and started the kissing too; Dor had been relatively innocent. Now he had just discovered how interesting Irene could be—and he was being banished to the worst of regions, drear Mundania. Were the curse fiends trying to show how unfair human beings sometimes were?

The curtain lifted on the third scene. The play continued, showing Dor in Mundania, unable to use his magic, miserable, while Irene was miserable at Castle Roogna. Love denied—and Esk did feel it, though he knew this was only an imitation of history, something that might or might not have happened a generation ago. He wished he could reach even the first stage of this tragedy: having a girl to love.

Finally, in the play, Dor had a revelation. "I love her!" he declared. Then he marched back to Xanth and charged in to face King Trent. "I love your daughter and I'm going to marry her!" he said, sweeping Irene into his arms. It was amazing how conveniently near she happened to be.

"Well, why didn't you say so before?" King Trent demanded grumpily as the scene closed.

Esk knew it was all arranged and rehearsed, but Dor *had* married Irene, and they now had two children, so it could have happened somewhat like this. At any rate, he felt exhilarated by the conclusion, being glad that the two had finally gotten together.

Now a man appeared. "Very good," he said. "I believe you will make a credible sample audience. I have only one question."

"How did I like the play," Esk said for him. "Well, I did—"

"I will ask for the information I require," the man said curtly.

"But I'm trying to tell you—"

"That is unnecessary."

"But how can you find out how I liked the play, if I don't tell you?"

"We know how you liked the play. It is only a technical matter I am concerned with."

"A technical matter?"

"I see I must explain," the man said gruffly. "Very well, pay attention. We do not need to ask you how you reacted to the play because you were under continuous observation. Your reactions were catalogued and matched against the standard reaction chart. We now know that they are essentially normal for your sex and age and culture. You will make an adequate audience."

"You were watching me? I didn't see—"

"Naturally not. It's a one-way curtain. We recorded every fidget, every nose scratch, every smile and frown and vocal expression. We know which parts you enjoyed and which you did not. Now that we have aligned your individual reactions to this standard presentation, we can verify their applicability to those plays we have not yet put on tour. We have zeroed you in."

"Zeroed me in," Esk repeated, wondering how many times he had scratched his nose while watching the play. "You say this was an old play?"

"Standard boy-meets-girl, boy-loses-girl, boy-recovers-girl, always good for a simple audience. Now the only question I have for you is why you frowned at the wrong place in scene two. When Cherie Centaur was reporting how Dor had stripped Irene's clothing from her. Did you find that historically inaccurate?"

The man had been watching, certainly! That was exactly where Esk had objected. "Centaurs aren't like that," he said. "They don't care how much of a person's body shows. She wouldn't even have noticed, and wouldn't have cared if they had gone completely naked in the moat."

"You are conversant with the attitudes of centaurs?"

"Well, some. I do know that much."

"How many centaurs have you known well?"

"Well, only one, really. But she is Cherie's grandfilly."

"Only one," the man repeated coldly. "On this basis you extrapolate an attitude for the entire species?"

It sounded inadequate, now. "You asked me why I frowned," Esk reminded him. "That's why."

"A note shall be made." The man turned away. "That will be all. Your next audience will be in the morning; the wench will conduct you to it."

"The wench?" Esk asked somewhat blankly.

"The servant who brought you here." The man snapped his fingers, and immediately the girl appeared.

The man departed, and the girl showed Esk back to his room. That was just as well, because he would have been lost in the maze of passages by himself.

"Was it rough?" the girl asked.

"I'll survive," Esk said.

She flashed him a quick smile. "I will wake you in the morning." Then she was gone. She was evidently no vamp, just one of the nothing folk of this realm.

*   *   *

The next two days were full of plays. Esk enjoyed them, generally, and soon was used to the knowledge that he was being scrutinized as closely as he scrutinized the plays. He did feel that he was performing a useful service for this community, and that his reactions would help them to refine their plays for their outside tours. For it seemed that the curse fiends, though largely self-sufficient economically, had a desperate need for the approval of others, in their chosen art form. They wanted their plays to be recognized as outstanding, and to have their audiences eager for the next season's offerings. Promotion within their hierarchy was based on this; an effective actor became a leader of their society.

Well, why not? It was a system he could live with. He regretted turning Doris off. A girl like that, in a comfortable place like this . . .

But he had a mission to accomplish, and another society to help save. Thoughts of remaining here were idle; the curse fiends would not accept him anyway. They were treating him nicely now only because they valued his input as an ignorant audience, and soon that would be done, as he completed their current repertoire of plays.

The final play impressed him for a reason other than the fiends intended, however. It was about a man's interaction with a demon. Abruptly intent, Esk watched it closely.

It was, as the fiends put it, a standard pact-with-demon narrative. A young man with whom Esk readily identified (the players were very good at that sort of thing) went to Good Magician Humfrey with a Question: how could he safely tame a demon? He served his term of service—the intermission between scenes served to abbreviate that year for the audience—and received his Answer: a talisman, a diagram, a verbal spell, and a parchment on which was written a contract. "Now this will only work once, because the elements are self-destructing," the Good Magician cautioned him. "But this combination will summon and control a demon, and the demon will then have to negotiate with you for its freedom. You can compel it to do anything you wish."

"Anything?" the lad asked eagerly.

"Anything within its capability. What I have provided will

handle one of the most powerful demons, so it will be able to do a great deal, but it is not omnipotent. However, it will not be able to deceive you, so you may ask it what its capabilities are before you decide. Just make sure that it signs this contract, after you have filled in the details of your deal."

"I will!" the youth exclaimed. Esk felt as if he were there himself, talking to the Good Magician. How nice it would have been if he could have asked a similar Question. But of course the problem in the Vale of the Vole was that there were many demons; controlling one demon wouldn't do the job. Still, he was really caught up in the play; perhaps he would learn something helpful.

The boy took the things home and set the process in motion. First he traced the diagram, which was a strange five-sided affair, onto his floor, and when he had it exactly right he painted it there so that it could not be scuffed out. Then he took the talisman and held it aloft: "Demon of the Day, I summon you!" he intoned. "By this spell, appear in the pentagram!" And he spoke the spell, which sounded incomprehensible to Esk, but potent all the same.

The stage darkened. The music swelled ominously. Sparks flashed. The air above the pentagram filled with smoke. There was a horrendous roar, making Esk wince. He was sure that the one watching him was making a note: special effects were being effective for the audience.

The smoke dissipated, and within the pentagram stood a glowing demon. Esk could see that this was an actor in a demon suit, not a true demon, but of course no real demon would have cooperated unless truly compelled by such magic. At any rate, the figure was suitably horrendous, and Esk wondered how it had been brought onstage in this manner. Maybe the smoke had concealed a trapdoor entry.

"Ha! Gotcha!" the boy exclaimed. "Now you have to do my bidding."

In response, the demon roared, and a flame shot out of its mouth. Esk was delighted; that was another marvelous special effect. Metria had never done that; now he wondered whether she could have. Dragons of the right variety could breathe out flame, but he wasn't sure whether demons could do likewise. This might be an error.

The lad, visibly daunted by this display—things were delightfully visible onstage—rallied his courage. "You can't get out of that pentagram until I let you out!" Then, as the demon swelled up angrily: "Can you?"

The demon pounded its fist at the air above the pentagram, and made it look just as if there were an invisible wall there. It tramped around, poking at the floor and at the ceiling, but met resistance everywhere. So determined was it, that Esk found himself worrying that it would discover some trifling gap in the magic shape, so that it could get out and go on a destructive spree.

But the pentagram was tight. The demon could not escape. Finally it stood still, defeated and outraged. "What do you want, dunghead?" it demanded of the boy.

Esk smiled. It was always fun to hear language on stage that it would not be feasible to use in life.

"I want a fine house to live in for the rest of my life, a cornucopia that never grows empty, and a totally beautiful woman to love me utterly," the boy said bravely.

"What? This is impossible!"

"No, it's possible. I verified it. A demon of your power can do these things, and I won't let you go until you sign the contract that specifies that you will do them all."

"Never!" the demon swore.

"Then stay there forever," the lad said, and turned his back as if to depart.

"Be reasonable!" the demon cried. "It takes time and expertise to make a fine house, and I know nothing about construction."

"You don't have to make it, just get it for me. I don't care how you do it."

Esk appreciated the fine point, but was losing sympathy for the boy. Evidently he didn't care who else suffered as long as he got what he wanted.

"Cornucopias don't grow on trees, you know," the demon continued. "The only one I know of is being used by an orphanage to feed its children."

"I don't care where you get it, just bring it to me," the boy said.

Esk lost further sympathy.

"And beautiful women don't love folk like you," the demon said. "I may be able to do some physical things, but I can't change the heart of a woman!"

"Find a way," the boy said coldly.

"I tell you, there *is* no way! I might get a woman to say she loved you, but her heart would still be her own."

Esk nodded. That demon was making some sense. He was almost having some sympathy with it.

The lad considered. "On further thought, I don't really care what's in her heart. Just have her completely beautiful, and willing to do anything I ask, anytime, with a smile on her face, and her heart can be whatever it wants."

"Ah, so you will settle for the semblance of a woman, provided she performs to your specifications."

"Exactly. No questions asked."

"Then perhaps we can do business."

The boy passed in the contract, and the demon signed. The deal had been made. The curtain dropped.

Esk spent the brief time between scenes pondering his own situation with the demoness Metria. He had not summoned her, she had come unbidden to his hideout, setting off this whole adventure. She, too, had offered him the semblance of a woman, a deal to get him to vacate his premises. Should he have made that deal? Perhaps this play would help him to come to a conclusion.

When the curtain lifted again, the youth reclined within the open-face mockup of a fine house. The demon entered from the side, carrying a huge cornucopia from which fresh fruits tumbled. In the distance came a cry, as of a hungry orphan child. The demon put the horn of plenty into the youth's hands.

"Well?" the youth demanded.

"Sir?" the demon asked respectfully.

"Well, where's the woman?"

"The semblance of a woman," the demon muttered.

"I don't care what you call her! The deal's not complete until you deliver her, and then leave us alone forever. You can't do a thing to me, because of the contract."

"True, sir," the demon said. "I will send in the woman."

By this time Esk's sympathy had transferred pretty much

to the demon. The youth was a spoiled brat, while the demon was honoring the letter of his contract.

The demon walked offstage, while the boy pulled luscious fruits from the cornucopia, bit once into each, and tossed them away, reveling in the horn's plenty.

In a moment a truly striking woman walked onstage. She undulated in her revealing gown, she almost flowed from her long golden tresses to her dainty slippers; she was the most luscious creature Esk had seen in all his life. He was half smitten with her himself, foolish as he knew this to be. The curse fiends had produced an actress to portray the most totally beautiful woman alive—and she was that.

"I have come to please you, you handsome man," the woman announced in a sensuous tone.

The youth looked at her. His eyes widened appreciatively. "You're the one?"

"I am the one," she said, doing a little pirouette that flung her gown out, showing a flash of her awesome legs. "The semblance of the perfect woman."

"You'll do anything I want?"

"Anything," she breathed.

"Take off your dress."

"As you wish, O virile man," she said, and opened the upper section of her gown as the light dimmed and the curtain came down. Esk strained to see her body, but could catch only the most tantalizing glimpse as the scene was cut off.

When the curtain lifted again, the two were in bed, having evidently completed a scene Esk wished he could have watched. But this was a family-rated play, where suggestion was prevalent over reality. The youth was asleep, the woman awake. She stage-whispered in his ear: "Is the contract safe? Is the contract safe?"

The youth stirred. "The contract!" he muttered blearily. He lurched up in his nightclothes and lumbered to a cabinet, where he drew out the scroll.

"Is it the right one? Is it the right one?" the woman whispered.

The youth peered at it. "I can't read it in this light!" he exclaimed. "If anyone stole it, and put another paper here—"

He fumbled for a candle, and lit it from a live coal in the fireplace, almost singeing his fingers. He held the candle above the parchment. "Yes, it's the right one," he said, peering down.

"Does it protect you from the demon? Does it protect you from the demon?" the woman whispered.

He looked more closely finding his place. The candle tilted precariously. "It says ' . . . said demon shall not harm said beneficiary in any way, nor seek to have any other party do so.' That's tight; the demon can't touch me."

"Are you sure? Are you sure?" the woman whispered.

"Sure I'm sure!" he said irritably. "See, right here it says— oops." For a drop of wax had fallen from the tilting candle, landing with a splat on the parchment. There was a puff of smoke as the hot wax interacted with the ink.

With a curse of annoyance, the youth grabbed at the solidifying wax with his fingers and yanked it off. A bit of the parchment adhered. "Only a spot," he muttered.

"Where did it strike? Where did it strike?" whispered the woman.

"Damn! It blotted out a word! Now it says . . . said demon shall . . . harm said beneficiary. The word 'not' is gone."

"Well now, isn't that a coincidence!" the woman said. But she wasn't the woman anymore. From the bed rose the horrendous shape of the demon. "I wonder how that drop of wax could have landed right at that particular spot?"

The youth looked at it with appalled realization. "You did it!" he cried. "You used your magic to make the wax fall right there! You cheated!"

"I did not harm you," the demon said. "I only guided a little wax so that it would not burn your hand. I honored the contract, and shall continue to do so."

"You will?" the youth asked with sudden hope. "Then turn back into the woman!"

"But now the wording of that contract has a new directive for me," the demon said. "It directs me to harm you. So—"

The youth screamed as the demon advanced menacingly on him, but the curtain dropped, concealing what happened next. The play was over.

Suddenly Esk was glad he had not made the deal with

Metria. Demons were too clever, too slippery! The youth in the play had deserved his fate, but it was still a scary reminder.

And the Vale of the Vole was overrun by demons. Now Esk appreciated Volney's quest much more directly. They had to get those demons out!

"Your visa has expired," the Magistrate informed him. "You must now depart."

"But first I must ask my favor," Esk reminded him.

"Oh, that. Very well, let's hear it."

"I want the curse fiends' help in ridding the Vale of the Vole of demons."

"Get rid of the demons? Why?"

"So that the voles can restore the nice curves to the Kiss-Mee River."

The Magistrate laughed. "What do we care about the voles? We have problems enough right here at Gateway Castle! The level of the lake rises and falls erratically, alternately flooding our farmlands and dehydrating them. Our crops suffer, and wild animals run amuck. We are hardly about to sacrifice valuable manpower to help stupid animals put curves in a stupid river!"

"But I served as a good sample audience for two days!" Esk reminded him. "Now you folk know how to tailor those new plays more precisely to your audiences. Don't you feel you owe me anything?"

The Magistrate frowned. "Perhaps there is a small debt owing. Very well, we shall assign you a person to investigate the situation."

"A person?" Esk asked doubtfully.

"I'm sure she can do what is required," the Magistrate said with a quirk of a smile.

"She?"

"Her name is Latia. She will meet you at the exit."

Esk groaned inwardly. How could a single woman help against demons? But it seemed that this was the best he could get. "Thank you," he said, with what grace he could muster. The effort strained his own acting ability.

"You will depart these premises in the morning. I am authorized to extend to you the appreciation of Gateway Castle for your service."

"Gateway Castle is welcome," Esk said shortly, his ability exhausted.

He had some spare time, so he took a tour of the castle. The servant wench was happy to guide him. The castle was entirely underwater, with windows that showed the fish swimming by, and in its center was a massive glass wall that circled a depression in the water. In fact, this was a whirlpool that spun its way savagely down to unseen regions beneath the bottom of the lake.

"But where does it go?" Esk asked.

"No one knows," the girl said. That was it; not only did she not know, she was not curious. Apparently that quality had been largely bred out of the curse fiends.

The woman was waiting for him at the dock. She was ancient. Her body was stooped and ugly, her hair stringy and gray, her skin so wrinkled that it almost buried her features. "Well, let's get going, youngster," she snapped.

"Uh, do you know what I asked for?"

"No. Does it matter?"

Esk sighed. Perhaps it didn't. She was unlikely to be of much use regardless.

They climbed down into the boat and took seats. Soon a bevy of girls joined them, their legs flashing prettily as they descended the ladder. "Say, it's Esk!" one exclaimed.

"And Crone Latia," another added with distaste.

"Don't let it bother you, wench," the old woman snapped. "I'm leaving Gateway."

"Oh." The girl was disconcerted. "Well, good luck, I guess."

"Don't be facetious."

That dampened things, and they rode in silence as the cable hauled the boat to the outer pier. Then the girls climbed out and headed off to their harvesting duties of the day, and Esk and Latia started on the way to Castle Roogna.

"I have two pills," Esk said. "They will enable us to travel without much resistance, so that we can cover the distance in a single day."

"Hmph," she remarked. "I'll believe it when I see it."

So he gave her a pill, and took the last one himself, and she believed. They traveled rapidly northwest, but she was old, and unable to move as rapidly as he could, so they did not get the whole way after all. Esk tried to hurry her along, knowing that their trek on the following day would be much slower; he wanted to cover as much as possible while it was easy. But she would not be hurried, and when the evening came they were still some distance from Castle Roogna.

They stopped at a suitable glade near a spring, making camp. Latia mellowed some, now that they were well clear of the home of the curse fiends. "Do you know why they assigned me to go with you?" she asked.

"No. I admit to being curious."

"It's because they wanted to get rid of me anyway, and they believe that I am unlikely to return from such a wild mission." She glanced sidelong at him. "What *is* the mission?"

"To get rid of the demons, so that the Kiss-Mee River can be made curvy again, so that the Vale of the Vole will be nice."

She snorted. "That figures, Mortals can't do anything about demons."

"Unless they get the right talisman and spell and diagram and contract."

"Those are known only to the Good Magician, who is as grumpy as I am. And they don't necessarily work as advertised."

"I know. I saw the play."

"Well, I'll try to help you, because that's what I'm here for, but I am obliged to advise you of the risk."

"The risk?" Esk asked.

"You know how we curse fiends all have the same talent? That of cursing?"

"Yes. I haven't actually seen it in action, but I understand it can be pretty bad. My grandmother was a curse fiend."

"She was?" The old woman showed greater interest. "What was her name?"

"I don't know her curse fiend name. She married my grandfather, an ogre."

"Oh, that one! I remember her. A fine actress, but impatient with convention."

"You knew her?" Esk asked, amazed.

"Of course I knew her! How young do you think I am? I'm glad she managed to make a good life for herself."

"You consider marrying an ogre good?"

"Certainly. Ogres have their points."

Esk was getting to like this woman better. "So you don't look down at me because I'm the grandson of an ogre?"

"Not if you don't look down on me because of my defective talent."

"Defective talent?"

"I was about to tell you my liability. My curses have become erratic. One in three turns out to be a blessing."

Esk laughed. "A blessing! What's wrong with that?"

"It interferes with a regular existence. Once when we were stunning a marauding dragon, and combined to hit it with the strongest possible curse, my blessing played havoc with the curses, and the dragon not only survived, it got stronger. We were lucky we were close to the pier, so that we could escape underwater."

"Oh. I can see how that would be a problem."

"So if something attacks, and I curse it, that may only make the situation worse. Of course, the malfunction is fairly regular; my last two efforts were good strong curses, so I have refrained for six months from making another. The Magistrate was aware of that, and eager to get me away from Gateway."

"Smart of him," Esk said cynically. "Maybe you can bless us and make the rest of our journey easy."

"I can't curse or bless myself, only others."

"Well, maybe you should curse me, then, and if as you say it is really a blessing—"

"That would be dragon roulette," she said. "I can't be absolutely sure it's a blessing; it is merely a strong probability. Whatever it is, it will be extremely powerful, because of the accumulated backlog."

But now Esk was thoroughly intrigued. "I'll risk it. Curse me."

"No, there is that element of risk."

"But if you curse me, and it's a blessing, then you'll know

your next two curses will be true curses, and you can depend on them for protection. That would be an advantage, because we have some rough country still to cover."

She was thoughtful. "There may be something in what you say. Consider it overnight, and if you still wish to experiment in the morning, I'll do it."

They slept, and in the morning it still seemed intriguing to Esk, so he repeated his request. Latia hesitated, but finally wound up and delivered a round curse.

There was a wash of something across him, that made his hair lift slightly, but it wasn't painful. "That's it?" Esk asked. "I don't feel better or worse."

"That's strange," Latia said, as mystified as he. "It never misfired like that before. Maybe my talent has finally gone into complete remission, and I can neither curse nor bless anymore."

"Maybe," Esk agreed, with mixed relief and regret. "Well, let me do something private, then we'll get moving."

She nodded. Curse fiend conventions were akin to the human ones in this respect, rather than the centaur ones, and he was just as glad. He made his way to a private copse and got ready to do his business.

The ground gave way beneath his feet. Too late he realized that the thick brush concealed a sinkhole. He flailed, trying to catch hold of something to support him, but failed; then he plunged down into the hole.

It was a long-term sink, not a new one; light came down, and vines grew everywhere. Esk slip-slid on the smooth enamel surface to the bottom, rolling. He saw the drain; fortunately it was clogged with vines. Finally he fetched up with his face wedged against a cool surface. He blinked, and looked.

It was a hypnogourd, and his right eye was right by the peephole. Before he realized, Esk had looked in—and was caught there, his consciousness locked within the gourd.

Only interference in his line of sight to the peephole could break his trance, for that was the nature of the gourd. It was unlikely that Latia would find him in this hidden recess of the ground; the sinkhole was invisible from a short distance beyond its rim.

Now at last the nature of Latia's effort seemed clear: it was after all a potent curse, its action delayed just long enough to make it truly effective. Esk was stuck here for the duration.

# 8

# DIGGLE

Volney swallowed one of the strength pills Ivy had given him, donned his heavy-duty talons, and started digging. The result was amazing; the earth flew back, and he made progress at twice his normal rate. If he had had a pill like this when they were trying to pass the chasm in the illusory mountain on the way to the Good Magician's castle, he would have been able to bore way down below the level of the water and pass under it. How nice of the little human girl to do him this favor; he was not really partial to human folk, but he did like Esk and now this child.

He was headed for the realms of the lesser voles. The Kingdom of Voles in Xanth comprised all manner of digging creatures, ranging from the monstrous diggles to the minuscule wiggles' larvae, with various shades of squiggles between. Back in the dawn of creation, so it was said, the Demon L(I/T)ho, Maker of Earth, devised all the species to inhabit the fertile region between the flighty surface and the depressive depths. The huge diggles took the large expanses of rock far down, and the swift squiggles took the loose superficial earth, and the wiggles took the limited veins of super-hard metallic stone. Litho's chosen creatures were the voles, and they were granted their choice of all the regions of the earth, and they prospered beyond any of the others. So while all the digging creatures were technically voles, the voles of the Vale were the archetypes, the envy of all others.

But Litho had reckoned without the demons. Just as the voles differed in type and degree, so did the demons. The original Demons were omnipotent entities, but the lesser demons were mere nuisances, bearing about the same relation to Litho as a worm did to a vole. Unfortunately, both worm and demon could be a lot of mischief in the wrong place. That was of course what had started Volney on his quest for assistance. If only the Good human Magician had been home!

Volney made excellent progress, but he had a way to go, for first he sought the largest creatures, the diggles. They tunneled without using claws, boring through the rock magically. They could leave a tunnel behind, or leave the rock as solid as it was before, depending on their mood; normally they left it solid so that they could have the pleasure of boring through it again and again. If they agreed to come to the Vale and bore, the demons would be unable to prevent them, because a tunneling diggle was physically insubstantial. Indeed, the diggles would be able to bore new and curvaceous channels for the river faster than the demons could straighten them. The demons would have to give up the futile effort and find another place to reside.

He reached the deep level of the diggles. Now all he had to do was intercept one, and ask it to take him to its leader.

Easier thought than done. He had no notion of the schedule on which individual diggles traveled. He would just have to wait until one passed within hailing range.

Meanwhile, time to eat. He had brought some fruit from above; he was developing a taste for it. When the Vale was restored, he would have to see about harvesting fruits and nuts there. He doffed his heavy digging claws and ate.

After a bit, his little ears perked. Voles did not depend to a great extent on sound, but at times it could be important. There was some type of scraping in the tunnel he had left behind.

He listened carefully, trying to identify the source of that sound. If some predator from above had happened on his

tunnel and was pursuing him, he would have to fight. He had
of course plugged the end of it, so that no creature would
encounter it by chance, but a predator such as a big serpent
could sniff it out. Actually, the advantage would be Volney's,
here deep in the rock, because the predator could not maneu-
ver, and Volney's artificial talons could gouge flesh as readily
as stone. Very few creatures preyed on voles, in the deep
earth. It would be another matter on the surface, where space
was unlimited and predators could grow to enormous size.
That was why voles normally stayed clear of the surface.
Besides, the light was too bright up there. He wondered how
the surface creatures were able to stand it. Only his volish
ability to change his fur and eyes for the surface conditions
permitted him to handle it. Now, in his brown subterranean
coat and gray lenses for maximum effect in near darkness, he
was more comfortable.

But this did not sound like a snake. It seemed to consist of
many tiny scrapings, as of insect legs . . .

Suddenly he realized what it was. Nickelpedes!

This was disaster. He could not use his talons effectively
against those little predators; nickelpedes were too small and
numerous. They would scramble under his defense and start
gouging nickel-sized disks from his tender anatomy. It was
not possible to reason with them; all they knew was hunger.
His tunnel down must have passed close to one of their nests,
so that they heard him, and scouted about until they found
his hole. Now they were on his trail, following the tunnel to
its end, which was where he was.

He could not hope to escape them by dashing back up his
tunnel; they would swarm over his body as he passed. He
could not hide from them in the darkness, for they needed no
light; indeed, bright light killed them. They were guided by
touch and smell, as he was, and they could go anywhere he
could dig.

He would have to go forward. If he intersected another
tunnel, he could go along it and outrun them, for they were
too small to travel rapidly. But what other tunnel would there
be, here? He was below the normal vole level, into the diggle
level, and the diggles had left this rock solid. He could tell
by the sound of it when he tapped. He would have to dig his

own tunnel, and that would slow him down to nickelpede velocity. Eventually he would tire, even if he took another strength pill, and they would catch him and feed on him. His situation was abruptly desperate.

The noise grew louder. One nickelpede had outdistanced the pack, and was homing in on him. Volney donned his enhanced talons, oriented, and struck savagely down. His sonar-location was accurate; the claw speared the nickelpede, killing it. The things were hard to kill; the strike had to be just right, and with sufficient power, or it merely bounced off their hard shells.

One down—thousands to go! He had to move.

He took another pill. Immediately the strength spread through him. He resumed digging, knowing that this would only prolong the chase; he was too far from the surface to reach it before tiring and slowing and getting caught, and indeed, the 'pedes might well be faster than he, traveling up. But he couldn't just wait to get eaten alive!

If only a diggle would come! Then he could hitch a ride, and be phased through the rock as if it were air, and the miniature monsters would just have to clack their pincers emptily and remain hungry. But there was a characteristic sound the diggles made when traveling, and that sound was not here; he could not depend on finding a diggle.

The rock fairly flew out behind him. Normally he let the debris accumulate behind, blocking the tunnel loosely. But the nickelpedes would have no trouble navigating this, they would simply scramble through the crevices between the fragmented rocks. A serpent he could have balked somewhat by packing the plug more tightly, and then striking at its emerging nose. Small size was an advantage to the little gougers. If only he could pack it so tightly as to make it completely solid again—but that was beyond his power. It was a maxim among his kind: only magic could restore bored rock.

He paused for a moment, listening. The sound was there, pursuing. All he had done was maintain his lead, or perhaps improve on it a little. He had to have some better way! But what better way was there? His thinking was going in circles.

Circles . . .

Then he had a notion. He wasn't sure it would work, but it might. Certainly he had to try it.

He resumed his digging, forging through the rock, not even trying to make a plug behind. He wanted velocity, even though the nickelpedes might gain. He dug in a curve, bearing left. He stayed on the same level; that was important.

In due course he could tell by his sense of location and the manner the rock ahead vibrated that he was about to intersect his own tunnel. He dug until only the thinnest wall separated the two. Then he reached up and excavated a hole in the top, forming a vertical tunnel. He made this go straight up for a short distance, then curved it to the level, above the original tunnel. He worked as quickly as he could, though he was tiring; he had little time to spare.

Then, just as the first of the nickelpedes caught up to the end of the lower tunnel, he scooted back down. He speared the nickelpede with a claw and threw its body back. Then he resumed digging, quickly breaking through the thin wall and making a complete intersection of tunnels at the bottom level.

There were nickelpedes massed in the other tunnel, of course. They turned, smelling him, and poured back into his new opening. But Volney scrambled up and away the moment the breakthrough was complete, into his vertical hole. He made the turn to the horizontal level, then stuffed refuse into it, plugging it behind him, so that what remained was a hole up that dead ended.

Now he settled down and waited, resting. If this worked, he had saved himself. If not . . .

It worked. The nickelpedes were not the smartest of creatures. They were tracking him mostly by following the tunnel. As long as it smelled of him, they would pursue it to its end. It was a system that was normally effective. But now the tunnel was a loop, and so it never ended. They were going around and around forever. If any tried the hole in the ceiling, they stopped when they discovered that it went nowhere; obviously he wasn't there. Some few might work their way through the plug and reach his hideout, but those few he could spear with the talon. The great majority were stuck in the trap he had devised: circularity.

Volney rested, recovering his strength. It was important

that he not attract attention to himself; if he moved too much, the nickelpedes might feel the vibration and start searching for it. A few did come through to him, and these he did quietly spear. When he was sure he was sensitized to their entry, he slept; any coming through would wake him long enough for spearing.

Then, finally, he heard a diggle. His wait was over! It no longer mattered if the nickelpedes became aware of him.

He started digging, going in a direction that would put him directly in the path of the diggle. When he got there, he waited.

The diggle was traveling slowly. Its wormlike nose projected into the chamber Volney had formed. "Ho, Dig!" he cried in the language common to all the members of the great family of voles. The magic of Xanth made communication intelligible to all the members of a particular group, such as the voles, or the humanoids, or the dragons. Unfortunately it did not do the same between groups, which was why Volney was unusual; he had learned the humanoid mode. It had been a terrible struggle to master the peculiar conventions of the alien system, but he had persevered, and succeeded better than the other voles in the class. They had known that the Good Magician was humanoid, so this study had been a necessity. If only they had also known that the Good Magician would be absent!

Meanwhile, the diggle had been considering. Diggles were not especially rapid of wit. Now it responded. "Ho, Vole!" it replied.

"Take me to your leader."

It considered again. "Where is your song?"

Oh, yes—diggles liked songs. Unfortunately, that was not Volney's strength. What should he do?

A nickelpede scrambled up behind him. His activity had attracted their attention, and now the little monsters were working up another horde.

"Vong!" Volney cried in the humanoid mode. "Vong, song, vooongg!"

And the diggle was satisfied. It was too slow to realize that this was not a very good song.

Volney climbed onto the diggle's cylindrical back and dug

in his talons. This was necessary to hold his position; the diggle's skin was so thick and tough that it suffered no discomfort. "Vong-vong-voonngg-vong!" Volney continued, getting into the swing of it.

The diggle resumed its motion, phasing through the rock and the crowding nickelpedes as if both were fog. It made a turn, orienting on the diggle leader.

Soon they were there. The leader, being old, no longer phased readily through rock, so preferred to remain in a network of physical diggings. Volney was well satisfied with this; it put him on the same footing.

"I come to ask diggle assistance for the voles," he said in voletalk.

"But the voles talk only to themselves!" the leader protested. Indeed, it was said among the digging species that the squiggles talked only to the diggles, and the diggles talked only to the voles, and the voles ignored them.

"That situation has changed slightly," Volney explained. He went on to tell of the problem in the Vale of the Vole.

"So you wish us to go and bore out new curves, to make the river friendly again."

"Exactly. The demons cannot stop you, because you are insubstantial when you bore."

The diggle leader pondered, after the fashion of his type. After an hour he replied: "We diggles have no quarrel with the demons, and would not wish to antagonize them. Therefore we shall not interfere in this business."

Disappointment smote Volney. He knew that this decision was final. "I thank you for your consideration," he said heavily.

"But perhaps the squiggles will have another attitude," the diggle said. "They are smaller than we, and move more rapidly, so their minds are more flexible. I will give you a guide so that you may seek their leader."

"I thank you for that notion," Volney replied. He had planned to ask the squiggles next anyway, but this would make it easier.

The diggle gave him a pebble. "The taste will guide you."

Volney took the pebble and put it in his mouth. He made a circle. When he faced one way, the taste became increasingly good; when he faced another, it became bad. No problem understanding this guide.

He bid parting to the diggle leader, and set off toward the good taste.

The route, to his surprise, was level rather than upward. The squiggles normally lived very close to the surface—so close that they often deposited their refuse dirt *on* the surface, instead of having it plug the tunnel. Deep rock wasn't their specialty, as they liked to bore with blinding speed. The light dirt and unplugged tunnels contributed to their velocity; dense hard rock inhibited them. Well, maybe there was a deep valley or an offshoot from the Gap Chasm that brought the surface down to this level; the squiggle leadership might indeed prefer to reside in such a secluded region.

It was growing warmer; Volney found himself panting. Surface creatures such as humanoids and centaurs had a crass way to dissipate heat: they exuded moisture from their skin, and this liquid evaporated and cooled them. This led to residues on their bodies and in their fur or clothing that built up a typical and not necessarily delightful odor. Voles, like most other creatures, did it more delicately: by sticking out their tongues and letting the breeze take the heat. However, it had to be conceded that there were times when the humanoid's allover bath of sweat might do the job better.

He paused so as to abate his body's generation of excess heat. But the heat remained; it was radiating at him from the stone. That was surprising; this was supposed to be a cool level. Where was it coming from? Surely the squiggles didn't like it this hot.

He turned away—but immediately the pebble in his mouth turned foul. That was not the direction. So he faced forward again and resumed boring.

The heat increased, and now there were rumblings in the rock whose nature he didn't trust. He had heard of volcanoes, which were great local upheavals from the heated depths; could one of those be in the vicinity? Yet why would the squiggles choose to live in such a dangerous region?

As he finally felt the pattern of an opening in the rock, the heat was almost unbearable. Just in time! He broke through and popped into a large subterranean cavern.

He paused again. There was no sign of the squiggles. The arches and chambers were entirely natural, as were the irregular grooves in the floor, which seemed to have been made by the dripping of hot liquid from the ceiling. The floor was actually cooler than the ceiling; the drippings had solidified into layers of colored stone that in light would surely be rather pretty. The source of the heat was above.

Yet that was where the pebble indicated the squiggles were. When he lifted his head it turned sweet; when he sniffed the floor, it turned sour. This was strange indeed.

Well, either he accepted the validity of his guidestone, or he didn't. Volney lifted himself on his hind feet and reached up to dig into the ceiling. The stone here was relatively soft, and his talons quickly gouged out a fairsized hole. In fact, the digging became easier as he progressed, and soon he was able to lift himself into the new hole, wedge his hind feet against the stone sides, and pull out big globs from above.

But it was also getting hotter. Volney's tongue was lolling against his fur, inadequate; he could not remain in this environment much longer. He gave one final swoop with his talons, then slid back down; he had to cool.

The rock above sagged, then melted. A gob of it dropped. Volney barely dodged it; this stuff was molten!

He landed on the relatively cool floor, panting. More hot rock dropped from the hole, splatting against the floor. It was getting worse! Surely there could be nothing up there fit for a living creature to exist in.

Something gave way. Then lava pored out of the hole, so hot it glowed, illuminating the cavern. The layered stone was indeed pretty, the moment before it was buried under congealing lava. Volney scooted back—and the pebble in his mouth gave him a nasty taste.

Something was definitely wrong. That pebble was guiding him into a scorching death in a pool of molten rock! Had he not quickly retreated from the hole he was boring, he would have been fried alive—and now that he was retreating to safety, the pebble was objecting.

But the lava gave him no time to consider the implications. More of it was pouring down, hotter yet and increasingly liquid and bright. It flowed across the floor, filling a channel.

Volney decided to forget the foul taste of the pebble and retreat the way he had come. But by a most unfortunate mischance, the lava was now flowing in a channel between him and his hole. It had cut him off.

Should he try to tunnel under it? The floor was cooler than the ceiling, so he might do this. But the way the stuff was flowing, he had no certainty that it wouldn't flow into the hole he bored and catch him there. He couldn't risk that.

Had he been a jumping creature, like Chex Centaur, he could have hurdled it and gotten away. But he was not; that channel, narrow as it was, had become an absolute barrier to him. He would get severely burned just approaching it.

He looked back at the hole in the ceiling. It had become a fountain of lava, the fluid splattering down and spreading out along several channels like the tentacles of a glowing kraken. Soon he would be blocked off from escape in any other direction.

He hurried in the only direction he could go, past the glowing column of falling lava and down the slight incline of the floor of the cavern. There was a bright channel of lava on his right, picking its way along.

Suddenly the lava veered toward him. Volney froze, alarmed; had he not stopped, the lava would have singed his feet, for it had gone right into the channel he was in. Then, feeling the renewed heat of its closeness, he stepped left to get around it.

The lava flowed left, cutting him off.

Volney paused again. That was almost as if—

The lava flowed back toward him.

Volney came as close as a vole could to jumping. He lifted his front feet clear of the reaching lava and stretched to the left, then dropped his front feet and sort of hunched his rear feet into them. The lava paddled where his feet had been. A tiny patch of shed hair puffed into smoke as the molten rock touched it.

He ran on, getting around the lava. But now a new channel was converging from the left. He dodged right, and the first string of lava resumed its forward flow, about to intercept him again.

It was! The lava was actively seeking him out, trying to

catch him! It was limited because it had to flow downhill or on the level, but so was he.

Volney scrambled between the converging channels and managed to get beyond just before they met. This was getting very uncomfortable.

He ran on down, but the several channels of fire paced him. They were definitely trying to trap him—and if this cavern ended, he would have no way to escape. There was no time to cut a new hole for himself, assuming he could reach a wall; there were lava lines between him and any wall he saw. If he tried to dig out through the floor, the lava would simply pour in after him. He had no further doubt of that. The ceiling— no, he could not risk that.

He saw a flicker ahead. Oh, no—more lava! In fact, more lines of lava, coming from the other direction. He was caught between them, doomed.

Then he realized that the fire ahead was a reflection. There was water there—a subterranean lake. It filled a depression in this part of the cavern, and bubbled gently.

And Volney couldn't swim.

He came to the lip of it and dipped a paw. The water was pleasantly cool; the bubbling was from air coming up through it, not from boiling. It wasn't deep; the light of the lava shone right through, showing that this was really only a large puddle. He could just about wade through it, if he had to.

The lava poured down, twin tentacles stretching forth to hiss against the lake to his left and right. Now he had no choice; he had to wade.

He waded in, and the lava did not. It didn't like the water, and drew back angrily at the brink, hardening. He felt the bubbles passing up around his body, innocently tickling him. Reprieve at last!

Then the light brightened. Volney looked back and saw with horror that a huge sheet of lava was sliding down behind him. It intended to press right on through the lake, boiling it away, so that it could finally nail its prey. He had to get beyond!

But he could not. Already streamers of lava were flowing around the lake to either side, enclosing it. Volney tried to wade faster, but saw that he was too slow; by the time he crossed, the lava would meet itself at the far side, and the escape route would be gone. If only he could swim, then he could move rapidly enough through the water.

He tried, splashing valiantly, but only succeeded in causing an enraged hissing at the rim as the splashes landed. It was no good; he could not make sufficient progress. He had lost this race.

He looked up. That was worse; not only was the ceiling out of his reach here, it was beginning to glow on its own. That meant that the main mass of this molten monster was closing in from its horrendous pool, ready to melt through and drop directly on him.

Was there no escape? Above and around was doom; below was water. He would drown if he tried to hide under the surface; he would burn if he did not.

But there was one chance. Volney didn't even pause to consider how well it might work; since it was his only course, he plunged in.

Literally. He took a breath and ducked below the water. One of the reasons he couldn't swim was that he was too dense to float; his feet were always on the bottom. Voles had to be dense, in order to bore through rock. Now this property of his body served him well; he was able to dig in the bottom much as if he were digging into dry ground. He scooped out the muck and soon encountered the firm stone below; this pond *was* a mere puddle, an accumulation at a low spot.

But the bubbles were still coming up. The stone was porous, and water and air extended down into it. That was now important.

He did as much as he could on one breath, then flipped over and poked his head out of the water. The ring of fire was flaring higher, and the ceiling was glowing; not much time remained. Volney took another breath and ducked down again.

He bored down farther, stirring up muck so that the water was cloudy; it was fortunate that he required only the sensation of touch, not vision. He got as far as he could, then shot up again for more air.

This continued breath by breath. The hole deepened rapidly, but the deadly lava loomed closer. The edge of the pool was hissing steadily as the lava encroached, destroying it in steam; soon the lava would make its major move and overwhelm the pond entirely.

Volney dug as deep as he could, then curved his tunnel, as he had when leaving the circle for the nickelpedes. He dug horizontally, then slanted up. It was getting harder to make progress on a breath, because of the time it took him to crawl along. But if this worked—

It worked. The bubbling air was catching in the upper part of the new tunnel, forming a bubble rather than pushing on through the rock right away. Air, like water, generally took the easiest course. Each time Volney returned, there was a larger bubble, until at last it was large enough for him to fit his snout into and breathe. Now he no longer had to retreat all the way to the surface of the pond; he could recharge right here.

That was just as well, because at last the lava was striking. There was such a horrendous hissing that he heard it right through the rock. He could no longer go back there.

Volney continued his boring, operating from his new base. The work was faster, now, because of his closer air supply. He had a lot of work to do, yet, and he was not yet safe from the lava, but he knew that the corner had been turned; he was on his way to escape.

Now he pondered the matter of the guide pebble. It had led him exactly wrong! How could that be?

Had the diggle leader betrayed him and sent him to his death in the living lava? He found that hard to accept; diggles were slow but honest, if only because the complexities of deception were too much for them to manage. This pebble was an example: a diggle could not understand intricate directions, and would inevitably get lost if it depended on instructions. But the pebbles were easy to understand: just proceed toward the good taste. Even the most worm-witted diggle could follow that system. When it got where it was going, it could take a new pebble that would guide it to the new destination. The smarter diggles would see to the distribution of the pebbles, thus directing traffic. The diggle leader had done for Volney what it did for its own kind: given him a pebble oriented on his particular destination.

How, then, could it have directed him so badly? He really needed to understand, because he wanted no more encounters with lava flows! Was it a bad stone? Yet it seemed to be working well, just wrong. It had guided him to doom, not to his destination. To the very place diggles as well as voles should avoid at all costs.

The pebble must be operating in reverse! It must have sweetened on the forbidden region and soured on the proper one. Yet why should this be?

He considered and concluded that he must have run afoul of a difference in taste. Diggles were wormlike, and their idea of a feast was a vein of coal. Voles were more like the surface creatures, and they preferred sweet foods. So to a diggle, bitter or sour might be positive, while sweet could represent spoilage. The pebble had been warning him with an ever-sweeter taste that he was going wrong, but he had misunderstood.

What a difference taste could make! This minor distinction between diggles and voles had very nearly killed him.

Volney oriented on the bad taste. It was an awful experience, but he was glad to do it; now at last he was going right. He hoped.

Soon enough he arrived at the squiggle headquarters. Here the creatures were as much smaller than he as the diggles had been larger. They were correspondingly more alert. He did not have to wait for one to come along; they tunneled out to meet him. "What brings you here, O volish one?" they inquired, quivering their whiskers expectantly at him.

Volney explained that he was seeking help for the Vale of the Vole. Their leader was apologetic, but explained that though he personally would like to help, he hardly knew how; and that there were elements among them that thought that it was high time the lordly voles were brought down to smaller tunnels. He was the soul of discretion, but it was evident that there was considerable resentment of the voles, historically by those who had had to yield the best pastures to them, and that history extended into the present. Thus the squiggles probably would not have helped, had they had the ability to. Volney really couldn't blame them.

However, the squiggles said, they would be happy to give

him a pebble to guide him to the nearest wiggle, who happened to be a female in quest of a mate. Volney demurred; voles had no truck with wiggles! Take the pebble anyway, they urged, in case he changed his mind. So Volney, avoiding rudeness, accepted the pebble and put it in his travel pouch.

Then, with heavy gizzard because of his failure to find help, Volney bored toward the surface.

He broke ground some distance from his starting place, deep in the surface jungle, and changed to his surface suit and eyes. Because he had a good sense of direction, he knew where Castle Roogna was. He did not really enjoy pottering along on the surface, but it was faster than tunneling, and he did not have a great deal of time left; his nether excursions had taken most of his week.

He reached the agreed rendezvous spot in the orchard on schedule. Chex was already there, and so was little Ivy, who it seemed was always to be found where things were happening. "Here'ss Volney!" Ivy cried gladly, running up to give him a hug. He wasn't sure how she managed that, but she did.

"Where's Esk?" he asked.

Chex spread her hands. "There hass been no ssign of him," she said with the hiss of the surface folk. "But I'm ssure he'ss on the way."

They exchanged stories of their searches. Volney was amazed to learn that she had not only entered the gourd, but had done so physically. "I did not think that was possible," he remarked.

"Oh, ssure," Ivy said eagerly. "I've done it! I had a night mare sshoe that let me go in, and I came out at the Good Magician'ss casstle, but I losst it."

"Lost the castle?" Volney asked, startled.

"The mare sshoe, dummy! Too bad, 'causse it'ss ssort of interessting in the gourd, if you can sstand the icky sstuff like the bug housse and the lake of casstor oil. There'ss a garden of candy, and—"

"That sshould be no horror to you!" Chex exclaimed.

"Well it wass, 'causse I think if I ate any, I'd maybe get

caught forever in there, so I had to pass it by, and *that* was the awfullesst thing I ever did!"

Chex smiled understandingly. "The gourd iss the repossitory of bad dreamss," she reminded Ivy.

"Yeah." Then, as Chex began to speak: "Yess!" And a giggle.

Time passed, but Esk did not return. Now the time for rendezvous was past, and they were getting alarmed. "If ssomething happened—not that anything could have!" Chex said nervously.

"Yes," Volney agreed as nervously.

"We might go out to meet him if he'ss a little late."

"Where?" For Esk could have taken any route to Lake Ogre-Chobee and any route back; they had virtually no chance of intercepting him.

Then an old woman staggered up. "Ah, a winged ccentaur and an esstinct vole!" she exclaimed. "You musst be Essk'ss friendss!"

"We are!" the three of them chorused.

"I am Latia, of the cursse fiendss. I curssed him, without meaning to, and now he'ss lost. I looked all over, but could not find him, sso finally I came here, hoping that you would know how to locate him."

Volney looked at Chex. Esk—lost!

"There'ss a finder sspell in the arssenal!" Ivy exclaimed. "I'll get it for you!"

Volney relaxed. Maybe it would be all right after all.

# 9

# GOURD

Esk found himself in a tangled mixture of glade and jungle that was strange in ways he could not quite fathom. About one thing he was not confused: he was in the world of the gourd. He had never been here before, but his father had warned him about it. When a person looked into the peephole, his spirit entered the gourd, and could not escape it until some other person came and broke his line of sight. If no one came, he would remain indefinitely, and his body would slowly starve. According to Smash, it could be a lot of fun in the gourd. But Smash was half ogre, and what an ogre thought was fun was not necessarily what Esk would.

He had been smitten by the curse, and fallen in a sink, and landed against a gourd. That meant that Latia would have trouble finding him—and might fail. Since her curse really had been a curse instead of a blessing, and it was by her own estimate a singularly potent one, it meant she probably would fail. He was in deep trouble.

Could he escape on his own? He struggled to remember what else Smash had said about the gourd. It was the home of the night mares, who were the couriers of bad dreams; the mares delivered them to deserving sleepers, and could pass freely in and out. No other creature could, except by means of the peephole.

Well, perhaps he could find a night mare and ask her to help him. If she went out and put a dream in Latia's head that showed exactly where he was, then the old woman could locate him. This would take time, but at least it was a chance.

It seemed to him that there was some terrible price that a mare required for such assistance, though. What was it? He couldn't remember. Well, he would find out in due course.

Where could he find a night mare? Smash had said something about a pasture where they grazed, somewhere beyond a haunted house and a city of moving buildings where the brassies lived. Esk didn't know what a brassy might be, but hoped he would recognize it if he saw it. So he would start looking for those things.

Now he examined his environment more closely. He perceived an assortment of paths, all tangled together like a helping of spaghetti. Did one of them lead to the haunted house, or the brassies, or the night mares?

There was one way to find out. He set foot on the clearest path and walked along it. The tangled terrain seemed to retreat slightly, reorienting to accommodate the perspective of the path he had chosen.

But Esk was cautious. He distrusted, as a matter of principle, any path that was too easy, because that was exactly the kind that could lead to a . . .

And there it was: a tangle tree. Just as he had feared.

Esk backed off—and discovered that this was a one-way path. It was clear and open ahead, and did not exist behind; the brush had closed in, girt with glistening thorns and slime-coated leaves. In normal Xanth such foliage would be dangerous; here in the gourd it was surely worse.

He hesitated. Certainly he did not wish to go forward into the tangler, but he couldn't go back, and the sides looked no more inviting.

The tangle tree had no such concern. Already it was reaching for him with its tentacles. They were stout and green and moved with a dismaying sinuousness; this was the largest and most aggressive tangle tree he had encountered, the stuff of a bad dream.

A bad dream! Of course! The gourd was the repository of horrible dreams. The night mares surely came here to pick up the dreams of tanglers, which they then carried to the Xanth-side sleepers. Dreams, like other forms of art, required effective original models.

Maybe this would be a good place to stay, so that when a mare came, he could ask her to take his message.

The first tentacle reached for his face. Esk ducked, but it pursued him. The tip of it caught in his hair and coiled it tight, drawing him up.

Esk drew his hunting knife. He reached up and sliced off the tip of the tentacle, freeing his hair.

Green goo spurted from the severed tentacle. "Ooo!" the tree groaned. Then, wrathfully, it intensified its effort. Six more tentacles swooped in.

Esk knew he couldn't fight all these off with his knife. So he ducked under and ran in the direction that surprised the tree: straight down the path toward it. Behind him the path dissolved and the jungle closed in—just in time to get grabbed by the tentacles that had aimed at Esk.

Suddenly the tangler was in a struggle with the thorn vines and poison slime leaves. Horror against horror! Esk ran on, directly into the embrace of the tree, while the tree was distracted by the outside action. Tanglers, like most vegetation, were not unduly bright; once launched into a grab, they tended to fight it through without regard to the nature of what they had grabbed.

The path led right to the huge wooden maw of the tree, which was now grimacing with concentration. Above it was a bole that opened into a giant eye. Normal tanglers did not have eyes, as far as he knew, but this was no normal plant; this was a bad dream. Esk stopped, hoping the eye would not spy him.

There was the sound of tearing. The tentacles ripped out the thorn and slime plants by their pallid roots and hauled them into the wooden orifice. The tree took a big bite—and of course got a mouthful of thorn and slime.

Now was as good a time as any to sneak away. Esk sheathed his knife and started out on another path, one of several that led in to the tree. But the moment his foot touched it, it vanished. These were all one way: in. How could he get out?

He would have to use his magic. He chose another path, and as his foot came down on it, he murmured "no." This balked the path's natural inclination, and it remained as it was. Esk had not thought to use his talent quite this way before, and hadn't been sure it would work in the gourd; he was now reassured.

The path gradually diminished as it got farther from the tree, and finally petered out amidst a confusion that was similar or identical to the one he had started at. He had accomplished next to nothing, apart from ascertaining that the easiest path was not necessarily the best.

He looked at the other paths that now offered. They couldn't all lead to tangle trees, because tanglers were notoriously isolationist; they reserved hunting territories and resisted encroachment by others of their kind.

He shrugged and stepped across to the best looking of the other paths. It couldn't lead to a worse evil than the last!

Again the surroundings reformulated to accommodate the new perspective, and it seemed that this was the only natural path for any person to take. But Esk was more cautious than before. He turned around and followed it back the way he had come. It did not vanish; it was a two-way path. Good. He turned again and proceeded in his original direction.

Soon enough he discovered its bad dream. This was a monstrous (of course!) kraken, the nefarious seaweed monster that snared unwary swimmers. But this one was swimming in the air above the path. Its tentacles were just as long and sinuous as those of the tangle tree, and had saucer-shaped suckers.

Even as he spied it, it spied him. It floated toward him, tentacles reaching.

Esk drew his knife again, knowing that this was hardly a threat to a creature such as this. He ran along the path, knowing that escape would not be feasible either. He was correct on both counts; the kraken paced him without seeming effort, its tentacles extending toward him in a leisurely manner. It knew it had him; it was supremely unworried about his effort either to fight or to escape.

He could tell it no, of course. But Esk was annoyed by

these trouble-leading paths, and now that annoyance burst into anger.

As the tentacles touched him, he sheathed his knife and tackled them bare-handed. His ogre strength manifested. He caught one tentacle and squeezed it and its sucker to a painful pulp; he caught another and yanked violently.

The kraken reacted as had the tree, keening in momentary pain, then throwing half a dozen more tentacles into the fray. This time Esk did not avoid them; he grabbed them and tied them into knots. He knew he was taking out his private frustration on a weed that was only trying to do its job, but his ogre nature didn't care. Nothing in its right mind messed with an ogre!

Very soon, the kraken had had enough; the bad dream had turned on it. It jerked away and fled, leaving Esk in command of the path.

He relaxed, feeling a bit guilty. He should have told the weed no, and passed on unmolested. He should not have taken out his frustration at being trapped in the world of the gourd on a relatively innocent creature.

Soon he came to the end of the path. It simply stopped, and the mess of thorns and poison slime resumed. So he reversed, and followed it to its other end—which terminated similarly. This was a path that went nowhere; it was simply the kraken's run. Again, he had gained nothing.

Well, there were other paths. He walked back toward the center of the limited one he was on, casting his gaze about until he saw another that departed at right angles. He found a stick and used it to push the thorns and slimes to one side, and stepped carefully across.

The perspective shifted again, centering on the new path; the one he had just left was now almost invisible, and what he could see of it seemed twisted, while it had been fairly straight before. The floating kraken was nowhere to be seen. This was certainly a deceptive region.

This present path wound pleasantly around and down, following a contour he had not noted before. Soon it presented a clear spring, whose water sparkled without moving.

If Esk had not known that this was the region of bad dreams, his experiences with other two paths would have warned him. He did not trust this water at all. Obviously the traveler was intended to drink from it. What was the trap? What could be so bad about it that it was part of the source region for sleeping horrors?

He heard a commotion. Something was coming down the path. He stepped carefully off it, avoiding the big thorns, and made himself as inconspicuous as he could.

It was a desperate bunny, fleeing a gross, slavering wolf. The bunny hopped down the path, its soft pink ears thrown back by the wind of its velocity, its little nose quivering. The wolf charged straight after, fangs bared.

Esk would have stopped the wolf's pursuit by telling it no, but the pair was moving so fast that both animals were by him before he worked up the thought. He simply had to watch as the bunny made it to the spring and leaped in, barely avoiding the wolf, who screeched to a halt at its brink. Apparently bad-dream wolves did not like water, so the bunny was safe.

But the bunny, having plunged into the water, suffered a transformation. Its appearance didn't really change, but its aspect did. It emitted a peculiar keening growl, then swam purposefully toward the waiting wolf, who seemed hardly to believe its luck. The crazy bunny was returning to its jaws!

The bunny scrambled to shore and shook itself. It growled again, and its eyes blazed red. It bared its teeth. Then it leaped on the wolf, who was so surprised it didn't move. The bunny's teeth snapped closed on one of the wolf's ears, and its two feet thumped hard against the wolf's nose.

The bunny was savagely attacking the wolf! The wolf, amazed, leaped back. The ear tore free of the bunny's teeth, leaving a splatter of blood. The bunny leaped again, toward the wolf, teeth snapping.

The wolf should have been able to dispatch the bunny, but its confusion was such that it turned tail and fled, the bunny pursuing.

Esk watched, as amazed as the wolf. What was in that water?

The bunny's nose wiggled. The creature paused, winding Esk. It stopped, turning toward him. It growled again, and its eyes ignited. It leaped.

"No!" Esk cried.

The bunny was in midair so could not change course, but
it did change its mind. Instead of biting Esk, it simply landed
against his chest and immediately jumped off. Then it resumed its progress up the path, following the wolf.

Esk looked at the spring. There was only one thing he
could think of to account for what he had seen. He knew of
love springs, that caused any creature drinking them to fall
violently in love with the next creature of the opposite sex it
encountered. It was understood that the most prominent crossbreeds had arisen because of the intercession of love springs:
centaurs, harpies, merfolk and so on. But here in this realm
of bad dreams, this must be the opposite: a hate spring. Thus
the bunny had imbibed, and been filled with such hate that it
had lost all fear of the wolf. It had hated Esk, too. It was no
longer gentle and frightened; now it was vicious and bold. Its
personality had changed radically.

Esk concluded that he did not want to drink from that
spring. He walked slowly back along the path, seeking some
other route.

He had tried three obvious, well-formed paths, and each
had led him to mischief. It was time to change his approach.
What about a hidden, devious path?

He almost missed it. The path was so inconspicuous that
it was virtually lost in the tangle. It might not be a path at
all. But he decided to try it. He stepped carefully across.

Once more the perspective shifted, and the path became
more evident. But it was in poor repair, and was so convoluted as to seem to make loops in places. Brush overhung it,
and stones intruded on it; he had to watch his step, every
step. Was it worth it?

He decided that it was. After all, if nothing had used this
path recently, then it probably was not being maintained by
some monster for a bad dream. Its very difficulty made it
safer. He proceeded with improving confidence.

Then, abruptly, he encountered a human skeleton. It lay
athwart the path, its skull on one side, its leg bones on the
other. There was no flesh remaining on it at all.

Esk sighed. "Obviously this path is not safe either," he said.
"This poor fellow—" He touched a hipbone with the toe of
his boot.

The skeleton stirred. Esk leaped back, though he knew that he had probably just caused the bones to shift and collapse. After all, bones could not move on their own!

The skeleton twisted around and sat up.

Esk retreated farther. *It was moving!*

The skeleton got to its feet, somewhat unsteadily.

"All right!" Esk exclaimed. "I'll vacate your path! I don't need to fight another bad dream!"

The skull turned on the neck bones, and the hollow eye sockets oriented on him. "You found me?" the toothy jaw-bone asked.

"I found you, and now I'll leave you," Esk agreed. "Really, I'm not looking for trouble, just for a way out of here. No need to chase me."

"Please, keep me," the skeleton said. Its lower jaw moved as it spoke. Esk wasn't sure how it could speak with no flesh to guide the air, but it did.

"Keep you?" Esk asked blankly. "What for?"

"So I will no longer be lost."

"You are lost? I thought you were dead!"

"No, I'm lost," the skeleton said firmly. "This is the Lost Path."

"How can a path be lost?"

"When no one finds it," the skeleton said. "Please, I must find my way back to the Haunted Garden, but I cannot unlose myself. Take me by the hand and help me be found."

Esk's initial horror of the skeleton was fading. After all, this was the place of bad dreams, and the skeleton was no worse than others. "But I'm lost too."

"No, I can see you are of mortal vintage. You must be peeping."

"Uh, yes," Esk agreed. "I fell, and my eye came up against a hypnogourd. I'm trying to find a night mare so she can take a message out, so that my line of sight can be broken. But until then, I'm stuck here."

"Yes, you are only temporarily mislaid. But I am properly lost. Therefore I must plead for your help; if you do not unlose me, I may never recover my station."

"Your station?"

"I am part of the skeletal set, adjacent to the Haunted

House. Some horrendous ogre came through and—"

"That was my father!" Esk exclaimed, remembering what Smash had said.

The skeleton drew away from him with alarm. "Oh, no! I thought you might be a rescuer!"

"Wait, skeleton," Esk said quickly. "I suppose if my father was the cause of your getting lost, I should try to get you found. What's your name?"

"Marrow," the skeleton said.

"My name's Esk." Then, somewhat awkwardly, he extended his hand.

The skeleton took it. "Oh, thank you, Esk! I will make it up to you! I am lost, but I do know something of the environs. If there is any way I can be of assistance . . ."

"I think you have already helped me," Esk said, disengaging from the bones of the hand as quickly as he could do so without affront. "I was looking for the haunted, uh, set, because my father mentioned it; if I can find that, maybe I can follow his route to the pasture of the night mares."

"That certainly might be true!" Marrow said with bony enthusiasm. "I cannot tell you the way because I am lost, but I can tell you anything else about it, and I'm sure my associates will have information."

"Good; let's get going."

But the skeleton hung back. "You must take my hand; I can not unlose myself."

"Oh." Esk took the hand again, realizing that he had to follow the strange rules of this place. Actually, the bones were firm and dry, not slimy as he had feared. "Do you know the proper direction?"

"Alas, no," Marrow said. "When that ogre started throwing bones—no offense intended—I fled, and I lost track of location. I tried to find my way back, but somehow I had stumbled onto this path, and that was it. I have remained lost ever since. Finally I just lay down to rest my weary bones, so to speak, and then you came."

"But once you were on the path, it wasn't lost any more," Esk said. "So you should have been able to find your way out."

"Not so. Once I was on it, I became part of it, because I did not find it; I merely stumbled on it."

"I'm not sure I did much better. I tried three other paths, and all were bad, so then I looked for a different kind—"

"And found it!" Marrow exclaimed. "So you are not lost. Even though you cannot directly escape this world, you can find your way from this path."

"Are you sure of that?"

"No," Marrow confessed.

Esk shrugged. The thesis made as much sense as anything else, and it was more encouraging to believe in the chance of escape than in the lack of any chance.

The jungle thinned, becoming more like a forest. That was a relief; Esk felt more at home in forest. Perhaps he was finding the way out. If he returned Marrow to the garden of the walking skeletons, and if one of the others did know the way to the pasture of the night mares—

Something bounded away, startling him. It looked like a mundane deer, but it was bright red. "What was that?"

"Only a roe," Marrow said. "Didn't you see the color?"

"Yes. That's why I couldn't be sure what it was."

"Roes are red," Marrow said. "I thought everyone knew that."

"I happen to be a stranger here," Esk said somewhat shortly.

They came to a potted plant. It was bright blue, and had knobs on the ends of its stems. As they approached, it lifted the knobs menacingly; obviously it intended to punch at anyone who came too close. "What is that?"

"A violent," Marrow said. "Didn't you note the color?"

"Oh, I see," Esk said, irritated. "Roes are red, violents are blue."

"I think he's got it!" Marrow exclaimed.

"Just who are you talking to?"

"The violent, of course. Didn't you hear?"

"I guess I don't speak the local dialect. What does it say?"

"It says it isn't its fault it got lost. They were planting violents on the median strips between major paths, but they rejected this one and threw it away."

Esk began to have some sympathy for the blue plant. "Why did they reject it?"

"Because they didn't want any more violents on the media."

"Oh." He should have known that no explanation would make much sense here.

They continued along the path. In due course they had to pass under a kind of woven vine that seemed to have eyeballs set into it. "Say, isn't that an eye queue?" Esk asked. "My father encountered one of those; it made him very smart for a while. What's it doing here?"

"Maybe I can find out," Marrow said. He reached out, caught the vine, and set it on the top of his skull. "It says it was lost from the Lexicon," he reported.

"The Lexicon? What's that?"

"The eye queue says that some ass from Mundania came through with a secretary and listed all the things of Xanth— except the eye queue vine. So the vine is lost."

"Too bad," Esk said. "Now nobody will be smart."

Marrow stepped out from under the vine, and it fell back into place over the path. Apparently it could not become a part of the skull, probably because there was no brain to enhance.

Farther along was a little squiggly thing, hardly large enough to see. "What's that?" Esk asked.

"A lost vitamin, I think. Let me see." Marrow put out a finger bone to touch the thing. "Yes, vitamin F."

"What's it for?"

"Oh, it has potent F-ect."

"Potent effect?"

"F you make the right F-ort."

"Let's find vitamin X instead," Esk said grimly. "Then maybe we can become X-pert in finding the X-it, if it X-ists."

"X-actly," Marrow agreed, not catching Esk's irony.

They continued past other lost items: a lost fossil bone that Marrow greatly admired, as it was of a species of creature unknown in Xanth or Mundania, whose discovery would revolutionize the understanding of both; a lost band of the rainbow, more wonderful than any other; a lost stream of consciousness; and a lost dire strait. Esk would have found all these things considerably more interesting if he hadn't been so acutely concerned about finding his way out of the gourd before his body got into trouble in Xanth. Suppose a dragon sniffed it out? He could wake up to find himself chomped.

Then they came to a young woman sitting in the path. She was of metallic hue, and quite nicely proportioned. Esk could tell because her only clothing seemed to be a metallic halter covering her front.

She jumped up as they approached. "Oh, good!" she exclaimed. "Found at last!"

"Uh, hello," Esk said, trying to keep his eyes above the level of her chest. He knew that Chex Centaur would have called his attitude foolish, but the attitude was one of the things that had not gotten lost. "I am Esk, and this is Marrow."

"Hello, Esk and Marrow," she said brightly. "I am Bria Brassie."

"You're a brassy!" Esk exclaimed.

"That's brassie," she corrected him. "I'm female, as you evidently hadn't noticed. A male is brassy."

"Oh. Sorry. I, uh, noticed, but—"

"That's not much of an apology," she muttered.

Esk plowed on. "I've been looking for you!"

"Well, you have found me. Have we met before?" She gave her brass hair a shake so that it glinted prettily.

"I mean, I was looking for where you live, because I think that's near the night mares' pasture! Do you know where—?"

"No, I'm hopelessly lost. I thought *you* knew. Didn't you come to get me out of here?"

"I came by accident," Esk admitted, glancing down, then wrenching his eyes up again. That wasn't much better, because her bosom was full and her brassiere was scanty.

"He's a peeper," Marrow explained.

Esk felt himself starting to flush, though he knew that the skeleton was referring to the gourd, not what Esk was trying not to stare at. "Yes, yes," he said quickly. "I fell, and landed against a gourd before I knew, and now I'm stuck here." He swung his gaze around, to indicate the surroundings.

"Are you having trouble with your eyes?" Bria inquired.

"Uh, some, maybe. Do you have any information about the terrain? Anything that might help us get, er, unlost?"

She turned, looking away from him. In the process she showed her pert brass bottom, that flexed exactly as if made of living flesh. "I'm afraid I don't. I like to explore, and was seeking a way to visit the outer world, but as you can see, I got lost." She completed her turn, and Esk hauled his eyes up once again. "Are you sure you're well?" she asked solicitously. "You seem flushed, which I understand is a signal of distress among living folk."

"Uh, yes, I am distressed," Esk agreed quickly. "My body is stuck in that pit, and I'm very much concerned that something will happen to it before I get rescued. If I can just get to a night mare—"

"Yes, it must be quite a problem, being alive," Bria said. "Is it true that you have to eat and eliminate, just to keep going?"

"Brassies don't?"

"Of course not. Why bother with all that inconvenience and mess if you don't have to? I suppose you have to wear all that clumsy clothing to keep you warm, too."

"You shouldn't embarrass him by remarking on his weaknesses of the flesh," Marrow reproved her.

"Oh, that's right," she agreed. "I apologize, Esk." She stepped into him, put her arms around him, and kissed him on the mouth. "Is that enough?"

Stunned, Esk just stood there, for the moment as still as a metal statue himself.

"It seems it is not," Marrow said.

"I'll just have to try harder, then," she said brightly. "Esk, I apologize for anything I may have said to offend or embarrass you, and hope you will forgive me that transgression." Then she embraced him so closely that he started to lose his balance and made an involuntary grab for support, reaching around her. Then she kissed him again, deep and long. She was made of metal, but her lips were warm and soft and firm, and so was her body.

Finally she drew back her head a little. "Is that enough?" she asked again.

Esk felt as if he were floating at treetop height. All that anchored him was his grip on her body. Then a mound flexed under his hand, and he realized where that grip was. He froze again.

"Apparently you are not putting enough into it," Marrow said.

Bria made a cute little grimace. "Apparently not. Well, I'll make sure it takes the next time." She inhaled, preparing for the supreme effort.

"No-no!' Esk stammered. "I-I—I accept your a-apology!"

She cocked her head at him, and her hair shifted with a coppery sheen. "Are you sure? You still look flushed."

"Ab-absolutely sure," he said uncertainly.

"That's a relief. Be sure to tell me if I embarrass you again."

"Uh, yes, certainly," he agreed, as she disengaged, and his hand finally slipped from her buttock.

"Apologizing is such a chore," Marrow said. "I don't know whether it is worse for the offender or the offendee."

Now it was not just his gaze, but his fancy that had to be sternly reined. Esk's experience with women was quite limited, but he was discovering that the nuances of such interaction could carry a formidable charge. He had met Bria only a few minutes ago, but already she had opened a dramatic new dimension to his imagination.

"We had better just walk along the path," Bria said. "Since Esk is not part of our world, he should be able to unlose us, if we maintain contact with him."

"My sentiment exactly," Marrow said.

Bria took Esk's right hand and Marrow his left, and they walked on along the path, which was wide enough at this stage to accommodate them in this formation. Esk suffered himself to be guided, for his thoughts were not properly on the subject. How could a creature of metal be so soft?

The path jigged and jogged, becoming narrow and then wide again, but they maintained their linkage and advanced resolutely along it.

Bria spied something in the path, perhaps a tiny pebble, and bent quickly to pick it up with her free hand. "Just what I've always wanted!" she exclaimed.

"Oh? What is it?" Esk asked.

She glanced sidelong at him. "Nothing of consequence, perhaps. Just another lost item I think I'll save, just in case I should one day need it."

Esk shrugged. Of course she could pick up anything she wanted. A stone as small as that was hardly worth the effort, though.

The scenery was changing, so they knew they were getting somewhere. Now they seemed to be approaching a region of more orderly plants, that—

Light flared, interrupting his observation in mid thought. "Oh, I'm so glad we found you in time!" Chex exclaimed. "Are you all right, Esk?"

"What'v thiv?" Volney asked.

"A bare-bottomed hussy!" Latia exclaimed. "And a bundle of bones!"

Esk snapped alert. "Don't say anything embarrassing!" he cried. "These are my acquaintances in the gourd!" For Marrow and Bria were with him, still holding his hands.

"That's right," Chex said. "Whatever a visitor to the world of the gourd is in contact with when he departs it, accompanies him. These are gourd folk."

The skeleton and the brassie seemed dazed now. It was Esk's turn to take charge. "On my right hand is Bria Brassie," he said. "On my left, Marrow Bones. They were on the Lost Path. Bria and Marrow, these are my friends in Xanth normal: Chex Centaur, Volney Vole, and Latia Curse Fiend."

The several named parties nodded in turn. Then Chex assessed the situation. "I believe we can return Marrow and Bria to their own world. Esk, you have simply to hold their hands and look into the peephole; then, inside, release them, and we shall break your eye contact so that you return alone."

"And where will that leave us?" Bria demanded indignantly. "On the Lost Path—where we can't escape?"

"But this is not your world," Chex protested. "Everything is different here."

"I wanted to explore this world anyway," Bria said.

Marrow shrugged. "I think I am no more lost here than I was on the Lost Path. At such time as some one of you peeks in a gourd and locates the Haunted Garden, you can return me there directly."

"But the gourd is locked onto the same scene," Chex said. "Each time Esk peeps, he will find himself exactly where he was before."

"Agreed," Marrow said. "But you others will have different scenes, and perhaps one of them will be the one I require."

Chex nodded agreement. "Yes, we can do that now. Ordinarily I would not voluntarily look into a hypnogourd, but this seems to be a constructive exception." She reached down and picked up the gourd. "Free me after only a moment, please," she said, and put her eye to the peephole.

She froze in place. Esk disengaged from Bria and Marrow, and put his hand over the peephole, interrupting Chex's vision.

The centaur resumed animation. "I was in a region of paper objects," she said. "Some exceedingly elaborate constructions; I had no idea that paper could achieve such configurations!"

"Wrong set," Esk said. He took the gourd and held it down for Volney.

The Vole looked, and froze. Then Esk covered the peephole, and Volney returned to life. "An endlevv vheet of fluid," he reported. "Very pretty, but I think not correct for theve folk."

Esk held the gourd up for Latia. She looked, and froze; then, when Esk broke the line of sight, she grimaced. "A great wide plain, with black equine shapes on the horizon," she said.

"The pasture of the night mares!" Esk exclaimed. "Just what I was looking for—but no longer need!"

"It seems that we cannot help these visitors at the moment," Chex said. "Perhaps if they do not mind remaining with us for a time, we can find some other person whose gourd orientation is more relevant."

"That's fine," Bria said. "I shall be happy to spend some time here."

"But you will have to dress decently," Latia said.

"What?"

"Different conventions!" Esk said quickly to Bria. "She

only means that here it will be better if you wear a dress."

"That's right," Marrow said. "You do wear clothing here."

"I don't," Chex said.

"Humanoids wear clothing, mostly," Esk said.

"I suppose we shouldn't embarrass the world we visit," Bria said reluctantly.

"There is a broadcloth tree close by," Latia said. "I can readily make you clothing from that." She glanced at Marrow. "And if I can find some herringbone material, that should do nicely for you." Latia set off for the fabric, trailed by the two from the gourd.

"Broadcloth and herringbone," Chex murmured. "She has a special sense of alignment."

"The curse fiends are very conscious of the proprieties," Esk agreed. "I gather she rendezvoused with you and Volney, and then Volney sniffed me out?"

"Exactly. We did not realize that you would return with company, but perhaps it is for the best. I gather you were unsuccessful in your quest for a solution to the problem of the Kiss-Mee River?"

"Unfortunately, yes. But I can still ask the ogres for help."

"We must eat and compare notes," she said, "then decide what to do in the morning."

"Yes. I am eager to hear how the two of you fared." Indeed, he was glad to be back with familiar company. But still his mind kept flirting with the experience he had had with Bria's mode of apology. He had returned from the gourd, his body intact, but his mind had hardly settled yet. He wished he could talk to someone about that.

"She seems like a nice enough girl, and quite well formed," Chex remarked, as if reading his mind. "But she is not of your world, Esk."

# CHEIRON

Chex trotted south, carrying Marrow on her back. She was headed for her sire's region, and the skeleton would not have been able to keep up afoot.

Actually, Marrow did not look like a skeleton now. Latia had worked up an effective suit of herringbone cloth, and picked him a pair of stout slippers and a pair of thick gloves that extended well up past his wrists. He looked very much like a living man, except for his skull, and even that could be masked by the hat and scarf. Fortunately he did not weigh very much, even bundled up like this, because he was all bone.

They had discussed it the prior night, after exchanging stories of recent adventures. They had decided to distribute the new additions to the group among the original members, with the fiend woman and brass girl accompanying Esk, and the skeleton accompanying Chex. The vole was tunneling alone, again; it was too difficult for any of the others to keep pace with him deep underground. Perhaps this time they would be able to obtain some more solid commitment of assistance. They would meet in seven days, as before, and see where they stood. One way or another, they intended to rescue the Kiss-Mee River from its unhappy plight.

It was possible that Marrow would not remain with her long, for they had agreed to ask any other folk they met to look in a gourd, and to conduct Marrow there if either the horror house or the haunted garden were found, because the two were adjacent. Meanwhile, she was happy to talk with him, because like all centaurs she was curious about anything that was out of the ordinary.

"How is it that you hold together without flesh or tendons?" she inquired.

"That is the nature of skeletal magic," he explained. "The toe bone is connected to the foot bone, and the foot bone is connected to the ankle bone, and the ankle bone is connected to the leg bone—"

"I grasp the connection," she cut in wryly. "I suppose it is that same magic that animates you?"

"Of course. Just as the magic of life animates your flesh. Doesn't it become quite hot in there, with such a ponderous mass of flesh encasing you?"

"We have become acclimatized to it," she said with a private smile. "How is it that you are able to speak, when you have no lungs, no throat, no mouth?"

"It is just part of the magic. Certain motions of the jaw produce certain sounds, and we learn to control these when young, until we become proficient. The full process takes several years, but we consider it part of the art of growing up."

"Of growing up? You mean, there are child skeletons too?"

"Of course. Did you suppose we were fashioned whole from air?"

"I thought you were the remains of formerly living folk."

"The remains of living folk? What an appalling notion!"

"No offense was intended, Marrow," she said quickly. "We of the outer world don't have much direct contact with you of the gourd, so are ignorant about many things. I apologize if—"

"No apology required," he said quickly. "Of course you did not know; that is why you asked."

Chex remembered something that Esk had mentioned in

passing. "About apology—is it true that your kind does it by kissing?"

"Of course not! Whatever gave you that idea?"

"Perhaps I misconstrued a reference. Esk said something about the brassies—"

"They do it their way, of course. Bria embarrassed Esk, so she kissed him."

"Skeletons don't do it that way?" This was interesting!

"Certainly not. How could we kiss?"

"I see your point. Yet in that case—"

"We knock skulls."

"Doesn't that hurt?"

"Hurt?"

She realized that pain would be a foreign concept to creatures who had no soft flesh. "I think I understand that it does not. But suppose a skeleton embarrassed a brassie? Would they kiss or knock heads?"

"How could a skeleton embarrass a brassie?" he asked.

That stumped her, so she moved on to another subject. "You said there were small skeletons. How do skeletons reproduce?"

"Very simple. He strikes her so hard she flies apart. That is known as knocking her up. Then he selects some of the smaller bones and assembles them into a baby skeleton."

"But doesn't she need those bones for herself?"

"Well, how does a living creature reproduce?"

"He inserts his seed in her, and she grows a foal from her flesh."

"Doesn't she need that flesh for herself?"

Chex considered. She concluded that Marrow had made his point.

In due course they reached Xap's stamping ground. The hippogryph was there, snoozing. He had the body of a centaur and the forepart of a griffin, with great golden wings and a golden bird-of-prey head. He was evidently past his prime, but still a powerful figure of a winged monster.

"Hello, sire," Chex called.

Xap snapped his head out from under his wing and squawked.

"He doesn't talk much," Chex explained to Marrow. "But

I understand him well enough." Then, to the hippogryph: "Sire, this is Marrow Bones from the gourd. He would like to return if he can find a normal person oriented on his region."

Xap squawked again. Chex turned to Marrow, who remained on her back, swathed in his herringbone. "Sorry; my sire says the last time he looked in a gourd, all he saw was a lake of purple manure. I don't think you'd care to go there." The skeleton nodded agreement; manure made bones smell bad.

"Sire," she continued, "I am looking for help for a friend. I would like to ask the winged monsters for that help. Do you suppose I could meet with them?"

Xap squawked. "Who? Cheiron?" she asked. "No, I don't know him or of him, but I doubt that I need to. Sire, I wish you'd stop matchmaking! I've told you before that no ordinary centaur wants to mate with a winged one; most won't even speak to me. My centaur granddam won't, and she's typical. I feel more comfortable with the winged monsters. At least they don't treat me like a freak. That's why I'm hoping they might help, when the centaurs refused."

Xap squawked again. "But I can't go up there!" Chex protested. "It's inaccessible to landbound creatures."

But it turned out that the winged monsters had a firm policy: they would not deal with any creature who would not meet them on their turf. Xap could help by notifying them of her coming appearance, but she would have to get herself to the turf.

Chex nerved herself. She dreaded the effort, but knew it was the only way. She knew the route, but doubted she could travel it. About the best she could do was to die trying.

She explained this to Marrow as she started for the mountain trail. "But isn't dying awkward for fleshly creatures?" he inquired.

"Very."

"Does it require courage for a fleshly creature to risk it, then?"

"I suppose so," she agreed. "Fortunately, centaurs are noted for their courage." But her tongue was drying up in her mouth. How she wished she had been able to find the Good Magician and had learned how to fly.

At the foot of the mountain she paused to defecate and urinate; there was no sense carrying any inessentials up. Marrow found this process quite interesting; his kind had no experience with it. "Life seems like such an inconvenient business," he remarked.

The trail proceeded steeply. Soon it came to a rushing torrent of water: the mountain's own process of urination. "Hold on," she warned Marrow. "There is no bridge; I'll have to ford this."

Marrow hung on, and she waded into the stream. The water was frigid; in a moment her legs were getting numb. Then the current intensified, doing its best to dislodge her footing, but she maintained it.

Then, in the center, the channel abruptly deepened. She was unable to find the proper footing, and the rush of water was too fierce to permit her to swim.

Frustrated, shivering, she backed out. "I can't pass!" she said, uncertain whether the droplets on her face were from river spray or her eyes.

"Allow me to inspect the situation," Marrow said. He climbed off her back, doffed his clothing, and walked along the bank, swinging his skull from side to side. "Yes, as I thought, there is a cave."

"A cave? Here?" she asked. "How do you know?"

"Skeletons have a sense about things underground," he explained. "There is water in this cave, not as cold as the river, with very little current, and it is large enough for your body. I can guide you through it, if you wish."

"Yes!" she exclaimed, gratified. Then, realizing that there was a detail he might have overlooked: "But I have to breathe, you know. Is there any air?"

Marrow angled his skull, orienting on the hidden cave. "Some. In bubbles. Several paces apart. I can guide you."

Chex decided to take the plunge. "Then guide me! Just remember, I need to breathe every minute or so; if I don't, I'll drown."

"What is drown?"

"Dying because of insufficient air."

"Oh, yes; you don't find that comfortable. I will try to remember that: air every minute."

"Exactly where is this cave?" she inquired, not completely at ease about this, but seeing no better alternative.

"Just a few paces upstream. It is quite convoluted."

Another problem occurred to her. "That means you will have to direct me constantly—but if it is underwater, you won't be able to speak."

"Oh, I can speak; you merely may have difficulty hearing."

"I appreciate the distinction. Let me explain to you how to direct me without words." She proceeded to drill him as she had Esk, so that he could guide her accurately with his knee bones and feet bones. Now the interference of his speech (or her hearing) would not put her at risk of drowning. Perhaps Marrow did not properly appreciate her concern about this detail, but she was greatly relieved anyway.

*Whoa*, his leg bones said.

Chex halted. "Here? But I don't see it."

*Turn*, the left knee said. Marrow was already good at this! She turned to the stream. *Caution*, his knees said.

He was getting very good. She hadn't known that that directive existed. She stepped into the river, experiencing the deadly chill of it.

The bed fell sharply away; it was surprisingly deep here. Guided by his leg bones, she made her way around and down, discovering a big hole below the water's surface, slanting back under the bank and curving to be parallel to the river. Here was the cave.

She had to duck her head to get completely into it, but it was big enough to accommodate her. Before she did that, she turned one last time to face the skeleton. "Remember, you must direct me to air within a minute. How good is your time sense?"

"It is excellent," he assured her. "We must have precise timing when we dance, just as we need thorough coordination when we gamble."

"You gamble? How do you do that?"

"We roll the bones, of course. It's a great way to pass the time between gigs."

"Gigs?"

"Assignments. When an order for a bad dream comes in, and we have to perform. They never give us enough advance notice, so it can be a real scramble. So our existence consists of long periods of boredom punctuated by brief flurries of terror. It's just like war."

"Terror? What are you afraid of?"

"Not us; the recipients of the bad dreams."

"Well, just don't gamble with your timing! I'm about to undergo a brief period of terror myself, and I don't need any help in that!"

"The first air bubble is just fifty-two seconds distant," he said.

Chex realized that she would just have to trust that. She inhaled deeply, causing a local fish to goggle at her chest, held her breath, and ducked under the surface and into the cave.

Now she remembered her claustrophobia. She was heading into a confined region.

But it was filled with water, she told herself. That was different. The cave would not collapse, because it wasn't under pressure; the water sustained it. She had to believe that!

She tended to float, so that walking was difficult; she had to reach up with her hands and more or less pull herself along the roof of the cave. Marrow's firm knee pressure guided her, so that she encountered no dead ends or tight squeezes. He was correct about its temperature not being as cold as the river, though it was still uncomfortable. Her wings also helped; their feathers were insulative and protected that part of her torso. But she worried: had he assumed that she would be walking at her land-bound pace when he judged the time to the air bubble? If so, it would take her several times as long, and that would be a disaster. Should she turn back while there was still time?

She decided to gamble. After all, if the air turned out to be too far away, she would have no way to cross the river. Besides, if she turned back now, her claustrophobia would think it had the victory and would never let her try it again. So it was this or nothing. The bubble had to be within range.

Precisely fifty-two seconds after her start, her head poked into a bubble of air. She took an eager breath, her emotional relief greater even than her bodily relief. Marrow had been right about his excellent sense of timing.

The air was quickly turning bad; this was not a big bubble. She held her breath again and moved on, this time remembering to expel the spent air slowly from her mouth; that would save time when she hit the next bubble, and also give her a gradually increasing density so that her hooves would have slightly more traction.

The chill of the water was now numbing her eyeballs, causing blurring vision. It was so dark here that she really wasn't seeing anything, so she got smart and closed her eyes, protecting them. Now she was completely dependent on the skeleton's guidance. This, oddly, decreased her fear of enclosure; it was as if she were no longer herself, but a mere vehicle answering to directives.

In forty-one seconds she came to another bubble of air. This one was larger, so that she was able to breathe more thoroughly before moving on.

Now Marrow guided her in a sharp turn to the right. The cave descended, then hooked up just in time to give her another bubble. She realized that they were not necessarily following the most direct route, but rather the one that guaranteed an air bubble within every minute. The skeleton was doing an excellent job.

Just about the time she feared she would lose control of her limbs because of the deepening cold, the cave angled up, and her head broke the surface of the river near the other bank. They had made it across.

Chex stumbled out and stood shivering. Her body was in an awful state, but there was a warm core of gratitude to Marrow for getting her through. She had just navigated an otherwise impassible barrier. She had mastered not only the challenge of the river, but of the cold and her own claustrophobia. That was in its fashion a triple victory.

"You know," she gasped as her neck thawed, "if we find someone up on the mountain who orients on the haunted garden, we may have to wait to return you to the gourd, so that you can guide me back through this cave."

Marrow shrugged. "Why not? It is a very pleasant cave."

A pleasant cave! But of course the skeleton was immune

to cold and accustomed to operating in darkness.

They resumed their trek up the mountain. Very little time had passed; it had merely seemed like an eon to her, as she had progressed bubble by bubble through the cave. Already she was warming with the exertion. Maybe she really could make it to the top.

Time: just how much did she have? It had taken one day's travel to reach her sire, and another to reach the base of the mountain. If she made it to the top in one day, that would leave her one day there to convince the winged monsters to help. Then the three-day trek back to the rendezvous with Esk and Volney. She was on schedule, so far.

The thought of Esk reminded her of the manner he had missed their prior rendezvous. That had been an ugly occasion. Had the curse fiend Latia not had the wit to seek them herself, it could have been the end of Esk. All because he had foolishly asked her to curse him, thinking that it would be a blessing. Human beings did have an erratic streak that caused them to act in irrational ways. Some blessing!

Yet he had survived it, and even brought out a denizen of the gourd who was proving to be of considerable assistance to her now. What might have been a curse to Esk was, ironically, a blessing for Chex.

But the other party he had brought out was the brass girl. Her kind, it had turned out, atoned for incidental offenses by kissing, and evidently she had performed such an atonement for Esk. Human beings tended to be unduly influenced by appearance and action, rather than being guided by practical and intellectual considerations as centaurs were; that was another of the human liabilities. Sometimes she wondered just how the human species had survived so well in Xanth. On the other hoof, they did have some endearing qualities. Esk had accepted her immediately and used his magic talent to help safeguard her from mischief; in fact, he had been more generous to her than the centaurs had been. So she was not about to condemn the human folk; probably their assets did balance out their liabilities in the long run.

So Bria Brassie had kissed him, and the boy was obviously smitten. That was a curse indeed! Yet, with a further and exquisite irony, Esk evidently did not perceive this as an aspect of the curse. Could it be that his entry into the gourd really had been a blessing? If so, it had to be a powerful one, because Latia had explained the manner in which her curses strengthened when allowed to accumulate.

This intellectual riddle was intriguing, so she continued to divert herself with it as she progressed up the steep trail. Assume that Esk had been struck by a very potent blessing. Then her advantage of Marrow's help was only peripheral, part of that blessing, facilitating her mission, and therefore Esk's mission. And Bria—she could be a good deal more important to that mission than they had supposed.

But she was a creature of the gourd. That meant that she had to return to it, for her existence in this world was no more substantial than Esk's had been in the gourd. She had to rejoin her world, or she would eventually perish. What, then, of her interaction with Esk?

Assume that such an interaction was feasible. After all, Bria did look human, when allowance was made for her metal. Suppose Esk did not want to give her up? That was where the zombie's huge gourd came in: Esk could enter that physically and go after her, and perhaps bring Bria out physically.

No—if Marrow and Bria remained physically in the gourd, then it should not be feasible to return them to their home regions within it merely by having some person or creature of the outside realm look in through a peephole and take them along. So they must be physically outside. But Chex was sure that no denizens of the gourd had settled outside it, historically; her dam would have informed her of anything like that. So there had to be a reason that they could not survive indefinitely outside. What could that be?

Well, she had a source of information. "Marrow, what would be the consequence if you did not manage to return to your realm in the gourd?"

"I would slowly fade away," he said promptly. "I am after all, merely the stuff of bad dreams."

"Then if Bria, to take a random example, wished to remain here, she could not?"

"She could not—unless she got access to a soul."

"Access to a soul?"

"We creatures of the dream realm have no souls, of course.

That is our primary distinction from you living folk. If we had souls, we would come alive, and be able to survive normal terms here."

Now Chex remembered: there was a great demand for souls in the gourd! The reason was suddenly clear. "My dam gave up half her soul to the night mare Imbri."

"Yes, half a soul becomes a whole soul, as it fills out. This takes time, but is done on occasion."

"So if someone were to give you half a soul, you would be able to live here indefinitely?"

"True. But of course I have no wish to live. I am surprised that you folk put up with the awkwardnesses and occasional messiness of it."

Chex nodded. She believed she had worked out a solution to Esk's problem, if it developed. If she survived this mountain hike. She was sure that Esk would not be able to devise a solution on his own; he lacked centaur rationality.

She came out of her reverie to discover the trail narrowing. They were well up the mountain now, and the slope was becoming sheer; there was barely room for her hooves on the slightly diminished slant that was the path.

Then it became too slight for her, the girth of her body caused her center of gravity to be too far out from the face of the mountain to remain stable. If she tried to go any farther, she would inevitably fall.

She stopped; she had to. The suggestion of the trail continued on around the curve of the mountain, with an awesome height of wall above, and a mind-blanking depth of drop below. She could not climb that cliff, and would certainly die if she fell. What could she do?

"I don't suppose you know of a nearby cave?" she asked Marrow.

"No cave," the skeleton replied.

"Then I fear we cannot continue. This is, as far as I know, the only trail, and it is too narrow for my body."

The skeleton considered. "It does not appear to be too narrow for my body."

"That may be true. But I am the one who must reach the meeting plateau and address the winged monsters; they would not listen to you, as you are not winged."

"Still, I think I might assist you. Could you manage that path if you had a line to cling to?"

"Yes, I suppose I could. But I don't carry a line; I'm a bow and arrow centaur. My arms aren't strong enough to sustain my full weight on a line, you see. My grandsire Chester has very strong arms; he could do it, but not me." She clenched her teeth with frustration. "Oh, how I wish I could fly!"

"But you could hold on, with support for your feet."

"Yes. But even if I had a line, I could not attach it, because I can't even see the other end of the trail."

"I shall look." Marrow dismounted and walked along the trail. As the ledge narrowed, he had to turn sidewise and step carefully, but it was evident that he had no fear of heights or of falling. That seemed to be another advantage of being non-alive. He moved on around the curve and disappeared from sight.

After a while he returned. "There is a rock that I could cling to," he announced.

"How nice for you," Chex said, trying not to be cutting.

"So if you will just kick me apart, then swing me around so that I can grasp on with one hand, it will be all right."

Chex's dismay received a jolt. Was Marrow proposing suicide in his fashion? "What?"

"Just let me take hold here, so I don't fall off the ledge," he said. "Now kick me hard."

"But that would destroy you!" she exclaimed, appalled.

"Oh, no, we can re-form readily, when prepared. Kick me apart; then I will explain the next step."

Chex had considerable difficulty accepting this, but finally did what he asked. She retreated along the trail until it widened, turned around, and backed up to the place where he was holding on to a solid rock. Then she gave him a tremendous kick on the hipbone with a hind foot.

The skeleton flew apart. The bones sailed into the air, disconnecting. But then something strange happened. The bones did not disconnect all the way; instead they formed into a line that flopped down the mountainside.

"Now haul me up," Marrow's voice came.

She walked back to the turnaround point, then came forward again. She braced herself and peered down over the ledge.

The line of bones extended well down the slope. About halfway along it was the skull. "Haul me," it repeated.

This was strange magic! She took hold of a bone and drew it up. Marrow's finger bone was no longer connected to his hand bone, or his hand bone to his wrist bone; one finger bone was connected to another and another, forming the line. She hauled the line up hand over hand, noting that the finger and arm bones connected to rib bones and neck bones and finally the head bone.

"Now swing the rest out around the mountain," the skull told her. "Up to the level of the trail; the rock is not far beyond your vision."

Chex obeyed. She started the line of bones swinging back and forth, pendulum fashion, until she was able to bring the end of the line high enough. Then, just at its height, she let go, and it flung out, slapping against the mountain.

"Got it!" the skull exclaimed. "Now pull me tight."

Chex gazed at the arc of bones. "But if I pull too hard, won't you come apart?"

"I don't think so. I will warn you when my limit approaches."

So she hauled on the line again, and the line tightened, until when she held an arm bone the skull called out "enough."

"What now?" she called back.

"Touch the arm bone to the hand bone."

She held a loop of the bone line. She brought the arm bone to the hand bone—and immediately the two snapped together as if magnetized.

"Now use me to keep your balance," the skull called. "Try not to put too much strain on me."

Chex looked at the narrow path, with the bone line now stretched above it. It seemed perilously precarious. But Marrow had known what he was doing before, so she had to trust him now.

She held on to the line and walked out along the precipice. The wall shoved her solid equine body out, and she could not brace with her feet. Her wings made it worse, because they added to the breadth of her body when folded, and there was no room to open them here. She clung to the line, her body increasingly off-balance, leaning out over the gulf below. She had never been afraid of heights, just of depths, but it would be easy enough to cultivate such a phobia now.

Her hands were becoming somewhat sweaty, but she could not clean them. She hoped the bones weren't ticklish.

"That's very good," Marrow's skull said, right under her hand.

Startled, Chex almost let go of the line. She had for the moment forgotten the nature of it. "Thank you," she muttered tersely.

She handed herself on along the rib bones and the backbones and the hipbones, closing her mind to the precise nature of them, not from any humanlike skittishness, but because she did not want to raise any question in her mind about how they were able to hold together in this format. Marrow was a more surprising creature than she had first thought.

Finally she reached the end, where the trail widened and the endmost finger bone clung. It had found a niche in the stone and hooked into it. Had she realized that this was all that supported the line, and therefore her tilting body, she would have been even more concerned than she had been.

She got her footing and let go of the line. "I'm across!" she called to the skull. "What now?"

"Haul me in," the skull called, as the line swung down from the other side. The far finger had let go.

She hauled in the bones, hand over hand. "That's good," the skull said as it arrived, giving her a momentary stare with an eye socket.

"But how do you get back together?" she asked.

"For that I will require some assistance," the skull admitted. "You will have to set the bones together in the proper order."

"But I don't know the proper order, except in a very general way!"

"I will direct you."

And so it was. She touched each bone to the one the skull called out, and it anchored in place. Before too long Marrow was back in proper skeletal shape.

"The more I learn about you, the more I respect you," she

told him as the job was completed. "I never realized that bones could be so versatile."

"Thank you. I must confess that your flesh is not nearly as clumsy or repulsive as I had anticipated."

"Thank you," she said with the trace of a smile.

They moved on up the mountain. The way was easier now, as the slope gradually leveled; they were nearing the crest. Just as well, for the day was drawing toward its close, and she did not want to be on the trail at night. If any of the winged monsters mistook her for nocturnal prey, her situation could become difficult.

Then they came to a cleft in the mountain. It cut right across the path, as though it had started as a crack and widened with time, until now it was a formidable gap. How was she to get across it?

She looked around. There were a few scrubby trees, and some dead wood, and some weeds, and assorted loose rocks. That was it. She looked again at the cleft. It was plainly beyond her jump range. There seemed to be no narrowing of it to the sides; in fact, this was its narrowest part. The entire top of the mountain was split, and the meeting plateau was on the other side.

"I can perhaps throw you across," she told Marrow. "But it is too far for me."

"I see no handholds," the skeleton said. "And if there were, I fear I could not sustain your full weight. Cohesion only goes so far."

"To be sure," she agreed. "You have done more than enough; I would not ask you to attempt that, even if I had sufficient arm strength to manage such a crossing. There has to be another way."

But was there? None of the items of deadwood were large enough to form a bridge, and certainly the stones would not do it. Unless—

She got to work, not letting herself think about how risky it was. She picked up wood, and rolled rocks, forming a pile at the brink of the cleft. She packed them in as solidly as she could, fashioning a ramp whose height rose significantly above the ground.

Marrow appraised this activity with a tilted eyeball socket.

"Isn't this a diversion of the strength you need to cross the cleft?" he inquired.

"I'm building a ramp," she explained. "My hope is that it will enable me to achieve a broader leap."

He considered. "Judging by your demonstrated power of foot and present mass, I believe you will fall short of the far landing by this amount," he said, holding his hand bones about a body width apart.

Chex remembered how accurate his estimate of her progress in the water cave had been. That dismayed her. She had hoped that the added elevation would do the trick. She had used up all the available materials; she could build the ramp no higher.

But she had one other chance. "I cannot fly, but my wings do provide some lift," she said. "Will that extend my distance enough?"

"I have no knowledge of the parameters of flying," he said.

"It will have to do," she said. "Let me toss you across now, and I will join you in a moment."

"As you wish."

She picked him up by the neck bone and hipbone, swung him back, then heaved him across. He landed in a pile, but in a moment straightened out; he was not subject to bruises. Then she tossed her bow and quiver of arrows across, and her supply pack; she wanted to carry no weight she could avoid on the jump.

Then, reflecting, she caught up again on natural functions. That was one more way to reduce weight. She had not eaten during this climb and was hungry, but at the moment that was for the best.

It was time. She trotted to the other side of the crest, then started her takeoff run. She accelerated steadily and smoothly, saving her peak effort for the conclusion. She hit the ramp, put forth her full strength, and galloped up it. At the very brink she leaped into the air.

The moment she was over the cleft, she spread her wings and flapped them mightily. She felt their downdraft, but knew it was not enough; her effort at flight was mere pretense.

Then her front hooves came down on the rock, and she knew she had made it. She brought her rear hooves up to overlap the prints of the front ones, securing her landing, and made a small secondary leap to reorient. For the first time in her life, her wings had made a significant and positive difference. How glad she was that she had built up her pectorals.

She came to a halt, then turned to face Marrow, panting. "I hope that's the last hazard of the trail!"

"Interesting," he remarked. "Your wings did extend your distance significantly."

"Most interesting," she agreed wryly. It seemed that skeletons were not much for emotion, other than the generation of terror in bad dreams.

She ate some fruit from her pack, then donned her knapsack and bow and quiver. "It can't be far now," she said.

"It is not," Marrow agreed. "They are just beyond the next crest."

"How do you know that?"

"I can feel the quiver of the ground as they land."

Skeletons were evidently very sensitive to quivers of the ground! "Good enough! I'll go make my pitch."

"Pitch? You plan to fashion another ramp?"

"Ramp? Not unless there's another jump!"

"Pitch is the inclination of a declivity."

"It is also the inclination of a presentation."

"Amazing."

They crested this portion of the mountain. The lofty plateau opened out, and there were the winged monsters.

They were of all types: griffins, dragons, rocs, sphinxes and assorted less common creatures, such as the hippogryph.

Xap stepped forward. He squawked.

"I understand," Chex said. "I had to make it on my own, or they would not listen to me. Will they listen now?"

He squawked affirmatively.

"O winged monsters," Chex said. "I come on behalf of the voles of the Vale. The demons have straightened the Kiss-Mee River and turned it ugly and mean, and prevent the voles from restoring it to its natural meandering. Will you help hold off the demons so that the river can be restored?"

There was a babble of squawks and hisses and growls. Then Xap squawked.

"They will decide tomorrow," Chex repeated.

Xap squawked again.

"I must meet Cheiron?" she asked. "You mentioned him before. Sire, you know I have trouble with centaurs! My granddam refuses even to talk to me, and the centaurs of the Isle would not let me address them."

The hippogryph shrugged and dropped the subject. He helped her forage for her supper and showed her to a suitable place to spend the night. Marrow, who needed no sleep, spent the night walking around and making the acquaintance of the various monsters. "A number of these would do well in bad dreams," he remarked, impressed.

In the morning Xap explained the mechanism of the decision. Because language was a problem with many of the monsters, and so was logic, they would abide by a presentation made by champions. She would represent the cause of the voles, and Cheiron would represent the cause of the winged monsters. The cause that was most persuasive would win.

Chex realized that she, in her fatigue of the prior day, had blundered. She had rejected an introduction to the centaur, and now Cheiron was angry, and she had to oppose him formally. She was confident that she could have made her case successfully against one of the bird-brained monsters, but a centaur was a different matter. Now she had to go up against an intellect comparable to her own.

Well, what was done was done. Perhaps Cheiron would appreciate the plight of the voles despite his private affront. She would just have to do the best presentation she could.

But when she stepped out to meet Cheiron, there was only a great wash of darkness hovering over the plain. It was as though a storm cloud had moved in. "What is this?" she asked, perplexed.

Xap squawked.

"Light and darkness?" she repeated. "I am the light, he the dark? How can I make my presentation?"

Xap squawked again.

"With my mind?" Yes, that was it. She had assumed that the presentation would be verbal and logical; now she realized that it was not merely a matter of having champions to make the presentations; the presentations themselves had to be in a form intelligible to the less sophisticated monsters. Thus light and darkness; flying creatures were good at determining shades.

The winged monsters were positioned in a circle covering the plateau. All of them faced in toward the center. They were as still as statues, waiting.

She thought of the Vale of the Vole as Volney had described it, in its original state: verdant, peaceful, pleasant, the Kiss-Mee River caressing it with its meanders. Of how any creatures that drank from it became suffused with good will and affection, though not compelled into embarrassing or awkward romantic relationships as happened with love springs. Light flared around her, diminishing the darkness above, and at the interface between the two the contrasts formed a picture that showed her vision.

Then she thought of the way the demons had come, channelizing the river, replacing its soft curves with hard, straight lines. The picture shifted to show the meanness of the present Vale, where vegetation was dying and creatures shunned each other, and the motto was Kick Mee or even Kill Mee.

Finally she made her plea. The images of flying monsters manifested in the picture, swooping down on the shapes of the demons, harrying them, driving them out of the Vale. Vole shapes appeared, tunneling through the dikes and walls, letting the captive water out, so that the Kiss-Mee could return to its natural state and nourish the Vale of the Vole again.

Now Cheiron's countercase developed. The flying monsters descended on the demons, but the demons fought back, dematerializing and re-forming behind the monsters, throwing rocks at them, stabbing them, pulling the feathers from their wings. Soon the poor monsters were in a big pile on the ground, wounded and dying, while the voles remained unable to do their work on the dikes. Then the demons piled brush on the pile of injured creatures and set fire to it.

When Chex had made her presentation, the light about her had expanded, until the whole plateau was illuminated, and the darkness above had diminished. When Cheiron made his response, the darkness grew, reaching down, squeezing out the light. Even the fire in the picture blazed darkly, with the smoke roiling up like a bad dream of the gourd and merging with the darkness. The light remained strong only around Chex herself; she had lost ground.

She tried again. She thought of the way Esk was going to see the ogres, who were his ancestors just as the winged monsters were hers, to ask for the help that his human kind refused to extend. She thought of Volney Vole, tunneling down to visit the most dreaded of his kin, the wiggles, on a similar mission. If either of these agreed to help, then the winged monsters would not be alone, and might after all be able to prevail against the formidable demons.

As she thought, her light brightened and pushed back the darkness, farther than before, and the images in the picture glowed. The marching ogres seemed almost noble, and the demons looked affrighted as the forces of both ground and air advanced. Victory was possible!

Cheiron's return sally came. The darkness swelled against the bright picture, and the picture grew smaller, as if retreating, until it was tiny and far away. What did the winged monsters care what the land-bound monsters did? The demons were no threat to the creatures of the air.

Chex did not wait for that case to be complete. She surged back with an impromptu thesis of emotion. The winged monsters did care, they *had* to care, for what harmed one part of Xanth harmed all parts, and what harmed the monsters of the land also harmed those of the air. Human beings might be callous about the problems of a nonhuman region, and centaurs might be indifferent to noncentaur matters, but surely the winged monsters wanted to have a better rapport with other creatures than this.

As she projected those thoughts, the light rallied and pushed back the darkness. But the darkness forged back. There was no point in having the winged monsters be as foolish as the ground-borne monsters; all of them could perish on this foolish quest.

But Chex would not abide that. Even if the quest were hopeless, still it was a worthy one. The deed should be done because it was worth doing, without regard to possible failure. Other creatures might mask their cowardice with expressions of indifference, but this should not be the way of the boldest of all creatures, the winged monsters. Better to die in such an honorable quest, than to live in the dishonor of noninvolvement, the way the humans and centaurs were. Human folk did not seem to care about the plight of volish folk, but other animals should.

Her light brightened and spread with every point, beating back the darkness, until little was left of it except a small cloud. Now secondary sources of light were starting up, like flames ignited by flying sparks. These were from the monsters that rimmed the plateau; they agreed with her!

The dark cloud shrank, until at last the figure hovering within it became visible. And suddenly Chex felt faint.

*Cheiron was a winged centaur!*

Of course she should have realized that before. She had correctly identified his name as typical of centaurs, but had failed to connect this with the fact that every creature on this plateau was winged. The path she had taken up had been little used, and there had been no centaur prints showing on it. The only way Cheiron could have come here was by flying. This should have been obvious to her instantly; she had blundered personally as well as tactically. She had alienated the only other creature of her precise kind.

The last of the darkness above dissipated, and the sun shone down. But in Chex's heart new darkness was welling. How could she have been so wrongheaded!

Cheiron flew down toward her, and the sunlight highlighted his silver wings and his golden hooves. He was the handsomest centaur she had even seen. He appeared to be of mature age, certainly older than she, well muscled and sleekly structured. *And he could fly!*

He landed before her and folded his wings, but she was too chagrined to meet his gaze. "I like your spirit, filly," he said. "You fought your way up here, and you fought your way through the darkness I spread. Your sire was right about you: you are worthy not only because you are the only other of my kind in Xanth. I came here from afar when I heard of you, hoping you were worthwhile."

Timidly, flushing in the atrocious human manner, she looked at him. He was smiling. "You—you are not angry that I did not meet you before?"

"Furious," he said. "But you are young yet, and cannot be

expected to have mastery of all social graces, especially when most centaurs shun you. I know how that is; believe me, I know! At least it gave me the pretext to try your mettle. The winged monsters will travel to the Vale of the Vole; you have persuaded them. And I—"

She gazed at him, smitten the manner of any adolescent in the presence of wonder. What a creature he was! "And you—?"

"I will welcome you—when you fly to me." He turned, spread his wings, and took off, leaving her in the downblast of air that was scarcely more tumultuous than her emotions.

*She had to learn to fly!*

# 11
# OGRE

They walked along the path to Castle Roogna. Chex had promised Princess Ivy that she would send Esk in for a report once she found him, and Ivy had promised in return to dig out something else to help them get help for the Kiss-Mee River. As it was turning out, little Ivy was doing almost as much good for them as her parents might have.

"Who is Ivy?" Bria inquired.

Esk explained, for of course Bria had very little information about the normal Xanth hierarchies.

"Oh, she's Irene's daughter!" Bria exclaimed. "My mother Blythe knew Irene."

"She did?" Esk asked, startled. "How could that be?"

"After your ogre father tore up Marrow's folk, he went on to tear up the brassies, and he abducted Blythe to this world. There she got to know several interesting people, including your mother Tandy, and later she came to help Mare Imbri rescue your kings."

"Why didn't you tell me that before?" he asked.

"I didn't think it was relevant. Besides, a girl has to be careful around ogres. Your father put a dent in my mother!"

"He wouldn't do a thing like that! He's always been loyal to my mother!"

"Are you saying it's not true? You embarrass me."

Esk paused. This promised to become complicated. "Uh, no, I'm not saying that."

"Then what are you saying?"

"Just that there must be some misunderstanding."

"Oh." She seemed disappointed. "Anyway, later she married my father, but I think she missed the outside world some. I grew up very curious about it. That's how I got lost; I was looking for a way out."

Esk smiled. "Well, you found a way out!"

"No, *you* found it. I'm not really out, though; I'm trapped here the same way you were trapped inside."

"You mean your body is still there on the Lost Path?"

"No. But I'm not really out, either, because the moment you go back into the gourd, I'll go back too, or fade out, or something—I don't know exactly what happens, but it isn't good. What I need is a way to get stabilized, so I don't get into trouble here."

"Chex found a physical way into the gourd!" Esk exclaimed. "Through the zombie gourd! Maybe if you went back in through that—"

"Going *in* won't do me any good."

"But I thought—"

She glanced at him appraisingly. "You shouldn't try to think, Esk. It's bad for ogres."

"Well, maybe you could go back in with me, and then go out through that big gourd. Then you'd be out on your own, and not dependent on me."

"That won't work either. I'm on the Lost Path, remember."

"Yes, but if we find someone who enters the gourd at your home region, then that person can take you back in, and you won't be lost anymore."

"But I still wouldn't know where the zombie gourd is. I would just get lost again, trying to find it."

"That's ridiculous!" he snapped. "You could get a map or something, and find it. Someone in there has to know where it is!"

"You think I'm ridiculous!" she exclaimed, her brass face clouding up. "You embarrassed me!"

Oops. He had been trying to avoid trouble, but had somehow walked into it anyway. "I'm sorry. I didn't mean—"

"That's no way to apologize!"

Esk glanced at her, then at Latia, helplessly.

"Go ahead," the curse fiend said shortly. "Apologize the proper way."

"Uh, yes," Esk said. He stopped walking, and Bria stopped walking. He took her in his arms. "I apologize for embarrassing you," he said, and gave her a quick kiss.

She stood motionless, seeming to be a brass statue. "I don't think you did a good enough job," Latia remarked.

Esk tried again. "Bria, I'm very sorry I embarrassed you, and I humbly apologize," he said, and kissed her somewhat more authoritatively.

Still the brassie girl stood, absolutely frozen. It was as if she had been cast in metal and allowed to harden in place.

"You need instruction in kissing," Latia snorted disdainfully.

Stung, Esk wrapped his arms about Bria, swung her around, and gave her a kiss that threatened to bruise his lips.

Then at last Bria melted. "Accepted," she murmured.

"Now *there's* a girl who would be excellent on the stage," Latia murmured. "I have seldom seen better management."

"What?" Esk asked.

"Nothing," the old woman said, with the suggestion of a smirk.

They resumed their walk toward Castle Roogna, but now Esk's head was spinning in much the way it had the first time Bria had kissed him. He tried to remember exactly how he had embarrassed her, but was unable. He tried to figure out what the curse fiend woman meant about management, but drew another blank.

Before long they reached Castle Roogna. Princess Ivy danced out to meet them. "You found him!" she cried happily.

"Volney Vole sniffed him out," Latia said. "The centaur and the vole had to go on additional searches, but we brought him back here."

"He looks sort of dazed," the girl said.

"He was some time in the gourd."

"Oh. That would do it." Then she noticed Bria. "Hello. Who're you?"

"Just something he fished out of the gourd," Bria said.

"You're a gourd folk? How exciting!"

Esk found his tongue. "She's Bria Brassie. Her mother knew your mother."

"A brassie? Then her mother must be Blythe Brassie, who got the dent from Smash Ogre!"

Bria glanced sidelong at Esk, who almost choked.

Fortunately Ivy was prancing on to a new subject. "I found something to help! A pathfinder spell!"

"A pathfinder?" Esk asked, accepting the object she gave him. It looked like a bit of twisted wire.

"It's a spell, and it finds your path for you," Ivy explained. "Wherever you want to go."

"That's easy. I want to go and ask the ogres if they will help the voles. But I can't walk there and back within a week, unless you have some more of those speed pills."

"No, I don't dare take any more; someone'd notice. But this is just as good. Ask it for the path to the ogres!"

"You don't understand. I can find the ogres; I just need more time than I have."

"Then ask it for the path that'll take you there in the time you have," Ivy said brightly.

"That spell can do that?"

"Sure. But there's one problem. It works only once for each person."

"Well, I can follow the same path back; that's no problem."

The girl's forehead wrinkled. "I'm not sure it's like that. I don't think you can find the path again without it."

"I know a path like that," Bria remarked. "Only you can't find your way *from* it."

"Gee, that must be fun!" Ivy said.

"I suppose I could use the spell to get there," Esk said. "Then hope to make it back the regular way in time. Maybe it can be done."

"You can get back, stupid," Ivy said. "Just have a friend use the spell to find the return path."

"Why that's right!" Esk exclaimed. "I'm embarrassed! I should have thought of it."

"Uh-oh," Latia muttered.

"You embarrassed him," Bria said to Ivy. "You will have to apologize."

Ivy was interested. "Gee—how do I do that?"

"Like this," Bria said. She put her arms around Esk. "I apologize," she said. Then she kissed him.

"Extraordinary!" Latia murmured admiringly. "No opportunity wasted!"

"That looks like fun," Ivy said.

At that point there was a splash and yowl from the moat. "Oops—Moatie's teasing someone again. Gotta go!" Ivy dashed off.

Esk examined the spell. "I'll need someone to go with me, I suppose," he said.

"Have no fear; we are both going with you," Latia said.

"But I'm going to ogre country!" he protested. "It may be dangerous."

"That is why we're going with you," Bria said. "Men always do get into trouble on their own."

Esk wasn't completely certain of her logic, but he was still slightly unbalanced from the last kiss or two, so accepted it. He knew that Bria was mainly teasing him with those kisses, because she was of a different world, to which she would in due course return, but still the kisses had their impact. If only he could find a real girl like her!

"Then I'd better figure out how to use this spell," he said, looking at the pathfinder.

"That's no problem," Latia said. "We curse fiends have used them on occasion. Simply hold it up, focus on it, and say the name of the place to which you wish to find a path."

"Oh." Esk held out the wire and opened his mouth.

"But also specify that you want the shortest path," Latia added. "Otherwise you might get the scenic route; that would be longer than the one you would find on your own."

"Thank you for that little detail," Bria said.

Latia glanced at her. "Are you being snide, girl? That would embarrass me."

"No, not at all," Bria said quickly. "I was only being appreciative!"

"I thought as much."

When it came to management, Esk realized, the old woman was no slouch. Women of all ages seemed to be better at that than men were; even little Ivy had managed to get around her father's restrictions without much difficulty.

He addressed the pathfinder spell again. He focused closely on it. "The shortest path to the Ogre-Fen-Ogre Fen," he said.

He blinked, for there before him was a path he hadn't seen before. It was reasonably wide and firm and clear; there would be no trouble following it. But it was headed south.

"The ogre fen is in the north!" he objected. "This is the wrong path!"

"Poppycock," Latia snapped. "Pathfinders never err. Trust it instead of your private judgment."

Esk realized that he had no particular choice, because if he didn't take the proffered path, he would have to find his own way, which would take him a week or so one way. He stepped out on the path.

Latia and Bria followed. The path bore contentedly south, entering the thickest jungle. Then, safely out of sight of Castle Roogna, it changed course, curving back to the north. "See? It knows where it's going," Latia said.

"But how can it be the shortest path, when it just added this extra loop south?" Esk asked.

"Maybe it has a sense of privacy."

The path curved left, and continued curving, until it intersected itself slightly above its prior level. The curve tightened, completing a second loop, coming in just above and inside itself.

"This path is just playing with us!" Esk said. "It's not going anywhere."

"It probably has its reasons," Latia said. "Don't criticize it too sharply; you might embarrass it."

Esk didn't want to kiss the path, so he refrained from further comment. The spiral continued, until it became quite high and tight; they were circling in a narrow radius at treetop level.

Then at last the path took off to the north again, along the branch of a giant tree. "See, it just needed to wind up to its elevation," Bria said, pleased. "It must be a female path; it knows what it's doing, even if others don't."

Esk hoped so. The branch gnarled down into the depths of the foliage, and the shade deepened, so that they had to watch carefully to make sure of their footing. There were many side branches, but they could tell which one that path followed because it was well worn. Esk wondered about that; the Lost Path in the gourd had been tricky to follow in places because of disuse. Who used this one so much?

"Probably there are several standard paths," Latia remarked, answering his thought. "Maybe segments of them get assembled, end to end, to make a particular route to a particular destination. So this segment has been much used, but only by folk going to other regions. It hardly matters, so long as the programming is accurate for us."

They came to the trunk of the tree. There was a hole in it, and the path entered the hole. The interior was like a tunnel, surprisingly extensive; it continued long after it seemed to Esk that it should have emerged from the far side of the tree. The sides grew smoother, and assumed a faint glistening as if moist.

Then Esk encountered a stalactite "Now wait a moment!" he exclaimed. "Stalacs are in caves!"

"That is curious," Latia agreed. She put her hand to the descending cone. "But this is after all wood."

Esk touched it. Sure enough, it was wood. The darkness had given it another semblance.

The tunnel finally emerged onto another branch. "Is this the same tree?" Bria asked, blinking in the sudden light.

Indeed, it seemed different. The bark was smoother, and the diameter of the trunk seemed smaller. Curious, Esk held on and worked his way around the outside until he could see the side they had entered.

There was no entry. The tree had a hole on only one side— the side from which they had exited.

He returned and peered back into the tunnel. It extended way back, and there was light at the end.

"You act as if you had never before seen a magic path," Latia remarked.

Esk was embarrassed, but struggled manfully to master it, fearing the consequence more than the embarrassment itself. He turned his face forward and strode out along the branch path.

This one had smaller branches that extended up, overhanging it, and some of these bore fruit. Esk reached up and plucked a plumb that was bobbing below a stringlike twig. Plumbs always grew that way, straight up and down, and bobbing when they were ripe. He bit into it, and it was juicy and good. So this was a plumb tree.

But farther along the branch were two matching fruits of a different type. They were greenish-yellow, and thickest through their bases. He plucked them both, for it was impossible to pluck a single one; that was the nature of pairs. These, too, were very good.

Farther along was a big pineapple. He let that one pass; that kind of fruit was apt to be explosive.

"This is a versatile fruit tree," Latia remarked.

At last the path passed from the tree. It stair-stepped down to the ground, and then coursed along to a small river.

Esk paused. "I don't see the continuation across the river."

Latia and Bria looked. The path intersected the river at a slant, and did not resume beyond it.

"Only one explanation," Latia said. She stepped into the river.

Her foot did not splash into the water. It landed on it as if encountering solidity. She took another step, and stood on the water. "Just as I suspected," she said. "The path goes on the river."

Esk, at this point, knew better than to question it. He stepped out on the water, and found it as solid as ice but not cold. This was the path, all right. He should have realized before, for the path from the Good Magician's castle had crossed water too.

Bria followed. "I think I like the ways of the outer world," she said, fluffing out her skirt.

Esk, looking at her, discovered that the water she stood on was reflective. He could see right up her legs. He turned again, quickly. Even though he had seen all of her legs in the gourd, before she put on the dress, he felt guilty about seeing them now. Guilty about *wanting* to see them.

"Did I embarrass you?" Bria inquired.

And there was the other aspect of that trap. He wanted to tell her the truth, that she had inadvertently embarrassed him, through no fault of her own, but he knew that would only complicate things. "I, uh, embarrassed myself," he said.

She laughed. "You're going to have trouble settling that!"

Trouble, indeed! He *knew* she was only teasing him; possibly she understood about the reflection. Why couldn't his emotion follow his intellect, and accept the brassie girl as a temporary acquaintance?

The river broadened, until they were walking well away from either shore. Now water lilies spread across its calm surface, obscuring the reflections, which was a relief. But where was the path going? It seemed to have little concern about its destination; sometimes it bore north, sometimes south, and sometimes east or west. Now it was heading out into what promised to become a lake. When would it get serious about its destination?

Abruptly it stopped. Latia, now leading the way, suddenly splashed into the lake beside a big green lily pad.

Esk dropped to his belly on the solid portion of the path and reached down to haul her out. His questing hand caught her bony ankle. He yanked on it—and felt the sting of a slap. What was happening?

Then Latia's head poked up. "Sorry, Esk—I thought you were a leech or something. It's all right—the path is down here. Just step down and reorient." Her head resubmerged.

"Did you notice—her hair wasn't even wet," Bria said.

Esk hadn't noticed, but now he recalled it. He had reached into the water, but his arm was dry.

He stepped off the end of the path, and dropped into the water. He was holding his breath, but it didn't seem necessary; he wasn't really submerged. In a moment his body twisted around, and he found his feet coming to rest against the underside of the lily pad. He was standing upside down, in the lake!

He tried breathing, and it was all right. He saw fish in the water, swimming normally, which was inverted compared to him, but to him the water was air.

He looked down (up) the way he had come, and saw Bria's legs. They were very nice legs, all the way up. Yet again he wrenched away his gaze and tried to stifle a blush.

Then Bria jumped in. She spun about and landed beside him on the lily pad, which bowed with their weight. "Careful," she said. "We don't want to break through and fall out through the sky!"

Esk stepped across to the next lily pad. He discovered that these pads had no stems; they were just there. He squatted and touched his finger to the lake surface between pads. His hand broke through the surface tension and dangled in the air.

"We'd better stick to the pads," he said. "I think they're the stepping stones."

They moved on, following the irregular trail of green pads. Finally the slope of the lakebed descended, requiring them to duck their heads. When it became so shallow that they could not walk, Esk tried stepping through the surface and resuming normal orientation.

He found himself thigh-deep in the lake, looking at a solid jungle of thorns. The path did not continue in this direction.

Latia emerged. "There they are," she said. "Cloudstones."

Esk looked. There above the lake was a small line of tiny clouds, the nearest and lowest within stepping range.

He shrugged and stepped onto it. It depressed a little, wobbling, but sustained his weight. He stepped quickly to the next, which was higher and larger, and this one was more stable.

Bria emerged. "Oh, I like this world better and better!" she exclaimed. "We don't have anything like this in the gourd!"

Esk refrained from pointing out that he hadn't seen it in this world either, until now. Maybe he just hadn't traveled enough, before.

The cloudstones took them safely across the lake and down to the far shore. Why the path hadn't gone directly there Esk couldn't guess, but he was in no position to question its rationale. Just so long as it got them to ogre country within three days!

At last the path resumed normal operation, proceeding directly north through mixed terrain—until they came to the mirror.

It stood across the path, a vertical full-length sheet of glass, big enough to reflect a complete man. Esk would have crashed right into it, because it reflected the path perfectly, making it look like a continuation—but he saw himself approaching and realized what it was before colliding. So he stopped, and admired his somewhat bedraggled image. Bria looked much better, but Latia looked worse.

He peered around the mirror. Beyond was a dense, impenetrable curse-burr patch. To the sides were itch plants. Above was the foliage of a poison acorn tree. This was a dead end that was really deadly.

"There has to be a way," Latia muttered. "Maybe this is a door." She poked her finger experimentally at the glass.

Her finger passed through it without resistance. "I think I have found it," she said, as her hand and then her arm disappeared into the mirror. The reflection showed only that portion of her that was on the near side.

"But we don't know what's in there!" Esk warned, for he saw that her arm was not emerging from the other side of the mirror. It was like the hole in the tree: it came out elsewhere.

"The other end of the path, obviously," she said, and put her head through. In a moment the rest of her disappeared, and the mirror was clear.

"You look a mess," Bria said, contemplating Esk's reflection. "Let me comb your hair." She brought out a brass comb from somewhere.

"Uh, but—" he protested weakly.

"Oh, did I embarrass you? I'd better apologize."

"No, no, that's all right!"

"It's best to be sure." She put her arms around him.

Esk knew he should protest some more, but he lacked the gumption. She squeezed him closely and kissed him, and she was warm and soft and fascinating. He closed his eyes, and knew that he would not have known she was brass from the present feel of her. Again he felt as if he were floating.

"If—if you are made of hard metal," he said as she released him, "how can you be so—so—?"

"Oh, I can be quite soft when I want to be," she said. "After all, we brassies couldn't move very well if we remained absolutely rigid."

"But your mother—that dent—"

"The ogre caught her by surprise. He picked her up by her brassiere, then dropped her on the brass hat of the man below."

Esk began to get a notion where the dent might have been. "I see. So it was an accident. But wouldn't the dent have undented when she turned soft again?"

"No, dents are the most permanent kinds of things. She's still got it; she pretends it's a dimple."

"I can see why you dislike ogres."

"No, I always thought it was romantic. I'd like to meet an ogre myself."

"Well, I'm part ogre."

"I know," she said softly. Then: "Oops, did I embarrass you? You're blushing again."

"No, no, it's all right!" he said.

But she decided to play it safe, and apologized in her fashion.

"Well," Latia remarked, stepping out of the mirror. "I can see that you folk were really concerned about my welfare while I was in the mirror."

"Uh—" Esk said.

"Don't tell me, let me guess. She embarrassed you."

"It's amazing how often I do that," Bria remarked innocently. "I must be very clumsy about outside world ways."

"To be sure," Latia agreed dryly. "Well, I'm here to report that the path continues beyond. It's an odd scene, but presumably it is what we want."

They stepped through the mirror. The other side was indeed strange; instead of being a mirror, it seemed like a clear pane of glass, showing the path they had just come from. A one-way mirror—what strange magic!

The path ahead was glass, too, reflective in the manner of the lake surface. The scenery to the sides was odder yet; it was all of glass. The brush was greenly tinted glass, and the trees had brownly tinted trunks and greenly foliage. A grayly tinted glass rabbit bounded away as they approached, and a redly tinted glass bird sailed overhead.

"It reminds me of home, a little," Bria said. "Only there everything is of brass."

"We'll get you home when we can," Esk reassured her.

"Oh, I'm not homesick! This is a wonderful adventure. I'm just comparing."

The glassy forest opened out into a glassy plain, with many glass blades. Creamly tinted glass animals glazed on it. They made glassy moo-sounds and moo-ved away, worried by the nonglass intruders.

Glazed? *Grazed*, Esk realized. Then again—

Then a glassy unicorn charged up, ridden by a glassy man. The man dismounted and strode toward the party, drawing a shining glass blade. He spoke with the sound of breaking cutlery, brandishing the weapon. "Your glass will be ass!"

"No," Esk said, realizing that the glassy man meant mischief.

The man changed his mind. He remounted his glass steed, and they galloped away, sending up a cloud of glass dust.

"Let's move on through here quickly," Latia suggested. "I don't think these folk are friendly."

They hurried on along the path. Soon they came to another sheet of glass. "This should be our exit," Latia said. "But I'll just check. You two can get back to what you were doing." She stepped through the glass, and they watched her walk around a curve in the path beyond.

"What *were* we doing?" Bria inquired brightly.

"Uh—"

"Oh, yes, I was apologizing to you. I don't remember what for, but better safe than sorry."

"But you don't need to—"

Her warm kiss cut him off. He decided that it was pointless to protest. Bria was correct: she could be very soft when she chose to be.

Yet her body was entirely brass, and some of her ways were brassy too. Any expectations he might have were foolish. He knew this; in fact he was absolutely sure of this. Yet somehow he doubted.

Latia returned, coming around the curve and stepping

through the glass. "Yes, it's our path," she reported. "And it seems to be near the ogre fen."

"Oh? How do you know?" Esk asked.

"Oh, nothing specific. Trees twisted into pretzels, boulders cracked with hairy fist marks on them, dragons slinking about as if terrified of anything on two legs. Perhaps I am mistaken."

Esk didn't press the case.

They stepped through the glass. Esk turned to look back, and it was a mirror, showing nothing of the glassies beyond. That had been another interesting experience!

Latia had described the terrain accurately. They were definitely in ogre country. Esk felt nervous; he had ogre ancestry, but little direct experience with full ogres. This could be a disaster.

Soon they heard a great crashing, as of trees getting knocked down. An ogre stomped into view, carelessly sweeping brush and rocks aside with one ham fist while picking his monstrous yellow teeth with the tenpenny nails of the other ham hand.

This seemed like a worse and worse idea. This was a plain animal brute! The ogre stood twice Esk's height, and was so ugly that clouds of smog formed wherever it glanced.

"Oooo, what a beast!" Bria murmured admiringly.

The ogre heard her. His shaggy puss swung around to aim at her. "What this me see—one tiny she!" he exclaimed.

"We came to talk to you ogres," Esk called.

Now the ogre spied the rest of the party. "He walk, to talk?" Ogres lacked facility with pronouns, because they were very stupid.

"Yes, we walk to talk," Esk said. "Please take us to your leader."

The ogre scratched his hairy head. Giant fleas dodged out of the way of his dirty nail. "Want to take, no mistake?"

"No mistake," Esk agreed.

"Okay, you say!" And the ogre reached out and grabbed Esk, hauled him up, and jammed him into the huge backpack he wore. Then he grabbed Latia and Bria and treated them similarly.

"I hope you know what he's doing," Latia muttered.

"I hope so too," Esk muttered back.

The ogre strode on, shoving brush and trees out of his way, while the pack jogged violently with his motion. The three clung to the rim and the straps, because getting bounced out would lead to a painful fall.

The ogre arrived at an ogre village. There was a huge fire in its center, beside which sat a great black pot.

"Heat pot!" the ogre bellowed. "Me got!"

"Uh-oh," Esk said. The pot was full of water, but he could see some bones in the bottom. They reminded him of Marrow, and that was not reassuring.

The ogre swung the pack off and brought it to the pot. He began to invert it.

"No!" Esk cried.

Perplexed, the ogre paused. "No so?"

"We came to talk, not to be cooked!" Esk yelled.

Other ogres had appeared, including several females. If the males were ugly, the females were appalling. "We look, not cook?" one inquired, scratching her head so vigorously that the lice scattered in terror.

"We want your help for the voles!" Esk cried, wishing he had never undertaken this foolish mission.

"Put vole in bowl!" another ogre exclaimed, smacking his lips with a sound that startled the birds from a distant tree.

"We came to impress you with the need for this," Esk said, knowing that the chances of impressing these monsters with anything they had to say was so small as to be worthless.

"Such mess, impress?" the ogre who had brought them demanded, and all of them laughed with a volume and crudity that only their kind could manage.

"Yes, impress," Esk continued doggedly. "For your help."

The first ogre thought about that. His cranium heated with the effort, and the fleas got hotfeet and jumped off. Finally he exclaimed: "Me say okay!"

The other ogres, glad to be relieved of the horrible effort of having to think for themselves, bellowed their agreement.

"Wonderful," Latia said. "Now all we have to do is impress them, and our case is won."

"Maybe we can do that," Bria said brightly. "We each have our natures and our talents."

"I'm not sure—" Esk began.

"For example, I can be very hard when I want to be. I'll show you." She climbed out of the pack, which the ogre had set on the ground beside the pot. "Eat me, ogre!" she cried. "Chew me up!"

The ogre did not wait for a second invitation. He snatched her up a moment before three other ham hands reached her, and jammed her feet in his maw. He chomped.

There was a pause. Then slow surprise spread across his puss from the region of his maw. For his teeth had crunched something much harder than bone.

He pulled Bria out and looked at her. She still looked edible. "She sweet; me eat," he concluded, and opened his maw wide and jammed in her head.

But the teeth crunched again on hard metal. Bria's head remained attached. "Can't you do better than that, ogre?" she cried from the vicinity of his tongue.

Confused, the ogre hauled her out. Immediately another ogre grabbed her and chomped on an arm. It was a powerful chomp; the sound of it rang metallically, startling a passing cloud so that it dropped a little water. A chip of yellow tooth flew out.

"Tough, she, me agree," the ogre confessed.

"Do I impress you?" Bria demanded.

The ogres exchanged glances. They were stupid glances, and traveled very slowly, so this took some time. The surrounding trees tilted away, worried when ogres acted strangely. But eventually they all nodded agreement; they were impressed.

"So that's how it goes," Latia said. "Well, let's see what I can do." She climbed out of the pack and addressed the ogres. "Who is the ugliest among you?" she asked.

An ogress leaned forward. As she did so, all the nearby plants wilted. "Me be ugly, me say smugly!"

She certainly was ugly; Esk had never seen a more horrendous puss.

"I can be uglier than you," Latia said.

All the ogres laughed at this, not even needing time for thought. It was obvious that nobody could be uglier than the ogress.

"Ugly is as ugly does," Latia said stoutly. "What can your ugly do?"

The ogress turned and lumbered into her hovel. A flock of bats flew out, looking stunned. She brought out a battered pitcher of milk. She grimaced at it—and the entire pitcher. curdled.

Esk gaped. That was ugly indeed! He had thought the stories about that sort of thing were exaggerated.

Then Latia put her hands to her head. She had powder and chalk, and was using these to make up her face.

"What's she doing?" Bria asked.

"She's an actress," Esk said. "All curse fiends are good at drama. They can make themselves quite pretty—and I guess ugly, if they want to."

Latia looked up. Her face, homely to begin with, had been transformed. Now it so ugly it was sickening. But the ogres just looked, undismayed; they were used to ugly.

Then Latia walked over to the big pot. "Lift me up," she said.

Curious, an ogre picked her up and held her over the pot. Latia aimed her face down, and scowled.

The water curdled.

Esk gaped. So did the ogres.

"Well?" Latia inquired, as the ogre set her down.

"We confess, we impress," an ogre muttered, still staring at the pot. He poked a ham finger in. The water was definitely curdled, not frozen. It clarified in the region of his finger, finding this to be relatively pretty.

Esk remembered how his grandmother, a curse fiend, had emulated an ogress and won his grandfather's love. At last he had a notion how she had done it.

But now it was his turn. What could he do to match what the women had done? If he got mad, he could develop ogre strength for a short time—but that would only match the strength every normal ogre had, not exceed it. That would not impress them.

Then he realized what would. "Who is stupidest?" he asked.

"Me!" the first ogre cried, forgetting to rhyme.

"Me, me!" another exclaimed, remembering.

There was a chorus of claims, for of course each was proud, and considered himself the stupidest creature of all time. But finally one emerged as dominant; the hugest and slackest-jawed of them all. He was so muscular that when he tried to think, the muscles bulged on his head, but so stupid that his effort to think couldn't even dislodge the fleas; his skull couldn't get hot enough.

"Well, I am stupider than you," Esk asserted. "I'll prove it."

Then he concentrated, and his terror of failure invoked his ogre strength. He marched across and wrapped his arms around the ogre's legs, and picked him up and swung him around, exerting all his ogre power, and cracked the ogre's head into a tree. The tree snapped off, but the ogre wasn't hurt, of course.

The ogre was, however, annoyed. Ogres didn't really like snapping tree trunks with their faces; they preferred ham fists. He snatched up the fallen trunk and swung it toward Esk, ready to smash him down into the ground with a single blow.

Esk stood his ground. "What could be stupider than doing what I did to an ogre like that?" he asked.

The ogres considered. Then, as the tree came down and Esk jumped aside; they started to laugh. The welkin shuddered with their haw-haws, making the sun vibrate and shed a few rays, and even the ogre Esk had attacked joined in. It was a good joke indeed. *Nothing* could be stupider than that!

"That was a darn fool thing to do!" Latia snapped.

"Totally idiotic!" Bria said.

"Precisely," Esk agreed. "It was the stupidest thing I could have done."

They were silent, acceding to the sincerity of his claim.

Thus it was that Esk's party impressed the ogres and won their support for the mission. Now all they had to do was survive the ogres' welcoming party and manage to explain how to reach the Vale of the Vole from here. The ogres would help.

# 12

# WIGGLE

Volney tunneled down toward the wiggle princess, guided by the locator pebble the squiggles had given him. This stone, like the other, was reversed for him; he had to orient on the foulest taste, avoiding the good taste.

The wiggles, as he understood it, were the strongest borers of all the clans of the voles. More correctly, their larvae were. When a pair of wiggles mated, the female went to a suitable patch of rock and made her nest, and when the larvae hatched they drilled out into that rock in an increasing radius until they found good locations for feeding and growth. Very few were lucky; the great majority of the thousands of larvae perished when they used up all their strength in the vain search.

The wiggles' problem was that their tastes were highly selective. Each individual liked only a particular flavor of rock, and would not eat any other. Since there were many hundreds of flavors, and the veins of rock were randomly distributed, the chances of a single wiggle larva happening on its particular flavor were perhaps one in a thousand. There were several thousand larvae in a typical swarm, so normally a few did find their homes. This was the reason that the ground was not overidden with wiggles; a female mated only once, and was thereafter sterile, because all the egg cells in her body were expended in the laying of the larvae. In any given year, there would be only one or two swarms, limited to their particular veins of stone. It might have helped if the stone that was suitable for swarming was the same as what was suitable for eating; then all the larvae would settle down immediately and eat.

But as he reviewed this in his mind, Volney saw why this was not so. If all the thousands of wiggle larvae ate the rock they swarmed in, they would soon finish it, and the vein would become a pulsing mass of partially matured wiggles. None of those would grow to maturity, because the food would be gone. All would perish, and the swarm would die out without descendants. So it was necessary for swarm taste and grow taste to differ; the swarm taste was identical for all the larvae, while the grow taste was different for each. The wiggle system really did make sense, when taken on its own terms.

But this particular wiggle princess, the squiggles had explained, was a mutant, or close to it. There was normally a good range of variation in a swarm, with the tastes of individual larva including the most mundane flavors of rock and the most exotic. The flavor required for swarming matched that of the princess's food; since she normally consumed most of the food in the process of maturing, she then had to find similar rock in another place for her nest. This particular female had an extremely exotic taste, so had been unable to find any more of her kind of rock. She could not mate until she was assured of a proper nesting site. Once she found that, she would summon a male, and they would mate, and she would go to the new site to make the nest.

The reason the squiggles, who were fairly canny creatures, thought Volney might be interested, was that this princess's taste was for air-flavored stone. She had found her vein and consumed it, but that seemed to be the only such vein available. Generally wiggles preferred rockflavored stone; she was a real rarity. But what she might not realize was that there was a good deal of air-flavored stone on the surface, because of the way the air contaminated everything it touched. In fact, a similar taste accounted for those few swarms that occurred at the surface, when a wiggle female happened on the surface and had a matching taste. The creatures of the surface believed that they had to destroy every wiggle larva in the swarm to prevent any from generating new swarms; that was their ignorance. The truth was that their effort made very little difference, apart from some temporary complications caused by the manner the larvae drilled through things, because none of the larvae would have the same taste as their queen-mother. Only those with some taste for deep rock, who managed to reach a suitable vein of it, would survive. All the surface creatures needed to do was ignore the swarm, and it would pass. Thus spake the squiggles, who had been more than satisfied to educate one of their lofty volish cousins on the facts of life at the other end of the spectrum.

All this was news to Volney, who had shared the conventional surface creature alarm about wiggle swarming. That showed that there was some justice to the attitude of the lower species of ground borers: the voles of the Vale had gotten out of touch, and were forgetting the nature of their relatives. He would have to reeducate his companions of the Vale, once this mission was over.

But first he had to *get* it over, and that was not a sanguine prospect. Though a wiggle swarm might not be the disaster he had supposed, it would still be devastating enough in the temporary sense, because of the way the larvae drilled through everything they encountered, leaving their little *zzapp* holes. Such holes could be quite painful for other living creatures, and even lethal. To loose a swarm on the Vale of the Vole—he remained uncertain how wise that might be, even if the voles and other creatures there had sufficient warning to evacuate the area until the swarm had passed. Concerns of this nature had caused him to dismiss the notion of seeking the wiggle princess out of paw, before. But now, with the failure of the other two members of the party to obtain help, he had to try it. He hoped he wasn't making a terrible error.

Such were his thoughts as he tunneled down at a slant, following the foul taste of the pebble. Periodically he rested and ate some fruit and root from his pouch, for this was an extensive dig. In due course he slept, keeping his whiskers alert for nickelpedes; he had no intention of being trapped that way again.

After two days, the sourness of the pebble practically numbed his tongue. He was getting close.

Indeed, in another moment he broke through to the tunnel network of the princess. He blinked, for it was lighted; bright fungus grew on the walls, illuminating the region in pastel shades. There was a definitely feminine aura here; he would have known immediately that this was the abode of a female even if he had stumbled on it by accident. He paused to prepare himself for the encounter, then sent out a call in voletalk.

She answered immediately. "Who intrudes on my network?"

Volney was taken aback. Her voice, in vole terms, was dulcet. He had expected a somewhat grating encounter, for his kind had very little contact with her kind.

"I am Volney Vole, seeking perhaps a favor." His words reminded him of the manner his human and centaurian companions hissed their "s" sounds, making their speech artificial; he was of course too polite to mention it to them, realizing that they probably suffered from infirmities of their palates.

She appeared, and he was surprised again. She was a surprisingly petite creature, reminiscent of a female of his own species, with gray fur that seemed to glow. She resembled a wiggle larva not in the slightest; she was definitely of the family of voles.

"And I am Wilda Wiggle," she responded. "I would be more than happy to grant you that favor, but I am not at the moment seeking a mate."

"So I have been informed," he said, surprised at her interpretation. He was not her type. A vole and a wiggle, however compatible physically, were incompatible genetically; they could only go through the motions of mating, never producing offspring. "My favor is not of that nature; I am not of your particular species."

"What is it, then?" She fluffed out her fur, looking very pretty. Volney became conscious of the grime on his own fur, because of his two days of boring. He should have taken time to lick himself clean. But he had a remedy: he shifted to his surface suit, his fur turning gray, his eyes brown. Because he had not been boring in that, it was clean.

"I am from the Vale of the Vole, and we have a severe problem. The demons are harassing us, and they have straightjacketed our formerly friendly river, the Kiss-Mee, and made it and the Vale unfriendly. We are seeking some way to drive the demons off, so that we can restore the river to its natural and superior state, so that our Vale may be pleasant again."

"That is very interesting, I'm sure," she said politely. "But I think it is no affair of mine."

"It occurred to me that if a wiggle swarming were to occur in that vicinity, the demons would be discomfited, and would depart, allowing us to restore the river."

"But wiggles do not swarm on the surface," she protested. "There is no decent-tasting rock there!"

"There may be," he said. "According to the squiggles, who bore both in the depths and near the surface, there is a good deal of air-flavored stone at the surface."

"Air-flavored stone?"

"I understand that the flavor you prefer is of that nature."

"I know what I like, but I never knew what it was called. Do you mean to say that there is stone in the flavor I require at the surface?"

"The squiggles seem to think so. When I first encountered them, they mistook me for you, because of the odor remaining on my fur. Therefore it seems that the particular atmosphere of the Vale may be compatible for you."

"You don't smell like my rock," she protested.

"It has largely dissipated now, for I have been some time away from the Vale. But perhaps some smell remains in my pouch." He opened his pouch.

She sniffed. "Yes! That is my flavor! Oh, I wish I had known before! I must mate and go there immediately!"

"There is a complication," he said. "The larvae of a wiggle swarm are damaging to the creatures of a region."

"Damaging? I know nothing of this."

"That is because your kind normally swarms in limited veins of specialized rock, where no other creatures live. On the surface the range of a swarm becomes virtually unlimited, because the larvae travel through the air, which offers little resistance. They leave holes in the creatures, which is awkward."

"Oh, I see. I suppose that could be awkward, as you say. But why don't you use a containment spell?"

"I beg your pardon?"

"A containment spell. This has been used historically by our kind on those rare occasions when our territory overlaps that of other creatures. It confines the swarm to a set radius, so that no harm occurs beyond it."

"But doesn't that interfere with your cycle of reproduction? If the larvae cannot travel freely, how can they find the rocks they need?"

"Not any more than a limited vein of swarming rock does," she pointed out. "We wiggles are accustomed to limitations. If the containment spell limits only the radius and not the depth, some larvae will find deep rock. Those that remain on the surface have no chance anyway, as they seek a different flavor."

Volney was highly gratified. "Then it appears we can exchange favors," he said. "Tell me where this containment spell is, and I will tell you where the Vale is."

She was visibly pleased. She fluffed out her fur some more, and gazed at him with eyes that shifted from brown to gray as her fur converted the opposite way. "It is lost at the moment; someone carried it into a gourd and failed to bring it out."

"Would that be on the Lost Path in the gourd?" he asked, remembering something that Esk had said.

"Why, yes, I suppose so. So if you go there, you should be able to find it." She gazed at him with those big eyes, that were now turning from gray to violet, while her coat became pleasantly green. It was evident that the wiggles were more versatile about coloration than the voles were. "You are a handsome vole, Volney."

"The Vale is—are you familiar with the outline of the land of Xanth?—it is in the central part, south of the Gap Chasm, north of Lake Ogre-Chobee."

"I am sure I can find it," she said. Her eyes were brightening to red, while her fur was turning silver. "I am so glad you came to see me!"

There was something about her attitude that nagged him. He looked into her face, and realized what an extraordinarily attractive creature she was. Those blazing red eyes—

Red eyes! That was the color of mating!

"I must dig on, now," he said quickly. "So nice to have encountered you."

"Remain awhile," she breathed. "We could have such a good time."

He realized now what had happened. Wilda had found a suitable place to nest, because he had told her of the Vale and confirmed it with a smell. That had moved her into her mating phase—and he was the closest male. Wiggles were not the brightest of voles, just as the diggles weren't; they were governed mostly by staggered instincts. First a wiggle found a place to eat and grow; then the males turned to prowling and the females searched for nesting sites. Once the sites were found, the females were ready to mate, and the first male who prowled their way was the one. That normally did not take long, because they put out a mating scent that attracted any males in the vicinity.

The mating scent! That was why she was becoming so attractive! She was starting to generate it, and he was feeling its initial impact. They might be of different species, but it seemed that this type of scent signal was universal. If he remained, he would soon be overwhelmed by it, despite the distinction of species, and—

And it was a trap. Not because there was any danger in the act itself; it was apt to be quite pleasurable. But because they were of different species.

"Remember, I am a vole, while you are a wiggle," he reminded her.

"Don't tell me you are prudish about cultures," she murmured, rubbing her fur against his. The process sent an electric tingle through his body.

He took a deep breath—and realized that the mating scent was getting to him. He would be overwhelmed all too soon, and then he wouldn't care about species.

"It isn't prudishness," he explained. "It's pointlessness. We would not be fertile; you would produce no swarm."

"I don't understand that," she said. "When one mates, one produces. One swarm; then one joins adult society, and subsequent matings are infertile."

"The genes differ. You need to mate with one of your own species, a wiggle male. I'm sure one will happen along soon." Because the mating scent could circulate through the fissures of the rock, reaching prospective males, who would delay not a moment.

"Let's not wait," she said, nuzzling his neck.

The scent was about to overpower him. Volney knew why this was wrong, but now he was having trouble remembering. Did it really matter? She was such a lovely creature!

Then he had a desperately bright notion. He took the guide pebble from his mouth and jammed it up his nose. Now the bitterness of it overwhelmed the alluring mating scent, and his mind reverted to normal.

Now it was clear to him why this was a dangerous trap. If he tried to mate with her, it would not take. Therefore she would not become gravid, and her mating instinct would not abate. She would continue her desire to mate, and her scent and appearance would reflect that desire—and he would find himself locked into a perpetual mating role. She would not seek any other while he was there, and no wiggle male would intrude, however eager, for no volish creature was wanton about mating; thus there would be no way for her to become gravid. And no way for him to escape, because a male could not deny the mating scent when it was in full strength.

He would never leave this tunnel, not even to eat. He would gradually starve, unable to wrench himself away, and his last act before he died would be another mating with her. Nature's natural curtailment would not be invoked, because of the genetic incompatibility. Other creatures of Xanth could crossbreed, but not the voles; they were pure strains, kept pure by this limitation.

Well, it might be possible for the mating to take, if enhanced by the elixir of a love spring, or by an accommodation spell. But neither was present on this occasion, so that was of no significance.

"Don't you like me?" Wilda inquired.

He did not want to affront her, because he wanted her co-operation when she did successfully breed with one of her own kind. A wiggle swarm, suitably contained, should banish the demons from the Vale, and certainly it would ruin the demons' dikes and let the water out of the Kill-Mee channels. "I simply want what is best for you," he said. "And that is a mating with one of your own species. I must go locate the containment spell." And that was most of the truth—about all she might be capable of assimilating.

"I really don't understand," she said. She tickled his nose with a whisker.

The tickle caused Volney to sneeze. The foul pebble flew from his nose, and was lost in the dust. Suddenly he was exposed to the full impact of the mating odor.

It was time for desperate measures. Volney held his breath and leaped for the wall. He jammed on his external claws and dug at the wall with extraordinary vigor. The rock powdered under the magic of the talons, and a new hole developed.

"What's the matter?" Wilda asked. "Did I say something to offend you? I apologize!"

"Don't apologize!" Volney gasped, remembering one more thing Esk had mentioned. Some folk had a most intimate mode of apology!

"But I only want to be nice to you!" she pleaded.

As Volney breathed, some of the scent reached him. Why not simply turn back and—?

But his rational mind still had enough sway to dominate—as long as he held his breath again. He continued his digging, getting his nose into the new rock, filtering out the scent.

"Ah, you wish to flirt," she said. "I will play! I will catch you!"

"Yes, catch me!" Volney gasped. He could dig his way out of her range, and before she found him, a wiggle male would pass within range of her scent, and would preempt the mating. Then, afterwards, she would remember the Vale, and feel no outrage at Volney's abrupt retreat.

But he had forgotten what good borers the wiggles were. Wilda started her own tunnel, parallel to his, pacing him, and she readily matched his progress. He had no more strength pills; he could not enhance himself with a spell to outdistance her. When she grew tired of playing, she would loop her tunnel and cut off his, and merge the two; and then her scent would overwhelm him, and they would be locked in the futile mating effort.

What could he do? She was tunneling above him, preventing him from going for the surface. She might not be bright about the details of genetics, but she was canny about tunneling, as all the members of the great family of voles were. It was inherent; any related creature who could not tunnel well was soon squeezed out of the ground. One of the shames of the surface creatures was surely their inadequacy as tunnelers.

Maybe he could double back, fooling her, and then head for the surface before she could catch him. She wouldn't brave the surface until after mating; it wasn't the wiggle way. He hoped.

He widened his tunnel, making room to turn his body around, then scurried back. It was much faster reexcavating refuse rocks than boring through solid virgin stone, and he made three times the speed. He soon intersected her original suite and scrambled through it.

"How nice," she murmured, wiggling her whiskers. "You have returned."

Volney held his breath and skidded to a stop. She had anticipated him! He could almost feel the scent caressing his fur. He spun about and plunged back into his tunnel. Soon he was back at its end, boring forward. Could he angle it up now, before she followed him back here?

He could not. She was already angling her tunnel toward his; he could tell by the sound of it.

Then he had a dark notion. He knew one place she wouldn't go!

Abruptly, he angled down. He had the excellent volish spatial memory that enabled him to orient on any region he had visited before. He knew where to go.

Wilda paced him, not closing in, evidently curious about this new ploy. She knew he couldn't dig down forever; eventually he would have to turn up again, and then she would end the flirtation and close in for the finale.

Wouldn't it be easier, he wondered, just to let her catch

him? But then he realized that it was the scent influencing him. Every time he bored through a fracture zone, a suggestion of that scent filtered through, and now it was filtering through the fracture zones of his will to resist and centering on his desire. If he let her catch him, he would never make the rendezvous with his friends on the surface, and the Vale of the Vole would not be saved. He had to fight on through!

Now he was nearing his current destination: the living lava flow. If he played this too close, he would suffer another type of fate; and as he fried to death, he would wish he had remained with the wiggle princess after all. For if he died in the lava, then Wilda would mate elsewhere, and go to the Vale—*and there would be no containment spell.*

He felt the heat. He did not know the full extent of the flow, but did know where his prior tunnel to it was. He angled across to intersect that, hoping that Wilda did not realize what he had in mind.

Her tunneling slowed as she felt the heat of the lava; this was not a region she liked! She was hesitating, while he ground on. Good; he didn't like this region either, and didn't want to go any further into it than absolutely necessary.

Then she came to her decision. Her tunnel angled to intercept his.

Volney increased his effort. He was tired from the two days of solid boring he had done to reach the princess, but he knew that he had to draw on any strength he had remaining. If she caught him, all was lost.

The heat of the rock increased. This made the boring easier for his magic talons, but also worried him; he was approaching the lava from the other side, and could not be sure of its limit.

Despite his effort, Wilda was gaining on him. Before he could locate his tunnel of several days ago, she cut him off. Her tunnel broke through into his, and her nose appeared before his nose.

"This is fun," she said. "But I don't like this region. Let's go back to my suite and make love." This was, in the circumstances, a virtually irresistible offer.

Volney tried to hold his breath, but his effort of boring had him gasping; he could not stop breathing now. He knew he had lost. He breathed in her fragrance.

But, strangely, he felt no overwhelming desire for her now. She was pretty, and she was nice; he found no fault in her. He did not blame her for her nature. In another situation he would have liked to associate with her more thoroughly. But he no longer felt the compulsion to mate with her. What had happened?

The scent that was strong in his nostrils now was that of the lava. It was very close, and the rock through which they were tunneling was hot.

That was it: the lava was burning off the mating scent! He had been saved by the flow!

"Princess Wilda," he said gently. "I like you, and find you most attractive. But I am not of your species, and I would do you no favor by attempting to mate with you. I must return to the surface to look for the containment spell, so that your swarm may flourish in the Vale without hurting any other creatures there. Go and find a mate of your own kind, and take my best wishes with you."

Her whiskers quivered unhappily. "You do not wish to mate with me?"

"I want to, but know it would only harm you," he said, and realized that he was not being insincere. "I am doing what is best. I will always remember you, with deepest regret for what I cannot do, for you are a delight among females."

Then he resumed his tunneling, heading up at a steep angle. She squatted where she was for a moment; then, forlornly, she turned and moved back toward her suite.

It was done. Somehow he was not thrilled. If only he *could* have yielded . . .

It took him three days to reach the surface, because he was tired; he suspected the fatigue was emotional as much as physical. The merest suggestion of that mating scent clung to his fur, and every so often he got a faint whiff, and it sent him into a daydream of regret. The princess was a wiggle, true, but she had been most delectable; now that his decision had been made, he was free to regret, endlessly, what might have been, foolish as that would have been. He could appreciate Esk's problem with the brassie girl; the sweetest temptation could be that which was known to be the most foolish.

He had one day remaining to make the rendezvous when he broke surface. It was not that far away, so he collapsed and slept.

On the next day he trudged on to Castle Roogna, and to the orchard. There were Esk and Chex, and the brassie girl and the skeleton man and the old curse fiend, and of course little Ivy, who dashed up and hugged him exactly as if he were one of her pets. The odd thing was that he discovered that he liked it; he felt much more volish in that moment.

They exchanged histories. It turned out that Esk had gotten the ogres to agree to help; already the gross humanoids were organizing in their dull fashion for their tromp to the Vale. Chex had gotten the winged monsters to agree, too; they would appear in due course.

Then Volney, with some misgiving, explained what he had accomplished. "A wiggle princess!" Ivy exclaimed with the characteristic humanoid problem with the "s." "How excssiting!"

Chex was far more sober. "A wiggle sswarm?" she asked, alarmed. "That'ss quite a risk!"

"We sshall have to ssearch for the containment spell on the Losst Path," Esk said.

That led to a discussion of ways and means. The gourd was very chancy; who should enter, by the Zombie route, and who should stay behind?

"I don't want to enter that way," Bria protested. "It might get me permanently fouled up."

"Readily ssolved," Chex said. "Let Essk return you to the Losst Path; then he will look for you from the insside, and resscue you again. Then you will be able to come to thiss world all the way physsically, or to return to your ccity. What iss your ccity called, inssidentally?"

"Brassilia," Bria responded. "But I may not want to return there."

"It will be your choicse, of coursse," the centaur said. Volney could tell by her manner that Bria's hesitation was no surprise to the centaur. Of course the brassie girl wanted to remain here; she was casting her scent for Esk. That was obvious to every member of the party except, of course, Esk himself.

Chex turned to the skeleton. "And you, Marrow—do you wissh to rissk the loop back in via the zombie gourd?"

"I confess to developing an interesst in thiss world," the skeleton said. "I am in no russh to return to the haunted garden. Sso I would like to travel with you, if you concur."

"But you rissk a convolussion whosse nature we do not properly undersstand," she reminded him.

Marrow shrugged. He was very good at that, because of the articulation and exposure of his bones. "It iss an interessting convolussion."

"Very interessting," the centaur agreed. "That makess our party four; I think that iss enough. Latia and Bria can wait here, and if we do not return in a week—"

"Then I will go in after you," Bria said. "And Latia will inform the voless of the Vale that the ogress and winged monssterss and wigless are coming, sso they can prepare."

That settled it. Tomorrow their party of four would set out for the huge zombie gourd Chex knew about. Volney knew it had to be done, but he was ill at ease. The notion of physically entering the gourd appalled him. But not as much as the notion of letting his folk of the Vale down.

# $\overline{13}$
# DREAMS

It took them one day to reach the zombie gourd, because the others could not travel as rapidly as Chex. They planned for a journey of two days within the gourd to find the containment spell, and the same time to return, giving them one day's leeway. The margin was the same, but the stakes were rising; the Vale of the Vole might well be hostage to their success.

Chex brought out the pathfinder spell. Esk had used it for the path to the ogre fen, and it would not work for him again, so Chex was taking her turn now. "The easiest and safest path for four folk to the lost containment spell," she enounced carefully. Esk recognized the wisdom of that; the gourd had its own difficulties and dangers, such as entrapment on the Lost Path. He had asked for the shortest path to the ogre fen, and it had been slightly harrowing in places; the gourd was bound to be worse.

The path appeared before them. As they had anticipated, it led into the huge peephole. Esk was nervous about this, because of his prior experience with the gourd, but he reminded himself that this was not the same situation; when they entered physically, they could depart physically, on their own initiative. Also, they had the guidance of the path. And of course he had not been hurt before, just confused. He had even emerged with a couple of new friends.

But the others were leaping in, and he had to follow before he got left out. He leaped—and found himself in the midst of rotting plants. It was as if some monstrous blight had descended on this glade and caused the vegetation to sicken and die.

"Vombie plantv," Volney muttered, evidently as bothered as Esk was.

Chex was showing the way along an overgrown and slushy path between depressions. Esk saw a fallen head-stone, and realized that these were sunken graves, with the sickly plants crowding them. He did not like this place at all.

"Watch the snake," Chex called.

Esk looked ahead, and saw a horrendous zombie serpent striking at Marrow's bone leg. But its aim wasn't good; it bit a plant instead. The skeleton walked on, unperturbed. He was back in his original state, having doffed the suit Latia had made for him at some point; indeed, it seemed like a pointless affectation for him.

Volney paused, watching the snake. He started to pass it, and it drew back again to strike; he scooted on ahead, and the snake missed and bit the plant again. It really was not particularly bright or swift, as snakes went, though perhaps was up to par as zombies went.

The oddest thing was that the plant was now becoming quite healthy. The venom seemed to enhance it.

"Zombies are afraid of health," Chex called back. "So the bite threatens to deliver what they fear. But we aren't zombies, and we can't be sure what it would do to us."

Indeed they could not be sure. Esk timed the snake, and zipped on by it, and ran to catch up with the others.

They were now at a region of slashing knives. "This is the route I took before," Chex said. "The path leads here, but it must diverge somewhere, because I was going to Centaur Isle then." She drew a knife from her pack, and threw it into the gantlet.

There was an instant melee as the knives attacked the intruder knife. They cut each other up in the process, going wild, and soon all of them were broken. The four of them should be able to pass this way—but the marks of the path-finder's path no longer seemed to go here.

Chex nodded. "It changes; the knife fight is merely a key, not a part of the path." She set out along a new path that proceeded back the way they had come.

The decaying vegetation had changed to decaying stone and other junk. Chex came to a green rock that was so far gone it resembled a fungus. She lifted a forehoof and struck it against this rock.

The thing flew apart. Where the pieces landed, they sank into the ground, and awful green fire rose up, spreading to the ground itself, consuming it. Before long something showed beneath: a platform of wood that did not burn.

Chex knocked the near end of the wood, and it dropped, and the far end swung up. There was a hollow beneath, with wooden steps leading down.

"Now the path should lead away," Chex remarked.

But it did not. The wear marks that signaled the proper route proceeded down those steps.

"I admit I was curious about this," the centaur said. "But it means the route will no longer be familiar to me. At least this has been enough to show you the way of it; the path can be devious."

Indeed it could be. "But reasonably safe and easy," Esk repeated. He wished he knew what was considered reasonable in the strange world of the gourd. If striking zombie snakes represented safety, what would represent danger?

Chex stepped down into the pit, somewhat awkwardly. It was evident that centaurs were not made for stairs. There was a landing below, large enough for the four of them. Beyond it, a broad lighted passage extended, and this was clearly the path.

They lined up four abreast and walked onward. This really wasn't very bad, so far, maybe the path *was* going to be easy by human definition.

Then they came to a rusty barred gate across the passage. Behind it stood four grotesque zombies. One was a rotting man, another a decaying centaur, another a moldy vole, and the last a tattered skeleton.

"This has abruptly become specific," Chex remarked. "Something knows we are here."

"I am not reavvured," Volney said.

"It is not unknown," Marrow said. "We of the gourd are animations of the concepts of bad dreams. Now that you— and it seems I—have entered this realm physically, those dreams are coalescing. I suspect this will become rather unpleasant for you."

"Not for you?" Chex inquired.

"I do not dream, of course, so cannot have a bad dream."

"But that figure before you looks very much like a spoiled skeleton."

"Yes. This is odd. It must have mistaken me for a living creature. I am not certain whether to feel flattered or insulted."

"But what do we do now?" Esk asked. "Break through the gate? It has no opening, and the bars are too closely set to let us through."

"If, as I conjecture, these are animations from our minds, it will be necessary for us to face them directly," Marrow said. "They are of course intended to frighten us away. Bad dreams lose their power when the subject fails to flee in terror." He glanced around. "I hope you will not repeat that in the outside world. Trade secret, you know."

Esk would have laughed, if his knees hadn't felt so weak.

"Then I shall face my doppelganger," Chex said boldly. She stepped up to the gate.

The zombie centaur stepped up similarly, as if it were a mirror image. It met her right at the gate. She put out her right hand, and it matched her with its left. She touched it— and her hand passed through its hand.

No, not through—into. The two merged, and disappeared.

Startled, Chex drew back her arm. So did the zombie, and both hands reappeared.

"Like water!" Esk exclaimed. "Like putting your hand into water! It disappears, and so does the reflection."

"That must be it," Chex agreed grimly. She spread her wings part way, as she tended to do when wrestling with a concept, and the zombie did the same.

Then she stepped forward, into the gate. The doppelganger duplicated the motion.

They merged. Their two front sections disappeared into each other, leaving a two-reared beast. Then the rears merged, leaving only the two briefly swishing tails. Finally, the tails drew together in the center and were gone.

Then a picture formed, superimposed over the gate. It was of Chex, galloping through a forest, casting worried glances back over her shoulder. What was she fleeing from?

She entered a field. Now the pursuit came into view. It consisted of a herd of centaurs: males, females, and young ones, brandishing spears and bows. They seemed intent on killing her!

The field terminated in a rough slope strewn with rocks. Chex had to slow to avoid cracking her hooves against the rocks, and the pursuing centaurs gained. One aimed his bow.

The descent became sharper, until she could go no farther without losing her footing entirely. Beyond was a drop-off to a raging river. There was no chance of fording that; if she tried, she would be dashed to death against the rocks in the river. Her plight and her terror were manifest.

"It's only a vision!" Esk called. "It can't hurt you! Just a bad dream!"

Chex heard him. She glanced at him with realization—and abruptly was back in the passage with them, the dream gone.

The zombie centaur was back on its side of the gate, unchanged. The way remained barred.

Chex was breathing hard; she had evidently had quite a scare. "You saw it?" she asked.

"We saw it," Esk agreed. "You were being chased by centaurs."

"They condemned me because of my wings," she said. "They regarded me as as a freak!"

"Exactly as the real centaurs do," Esk agreed.

"Then that is your deepest fear or shame," Marrow said. "The worst dream the night mares can bring you: rejection by your own kind."

She shuddered. "Yes. I try not to think about it, but it does hurt terribly. I want to be part of my species, and I cannot be."

"You must face it down," Marrow said.

"How can I do that? They will kill me if I do not flee them!"

"But a dream death is not a real death," Esk reminded her.

"I hope you're right," she said grimly. "Don't wake me, this time."

She marched back into her doppelganger. The two disappeared again into each other, and the dream reappeared.

Chex was fleeing through the forest, heading for the field. But this time she forced herself to stop, and to turn and face her pursuers. "You have no right to harass me like this!" she cried. "I am what I was foaled to be! It is no fault of mine!"

"Freak! Freak!" they chorused. "Death to all freaks!"

Then they stabbed her with spears, and shot her with their arrows, and carved her with their knives, until only a shuddering mass of flesh remained.

Chex woke screaming. The second dream had been worse than the first! The threatened violence had been no bluff.

Esk jumped over to her and opened his arms. She reached down and clutched him to her, heedless of the physical or social awkwardness. "Oh, it was horrible!" she cried. "I *died!* They killed me, and it hurt, and I was mutilated and dead!"

"Terrible," Esk agreed, holding her as well as he could, though her pectorals were squeezing against his neck.

. "That was evidently an improper way to face that fear," Marrow said.

"First I fled, then I faced them!" Chex sobbed hysterically. "Both were wrong. What else can I do?"

"Vhat iv for uv to convider," Volney said. "Vhe hav tried the ekvtremev; what remainv between?"

Chex disengaged from Esk. "Here I'm acting like a silly filly! Of course this is a problem to be analyzed and solved. I was reacting in blacks and whites, when reality is generally in shades of gray. But the dream had such verisimilitude, it overwhelmed me!"

"Such what?" Esk asked, daunted by the six-syllable word she had used.

"It was realistic," she clarified. "It made me believe I was there even though I knew better."

"It made *me* believe you were there, at first," Esk said.

"And I thank you for your support," she said. "I am coming to appreciate the value of friendship."

"Friendv," Volney said, nodding in his emulation of human idiom. "Could we join you there, and oppove the ventaurv?"

"Say, yes!" Esk exclaimed. "Four are better than one! And Marrow could give them a real start!"

"I appreciate the offer," Chex said. "But I wouldn't want to put you into that sort of danger. Perhaps you could not actually be killed, but believe me, you could be hurt; I felt that pain! In any event, I believe this is my personal challenge to surmount; if I should do it with help, it wouldn't count."

They saw the justice in her position. "But if you can't fight them, or reason with them, or escape them, what can you do?" Esk asked.

"Reject them," Marrow said.

Chex's eyes widened. "I think you're right! I was treating them seriously both times, and so they had power. I *gave* them that power!"

"Yet you knew they were figments of a dream," Esk said. "They still attacked you. I'm not sure that just telling them you reject them will do any good."

"No, it won't," she agreed. "I have to prove it. And, since this is a dream, I think I know how." She faced the gate. "Wish me luck."

"Mountains of it!" Esk said.

"Cavev of it," Volney agreed.

"Rib cages of it," Marrow said.

She nerved herself visibly, then strode into the gate. She disappeared against the zombie centaur, and the vision formed.

This time she ran to the field, then braked and whirled. The horde of centaurs charged up, brandishing their weapons.

"You have no authority here!" she cried. "This is my dream! I reject you and all you stand for—narrowness, intolerance, violence! That is not my way, and should not be yours."

They charged on her, weapons flashing. *Oh, no!* Esk thought. It wasn't working.

Then Chex spread her wings and leaped into the air. The wings stroked powerfully, the downblast stirring up a cloud of dust and blowing back the manes of the centaurs. She rose above them, slowly, grandly.

*She was flying!*

The centaurs gaped. This was entirely unexpected.

"I reject your land-bound ways!" Chex cried. "You have no wings, so you condemn those who do! That is your fundamental failing—sour grapes!"

Now the centaurs began to recover. They lifted their weapons—and Chex accelerated her wing beats and launched up into the sky, quickly passing out of range. "I don't need your approval; I don't fear your condemnation!" she called. "I have my own life to live! I leave you behind!"

Then she woke. She was back on the floor, panting flushed with victory, and the dream was gone.

"But in real life, I still can't fly," she said sadly. "I recognized that the terms of the dream were different, and that if I had awful liabilities, I also had wonderful abilities. They go together; the extremes are feasible, in the dream. So I drew on the positive, and vanquished the negative. And do you know, it's true! I don't need the centaurs anymore! I'm free of my liability of false desire; I no longer want to be like them or accepted by them. I want to explore my own horizons, which are so much greater than theirs! Their reality is valid, for them; I could not flee them as long as I desired their acceptance, nor oppose them as long as I knew that their dream presentation was merely an exaggeration of their actual way. I could not defeat them on their own turf. But when I invoked my turf, they were helpless!"

She paused, realizing that the others were staring at her. "What's the matter? Do you disagree?"

Esk found his voice. "You're through," he said.

"I—" She looked around. "Why, I'm on the other side of the barrier!"

"Your victory," Marrow agreed.

"I came to terms with my worst fear or shame," she agreed. "It no longer haunts me. The dream was only the representation of it. The barrier was only another representation. Neither exists for me anymore." And she walked through the gate without hindrance, turned, and walked through it again. The metal bars had no substance.

Esk stepped up to touch the bars—and his doppelganger matched him, reaching out to meet his hand from the other side. Esk jerked his hand back; that barrier remained real for him.

"The vombie ventaur iv gone," Volney said. "But the otherv remain."

"We must conquer our own bad dreams," Esk said.

"I vhall tackle mine," the vole said, and marched into the gate.

The zombie vole met him snout-on. The two merged, and the dream formed. It was of a tunnel whose walls glowed prettily with colored fungus. He entered it by boring through the wall, the magic metal talons on his front feet gouging through the rock as if it were mud.

Another vole was there—no, Esk realized that there were subtle distinctions of form and coloration. It was a female, and not of precisely Volney's species. Her eyes and fur changed color as his did, but she differed too.

"The wiggle princess," Chex murmured. She had crossed the barrier again and now stood beside him.

Oh. Esk thought of the demoness Metria, and began to understand the nature of the vole's deepest shame.

Volney came to stand before the wiggle. She approached, and they sniffed noses. There was a pleasant smell, as of blooming flowers. It reminded him somehow of Bria Brassie, and that was funny, because she was made of metal and smelled of polished brass.

Volney jerked away, and the dream ended. He was back in the passage, on the near side of the gate. "I wav afraid it would be that," he said.

"You desire the wiggle princess," Chex said.

"But the trap—"

"Yes, you explained," the centaur said. "But you avoided her, so you should have no shame in that connection. You did what you had to do, and we are on this quest for the containment spell because of it."

"Yet I came vo clove to failing," Volney said. "Because of my unworthinevv."

"Your what?" Esk asked. "You always struck me as a fine figure of a vole."

"I am not," Volney said. "The rejection by her kind that Chekv feared—iv alvo mine."

"This requires explanation," Chex said. "Aren't you on a mission for your folk?"

"I am—but it iv not becauve I am the bevt for it, but becauve I am ekvpendable."

"Expendable?" Chex asked. "How could that be?"

Volney sighed. "It iv the time for the baring of vecret vhamev. I was a vuitor for an ekvtremely volivh female vole, but vhe turned invtead to another."

"An extremely volish vole turned you down?" Chex asked. "Surely that is no fault of yours!"

"Yev it iv," Volney insisted. "Volve mate for life, and when I wav rejected, I became ineligible for any vubvequent matvh. There wav nothing for me to do but depart."

"One rejection makes you—taboo?" Chex asked. "That hardly seems reasonable."

"You are not a vole," he reminded her. "Think of me av having vprouted wingv."

"Point made," she agreed, grimacing.

"But then you were going—and helping your folk," Esk said. "Where is the shame in that?"

"I did not undertake the mivvion for the good of the Vale, but av a pretekvt to depart," Volney explained.

"Still, you did plan to complete it, didn't you?"

"Yev. But when I met Wilda—"

"You were tempted to forget your mission," Chex concluded. "Yes, I can appreciate that. But you *did* resist that temptation, so there is no shame."

"The vhame iv in the temptation," Volney said. "I vhould not have been."

"I doubt it," Marrow said. "You resisted that temptation both in life and in the dream."

Chex nodded. "I think you have not yet faced your deepest fear or shame."

Volney sighed with an exhalation of "v's." "Then muvt I fave it now," he said. He walked forward into his doppelganger vole.

The scene re-formed. Dulcet Wilda Wiggle came forward to meet him, sniffing noses. The smell of flowers grew strong.

Volney hesitated, then took the plunge. If seduction by her was not his deepest potential shame, what was? He moved in to embrace her in the volish way.

Her nose wiggled. She was smelling something. A picture formed above them, a scene within the scene: a female vole turning away from the Volney of the scenelet.

"She realizes he is a rejectee," Chex murmured.

Abruptly the wiggle turned away. The scent of flowers faded. Volney was left there—rejected again.

Abruptly he woke, back beside them in the passage. Now his deepest concern was clear: that his basic unworthiness as a vole would have alienated the wiggle princess, had he chosen to dally with her. Then he would have been guilty twice: of betraying his mission and his Vale, and of failing at that.

"There is only one solution," Chex said. "Complete your mission. Then if there is fault, it is none of yours, and you need have no further shame. The wiggle princess would not reject you then, but if she did, you would know that it was her error, not your own."

"But I am guilty of unvolivh weaknevv," he protested.

"Only in your bad dream," she said. "You are afraid of weakness; you have not practiced it in life."

Volney shrugged. Then he marched back into the zombie vole. The dream formed—and dissipated immediately, leaving Volney on the far side of the gate.

"Now you believe," Chex said. "The dream has lost its power over you. Thus it was unable even to form."

"Now I believe," Volney agreed. "I will complete my mivvion, regardlevv of temptation or rejecvion."

Esk took a breath. "My turn," he said.

The zombie man came to meet him. Esk merged—and his dream opened out.

It consisted of a swirling universe of stars and dust and moons, all moving in the splendor of their separate trajectories, rather than being fixed in their shell the way they were in reality. The moon, instead of being a mass of green cheese, was in this weird vision a monstrous ball of cratered rock. And, strangest of all, the Land of Xanth was but a peninsula on the surface of a giant mundane sphere. Esk would have known that this was a hallucination even if he hadn't already been aware that it was only a dream.

The scene kept coming toward him, the detail expanding, until it became a map of Xanth, on which he was standing. Then a parallel picture formed, identical to the first, except that Esk was not in it.

That was all. He stood disembodied, studying the two pictures, one with his image and the other without. There was absolutely no other distinction between them.

He screamed. In a moment he found himself back in the passage. Chex hurried across and embraced him, much as he had embraced her between her dreams, comforting him as his horror slowly faded.

"But what doev it mean?" Volney asked, perplexed. "I vaw no monvterv, no vhame. Merely two venev."

"There was no difference!" Esk cried. "None at all!"

"True," Chex murmured. "But this was no horror to us. Why should it be to you?"

As he thought about it, Esk came to understand it. "I am in one, and not in the other—and there is no difference. I make no difference at all!"

"Yes, Esk," Chex said.

"It doesn't matter whether I live or die," Esk said. "Xanth is just the same. *What justification is there for my existence?*"

"That is only your fear, not the reality," Chex reminded him.

"But maybe it *is* reality!" he argued. "I am nothing and nobody; what I do doesn't matter. I realize now that I set out to see the Good Magician because I needed some proof that I had some importance, some mission in life. Getting rid of the demoness, saving my folks from her—that was only a pretext. I hoped the Good Magician would somehow—make me worthwhile."

"But you are worthwhile!" Chex said. "How can you doubt that?"

"I tell myself I am," Esk said. "But deep inside, I'm not sure that it is so. What have I done to make any difference at all to Xanth? If I had never lived, would it matter to anyone or anything? The picture with me in it is just the same as the one without me."

She considered. "I suppose that could be. But it would be similarly true for all of us. Objectively viewed, we may all be unworthy. But I think there is an answer. You don't have to settle for what you are at this moment. You can work to *make* a difference. This is what Volney will do. Then the pictures will change."

Esk nodded. "When you say it, it does seem to make sense. But how can I make a difference? Xanth is so big, and I'm so small."

"How much difference would the Kiss-Mee River make?"

"A lot. But that's Volney's mission. We're only helping."

"But if he can't do it without you?"

"And if I could help him do it—then there would be something that would not be the same without me," Esk said, liking the notion.

He walked back into the gate. The zombie met him, and merged, and the dream came again.

"I am nothing now," Esk said. "But I can make a difference, and I'm going to try. If I succeed, I will be something. That's all I can do—all any person can do. To make an honest try. If that's not enough, then nothing's enough, and it's not worth having any bad dreams about."

The pictures shimmered. Then something wriggled on the one that had his image. A river that was almost straight on the other map was assuming curvature here.

That was all. It was only a dream, but it gave Esk tremendous satisfaction. He knew what he had to do to abolish his deepest fear. To guarantee that his life had some bit of meaning. His life was not necessarily empty until he failed to accomplish that mission.

The vision dissipated. Esk found himself standing on the other side of the gate.

Only Marrow remained on the original side. "It is my turn," the skeleton said. "But I hesitate."

"That is understandable," Chex said. "We have all had very difficult experiences."

"I have no concern about a bad dream," Marrow said. "I do not dream, because I am not alive. My concern is that either there will be no reaction, because there is nothing in me to generate it—no fear, no shame, no guilty secret—or that my attempt to cross will trigger an error that will blow the program."

"Do what?" Esk asked.

"This trial is geared to living folk, with dreams," Marrow explained. "If one without dreams enters it, the mechanism could clash, unable to orient, and the entire setting could be compromised or destroyed. I am uncertain whether this should be risked."

"He has a point," Chex murmured. "He is a creature of the bad dreams; how can he have one of his own?"

"What happens," Esk asked, "if the program, ah, blows?"

"This entrance to the framework of the gourd would be closed off," Marrow said. "You might be trapped here, with no route of escape. Or there could be emotional or physical damage to the three of you."

"Marrow iv a good guide," Volney said. "We may not complete the quevt without hiv advive."

"Then maybe we should risk it," Esk said.

Chex nodded. "Maybe we should. There is after all no indication of trouble; there is a skeletal zombie ready. Come on through, Marrow."

The skeleton shrugged. "It is, as the saying goes, no skin off my sinus cavity." He marched into the grate. The zombie skeleton met him, and the two merged.

A picture started to form. It showed Marrow, standing in the passage, exactly as he was. Then it dissipated, and Marrow was standing back where he had started.

"It tried to make a dream for him!" Esk exclaimed.

"And found nothing on which to fasten," Marrow said.

"I'm not sure of that," Chex said. "There had to be something even to start it, and I think we should understand what it is. It could be significant."

"He was bounced without a dream," Esk said. "It thought there was going to be a dream, so it started it, but then it found out there wasn't, so it ended."

"But there *was* a dream," she insisted. "A simple one, but nevertheless a dream. That suggests that Marrow does possess some reality on our terms."

Now Volney was interested. "What could vuch a reality be? He hav no life."

"The picture was just of him, unchanged," Esk said. "For a moment I thought it *was* him, until it faded."

"Indeed it was me," Marrow said. "Since I have no life, I have no dream. It was just a picture of me as I am."

"Yes, it was," Chex agreed. "Therefore, that must represent your deepest fear or shame."

"I have no fear or shame," Marrow repeated.

"That may be why you were rejected," Chex said.

"Because it accepts only those who can reconcile their dreams, and I had none to reconcile," Marrow said, nodding his skull.

"No. Because you refused to come to terms with it."

That amused Esk. "Why should he come to terms with what doesn't exist?"

"Because it *does* exist," she said firmly. "Had it not existed, he would have passed through without challenge. But there is a zombie doppelganger waiting for him, and he can't pass until he overcomes that deepest spectre within him."

"There is nothing within me," Marrow protested. "My skull and rib cage are completely hollow, as you can see." He knocked on his skull with a knucklebone, and the sound was hollow.

"So was the skeleton in the dream," she agreed.

"You mean he's afraid of *himself*?" Esk asked incredulously.

"Perhaps." She gazed at Marrow. "*Are* you?"

"What could there possibly be to fear in that?" Marrow asked, irritated.

"You are avoiding an answer."

"But there is nothing in me to fear by me," the skeleton said. "I exist only to generate fear in living human folk. I have no other reality."

"So your dream suggests," Chex said. "Does that please you?"

"Why should it? I have no right to be pleased or displeased. It is merely my situation."

"Again, you avoid an answer."

"How do you think I feel?" Marrow demanded.

"I'd be pretty upset," Esk said. "Here my deepest fear was that I counted for nothing in Xanth, so my life may have no meaning. You aren't even alive. That's one step below me, even."

"It would be foolish of me to wish for life," Marrow said curtly. "It involves messiness."

"How can a creature who isn't alive be foolish?" Chex asked.

"Life is just a mass of awkwardnesses about consuming substance and eliminating substance," Marrow said. "Of discomfort and pain and shame. The end is exactly what I already am: dead. It is pointless."

"But life has feeling," Chex said. "And you have feeling. Is your deepest fear that you can never be any more than you are now?"

"But I *can* never be more!"

"Why don't you try the gate again," she suggested.

Marrow shrugged and walked back into the zombie. This time a more substantial picture formed—of him, as he was.

"But I don't *want* to be like this forever!" Marrow cried abruptly. "And maybe I don't have to be! If Esk can make of himself something worthwhile, why can't I aspire to be more than a spook?"

The dream held for a moment more, then faded. And Marrow was on the near side of the gate.

"I will hug you," Chex said. She did so.

Marrow seemed dazed. Esk could understand why. The skeleton was coming alive, at least in aspiration. That was an enormous advance.

Esk marveled, privately. He understood how living folk could become dead, but not how dead folk could become alive. Was this a genuine process, or merely an illusion spawned by this realm of dreams? Suppose Marrow only *thought* he was starting to dream, and therefore to live?

"Let's move on," Chex said briskly. "We now have better notions of our motives and natures, but it will come to little unless we find that containment spell."

All too true! They moved on along the passage, which seemed brighter now.

"No more rot," Volney remarked, sniffing the floor. "We have pavved beyond the vombie region."

"I am glad of that!" Chex said. "Not merely because I am

not partial to rotting flesh, but because this means that this is indeed an access to the whole of the world of the gourd, not merely the zombie segment. This path is proving itself."

Then the passage terminated in a blank wall. The path went right up to that wall and into it, but they could not pass through that solid stone.

"What now?" Esk asked, dismayed.

Chex passed her hands along the wall, feeling for crevices or loose panels, while Volney sniffed at the bottom for any evidence of impermanence. Both found nothing. The wall remained completely solid and immovable.

"Any notions, Marrow?" Esk asked wryly.

"Perhaps. There is obviously a way through this barrier, as there was through the last. We have but to find that way."

Esk suppressed a sharp response about restatements of the obvious. "Then what is your notion?"

"This is the realm of dreams. Perhaps a dream is needed for the wall."

"You mean if we dream we can pass it, then we can?"

"More likely we shall have to handcraft a dream, as is generally done here."

Chex became interested. "How does one handcraft a dream of passing through a wall?"

"One designs it and implements it," the skeleton said seriously.

Chex showed signs of suppressing the same irate response that Esk had. "Could you be more specific?"

"Certainly. It is possible that if we portray a passage through the wall, it will operate as portrayed."

Chex seemed doubtful, but she scouted about the passage until she found a fragment of stone that was black and crumbly. She used this to mark a black line on the wall. She extended it into a crude picture of a door. Then she pushed against the door. Nothing happened.

"Let me try," Esk said. He took the rock and drew a doorknob. Then he made as if to grasp and turn that knob.

It turned. The door opened out of the wall.

Startled, they piled through. They entered a large gallery in which many lovely pictures were hung.

"Exhibitions at a picture," Chex remarked, looking around.

The path led past scenes of rivers and lakes and waterfalls, past scenes of deserts and badlands and dry holes, past scenes of snowy forests and flowering bushes, past scenes of strange houses, including one with chicken legs, until it stopped at a portrait of a gargoyle. A stream of water was issuing from the monster's mouth and splashing into a pond below.

Their path went up the wall and into the pond in the picture.

Esk sighed. "I'll try it," he said.

He poked his finger at the pond. His finger passed into the picture, and he felt the wetness of the water. He pushed his arm through, and it got wet too. Finally, he put both arms into it, ducked his head, and dived forward into the picture.

He splashed in the pond, which was deeper than it looked. He swam, and in a moment hauled himself out onto the pavement beyond the pond, dripping. He looked back, but saw nothing except the rest of this landscape, which was a pleasant country village whose source of water was evidently this fountain. The sun was high in the sky, buttressed by fleecy clouds. He had entered the world of the picture.

The path traveled on down a road, which led into an ordinary forest. There was nothing to indicate that this was the world of the gourd.

There was a splash behind him. Volney Vole appeared in the water. In a moment he caught the rim of the pond and hauled himself out, as Esk had done.

Then Marrow arrived, appearing from nowhere. The skeleton could not swim; he simply put his bone feet down and walked along the bottom until he came to the edge. Then Esk reached down and caught a bone hand, and helped haul Marrow up and out.

"There will be a splash," Marrow warned.

Indeed there was, as Chex landed in the pond. This time Esk was watching closely. She appeared as if jumping out of a mirror: first her front section, then her hindquarters. The mass of her body caused the water to rise and overflow. She had a difficult time climbing out of the pond; she got her forepart clear, but Esk had to catch her hands to help her brace and lift a hind foot, and Marrow grabbed that hind foot and lifted it to the rim. Then they helped roll her up and over that brink as she hauled her other hind foot up. She got on her belly, precariously poised by the pond, and finally managed to tilt her body away from it so she could get back to her feet.

"If this is the easiest and safest path," she grunted, "I would very much dislike the most difficult and hazardous one!" She shook herself, spraying water out. "I hope we don't have far to go yet!"

They walked down the road to the forest. As they passed the first trees, the path abruptly diverged from the road and plunged into the thickest tangle of vegetation.

Chex sighed. "I should have known."

But something was nagging Esk. "This path seems familiar, somehow."

"Naturally," Marrow said. "It is the Lost Path."

"And the lost containment spell will be on this path!" Esk exclaimed. "We're getting close!"

Buoyed by this realization, they piled onto the devious path. Only Marrow seemed apprehensive. "There will be no escape by having your eye contact with the window to the gourd broken, this time," he warned.

That chilled Esk's enthusiasm. But he saw no alternative but to forge ahead. If they became trapped on the Lost Path despite the guidance of the pathfinder spell, then their dream of saving the Vale of the Vole was vain. But if they did not take this path, the dream would be abandoned.

# 14

# ELEMENTS

The path was inordinately convoluted, but as they traveled it, it seemed clear enough, just as had been the case when Esk was on it before. Soon the familiarity was unmistakable; he remembered the contours. Before long they would come to the place where—

"Say, Marrow!" he exclaimed. "Will you be where you were?"

"I am here, of course," the skeleton said.

"I mean that if you entered my world the same way I entered yours, just in mind rather than in substance, your body should—"

"I doubt it. We magical creatures lack your grip on reality; we are entirely where we appear to be. So neither I nor Bria Brassie will be on this path; you found us, so we are no longer lost."

Chex nodded silently; she had evidently figured this out for herself.

"That makes sense," Esk said. But he remained nervous; suppose the skeleton *did* appear in the path?

But when they came to that spot, only the dent left by Marrow's hipbone remained in the ground. Marrow's explanation had been correct. His whole existence was where it seemed to be. There were indeed differences between the living and the magical creatures.

Before, he had to hold Marrow's bone hand to get him unlost; now Marrow was walking independently, because he had been found. Evidently the pathfinder's path superseded the qualities of the Lost Path, and none of them were lost.

Something red bounded away. Chex was startled, but Esk reassured her. "That's only a roe. Roes are red."

She gave him a peculiar look, but did not comment.

Then they reached the potted plant. "That's a violent," Esk said nonchalantly. "Violents are blue."

She looked at him again, and again stifled her comment.

"It was supposed to be planted on a median strip, but they rejected it," Esk continued.

She finally bit. "Why?"

"Because they didn't want any more violents on the media," he explained innocently.

"That does it!" she exclaimed. "I am going to throw you into the thorn bushes!"

"Please don't; that would nettle me."

She took a step toward him, but was interrupted by Volney's squeal of laughter. Embarrassed, she faced away instead.

"I suspect she is the one who got nettled," Marrow remarked. They went on in silence. Soon they passed the eye queue vine, and the lost vitamin F, and the other items, until they passed the place where Bria had been. Esk remembered her kisses of apology, and felt himself flushing.

"Here is where the brassie picked up that accommodation spell," Marrow remarked.

"The what?" Esk asked, startled.

"The lost accommodation spell. Elves and other creatures use them when they want to breed with folk the wrong size or type."

"How can it be lost, if the elves use it?" Chex asked.

"It's not listed in the Lexicon, just as the eye queue is not, so it is lost," Marrow explained patiently.

"Just how does an accommodation spell accommodate?" Esk asked, now quite interested. He remembered how friendly

Bria had become about that time, and wished he had realized the spell's nature before.

"If an elf wishes to breed with a human being, or an ogre or whatever, the accommodation spell, when invoked, makes them appear to be of similar size. Thus they can accomplish their desire with reasonable dispatch."

"Suppose they are different in type, rather than in size?" Esk asked. "If, for example, one were flesh and the other metal?"

"The spell would make them compatible," Marrow said. "Those elven spells are quite potent. They could breed."

"I suspect that someone has designs on someone," Chex remarked. She glanced at Esk's flush. "And that someone doesn't mind very much."

"Is it, uh, one of those one-time spells?" Esk asked. "Like the pathfinder, where one person can only—?"

"No, it's continually invokable," Marrow said. "I was haunting an elf once, in a dream, and he was living with a mermaid on a regular basis. He was afraid of death, not of loss of the mermaid, and he had been with her for years." He made a fleshless grin. "I assumed the semblance of an elven skeleton and chased him right to the edge of the water, but then the mermaid put her arms around him and shielded him from the fear I represented, and I had to retire. She had a bosom like that of Chex, except that it was glistening wet."

"My pectorals get glistening wet when I exercise in hot weather," Chex remarked.

"But what—what about an unreal person?" Esk asked with tormented excitement. "How could she—?"

"We have already seen some progress, with Marrow himself," Chex murmured. "Sometimes the unreal becomes real, in association with real folk."

They continued walking the path, but Esk was hardly aware of the other details along the way. Had Bria's apologies really been because of the nature of her culture, or to impress him? She had impressed him, all right! But what had been her motive? Was her true interest in him, or in getting unlost, or in trying to become real?

The more he considered it, the more it seemed to him that she had wanted some avenue out of her predicament, and he was what had been available. So she had left the gourd with him, and now had independence of a sort. She could use that accommodation spell with any other male; why should she bother with him? He wished that thought did not bother him so much.

"Well, look at that!" Chex exclaimed, startling him out of his reverie. "Our path diverges from the Lost Path!"

"But the containment vpell—ivn't it lovt?" Volney asked.

"Perhaps not in quite the way we assumed," Chex said. "Or perhaps there is a section of this lost path that is neither easy nor safe, so we must detour past it."

They followed the pathfinder's path. It led into a region completely different from their recent experience. Splashes of color formed in the air above it, spreading and changing and dissolving. Strange sounds sounded, groans and whines and unpleasant laughter. Smells wafted by, some like perfume, some like rotting brains.

"It is good to return to conventional horrors," Marrow said enthusiastically.

"That's right," Chex said. "This is the origin of bad dreams; I had almost forgotten."

"Yes. These are the sensations experienced by those alone and nervous. Aren't they lovely?"

"Lovely," she agreed with resignation.

Then a huge face formed above them, its eyes glowing. "Whoo invades theese mmy premisesss?" it demanded windily.

"Oh, go retire to the Lost Path!" Chex snapped at it. "We've been through enough already."

"Oooh, sooo?" the face asked, scowling. The mouth opened wide, impossibly wide, until it was larger than the face itself. From it came another entire face, uglier than the first, with a huge warty nose and daggerlike teeth.

"Tressspasssers!" this new face hissed.

"Look, would you *mind?*" Chex asked impatiently. "We are trying to get somewhere, and we're getting tired of routine spooks. Just let us alone."

"Aarrgh!" the face growled. It opened its mouth, and the dagger teeth flashed. From this orifice came a third face, even worse, with little dancing flames in lieu of eyes, and a beak instead of a nose, and a hole like a deep cave for a mouth.

"Will you leave off?" Chex shouted. She unslung her bow, nocked an arrow, and let it fly at the beak.

"Uh, that might not be wise," Esk said, somewhat too late. He was amazed at the facility with which she had attacked the face. He had known that centaurs were good with bows, but had not realized just how good.

The arrow passed right through the beak, for it was only an image in the sky. But the face reacted with outrage. It roared, sending down a blast of frigid air admixed with sleet, and lunged down at them. Before they could move, the gaping orifice closed on them. The monster had swallowed their party whole!

The temperature plummeted, and the sleet quickly coated them with ice. In a moment they found themselves standing on a snow-covered hill, with the wind howling around them, driving off any heat remaining in their flimsy bodies.

"You're right," Chex said, her teeth chattering. "I shouldn't have done that."

They huddled together for scant warmth, except for Marrow, who wasn't affected, though the snow was caking on his bones. The storm raged around them, blotting out the sun and, indeed, the sky. They were unable to look into the wind; the whole scene was just the rush of air. It was mean in the belly of the air monster.

And it was increasing. The force of the wind was threatening to sweep them right off the mountain, even before they froze to death. "S-some easy p-path!" Esk chattered.

"I believe this is the realm of the Element of Air," Marrow commented. "The gourd annex, of course. Air becomes quite stormy when aroused."

"Fanvy that!" Volney muttered from almost under the snow.

"Fancy that," Chex repeated. "Let's burrow down for some warmth until this passes."

"It will not pass," Marrow said. "When Air is offended, it will not rest until it destroys its offender."

Indeed, the storm was still intensifying. The sleet and snow blasted at them like sharp sand. Their huddle was not effective; there was too much exposed surface, and the wind and cold were too intense.

"We shall have to tunnel down below it," Chex said. "Only I am unable to tunnel well, and am afraid of close confinement. Only the knowledge that this is all the world of the gourd has enabled me to endure the subterranean passages we have navigated hitherto."

"I am able to tunnel," Volney said. He donned his special talons and more or less dived into the snow, sending up a shower of white. In a moment he disappeared into the hole he was excavating, with only the flying refuse signaling his activity.

"Your fear of confinement did not manifest in your bad dream," the skull remarked.

"That is true," she agreed, surprised. "I was more afraid of rejection than of getting squashed. If I conquered my deepest fear, I should be able to conquer my lesser fear." She squared her shoulders. "At any rate, I will try. I think at this point I would rather be squoze than froze."

"But it will take too long to dig a hole in the ground big enough for all of us," Esk said.

"We can make a snow fort to shelter us partially until the digging is complete," Chex said. She tried to move snow with her hands, but they quickly turned blue, and her activity slowed; she was freezing. "Oh, if only I had a shovel!" she exclaimed, tucking her hands under her wings.

"I will be your shovel," Marrow said. "Kick me."

"What?" Esk asked.

"Kick me apart and form my bones into a shovel," the skeleton clarified.

"Oh, yes!" Chex agreed. "Bend over."

Marrow bent over, and she turned around and delivered a powerful kick to his bone posterior. His bones flew apart, but as they landed they connected in a chain. Chex formed this chain into a crude shovel, with the long leg bones serving as the handle and the times of the rib cage serving as the scoop. There were a number of bones left over, so Esk formed these into a somewhat clumsier second shovel with the grinning skull as the scoop. There was a linkage of tiny bones between the shovels; it seemed that Marrow never came completely apart.

They proceeded to dig, and it went very well. The energy they expended warmed them, and the shovels worked very well despite their seeming clumsiness. Apparently the magic of the skeleton facilitated whatever task his bones were shaped to. Soon they had a massive excavation, and the force of the howling winds was first cramped and then cut off.

Meanwhile Volney was still boring down. Abruptly his head appeared in the hole. "I have found a cave," he announced. "However, it may not be wive to enter it."

"Why not?" Esk asked. "We can't stay here long; we'll freeze!"

"There may be another monvter."

Chex paused in her labor. "It is a warm cave?"

"Comfortable. But—"

"Then let's chance the monster!" she exclaimed.

"But what about the path?" Esk asked. "We have to follow the path!"

"The path iv there," Volney said.

"That does it," Chex said. "If I can scramble down your hole, I'm going to!"

"In a moment," Volney said. He resumed tunneling, and the hole widened rapidly. Soon it was wide enough to allow Chex to squeeze through—or so she judged.

"Push me when I need it," she told Esk, handing him her shovel. "Ignore me if I scream; I may foolishly panic." She had to lean her head and shoulders way forward, and grasp her front legs with her hands, and stretch her hind feet out behind. It looked like an extremely uncomfortable position for her, but she simply did what she had to to get by.

Volney helped pull her from below, and Esk helped push her from above, but the thickest part of her body wedged in tight and would not move. She was stuck.

"Now what do we do?" Esk asked rhetorically.

"Use one of my bones as a lever to pry her out," the skull said.

Startled, Esk almost dropped it. But why shouldn't Marrow talk when re-formed into a shovel? He spoke by magic anyway. He set his shovel, which had arm bones for its handle, at the end of Chex's shovel, forming a double-length pole. "Can you hold firm if I push at the side?"

"Certainly," the skull said. "We skeletons pride ourselves on our rigidity."

Esk slid the business end of the shovel/pole down where the centaur was wedged, then slowly leaned outward on the handle, trying to wedge her body in just that amount needed to enable it to pass. It didn't work.

"A little to the left," the skull suggested.

Esk tried again, to the left, beside one of her folded wings. "Yes, that's it," the skull said. "I can feel the give, here. A little more . . ."

Esk pushed a little harder. Suddenly Chex gave a wiggle, and her torso slid down a little. It was working.

Following Marrow's suggestions, Esk pried carefully in different places, each time getting the torso down a bit more. Finally it slid the rest of the way down. She was through.

Esk dropped down behind her. The hole debouched in a cave, where the centaur and the vole were now standing. In the light from the hole he had come from, Esk saw that Chex was touching up some scrapes on her hide. "I, ah, had to pry a little," he said.

"Good thing, too," she said. "I was in danger of suffocating, not to mention panicking." Indeed, she seemed shaken, but she had survived the experience.

It was warmer in the cave, and that was a blessing. He spotted the faint glow of the pathfinder path; it did indeed pass this way. But what was this about a monster?

There was an ear-grinding bellow from the direction the path led. There was, indeed, a monster.

They exchanged glances. "But we can't go back," Chex said. "Even if I could squeeze through, going up, I wouldn't care to; there's only the angry Element of Air up there."

"And it is supposed to be safe," Esk said. "So far, it has been scary, but we haven't actually been hurt."

"Vo far," Volney agreed, twitching his whiskers disapprovingly.

They moved on along the path. It wasn't long before they found the source of the roaring. It was a huge face set in the floor of the cave, whose mouth was a cave in itself, and whose eyes were steaming vents.

Chex paused at the chin. "The last face was that of the Element of Air," she said, "at least as personified here in the gourd. That should make this one the personification of the Element of Earth."

"Growerr!" the mouth roared, and sulfurous gases fumed up, making them cough.

But the path led into this mouth.

"Let's put Marrow back together while we consider," Chex said.

"No need," the skull said. "You may need a shovel or a lever again—or a weapon. Wait till we're clear of these difficulties, if you don't mind carrying me."

"I don't mind," Esk said. He was coming to respect the skeleton's properties increasingly. Marrow was a very versatile fellow.

"If we invult thiv fave, it could be movt uncomfortable," Volney warned.

That gave Esk an idea. "So let's flatter it!" he said.

Chex nodded. "Perhaps we could have had an easier transition through Air, if I had not lost my temper. That was a most uncentaurish thing for me to do."

"Have you ever seen a handsomer face?" Esk asked loudly. "One with more, uh earthy features?"

"Why, I'm not sure I have," Chex replied. "It is a most appropriate sculpture."

The huge mouth stretched into a smile. The roaring abated.

"Let's go in and see what other wonders are here," Esk said. "I'm sure it is even prettier inside than outside."

"That is certainly possible," Chex agreed. "We do tend to forget how much we owe to the Element of Earth. Without it we would have very little substance."

The smile stretched into a satisfied grin. A large stony tongue protruded, forming into a ramp.

They walked down this ramp, into the mouth. There was no squeeze at all.

After a short descent, the ramp leveled out into a winding road through a network of caves. Stalactites hung from the ceiling, and there were magnificent pillars rising from below, their points seeking those of the stalactites with uncanny accuracy. Some were of prettily colored stone, showing green and red and yellow in merging bands. Some were crystalline, translucent, seeming almost too delicate to survive any shudder of the ground in the region. Some glowed, providing soft light for the path. Now it required no stretch of imagination to compliment the beauty of this region; it was indeed lovely.

There were also chambers of broken stones, but even these were remarkable. The stones were assorted gems, ranging from multicolored quartz to scintillating diamonds. Here Chex's female nature asserted itself. "We are merely passing through," she said, "but I wonder—do you think it would be all right if I took one little fragment of this lovely purple amethyst? It is such pretty stone!"

"If the Element of Earth doesn't object," the skull said.

Chex leaned down to pick up one stone, from a mound half her height. "May I keep this one?" she asked. "I promise to treasure it forever, and my memory of this region."

From the walls of the cave there came a soft purring.

Esk resolved to try the positive approach first, in all future encounters with strange folk or forces. What a difference it had made in this case!

Finally they came to a wall of fire. "This promises to be more of a challenge," Chex remarked. "How do we enter the Annex of the Element of Fire without getting burned?"

"I suspect you will have to become flames," the skull said.

Chex laughed, then sobered. "That was not humor," she concluded.

"It certainly isn't funny," Esk said. "I don't want to get burned up."

"Perhapv more imaginavhion?" Volney asked.

"You mean make another picture of a door, and step through it?" Chex asked. "But if beyond is the realm of fire, we would still be burned."

Esk pondered. "We insulted Air, and almost got wiped out in a snowstorm. We complimented Earth, and had a very pleasant tour. Suppose we compliment Fire? These Elements have power, and they can make things hard or easy for us if they choose."

Chex nodded. "If Air could almost freeze us to death,

maybe Fire can refrain from burning us to death, if it chooses. But how do we compliment Fire?"

"You might try telling it the truth," Marrow's skull said.

"The truth?" Esk asked. "That we don't want to get burned?"

"That we have a mission to perform, and need its help."

It was Esk's turn to nod. "I'll try it."

He faced the wall of fire. "O Element of Fire," he intoned, "we are four travelers who must pass through your realm. May we talk to you?"

A giant face formed in the wall, with eyes like sunspots and a mouth like a monstrous magnetic flux. "Ooooh?" it inquired hotly.

"Yes, we have traversed Air and Earth, and now we come to you. We have used you in our cooking and to heat us when we are cold. We appreciate your power, but we cannot touch you without being hurt. Will you let us pass without being burned?"

The face considered. "You must be-come flame," it said, enunciating each syllable with a flare of fire.

"But—" Esk began.

"We can become flame—without being hurt?" Chex cut in.

"Yes—if you ac-cept," the fireface said.

"And we can go on to the next realm?"

"Yes."

"Then we accept," she said. "How do we become flame?"

For answer, the mouth opened into a big fiery circle.

"We have to trust the word of the Element of Fire," Chex said. Then she leaped into the circle.

She vanished. In her place was only a dancing flame in the shape of a centaur.

Esk stared, horrified. "It burned her up!" he whispered.

The centaur-flame turned and made a beckoning motion.

"No—that is her," the skull said. "She has become flame. Throw me in next."

Esk's hand was shaking, but he heaved the bone staff, through the hoop. It converted into a flame the shape of a skeleton.

"It musvt be true," Volney said. "The path iv vuppoved to be vafe, remember. Heave me up nekvt."

Esk leaned down and locked his hands together. The vole put a hind foot in, then heaved as Esk heaved, and managed to flop into the circle. He too disappeared in flame.

Now it was Esk's turn. He contemplated the ring of fire, and quailed. Was it really safe to pass through that hoop, or had the others been burned up and mocking flame images substituted? How could he be sure? Chex had conquered her claustrophobia and entered Earth; could he conquer his fear of being burned and trust his body to Fire?

He hesitated, unable to take the plunge. The three fire folk beckoned him from beyond. But fire demons would do that, too; it was no proof that his friends were all right.

Then he thought about how he might escape, if he did not enter the flame. The path that had brought them here could not be traveled the other way; there were too many barriers, blank walls, one-way pictures and such. He could not return alone; he had to be with someone who had the pathfinder spell that could ferret out a new path. So he was lost, by himself. He might as well perish in the flame.

That gave him the doubtful confidence to take the plunge. He took a breath, held it, and jumped into the hoop.

There was a flare of vertigo. Then he landed on a jet of fuel, and it buoyed him and sustained him.

"Welcome aboard," Chex said. "For a moment I thought you weren't going to rejoin us!"

Esk looked down at himself. He was fashioned of flame!

"Be careful not to stray from a source of fuel," Volney cautioned. "You can fade quickly if careless."

Esk did a double take. "You're not lisping!" he exclaimed, his body flaring brightly with his surprise.

"I never lisped!" the fire-vole said indignantly. "It is you who has corrected his hissing."

Esk decided not to argue the case. He quickly verified the fuel situation; if he stepped off his jet, his body became anemic and threatened to flare out. There were many jets here, so there was no problem; he simply had to step from one to another.

He looked at Chex. She was changing shape!

"Flame is malleable," she said, observing his look. He wasn't sure how any of them saw or heard or spoke, but they

did. "I have trouble keeping my posterior hot, so I am ex-
perimenting with a shape that is more efficient for this purpose." She continued to change, until she lost all semblance
of centaurhood and most resembled the flame on a big candle.
Then she extended a pseudopod of fire to an adjacent jet, and
flared up there, and let her prior self die out.

Esk tried it. He merged his two feet into one base, and felt
better; more of the fuel was pouring into his being. He
reached for the next jet, and saw that it was an extension of
flame rather than an arm; why take the trouble to shape a
useless arm, when all he needed was the connection?

Soon all of them looked like candle flames, even Marrow.
They commenced their trip across the realm of Fire. The path
showed in the form of a pattern of fuels, whether comprised
of just gas, or flowing liquid, or sturdy solids. They could
endure on any of it, though their color and heat varied as the
fuels did. The flavors of the fuels varied, and their reliability.
Gas was green and flickering, while coal was blue and even,
and wood was yellow and sputtering. They became connois-
seurs of fuels, for these were the stuff of life. To be without
fuel was to perish: a horrible thought.

They crossed the field of fire, and came to a sharp bound-
ary: water. A seemingly endless lake stretched across the
plain, terminating the fuel and therefore the fire. It seemed
bleak indeed. But the path continued into it.

"We thank you for your hospitality, Fire," Esk said. "Now
we must move on through Water."

A flame face appeared. "I don't envy you," it said, and
flamed out.

"Oh, Element of Water," Esk said, addressing the lake.
"We are four travelers who must pass through your territory.
May we do so in safety and comfort?"

A face formed on the surface of the lake, with eyes like
whirlpools. "Dive in," it mouthed wetly.

"But at the moment we are in the form of flames," Esk
said. "We fear being abruptly quenched."

The water mouth simply opened into a widening ripple
ring. There was no other answer.

"I will try it," Marrow said. "I have no life to lose."

The skeleton-flame leaped into the water, hissed hugely, and flickered out. "Oops," Volney said.

Then a bone-white fish poked its snout out of the water. It spouted a stream of water toward them, then turned tail.

Esk looked at Chex. "Marrow?"

"So it would seem," she said.

"Then I'll follow." Esk dived into the water.

He felt the shock of the cutoff of his flame. But at the same time he felt the pleasant pressure of the cool water. He inhaled—and felt the water surge through his gills. He was now a fish.

There was another splash, and a new fish appeared. This one had brown scales and a large body with white fins above that fluttered like wings. "Hello, Chex," he said in fishtalk.

"This is very like flying!" she replied, pleased.

"This is very like living," the bone-white fish said, wiggling its bony fins.

There was one more splash, and a squat fish with short fins appeared. "This is very like tunneling," it said, also pleased.

They swam across the Element of Water, following the glowing trail of bubbles that marked their path. They passed waving seaweed plants, and bubbling underwater springs, and regions where the sunlight speckled the upper surface, and shallows where white sand lay like a desert with dunes, and deeps where the seafloor was lost in the gloom of the unfathomable unknown.

It was, indeed, like flying. Chex fairly danced, her upper fins stroking like wings, moving up toward the surface and down toward the floor. Esk had never longed to fly, but now he understood how it was with her, there was a unique freedom in this mode that made landbound travel seem oppressively dull.

Other fish came to watch them pass, but these did not intrude on the marked path. Some were large and looked hungry, but the path was evidently enchanted to keep them off.

In due course they reached the far side of the Element of Water, gourd annex. The path lead through a translucent vertical wall, and there seemed to be no special challenge to passing through it, except for their fishly status.

"O Void," Esk spoke, "we are four travelers, needing to

pass through your territory on a quest. Will you—"

He broke off, horrified. "What am I saying? *That's the Void!* No one escapes from it!"

"Except the night mares," Chex agreed, equally horrified. "My dam was here once, and had to be carried out by night mares. She had to pay a fee of half her soul for that!"

"And my dam—my mother too!" Esk said. "And my father—they were left with no more than one full soul between them. We can't go there!"

"You forget," Marrow said. "This is not the true Void we face, but merely its annex. This is the dream of the Void, which horrifies sleepers, even as you are being horrified now. It is no more binding on you than the gourd itself."

Chex nodded, which was a nice accomplishment in her fishly form. "I suppose we can risk it then, since the path leads into it, and the path is supposed to be safe." She sounded extremely uncertain.

"We either trust it or we don't," Esk said. "Since we must pass through it to reach the containment spell, that is what we must do." He hoped he sounded more assured than he felt. His knees felt weak, which was alarming because he didn't have any knees at the moment.

Esk repeated his ritual address to the Void, but there was no response. They discussed this, and concluded reluctantly that if they could swim through the barrier, it was probably safe to do so, and they would assume appropriate forms in the next Element. Perhaps even their own.

This time, mutually nervous, they linked hands (fins), and swam forward into the barrier together.

They found themselves floating in the air above a featureless plain. The water was gone, but they remained fish.

"I thought I might revert to my own form," Chex said, surprised.

As she spoke, she did so, becoming a centaur, floating in the air without flying. "And be tied to the ground," she added, startled again. Whereupon she dropped to the ground, her hooves striking with clunks.

"Then why aren't the rest of us reverting?" Esk asked.

The rest of them reverted similarly. Marrow was in his assembled form, the complete skeleton.

"I think I would have settled for a fleshly state," he said wistfully. And became a living man, fully fleshed, naked.

"I think we have a special situation here," Chex said, with a certain centaurish understatement.

"Very special," Volney agreed, assuming the form of another man.

"This is like the Fire realm," Chex said. "There we could shape our forms, and Volney spoke as we do; but here it is more so."

"I had noted your amelioration of speech," Volney agreed. "I always wondered what it would be like to walk upright, as human folk do."

"Or to be fleshed, as living folk are," Marrow added, assuming the form of a male centaur.

"Or to be masculine," Chex said, turning male.

"Um, we may be in danger of getting distracted from our mission," Esk warned.

The others immediately reverted to their natural forms.

"I will be relieved when we finally reach the containment spell," Chex said. "We could be distracted for eternity in a place like this, and the danger of that might be similar to that of the gourd via the peephole, not to mention the risk to the Vale of the Vole."

"All too true," Volney agreed. "There are dangers other than physical."

They followed the path, which wound generally downward. At first the scenery was blank, but gradually trees and fields and bushes developed.

Chex paused. "At the risk of distraction, let me pose a question," she said. "Is it possible that there is no scenery, and that we are imagining it? If so, things may not be what they seem."

"Easy to test," Esk said. "Let's all concentrate on there being no scenery, and see if it disappears."

They concentrated, and it disappeared.

"My next question," Chex said slowly, "is, are we also imagining the path?"

Esk whistled. "We'd better find out!"

They concentrated, but the path remained.

"That, at least, is genuine," Chex said, relieved. "We can

imagine any scenery we want, just so long as we don't lose the path."

They proceeded, and the scenery formed again, this time more elaborately and less credibly. It seemed to be a joint effort, with voles and winged centaurs flying in the distance, and trees growing in the manner of bones and bearing skulls for fruit, and brass girls peeking from behind translucent metal curtains that showed their bronzed legs.

Then the path led into a loop. There was no question about this; they circled the loop several times, verifying that it went nowhere.

"I think we have come to the end," Esk said. "But where is the containment spell?"

"Abolish the scenery," Marrow suggested.

They concentrated, and their surroundings became blank again. Now they saw that the path's loop enclosed a deep hole. The terrain simply curved down until lost in a blackness so deep that it seemed to suck them in; they had to yank their gazes away.

"But what is it?" Volney asked.

"I suspect it is the center of the Void," Marrow said. "The black hole from which nothing returns."

"But if the spell is down there, how can we bring it out?" Esk asked.

"You forget again," Marrow said. "This is the Void annex, not the Void itself. This is a representation of the center. We might indeed be able to fetch something from it."

"But the path does not go into it, just around it," Volney said. "That suggests that the spell is not in it, but—"

"But *is* it!" Chex exclaimed.

"The containment spell is the Void?" Esk asked, confused.

"I think I see the logic," Chex said. "What contains a wiggle swarm?"

"Nothing," Esk said. "You have to catch and kill every one, or there will be another swarm later."

"Not so," Volney protested.

"Point taken," Chex said quickly. "But we agree that there is no wall that will bar swarming wiggle larvae; they *zzapp* through everything until they run out of energy or find their particular type of rock or get killed."

"True," Volney agreed.

"So the notion of a containment spell is a strange one," she continued. "It claims to contain the uncontainable. However, there is one thing that contains anything inside it, without exceptions, and that is—"

"The Void!" Esk and Volney chorused.

"The Void," she agreed. "My dam and Esk's parents escaped the outer region of the Void only through the intercession of the night mares, who alone can range such regions freely. So that outer wall of the Void should contain the wiggles too, not hurting them, just preventing them from escaping it, until they run out of energy and expire. They would die happy, imagining that they are in their favorite rock, but they would not reach beyond it. In due course all of them would be gone, except those who drilled down and actually found their type of rock within the enclosed region. The Void is indeed the containment spell."

Her logic was compelling. "But how can we take the—the Void with us to the Vale?" Esk asked.

"Obviously we can't," she said. "But perhaps we can take this representation of it, and it will do the job."

"Imagination won't stop a wiggle swarm!" Esk protested. "A wiggle larva has very little imagination; it is single-minded."

"True. But I suspect that this gourd Void operates like the peephole. If we take it to the Vale and set it up, it will lock the wiggles into the real Void, which is a region just like this only more permanent, and the effect will be the same. Then all we shall have to do is return it to the gourd, and—"

She broke off as the implication sank in. Marrow was the one who voiced it. "How do we set up the Void there without being trapped in it ourselves, and how do we return it to the gourd when we are done with it?"

"There must be a way," Esk said. "We really have two problems: getting it there, and getting it back—without being trapped in it."

Marrow leaned over the hole, peering at it. "Don't do that!" Chex exclaimed. "If you fall in—"

"It is only a representation," the skeleton reminded her. He reached down, picked up the edge of the hole, and folded the hole in half. Then, as the others stared, he folded it again, into a quarter, and continued until it was a small wad he could hide in one bone fist. "The problem of moving it has been solved. I was concerned that I would be unable to handle it, because the demon folk cannot handle anything of the gourd, but it seems I am not made of the same stuff as the demons."

"Evidently not," Chex agreed. "I did not realize that demons were limited in that respect."

"Demons, being soulless, are barred from handling things that relate intimately to souls," Marrow explained. "Most of the things of the gourd relate, for it is the living conscience, the guardian of the soul, that summons the dreams."

The blank scenery around them was gone. Now they stood in a large chamber, evidently the real-life setting for the illusion that was this aspect of the realm of the gourd. The illusion had faded with the folding of the central part of it.

"Uh, yes, so it seems," Esk agreed. "We can take it there, and back here the same way. But only if we can be next to it to pick it up, and when the wiggles swarm, we'll be so full of *zzapp* holes that we'll be dead."

"I am already dead," Marrow reminded him. "I shall be glad to remain beside the hole until the wiggle swarm is done."

"And the rest of us can remain outside," Chex said. "Marrow, I think you have made the completion of our mission possible!" She leaned down and kissed the top of his skull.

The skeleton seemed disconcerted. "Was that an apology?"

"An apology?" she asked.

"You either kissed me or knocked skulls, and that means—"

She laughed. "Yes, that was an apology for ever thinking that you were not as genuine a person as any of the rest of us!" She glanced about. "Now let's have—let's see—Volney use the pathfinder spell to find us a path to the zombie gourd exit. He hasn't used that spell before." She brought out the pathfinder spell and handed it to the vole.

"Gladly," Volney said.

# 15
# MONSTERS

Three women welcomed them back to Castle Roogna: old Latia, mature Bria, and young Ivy. Everyone else was tied up with the search for the missing Good Magician Humfrey.

Esk happened to be leading as they arrived at the orchard, so he got the first brunt of it.

"Did you get the containment spell?" Latia asked.

"Have I caused you embarrassment?" Bria asked.

"What was it like in the gourd?" Ivy asked.

Esk addressed them in order. "We got it. Yes, you have. It was weird."

Then Marrow showed his fist full of Void, distracting Latia, and Chex started giving a travelogue for Ivy, leaving only Bria.

"Then I must apologize," she said eagerly. "What did I do?"

"You used me to get you out of the gourd, and to try to become real."

She had been about to embrace him, but now she paused. "Yes, that's true. But you know, my mother, Blythe, always did rather regret that she never got to know the ogre, your father, better, or get out more into this world. She spoke of it sometimes, and I could see how sad she was. It wasn't that she was unhappy in the City of Brass, just that she wondered what might have been. I inherited that wondering; that's why I wandered, and finally got myself lost. I was looking for a way out, but I couldn't find it. Then you came, and I knew right away that not only could you get me out, but you were sort of cute too. Then when I learned that you were the son of Mother's ogre, I just knew I wanted you for myself. When I found the accommodation spell I knew it was possible. I knew you were looking for a flesh girl, and that you wouldn't like my type without a lot of encouragement, so I just had to act fast if I was to have any hope at all. That's the whole of it."

"I don't think so," Esk said. "Why did you think I wouldn't like you?"

"Well, I'm not exactly like the flesh girls."

"You're still holding back."

"Whatever happened to you in the gourd, you learned a lot!" she exclaimed.

"I learned my deepest fear, and now I can recognize that kind of fear in others. You must have good reason to think I won't like you if I know the truth."

"It's the soul," she whispered.

"The what?"

"We creatures of the dream realm don't have souls. We can't be real without them."

"You want my soul?" he exclaimed, shocked.

"Maybe—half of it?" she said timidly.

"You can't have any of it!" he exclaimed, outraged.

"Yes, of course," she said almost inaudibly. "Then let me apologize, and I will leave you alone."

"No! No apology! I've had enough of that artifice!" He spun away from her and stalked off.

The other dialogues were winding down. "We muvt move on to the Vale," Volney said. "The monvters will be arriving."

"Start in the morning!" Ivy exclaimed. "There's so much I want to hear!"

They agreed. They were tired from their day's trek. The path out through the gourd had been almost as convoluted as the one going in, and then they had had to walk from the gourd to Castle Roogna. It would be better to start fresh in the morning.

Next day they set forth, with Volney leading the way, then Chex, Esk, Marrow, Latia, and Bria. The brass girl had not spoken to him since his rebuff of her desire, and he felt a little guilty about that, but a lot angry about being asked for such a thing. Half his soul!

Then he remembered something Chex had said, and speeded up to walk abreast of her. "Didn't your mother lose half her soul? To get out of the Void?"

"Yes. That was the price of the night mares. Souls are in great demand in the realm of the gourd. Your folks paid it too."

"They never talked much about that aspect of their experience," he said. "I never thought they had half souls."

"Oh, they don't. The Night Stallion gave back a soul at the end, so they each had a full one again. They probably never thought about the matter since."

Esk wasn't sure of that. "But your mother—"

"My dam never got hers back. But she really didn't mind. You see, that was the half soul that went to Mare Imbri, and enabled her to become real and survive the loss of her body in the true Void and become a day mare. Chem grew her soul back in time, anyway, so really didn't lose anything."

"Souls—can grow back?" He had heard of this, but now it was important to get the matter quite straight.

"Oh, yes, if there's something to start with. That's how babies get souls, I understand; they take some from each parent, and grow the rest, and the parents grow back what they have lost. So, while I understand it is not fun losing part of your soul, it's not torture either. I would not have a soul of my own if my dam had not been able to grow hers back to full strength. Why do you ask?"

"Bria wants half mine."

Chex gazed down at him sidelong. "Oh, so it has come to that? I can't say I am surprised."

"That's why she's been playing up to me. For my soul, so she can become real."

"Oh, is that how you see it?"

"What other way is there to see it? She decided to use me to get her out of the gourd. I thought she liked me."

"Is there a conflict between the two?"

"Isn't there? You don't use someone you really like."

"I'm not sure of that. Liking and sharing—they can go together."

"I guess she'd like me to give her half my soul!"

"But she has a home in the gourd. Why would she want to remain out here?"

Esk spread his hands. "I guess she just likes it better here. She says she likes exploring, and her mother knew my father."

"But why would she like it better, when it's so strange for her?"

"What are you getting at?"

"I wouldn't want to go to a strange realm and stay there the rest of my existence, unless I had a very good reason."

"I really don't see any reason for her."

"If I met someone who lived in that other realm, and I wanted to be with him, and could not unless I stayed there, then I think I might do what I had to, to arrange to stay."

Esk considered. "Are you saying that it's the other way around? She's not using me because she wants to stay, but she wants to stay because she likes me?"

"Well, I do wonder why she hasn't asked any other man for his soul. Surely she had opportunity while we were absent, but Ivy said Bria just kept mostly to herself and didn't say much. That she did no exploring, and seemed depressed, until you returned."

Esk shook his head. "I wish I knew her true motive."

"Why?"

"Because it makes a difference!" he flared. "If she just decided I was the handiest idiot with a soul to take—!"

"Why should it make a difference? You don't have to give her anything you don't want to give."

"What if I gave her my soul and she just went off elsewhere?"

"Then the resolution of that indecision might be worth it. It would certainly be a way to ascertain her true motive."

Confused, Esk didn't answer. He dropped back, his thoughts in a morass.

The path reached the intersection that led south to the Good Magician's castle and north toward the Vale. Volney went north, and they trailed along after him.

This path soon narrowed and curved eastward, following the contours of the land. Volney proceeded with sureness, but evening fell before they progressed very far along it. They had to camp for the night.

They foraged for fruits and tubers. Marrow and Bria helped, though neither needed to eat. The sight of her stirred him, like a breeze lifting the curtains of his confusion. If all she wanted was his soul, and she couldn't have that, why hadn't she simply gone elsewhere? She hardly needed to help them if she didn't want to.

Why should it make a difference to him, Chex had asked. Because Bria had kissed him and been soft in his arms and he wished he could have more of that. Maybe he was a fool, but that was the way he felt.

Chex had told him exactly how to learn the truth.

He went to Bria. "I'll give you half my soul," he said.

"What, to get rid of me?" she snapped. "I don't want it!"

"Then why did you ask for it before?"

"I—" Then she turned away. "Oh, never mind."

This was not at all what he had expected. "No, I really want to know."

"Because I was foolish," she said. "I thought—" But again she broke off.

Esk began to see the answer. "Because you thought we could maybe—have a life together?"

"I should have known better! I'm just a brassie from the gourd! I'm not even alive! Why should anyone want to—to—" She dabbed at her face with a corner of her skirt.

She sounded exactly as uncertain of her value as he had been of his. And as prickly about admitting it. His understanding expanded. "Someone might."

"Oh, sure," she said corrosively. "Who?"

"Only another fool," he said. "I think I owe you an apology."

She gazed at him, a brass tear on her cheek. "You mean you want to—?"

"I misunderstood your motive, I think. I thought you wanted my soul, not me. It hurt."

"Oh, Esk," she said, abruptly softening. "I—"

"Take half my soul. Then do what you want."

"Let's just apologize for now," she said. "I want you to be sure."

They apologized to each other, her way, and Esk was sure already. But she wouldn't take his soul yet.

Chex saw them holding hands, a little later, and made no comment. Neither did any of the others. That meant they understood.

In the morning they resumed the trek, and this time Bria walked with Esk. The path continued eastward without unusual event; it did seem to be enchanted, and now that the little dragons had gone, there were no other threats.

By evening they reached the Vale of the Voles. It was a sorry sight: a broad valley overrun by scrub, much of which was dying. Through it ran a channel as straight as a metal pole, along which ugly brown water coursed. There was a bothersome humming sound throughout.

"That's funny," Esk said. "I thought only demons could hear the hummers."

"They have gotten worve," Volney replied. "Now there are vo many that everyone can hear them. But they bother the demonv worve than uv."

The demons were there too, cruising around recklessly. The voles were evidently keeping low, so as not to attract the notice of the irate demons.

"What a wasteland," Chex remarked.

A demon in the form of a small black cloud made a right-angle turn and zeroed in on her. "What did you call me, horseface?" it demanded.

"I wasn't talking to you," Chex replied. "I didn't even know you were there."

"That's a lie! You called me a wasteband!" the demon screeched. "I'll pulverize you!" A muscular arm sprouted from the cloud and formed a fist that cocked itself, aiming for her face.

"No," Esk said.

"Aw, you aren't worth the effort, mare-hair," the demon said, and drifted away.

"I may be mistaken," Latia said, "but I believe I see why the voles would like to be rid of the demons."

"They were not bothervome until the hummerv got bad," Volney said. "Now the Kill-Mee River makev everyone, vole and demon, bad tempered."

"The winged monsters and ogres may arrive any time," Esk said. "We'd better get a good night's rest before it gets hectic."

"Yes, indeed," Chex said. "We shall need to get organized too. Do we have any campaign plan?"

"Campaign plan?" Esk asked blankly.

"Who is going to direct the monsters? Exactly what are they going to do when they arrive?"

"Why, just wade into the demons and drive them off," Esk said.

"More likely the ogres will wade into the winged monsters, unless there is some organization."

"Uh, yes," Esk agreed, disgruntled. "But how do you organize ogres?"

"You establish an overall plan, then designate a liaison to their leader. The same for the winged monsters. Organization and discipline—that's the key to prevailing in any conflict. But first we need a leader."

"I guess, since you know how to do it—" Esk said, uncomfortably.

"A filly? Don't be ridiculous. It has to be a man."

"Why?"

"Because that's the nature of armies. They have male leaders."

"That's silly!" Esk protested. "The most competent one should be the leader."

"No. The most acceptable one must be the leader." She smiled. "And I think that is you, Esk. You are the only male human creature in this party, thus related to all others by blood or gender."

"Blood or gender?" Esk repeated, alarmed.

"Ogres, curse fiends, brassies, centaurs, and manlike skeletons all derive in some devious manner from human stock. That's blood, figuratively. Volney is male, as are you. So you have an affinity with each of the rest of us, and with those we are working with. You have some small basis for understanding each of our viewpoints, and we all know that, so we can accept you as our leader more readily than we could accept another creature. Does anyone disagree?" She glanced around.

The others shrugged.

"But I don't know anything about leadership!" Esk protested.

"A good leader asks advice, of course, and chooses as he thinks best. I suggest that you establish a campaign plan, and appoint liaisons to the several groups."

"Uh, yes," Esk agreed, still feeling out of sorts. "The plan is to wade into the demons and drive them out of the Vale. Any objections?"

"Yev," Volney said. "The demonv can dematerialive, and will do vo when threatened: How can we drive them out?"

"You're right," Esk said, chagrined. "How could I have forgotten! Uh, does anyone have a suggestion?"

"Yes," Latia said. "I happen to know a bit about demons. It is true that they can dematerialize at will, but it is also true that they cannot maintain that state indefinitely or they lose cohesion. I think they have to spend about ninety percent of their time in solid form. If they don't they start to dissipate into vapor, and cannot recover."

"But I thought demons were eternal!" Esk said.

"They are, but their material forms aren't. If they vaporize, and can't recover, they must remain vaporous, as clouds or similar, unable to have much tangible effect on physical things. They don't like that. I know of one case with a perpetually bad nature. He calls himself Cumulo Fracto Nimbus, the King of Clouds. He's really just a vaporized demon. He serves as a bad example for other demons; they don't want to be relegated to that state."

"But the demons can dematerialize for short periods," Esk

said. "So they can just do it when a monster attacks, then re-form. How can we get around that?"

"I was coming to that. If the monsters simply keep attack-ing, forcing the demons to constantly dematerialize, before long their vapor limit will be used up, and they will have to go. A concerted, continuous campaign should do it in a day or so. We just need to see that the demons get no rest in solid form."

"Say, yes!" Esk exclaimed. "And we'll have the monsters to do it! Thank you, Latia! That's a big help!"

"That's what I came for," she said, almost forgetting her dour nature so far as to smile. But not quite.

"Anymore objections or suggestions?" Esk asked, feeling better.

"Suppose the demons attack us?" Chex asked. "I mean not the monsters, who can take care of themselves, but those of this party who are vulnerable? They could disrupt our orga-nization, not to mention our lives."

Esk's feeling plummeted. "I never thought of that, either! We'll have to plan to protect ourselves. I can say no to those who attack me or anyone with me, and the others—I don't know."

"I can throw a curse," Latia said. "I have two bad ones stored up." She glanced at Bria. "That is presuming that the one I threw at you was, after all, a blessing."

"I think it was," Esk agreed, and Bria smiled at him.

"I can hide among my kind," Volney said. "The demonv cannot divtinguivh well between volev; we all look alike to them. I vhould be av vafe av any."

"Then I appoint you to be our liaison to the voles," Esk said. "And Chex to be liaison to the winged monsters, who should be able to protect her. I think Bria and Marrow can't be hurt. So maybe we aren't as vulnerable that way as we thought."

"Who will be liaison to the ogres—and to the demons?" Chex asked.

"The demons!" he exclaimed. "We're fighting them!"

"We need liaison to the enemy, too, so we can let the de-mons know what we want: their withdrawal from the Vale."

Esk considered. "Maybe Latia can be liaison to the ogres;

they were really impressed by her—uh, by the way she curdled water."

"By my ugliness," Latia said. "It's high time that paid off for me! Certainly I'll serve in that capacity."

"And for the demons, that leaves Marrow or Bria. Does one of you want to—?"

"I'll do it," Bria said. "I'll make myself extremely hard for them."

"Then I suppose Marrow is—is our reserve," Esk said.

"You will need a messenger, when you have information to impart or new directives to give to the scattered folk," Marrow said. "I can serve in that capacity."

"Yes, that's good," Esk agreed. "So I think we're pretty well organized, now. Let's sleep."

They did, but it took him a long time to relax. He was aware, now, of the formidable challenge ahead. He had somehow thought that once they got help and reached the Vale, everything would fall neatly into place. That wasn't so. People could get hurt!

Finally Bria came. "Put your head in my lap," she said. "I don't need to sleep."

He did so, and found her lap surprisingly soft. She stroked his hair, and it was very nice, and soon he slept.

It was stormy in the morning, which seemed appropriate. Ogres loved foul weather, and perhaps winged monsters did too. There was the sound of trees crashing down as something big and violent approached the Vale, and a big, winged shape sailed out of the swirling sky.

"Liaisons, get out there and intercept your folk!" Esk cried. "Before they encounter each other!"

Chex galloped off to the region where the winged monster was coming down, while Latia put on her ugliest face and clumped toward the forest crashing. "I will notify the volev," Volney said. "Can you find me if you need me?"

"Give me a hair of your pelt," Marrow said. "I can use it to orient on you."

Volney touched his flank with a talon, and several hairs came loose. The skeleton took one and put it to his nose. "Yes, I will know this scent."

"You can do that?" Esk asked, surprised. "Find one vole among hundreds, by smell?"

"Not exactly by smell," Marrow said. "I sense the essence of things magically, whether by light or by sound or by substance. I speak the same way. No offense intended, but it seems to me that your fleshly mechanisms are relatively clumsy."

"I suppose they are," Esk said. "We fleshly creatures do most things in the mundane manner, saving our magic for special things. That may be why we have talents. It has been said that in Xanth, some creatures have magic, while others are magic; I'm one of the former, and you are one of the latter."

"Yes, all my magic is needed just to handle my perceptions, communication, motion, and to keep my bones together. There is none left over for a separate talent. Perhaps that is why I would like to achieve the living state."

The skeleton's aspiration seemed to have evolved; usually before, Marrow had remarked on the inconvenience and messiness of the living functions.

"I think the same goes for me," Bria said. "Only I don't long for a magic talent, just for . . ."

"A soul," Esk said. "I told you, you could have half of mine."

"And I told you to wait until you're sure. I don't think it's the soul I want; that's just the means to the end."

"An end?" Esk asked. "What end?"

"Love. I don't think I can truly experience it without a soul. All I can experience is my futile longing for it."

"A soul," Marrow said. "Yes, of course that is necessary. I wonder whether anyone would share one with me?"

"Maybe if you got to know someone well enough," Esk said. "You certainly seem worthy of it."

Now Chex and Latia were returning, trailed by what turned out to be a stallion with a bird's head, and an ogre who—

"Grandpa!" Esk exclaimed. "Crunch Ogre!" For it was indeed he, the vegetarian ogre who had married a curse fiend actress, now grizzled with age but still the epitome of ogreishness: big, ugly and stupid.

"Me learn of plan, do what me can," Crunch said.

"And this is my own sire, Xap Hippogryph," Chex said happily. "He took this pretext to check up on me."

"These two can speak for their groups," Latia said. She grimaced. "Your grandfather says I remind him of his mate, who is beautifully ugly."

"That's great!" Esk said. "Now I know we'll have good contact with the ogres and winged monsters. Did you explain that they must not fight each other?"

The hippogryph squawked with distaste, and the ogre made a horrendous scowl. That was sufficient answer; they understood.

"But you will get to bash all the demons you want," Esk continued.

This time the squawk was joyous, and the ogre smiled, which was of course worse than his scowl.

Esk explained about the need to harass the demons steadily, until they departed the Vale just to find some place where they could put in some solid time in peace. Monster and ogre nodded; they were going to love this!

Now the forest behind shook with the horrible tread of many ogres, and the troubled sky darkened further with the arrival of many winged monsters. Crunch and Xap hastened to meet with their groups and explain things.

"You had better locate Volney and tell him that the action is about to begin," Esk told Marrow. "The voles will want to tunnel well out of the way."

"Immediately," the skeleton agreed, and headed off.

"How do I contact the demons?" Bria asked. "I don't know their leader, or even whether they have a leader."

"I think you will just have to go out and see whether any one of them looks like a leader, and then address that one. If he's not the leader, he can still act as liaison. Tell him that we won't leave until the demons do."

"I'll do that," she agreed.

"We had better rejoin our contacts," Chex said, "in case there are any questions or confusions."

"Yes," Latia agreed. "You know, I can see why my friend married that ogre. There's a certain splendor in all that brute power uncluttered by the restraints of intellect."

"Ogres do have their points," Esk said, feeling foolishly proud of his heritage.

They departed, and Esk found himself alone. It had been a long time since he had been alone, even for a minute, and he discovered that he felt uncomfortable with it.

Then the ogres waded into the Vale of the Vole, punching at demons with great gusto, and the winged monsters flew across the Vale, spearing demons with their claws with equal gusto. The weather continued to deprove, but Esk stood out in the wind and rain and watched the carnage with simple joy. The campaign to restore the Kiss-Mee River had begun!

A demoness appeared beside him. "So it *is* you!" she exclaimed. "Just as the brass girl said!"

Esk looked closely at her. "Oh, no—Metria!" he exclaimed. "What are you doing here?"

"I heard the forest shuddering, and saw the monsters massing above, so I was curious. Then I saw this strange metal woman, and she told me that you were running this show. Just what do you think you're doing, Pesk?"

"That's *Esk!* We think we're clearing the demons out of the Vale of the Vole." Indeed, as he spoke, there was a great splashing, as the ogres reached the channelized river and waded in, knocking out the retaining walls as they went. "You won't have the Kick-Mee River to kick around any more."

"Kick-Mee," she repeated. "That's almost clever, Esk."

"Thank you. Now go away. We have to restore the river you demons ruined."

"But we only did that to get rid of the hummers!" she protested.

"And did it work?"

"No," she confessed. "They're worse than ever."

"Well, we're only doing this to get rid of you demons."

"Do you think it will work?"

There was something about the way she inquired that bothered him. "Why don't you go back to my hideout and relax?" he asked nastily.

"It was getting dull there after you quit. We demons aren't happy unless we have someone to pester." She focused on him thoughtfully. "I think you're more of a creature than I

guessed, before. Let me do you that service we discussed."
Her dress dissolved, leaving her naked.

"Absolutely not!" Esk exclaimed. "You disgust me!"

"No, I never discussed you with anyone else. I didn't even remember you, till now."

"That's disgust as in ugh," Esk clarified. "You're confusing words again."

"Ugh," she agreed. "Thank you for that correction. Let's do this quickly, so I can still have time to bash a bird before they quit." She reached to embrace him.

He straight-armed her, but his hand passed right through her head without affecting her body. She embraced him hungrily, rubbing her lush torso against him. "Let me just get these clothes off you, you darling mortal man," she murmured.

"No!" Esk cried. This time it carried the force of his magic, and she had to desist.

She stood back slightly, considering him. "Why not, Esk? Don't you like women?"

"Sure I like women! I just don't like demons!"

She snapped her fingers. "That brass-ass! She's the one! I should have realized!"

"So what if she is?" he asked defensively, bothered that he should have to defend anything to a demoness.

"Esk, she's no more your kind than I am! She has no living flesh, no soul. Why be a fool?"

"What do you care what kind of a fool I am? You got my hideout; now leave me alone!"

"Well, I'll think about it," she said. "Meanwhile, I'll just serve as liaison to my folk."

"I don't want you as liaison!"

"Too bad," she said, and faded out with a superior smile.

The rain was easing, and the clouds thinning. But the melee was getting worse. Esk peered at the action, and discovered to his horror that the ogres and winged monsters were starting to fight each other. Even as he saw that, Marrow hurried back.

"I told Volney, then got caught in the scuffle," the skeleton said.

"Our monsters are starting to fight each other!" Esk said.

"Go find our ogre and winged monster liaisons and tell them to stop it! We haven't gotten rid of the demons yet!"

"Right away!" Marrow agreed, and hurried off again.

Bria ran up. "I found a liaison!" she cried. "A demoness who said she takes the message."

"I don't want that one!" Esk said. "That's the one I know from before! She came here and tried to—never mind."

"Oh, she did, did she?" Bria said with some asperity. "Well, two can play at that game!" She stepped out of her dress.

"What are you doing?" he asked, upset.

"I'm seducing you, of course." She came to embrace him.

"But there's a battle going on!"

"Yes, we'll have to hurry."

"But I thought you wanted half my soul!"

She paused as if startled, then recovered. "Yes, give me half your soul!"

Esk had promised, but he did not like this at all. This was not the way Bria had been before.

"Well, come on!" she said urgently.

"No. Not now," he said, feeling like a complete heel. Why was he reneging?

"Well, then, see if you get any of this!" she snapped, and her dress reappeared on her body. She stalked away, and was soon lost to view.

The campaign was falling apart, as the ogres and winged monsters fought each other instead of the demons. This had to be stopped—but how? He had *told* them not to fight each other!

Marrow returned. "The voles want to know why the monsters are fighting each other instead of the demons."

"I wish I knew!" Esk said. "Maybe the monsters lack discipline. Maybe a better leader would have prevented this."

Chex galloped back. "My sire says the ogres started it!" she exclaimed. "They just laid into the winged monsters they could reach!"

"We'll have to see what Latia reports," Esk said dejectedly. "Oh, everything is going wrong!"

"The battle, anyway," she agreed.

"With Bria, too. She—"

"There she is now," the centaur said.

Indeed, Bria was coming back. Esk decided that abjection was the best policy. "Bria, I'm sorry!" he exclaimed. "I'll give you my soul right now!"

She halted. "What?"

"I didn't mean to renege! I just—was confused."

"Esk, I told you I wanted you to wait. It's too big a decision to make on the spur of the moment."

"Yes, but then you asked for it right away, and—"

"I did not! How could you think such a thing?"

"But just now, when you were here—"

"What are you talking about? I've been down looking for a liaison demon the whole time."

"She was," Chex put in. "I saw her down near the river channel."

"But—" Esk said, his confusion getting worse.

"And I found one," Bria said. "A demoness, who said she would talk to her folk."

"Yes, that was Metria, the one who—"

Latia rushed up, gasping. "Crunch says the winged monsters started it! They just flew down and started attacking ogres, so naturally the ogres fought back! Why did they break the truce?"

"The *ogres* started it!" Chex protested. "My sire would not deceive me!"

"Crunch would not deceive an ugly curse fiend," Latia retorted, "even if he were smart enough to make the attempt, and she stupid enough to fall for it. The ogres didn't start it."

"Everybody blames the mischief on somebody else!" Esk cried. "But *somebody* must have started it!"

Then they all did double takes, coming to a common realization. "The demons can change form," Chex said.

"And they love mischief," Latia added.

"And they have motive to mess up our campaign," Bria concluded. "Once I talked to Metria, they knew what we were doing, and who our leader was!"

"So demons in the form of ogres attacked the winged monsters," Chex said.

"And demons in the form of winged monsters attacked the ogres," Latia said.

Esk snapped his fingers. "And Metria—she must have assumed your form, Bria! Now I remember—your clothes reappeared on you as if by magic! You can't dress that way!"

Bria pursed her lips. "She emulated me—and tried to get your soul?"

Esk was overwhelmed by new chagrin. He seemed to be flushing across his entire body.

"I think we had better hurry back and explain to our liaisons," Chex said. "And call a temporary retreat."

"Yes," Latia said. Both hurried away.

Bria approached Esk. "And you almost gave it to her," she said. "What a disaster that would have been!"

"How could I have been such a fool!" Esk moaned.

"Because you are a nice man with a nice soul who just doesn't want to believe evil of anyone," she said. "I think I had better stay close to you, after all. The demoness can bring many messages here."

"I thought she was you, and I told her no," Esk said, still overcome by guilt.

"And she took off her clothes," Bria said. "I suppose I should be insulted, but I'm not. I think maybe she wasn't acting like me, so you were suspicious, and that's why you told her no."

Esk brightened. "Yes! She wasn't acting like you! Only I didn't realize—"

"If I seem to ask you for anything, or offer you anything, just say no," Bria said. "Because it won't be me, it will be her."

"I guess I'm glad it wasn't you," he said. "I apologize for thinking it was you."

"Accepted," she said, and they kissed.

The battle was beginning to clear, as the ogres and winged monsters got the word and retreated. The demon ploy had failed, but the battle had not been won.

By the time the disengagement was complete, the day was late. To Esk it seemed as if only an hour had passed, but it had been many hours.

They discussed the day's events, and worked out a new plan for the morrow. Each monster would take a particular territory, and bash anything else found within that region, regardless of its appearance. That way the demons could not fool them, because each monster would know that no ally would intrude in his particular spot. Marrow would serve as an observer, but not as a messenger, because no messenger could be trusted. The demons would emulate the messenger, and carry false messages. But though there might be a hundred skeletons ranging the battlefield, only one would be the true Marrow, and Esk would be able to identify him by using his magic. He would simply tell any skeleton no, meaning that his appearance was wrong, and if it were a demon, that appearance would change. Only the true Marrow would be unable to change. Esk could have done this with Metria, had he thought of it in time. "So I will listen to Marrow, tomorrow," he concluded. "And I will talk to any others directly, showing my magic, so that I know they are valid, and they know I am."

Then they made their various preparations for the night. Bria joined Esk. "I want to give you something," she murmured.

"No," he said, alarmed.

She laughed. "Don't worry, I'm not the demoness! It's the accommodation spell. I want you to have it."

"Me? Why?"

"I can be very soft when I want to be, but not *that* soft. There are some things flesh can't do with brass. That's why the spell is necessary. Keep the spell; if you don't invoke it, I can't seduce you."

"Uh," he said, nonplussed.

"So if I succeed in doing so, you'll know it isn't me, it's the demoness."

"But—"

"I just thought you'd like the security of knowing that." She handed him the spell.

Esk looked at the object she had given him. It looked like a grain of rice. "This—is it?"

"Some of the elven spells are very small, but potent nonetheless." She smiled briefly. "So to speak."

"But I'll lose this!"

"Swallow it, then; you won't be able to lose it."

"But if I digest it, it will be gone!"

"No, it will be part of you for all your life. You will be able to invoke it anytime by gesturing like this." She made an encompassing sweep with her hands. "All you will have to do is be close to the one you wish to accommodate, whoever that may be."

"But I don't want anyone but you!"

"I was teasing you, Esk," she said gently. "Though it is true it would work with any female. If you get the wrong one, simply dissolve it by reversing the gesture."

"But it's *your* spell!" he protested. "You found it!"

"And you found me, so I am yours."

"But you're the one who needs it, not me. I mean, you're a brassie, in a realm of flesh, so—"

"There's only one I wish to accommodate, so he can have the spell."

"But this is so—"

"Esk," she said seriously. "I asked you for half your soul, so I could love you better and be more like you. You may give me that, when the time is right. You run the risk that if you do, and I am not what I seem, you will have lost half your soul and have nothing in return. Well, I want you to have something back, and I think this is it. I run the risk of giving it to you, and then you leave and I have nothing in return. So we are sharing risks, but if we win, we win together. Eat the spell; make it yours for always."

Esk ate the spell. Then he lay down and held her until he tired and fell asleep, after which she held him until he woke again. Somewhere between they exchanged an apology or two, but these might simply have been kisses.

Next day the campaign resumed. The ogres marched to their assigned quadrants, and the winged monsters flew to theirs. Latia and Chex went to make contact with their liaisons, and Volney with his. Then both groups commenced the bashing of demons, and if the demons resembled other ogres or monsters, so much the better. The voles, forewarned, lay low.

Marrow walked through the Vale, up and down its long length, inspecting the situation. Soon the skeleton returned.

"The monsters are bashing each other again!" he cried. "Sound the retreat!"

"Take my hand," Esk said.

Perplexed, the skeleton extended a bone hand, and Esk took it in his own. "No," he said.

The skeleton shimmered and changed, becoming a grotesque parody of itself. "Get lost, demon," Esk said.

"Demon*ess!*" it said, and Metria's visage formed. "How did you know?"

"Marrow wouldn't tell a fib like that," he replied.

She puffed into irritated vapor and dissipated.

"You really showed her," Bria said, taking his hand. "Come, let's entertain ourselves while the campaign proceeds."

Esk looked around—and saw Bria on his other side, seated a little way away. He looked back at the first. The two were identical.

"Ignore the demoness over there," the closer one said. "She doesn't matter." She drew him in toward her for a kiss.

Esk remembered what Bria had told him the last evening. He could distinguish between the brassie and the demoness— but only by doing something whose success would make him wish he hadn't, because it was possible only with the demoness. Unless he used the accommodation spell, which he had no intention of doing. That left him with no way.

Then he snapped the fingers of his free hand. "What a fool I am!" he exclaimed.

"For waiting so long," the Bria close to him agreed.

"No," he said, invoking his magic.

She fuzzed in outline, then reverted to Metria's form. "Curses, foiled again!" she exclaimed, disgusted, and vaporized.

Esk looked at Bria. "You never spoke!" he exclaimed.

"I knew you could distinguish between us if you wanted to," she said.

"I wanted to, but—" He shrugged. "Not the way you suggested."

"I know I shouldn't tease you like that! It could make trouble."

"Not anymore," he said. "Now that I've finally figured out the obvious."

"Your fleshly brains do seem rather inefficient at times."

"I'm insulted."

"Then I must apologize." She came to him and put her arms around him.

"No," he said.

She halted in place. "I wish you'd let me."

"Just making sure," he said. "You didn't dissolve into vapor, so you are the right one."

She nodded agreement, but still could not kiss him, because of his magic. So he kissed her instead.

The battle died down. The monsters were either tiring or running out of targets. "Do you think the demons have flown?" Bria asked.

"I don't trust them to give up so readily," he replied. "There must be some trick." But he couldn't think what it might be, because the demons certainly seemed gone.

The skeleton returned. "The action has died out everywhere," he reported. "The monsters have run out of demons."

"Give me your hand."

The skeleton extended his hand. "No," Esk said.

"I realize you don't trust this report, but that's the way it is," Marrow said uncomfortably.

"I know it is," Esk said. "I had a false skeleton come before, so I am verifying each."

"Oh, yes, of course. I had forgotten."

Chex and Latia were approaching. Esk touched each, using his magic, and each was genuine. There seemed to be no demon tricks.

"Maybe we had better verify this ourselves," Esk said.

"How can we do that?" Chex asked.

"Well, I can touch things to make sure they aren't demons, and I thought Latia might throw a curse. That could stir them up."

"I think it could," Latia agreed. "But I could verify only a limited region that way, and I have only two curses before I reach a blessing."

"That's my problem too," Esk said. "I can expose one demon at a time, but it would take forever to expose them all, and that wouldn't get rid of them anyway. So let's hope they're really gone."

They walked into the valley, to the nearest square governed by an ogre. The ogre stood and made a monstrous ham fist, ready to pulverize them.

"Oops, I hadn't thought of that," Esk said. "Of course it thinks we're demons pretending to be us."

"You stop the ogre, so I can get close enough to curse his territory," Latia suggested.

"Good enough."

When they reached the edge of the square, the ogre charged. "No!" Esk said sharply.

The ogre, dully surprised, backed off. Latia stepped in and hurled her curse.

A rock, a bush, and a pile of dirt wavered and vaporized. In a moment three demons manifested, rubbing the regions of their posteriors. This was evidently where the curse had scored.

"Go to it, ogre!" Esk cried, as he and Latia scrambled back.

With a horrendous roar, the ogre grabbed at two demons and bashed their heads together, while stomping on the third. The demons, of course, dematerialized. But their cover had been blown.

"If any new objects appear in your territory, bash them!" Esk called to the ogre.

"Me see, hee hee!" the ogre agreed, stomping gleefully. Meaning had returned briefly to its life.

Chex sighed. "Obviously the demons haven't vacated. They are getting plenty of solid-time by concealing themselves as inert objects. They can't hurt us that way, but neither can we drive them out. I fear we are losing this campaign."

Esk nodded glumly. "Fortunately, we do have another resource. I had hoped we wouldn't have to use the wiggle swarm, but it seems we'll have to."

"I vuppove we alwayv knew it would come to thiv," Volney said. "Otherwive we would not have vet up for it."

"But it means that the voles remaining in the Vale will have to evacuate," Chex said. "They won't like that."

"We will do what is nevevvary," Volney said grimly. "I will give the word now." He moved off to find his liaison.

"It seems ironic," Chex remarked, "that in order to save the Vale, we have to come close to destroying it."

"We seem pretty much like monsters ourselves," Bria said. They proceeded dejectedly back toward their camp.

# 16

# SWARM

Wake, Esk!" Bria whispered urgently.

"Huh?" he asked dully, finding it dark. "What time is it?"

"Midnight, or thereabouts," she said. "Esk, I hear something."

He grabbed her hand. "No," he said.

"Oh, don't doubt me now!" she cried. "I'm the real brassie! Just listen."

She was solid, and did not vaporize at his challenge. He had been afraid that Metria was trying to fool him at night, when he couldn't see her. He listened.

There was a kind of distant roaring noise. "Maybe the ogres, on their way home," he said. For they had dismissed the ogres and winged monsters, knowing that their efforts could not after all dislodge the demons.

"Ogres make crashes, not sustained roars. That's something else."

"Maybe Marrow will know. He's been scouting around. He doesn't sleep any more than I do."

"Where is he?"

"Out there somewhere. Should we call him?"

The roaring seemed louder. "Yes." Esk put his hands to his mouth and called: "Marrow! Marrow!"

In a moment they heard the skeleton approaching. "You heard it?" Marrow asked.

Esk took his bone hand and verified his identity. "Yes. Do you know what it is?"

"It is water, and it is coursing this way. Is that significant?"

"Water? From where?"

"From the Kill-Mee River, obviously, or the Kill-Mee lake. That is the only significant source in this vicinity."

"But we are uphill from the Vale! How can the water be coming here?"

Chex stepped up; there was no mistaking her footfalls in the dark. "The demons must be doing it. They are good at channelizing; they may have made a new channel that leads here, and boosted the water with a spell."

"But why?"

"My guess would be to get rid of us," she said. "We have caused them a lot of disturbance, and are planning more, so they may be launching a preemptive strike. I didn't think they had the organization for that, but it may be they do."

"You bet we do!" came Metria's voice. "We learned it from you. Too bad you woke up early."

"We'd better get out of here," Esk said.

"You'll break your legs, trying to run in the dark," the demoness said. "And if you don't run, you'll never escape it. We have a torrent coming! The whole of Lake Kill-Mee is pouring down here!"

"There is lowland all around," Marrow reported. "I believe she is correct; you cannot escape it in time. I am not threatened, of course, as I cannot drown, but the rest of you—"

"I cannot drown either," Bria said.

"Maybe we can throw up a barricade," Esk said, growing desperate.

"Fat chance, mortal," Metria said. "You've had it. My only regret is that you were too stupid to be seduced away from your stupid campaign."

Already the roaring was swelling to an alarming proportion. Water was surging along the lower channels to either side of the hillock they had camped on. "We've got to try!" Esk cried.

Then there was a new crashing. "Hoo, hee, where be?" Crunch's voice bellowed.

"Go away, you big ugly idiot!" Metria screamed.

"She nice too, demon shrew," the ogre bellowed back, pleased at the compliment. In a few more strides he arrived, his huge horny feet striking sparks from the groaning ground they hit. "It get wet, need help yet?"

"Take Volney to safety!" Esk cried, knowing that the vole, being lowest to the ground, was in the greatest immediate danger. Had there been more time, Volney might have tunneled down and made a closed-off chamber that would survive the torrent dry. But now he just had to be gotten away.

"Me roll, take vole," the ogre agreed. There was a sound as he found Volney in the dark and picked him up.

"Oh, phooey!" Metria exclaimed. "One's getting away!"

There was the sound of great wings, and a huge flying shape blotted out the few stars that dared to show their light on this awful night. "Squawk?"

"Sire!" Chex exclaimed. "Take Esk to safety!"

"No!" Esk cried. "Take Latia!" Because he knew that she was older and more frail than he.

Xap didn't argue. He found the curse fiend and got her mounted, then spread his wings and took off.

"Double phooey!" the demoness swore. "Two saved. But that's all, you fool; no other monsters are coming, so you're stuck!"

Indeed, the water was now attacking the hillock, gleefully gouging out chunks of it. By the sound, there was a great deal more coming. Marrow and Bria might survive the flood, being dead already, but Chex and Esk were in real trouble.

"Oh, how I wish I could fly!" the centaur cried over the almost deafening roar.

"I wish you could too!" Esk cried back. Then he had a notion. "Bria—could the accommodation spell make her able to fly?"

"It could make her able to mate with you, but that's all," Bria replied sadly. "Oh, Esk, I don't want to lose you!"

"Take my soul!" he screamed at her. "Take it before I lose it anyway!"

"No! That would only make me love you, and you'd be gone!"

"Then give it to me," Metria said. "No sense in wasting a serviceable soul."

Esk suggested that she do something with herself that perhaps only a demoness could manage; it would have turned a mortal inside out, or worse.

"Get on my back," Chex called. "I'll try to forge through the water."

"You'll never succeed, mule-mane!" the demoness screamed. "The water's too strong!"

Esk was sickly certain she was right, but he staggered through the shallow rushing water toward the centaur. "Where are you, Chex?"

"Here," she called back. Her swishing tail touched his right arm, which felt abruptly light.

He reached her and tried to mount, but the splashing water made her hide slippery. She had spread her wings for stability, and was flapping them, and the downdraft made it worse. He slid off with a splash.

"Try again," she urged. "Maybe Marrow or Bria can boost you." Her nervously switching tail caught him across the back.

Suddenly Esk felt impossibly light. He jumped—and leaped right over her back, landing with another splash on the other side.

"What's the matter?" she cried over the roar.

"I—I jumped over you!" he exclaimed, hardly believing it. "I feel so light!"

"That's true," Marrow said. "Her tail makes things light; I felt it when I rode her and it flicked me. I had forgotten."

"My tail makes things light?" Chex repeated, surprised.

"Chex!" Bria screamed, as Esk jumped again, more carefully, and made it to the centaur's back. *"Flick yourself!"*

"Why—" Chex said.

"That's right!" Esk said. "Your magic must be in your tail! It makes things light enough to fly! That must be why the biting bugs take off when you swish them."

Chex swatted herself with her tail. "Oh my goodness, I feel it! I feel it!" she screamed, delight overcoming her horror of the raging water. "I'm light—I think light enough to fly!"

"Take off!" Bria cried. "Marrow and I will be all right! Get into the sky!"

"Hang on!" Chex said, but Esk needed no warning; he was gripping her mane tightly.

She flapped her wings harder. Her body tilted, as if she were standing on her hind feet. Then it evened as her hind quarters lifted. They were airborne!

She continued to stroke strongly. Her body spun about in the air as it lifted, making Esk dizzy, but they were above the flood and therefore safe. "Just stay up!" he cried. "You don't need to go anywhere, just stay out of the water!"

"I wish I could see better!" she cried back. "I'm so afraid of crashing into something and falling!"

"Then fly straight up, toward the stars!" he replied. "You can see them!"

"Yes!" She pumped slowly on up. The roar of the water diminished slightly as they put distance between them and it. "But I am tiring!" she panted. "I've never flown before!"

"Call for help!" Esk recommended, not sure whether he was being facetious.

She took him literally. "Help!" she screamed.

There was an answering squawk in the distance.

"Sire!" she cried with glad recognition.

Xap Hippogryph flew toward them, and was soon hovering beside his filly. "Sire, I'm tiring, and must come down!" Chex cried. "Can you guide me to a safe landing?"

There was an affirmative squawk. Then Xap led the way, and Chex followed, getting the hang of navigation even as her wings lost strength.

"Flick yourself again!" Esk suggested.

She did it. "Oh, yes, that does help! Now I can make it, I think!"

It was true. The lightness caused by her magic flicking gradually wore off, but could be restored by repeated flicking. All she needed was wing strength, which would come naturally with practice.

Soon they reached the dry hill where Crunch and Volney

and Latia waited. The last thing Esk heard before Chex's hooves touched down in a clumsy but serviceable landing was Metria's anguished "Darn! Darn! Darn!"

They had survived the demons' counterattack.

By morning the water was ebbing. Even the full Kill-Mee lake could not keep the entire region inundated long; the water was running through new chnnels to rejoin the river and surge on down into Lake Ogre-Chobee, where it would surely agitate the curse fiends. Soggy refuse was everywhere, and high-water marks were on the trees. Huge tangles of battered brush were balled in the thickets, while small temporary ponds stewed as the sun heated them.

Gazing at this, Esk realized that he might have climbed a tall, stout tree and rode out the flood. But how could he have known what tree was secure, in the dark? A number of large ones had been undermined and toppled. Also, that would not have helped Chex. So the way it had turned out was best.

The four fleshly members of the party were safe and, thanks to the return of Crunch and Xap, were likely to remain that way. But the two creatures from the gourd were gone.

"They said they would survive," Esk said, trying to sound positive.

"They are all metal and bone," Chex agreed with a similar effort.

"Me look down brook," Crunch offered.

Xap squawked. "Sire will search by air," Chex translated. She spread her wings experimentally, but winced and folded them again. "My muscles are stiff from the night's exertion. I'm not ready to fly again, just yet." Then she looked surprised. "But they are stiff here," she added, reaching back to touch under her wings. "Not here in the pectorals." She cupped her breasts.

"You ninny," Latia said. "Did you really think those were *muscles* you were developing there? You have become a mature female of your species!"

"But I exercised!" Chex protested.

"You exercised, and strengthened your wing muscles, true. But you were also becoming a mare, or a woman, however you choose to call it. Any man could have told you."

Flustered, Chex looked at Esk, who could only nod. Her breasts had never looked much like muscles to him.

For the first time, he saw a centaur blush.

"Well, letv vearch where we can for Bria and Marrow," Volney said diplomatically. "We can vpread out and keep each other in vight, walking downward until we find them."

They did that. Chex walked closest to the Vale on the east, then Esk next west, then Volney, then Latia farthest west. They walked south, pushing through tangles, slogging through mudflats, and making generally messy progress. Far ahead they heard Crunch proceeding in the ogre manner, crashingly, and above Xap wheeled, his sharp eagle eyes peering down.

They searched all morning without success. Esk's heart slowly sank, as if caught in the mud he slogged through. What would he do if they couldn't find Bria?

By evening they knew it was no use. They had canvassed the region up and down and sideways, looking and calling, but had found no sign of either lost creature.

"But they can't die, because they aren't alive," Esk said around the lump in his throat. "They can't be hurt!"

"But they can be mislaid," Chex said. "Perhaps the water caught them and washed them all the way down into Lake Ogre-Chobee, and they are waiting for it to ebb before they slog back here."

"That must be it," Esk agreed. But he knew that it was as much of an effort for Chex to believe this as it was for him. Bria and Marrow should have been able to hold onto something and ride the rushing water out, then call out if stuck in a tangle. Indeed, they could have climbed a tree with far more confidence than Esk, because if it fell they would not be killed. Their complete disappearance was inexplicable.

"We have done what we can," Latia said briskly. "We must simply wait for their return in due course, and get on with our business. The wiggle will be arriving soon."

They foraged and ate and settled for the night. Esk slept alone, and didn't like it; it had not taken long at all for him to get quite accustomed to Bria's company.

As darkness closed, a figure appeared. "Hello, Esk."

"Bria!" he exclaimed joyously. Then he caught on. "Metria. Go away."

"Don't be that way," the demoness said. "You've lost your metal girl, but demon substance can be as good. Let me show you what I can do for you."

"You're trying to corrupt me, so I won't make any more trouble for the demons!" he said angrily.

"That, too. But I have developed respect for you, Esk. You're an interesting man. We could have a lot of fun together." She lay down beside him and drew his head into her bosom. It smelled faintly of smoke.

"I thought you just wanted to be left alone," he said grumpily.

"Yes, when I choose. And to have stimulating company when I choose. I misjudged you, before, so I'm making up for that now. Come, have a pleasant night with me; your companions need not know."

"No!" he gritted.

"Oh, fudge," she said. "You keep doing that, you fool." She dissolved into vapor and was gone.

So the demons knew of their loss. That did not make Esk feel any better. He knew he could not trust Metria, yet for a moment in his sorrow and loneliness, he had almost been tempted. He felt guilty for that.

Next day the water was down further, but there was still no sign of Bria or Marrow. There was, however, another arrival: Xap reported a pretty vole coming along the path from the east, looking good enough to eat.

"That'v Wilda," Volney said. "Now we muvt vet up for the vwarm."

Well, this might help take their minds off their lost companions. They plunged into this new aspect of their campaign with vigor.

Wilda Wiggle was indeed a very pretty figure of volishness. She wore her surface coat, gray, with intense brown eyes. Her fur almost glowed, and her contours were softly rounded. Esk was sure that if he had been a vole, he would have found her compellingly luscious. It was hard to believe that this dulcet creature could be the origin of the worst menace of Xanth: a wiggle swarm.

But it was so. "Have you the plafe?" she asked, speaking the humanoid language as well as Volney did, but with an accent.

"We have," Esk assured her.

"Have you the fpell?"

"We have."

"Ekfellent. I have mated, and muft foon make my neft."

"The way we have set it up," Esk explained, "is that you will select a site near the center of the Vale. Then, before the larvae hatch and swarm, you and all other vulnerable creatures will evacuate the Vale, and we'll lay down the containment spell, which is really an aspect of the Void, and leave it in place until the swarm is done. Then we'll fold up the Void again, and the voles will return to restore the river. The demon's dikes will be hopelessly ruined, of course, so the restoration will be easy."

Wilda considered. "I have two queftionf," she said, wiggling her nose delicately. "Are you fure the demonf will leave?"

"Well, we think they will, because they won't enjoy the swarming at all, and once their dikes are ruined they'll have to do the work all over again, and demons are not noted for their patience. If it doesn't work, we'll just have to think of something else."

"And who will fet out the Void, and fetch it back again?"

"Why, Marrow will do that," Esk said. "You haven't met Marrow yet; he's a—" He broke off.

"Oops," Chex said.

"Oh, my!" Latia said. "We forgot that we needed him for that little chore!"

"Do you folk have a problem?" Metria inquired, coalescing.

"You've been listening!" Esk said accusingly.

"Of course," she said. "I'm the demon liaison, after all. Your brassy girlfriend appointed me."

"That's brassie!" Esk snapped. "Not brassy."

"I don't think you're going to find your bone friend in

time," the demoness said, "or your metal one. Considering that we hold both hostage."

"What?" Esk gasped.

"Well, I really don't expect you to believe me, but it's true. We couldn't let you folk proceed with your plan unchallenged, after all. You can have them back the moment you agree to stop harassing us and go home."

"Damn you!" Esk swore.

"That's hard to do, just as it's hard to kill your dead friends. All we can do is hold them. Are you ready to deal?"

"No!" Esk cried in fury and anguish. "I'll handle that Void myself!"

"Esk, you'll be holed!" Chex protested. "You wouldn't survive!"

"I'm an old crone; I'll do it," Latia said. "It doesn't matter much if I die."

"I'll never understand you mortals' will to sacrifice," Metria said. "It won't work, regardless, because whoever remains in the Vale will be holed and killed, and won't be able to remove the Void anyway."

They exchanged glances. "She's right," Chex said. "A fleshly creature can't do it."

"But a demonic creature might," Metria said. "Why don't you ask me?"

"What?"

"I said—"

"I know what you said. Even if a demon could handle the Void, which no demon can, why would you? This is to drive you out of the Vale!"

"I can't touch the Void, 'tis true. But I could protect a mortal from the swarm, by making myself into an invisible shield."

"You know, she could," Chex said. "But—"

"But why? I'll tell you why," Metria said. "It's because we demons have nothing to fear from the wiggles. We can either vaporize or make ourselves too hard for them to penetrate. We just don't like the mess they will make of our dikes. But you mortals won't believe that, so we'll have to prove it the hard way. Are you ready to deal?"

"Deal?" Esk asked. He was getting bewildered, as he

tended to do when events became too surprising.

"I'll help you with the Void," Metria said. "And we will release our hostages to you. If."

"If what?" Esk asked guardedly.

"If, after you are satisfied that you can't drive us from the Vale, you will put the same effort into solving our problem that you have put into trying to get rid of us."

"Us help you?" Esk demanded. "That would be crazy!"

"Suit yourself," she said, beginning to fade.

"Wait!" he cried. "I didn't say I wouldn't!"

She resolidified. "Now you are getting sensible. It isn't much we ask, after all."

"Let me see whether I understand this correctly," Chex said. "You are allowing us one more try at getting you demons out of the Vale of the Vole, and if we fail, then we must try as hard to get rid of the hummers as we did to get rid of you."

"That's it," Metria agreed.

"But if we fail to get rid of you, we may fail to get rid of the hummers, too!"

"But you'll try as hard as you can, and you might have better success," the demoness said. "You fleshly creatures have souls, and therefore a degree of honor; we think it's worth the deal."

"And we get Bria and Marrow back," Esk said.

"The moment you start working for us," Metria agreed.

"All right," Esk said. "I'll make the deal."

"Now wait," Chex protested. "This isn't tight. If we do drive the demons out, we won't get back the hostages, and—"

"Never mind," Esk said. "I have my reason. I'm making the deal, not you." He turned to the demoness. "I will handle the Void; you will protect me."

"But vhe may not!" Volney said. "How can you truvt her with your life?"

"Because I'm making the deal," Esk said. "It's my responsibility. If I die, then the deal is off, and the rest of you can do what you want. So the demoness has some incentive to honor her part of it, and keep me alive."

Metria nodded. "You *have* gotten smarter, mortal."

"But then the hostages would not be freed," Chex said.

"I'm the one who is love with Bria, not you," Esk said. "If I'm gone, there's no such lever on you. And the demons don't want the hostages anyway; they're just using them against us. So if I don't make it, you just quit and go home, because the Vale will be locked forever in the Void, and of no further use to either the voles or the demons. We're playing for double or nothing, here; if Metria lets me die, the demons lose as much as we or the voles do. More, actually, because the demons already control the Vale, and the voles will be driven away if the demons remain."

"You've learned to play hardball," Chex said. The term derived from Mundania, wherein the ball might be soft, but the play bashed heads. Ogres were fans of Mundane ball games, as they were of Mundane politics, because of the extreme violence there.

"It will take me a day to build my neft, and another to lay my eggf," Wilda said. "Can the volef evacuate in that time?"

"They'll have to," Volney said. "Let'v get on it."

They got on it. They helped organize the evacuation of the voles from the Vale, while Wilda built her nest in the center beside the deleted Kill-Mee River. The voles emerged from their deep tunnels in families, with cute little ones scrambling along behind their elders. All of them changed from their subterranean outfits to their surface coats, whose gray color resisted the brightness and heat of the sunlight better.

The demons watched cynically. They didn't care whether the voles left or stayed; they intended to govern the Vale their way regardless. Similarly they watched Wilda at her labor fashioning her nest. She gathered sticks and stones and broken bones, and sand and mud and other crud, and formed a small round house, chinking every crevice tight. Then she climbed into that house and pulled the lid down securely.

The voles were only half evacuated then, but that was on schedule, because they had one more day. They toiled on out, all day and all night, until the Vale was entirely clear. The demons remained where they were, unconcerned.

Esk took the wadded-up Void, which Chex had saved in her pack, and carried it to a spot near the nest. "Where are you, Metria?" he called.

The demoness materialized beside him. "Here I am, mortal. What's on your foolhardy mind?"

"It's almost time. I just want you to be here with me when I open the Void."

"I will be as close to you as a second skin," she assured him with, it seemed, a certain relish.

The lid lifted off the nest. Wilda's head poked out. "I have an hour to get clear," she said, spying Esk. "If everything ready? No volef remain?"

"It's ready," Esk said.

Wilda scrambled out of the nest, let the lid fall back into place, and hurried toward the forest. She knew that the wiggle larvae had no discrimination; they would hole her as readily as anything else in their path.

Just as she plunged into the forest, Esk heard a noise from the nest. The larvae were starting to hatch!

He took out the Void and unfolded it. He laid it out on the ground and stepped away from the black hole that appeared. It might be merely an aspect of the Void annex of the gourd, but it looked deep, and he didn't want to fall in.

The sounds were increasing at the nest. "Time to shield me," he told Metria.

"That I will do, mortal man," she agreed. She wavered, and became a flat sheet. This sheet floated toward him, becoming translucent, then transparent. It brushed up against him, and passed through his clothing, plastering itself to his body.

"Hey!" he protested as it pressed against his face, threatening to smother him. "I have to breathe, you know!"

"So you do, mortal," she said. "I forgot." A wrinkle formed, so that the fit against his face was not quite tight, and air could get in from the sides.

The wiggles were definitely swarming now. Holes were appearing in the nest, and their *zzapping* spread out in all directions.

"How could you pass through my clothing, but still stop wiggles?" he asked nervously.

"I phased out and in again," the sheet replied. It continued to close about his torso, wrapping about his arms and legs. She had not been joking about being as close to him as a second skin!

"Hey!" he exclaimed, as the sheet abruptly tickled him in the crotch. It was conforming itself precisely to his private parts. "Stop that!"

"Make me, mortal!" the sheet replied, giving him an embarrassing squeeze.

Esk jumped, turned, and started to stride away. "Don't turn!" the sheet cried.

*Zzapp!*

"Ouch!" He clapped his hand to a buttock.

"I told you not to turn," the sheet said. "I am covering you only on the front. You got tagged by a wiggle."

Indeed, there was blood on his hand where he had touched his buttock. A passing wiggle larva had grazed him. He hastily turned to face the nest again—and felt something bounce off his chest.

"Just in time," the sheet said. "If that had struck your back, it would have holed you."

Now the *zzapps* of the wiggle larvae were all around him, passing so thickly that there was no way to avoid them. Metria was indeed protecting him. He just wished that she wasn't so conscientious about certain regions of his anatomy.

"I never promised you I wouldn't enjoy it," the sheet said, giving him yet another embarrassing tickle. Yet at the same time a *zzapp* bounced off there, so he knew that this closeness was necessary. She was teasing him, but also doing the job she had promised. She evidently did have a certain interest in his body, though he couldn't see why; if she wanted a body, why didn't she have a male demon assume that shape?

The carnage of the wiggle swarm was becoming horrendous. The shrubs and trees were getting holed and tattered as the tiny wormlike creatures *zzapped* through. Each wiggle larva would jump forward a short distance, then hover in place in the air, absolutely still. It was evidently tasting its surroundings to discover whether they matched its need. Then, unpredictably, it would jump forward again. If anything was in its path, it simply tunneled magically through. That was why wiggles were considered the worst scourge of Xanth; a swarm ruined just about everything in the vicinity.

Except the demons. The demons were ignoring the larvae, or at least were not alarmed by them. A demon in the vapor state could not be hurt by holing, and they were achieving such compactness when solid that the wiggles bounced off, as they did from Esk. Metria was right: this was no way to drive out the demons.

However, if anything happened to Esk, all the demons would be trapped in the Void, for they could not escape it. They weren't in any discomfort within it, they simply could not pass its outer rim, which was near the edge of the Vale. That would be one way to rid the Vale of them. The only trouble was that it would rid the Vale of serviceability for anything else; any voles who entered the Void would not be able to depart again, ever.

No, wait. He had miscalculated. Once the wiggle swarm was gone, anyone, human or vole, could enter, fold up the central hole, and abolish the Void. Why hadn't he thought of that before? He had never had to risk his life here.

But the demoness hadn't realized it either, or Chex, so at least he had company in his foolishness. That was a comfort. Anyway, *someone* would have had to risk his life, in order to place the Void, and that person would have been stuck in it with the wiggles, and he, Esk, was the only one Metria would have been willing to protect, so it all came out the same.

The hours passed as the carnage proceeded. The *zzapps* of the wiggles became fewer, here, as their radius of destruction increased, but Esk knew better than to take a chance; one holing by one tardy larva could still put him away. That meant that he remained in close—very close!—contact with Metria. After a long while she tired of nudging and tickling him in intimate regions, having evidently had as much fun as she wanted with him, but they were still stuck with each other's company.

"Why, really, did you make this deal?" he asked her.

"To get this close to you without your saying no, of course," the sheet responded promptly. "How else could I surround your flesh with mine for hours at a stretch?" She squeezed him in a localized region, making her meaning considerably clearer than be liked.

"I don't think so," he retorted. "Your sole object has been to embarrass me or subvert me so that I could not be an effective leader against the demons. Now that we're cooperating, there cannot be much pleasure for you in my company. You had to know you were letting yourself in for a long, dull day. So why did you do it?"

"You are getting smart again," she said. "I suppose now there is no reason not to tell you the truth. We really do want to be rid of the hummers; they are just about as bad to us as the wiggle swarm is to you. Every time we try to settle down in solid state to rest, they drive us crazy with their humming. We have tried everything we can think of to get rid of them, but they just keep getting worse. When we saw how determined and clever you were getting in trying to deal with us, it just seemed that you might even solve our problem with the hummers if you had reason. That is the truth. We're desperate, and we want your help. Without it, we're going to have to vacate the Vale anyway."

"You mean if we had just done nothing, you demons would have gone, and the voles' problem would have been solved?" Esk asked, chagrined.

"It is an irony, isn't it," she agreed complacently.

"You don't know how that makes me feel!"

"Oh, I know," she said. "Even if you can't solve our problem, I will have some delight in remembering how much frustration I caused you simply by telling you the truth."

Esk laughed somewhat bitterly. "You outsmarted me, all right! Yet if I had it to do over again, I probably would, because—"

"Because of the metal girl? You mortals do put inordinate stress on relationships."

"You do have her hostage? You weren't just telling us that to cause more mischief?"

"We do have them both. Remember, I was with you when you deserted them; we knew exactly where they were. We couldn't abduct you, because we wanted your help, but when you left them behind, they were ready prey. They thought we were actually rescuing them, at first, but then they realized who we were, and the girl started crying and saying your name. It was quite amusing."

"Damn you!" Esk repeated.

"We've been through that before," she reminded him.

Esk shut up. She was still baiting him, when she had opportunity. He was already committed to help her cause; there was no need to give her extra satisfaction.

Night fell, and he lay down and slept, carefully facing toward the wiggle nest. The demoness stroked his hair in the manner Bria had, using a flap of her sheet, but he refused to curse her again. Tomorrow he would be with Bria again; that made it bearable.

By noon the next day the wiggles had cleared, and it was safe to fold up the Void. Esk did so, and Metria gave him a final goose and separated from him. He had failed, as she had predicted, and now had a new chore to tackle.

The Vale was in shambles. The dikes made by the demons were rubble, holed so many times they had collapsed. The trees were tattered and many would die. The water had spread out, passing through the holes, and formed a great messy marsh. The whole region was deathly quiet.

Esk, about to fold up the Void, paused. "Metria—do you notice anything?"

She formed in her natural guise. "I notice you have ruined the Vale for vole and demon by your foolish exercise. It will be a real chore to rebuild those dikes."

"Why rebuild them?"

"To get rid of the hummers, of course."

"Listen, Metria. What do you hear?"

She listened. "Absolutely nothing. It's eerie."

"What about the hummers?"

She was so surprised that she dissipated into vapor, and then re-formed. "They're gone!"

Esk had been thinking fast. Now it burst upon him in much the way the sun burst out of a smothering cloud. "Don't you see, demoness—it is the environment that spawns the hummers! The spread of the water evidently stifles them. There used to be a lot of water in the Vale, because of the way the Kiss-Mee River meandered. Then you channelized it, and the land dried out, and the hummers increased. Maybe they need stagnant pools such as the ones you left in the cutoff meanders; flowing water washes them out. I don't know the exact pattern, but I'm sure now that it involves the disruption of the natural river. Now the hummers are gone—but if you channelize the river again, they will return worse than ever! *That's* the answer to your problem—to restore the Kiss-Mee River, and keep every meander!"

She seemed stunned, which was unusual for a demon. "When we straightened the river—the hummers got worse. Now they're gone. But we can't leave the Vale in a stew like this; even the voles wouldn't be able to use it. Demons and voles need dry land to camp on."

"You can have the dry land," Esk said warmly. "Just make it *natural* land. Let nature take its course. That means meanders, and occasional flooding. It may be inconvenient for you, but it must be devastating to the hummers, who probably need still, stagnant water to breed in, like that in your holding ponds, and dry land to forage on, like the Vale the way you made it. Let the river change its level as it wishes, and the land alternately flood and dry out, and you should have very few hummer problems. I'm only conjecturing, of course, but doesn't it make sense to you?"

She listened again, and heard no hummers again. "It does make sense to me, mortal. Let me consult with my kind." She vaporized.

Esk folded the Void carefully, and wadded it into a fist-sized ball. They would have to return it to the gourd, but one of their number who had not yet invoked the pathfinder spell could do that, perhaps Marrow. He, Esk, would have to remain here until the demons were satisfied about his solution to the hummer problem, but that was all right; he didn't have any other pressing destination.

As he walked slushily out of the Vale, Metria reappeared. "We'll give it a try, mortal. We'll even help the voles restore the river. Meanwhile, we'll release the hostages; they're a bother to keep anyway."

And there at the edge of the forest was Marrow—and Bria. The brassie girl rushed down to fling herself into his arms. "I was so afraid you had fallen and drowned!" she exclaimed. "The demons wouldn't tell us anything!"

"They're demonic," he agreed. "But I think I have solved their problem with the hummers. The demons are going to help restore the Kiss-Mee River to its natural state."

Then there was a flurry of discussion, as things were

worked out. Wilda Wiggle, having passed beyond her reproduction cycle, was now ready to settle down with a male for
fun and companionship, and she still liked Volney. The two
were conversing by the shattered riverbank, and it seemed that
some of the water's affection was returning, for they were
touching noses in a fashion that was surely the volish kiss.

Marrow was going to return the Void, then see what else
he could do to become real; he thought the folk at Castle
Roogna might be able to use his services in looking for the
lost Good Magician. Latia was returning to her people, her
mission completed; that success would ensure proper respect
for her during her retirement. Xap and Crunch departed together, evidently friends now. And Chex—

"I believe I have a date with a winged centaur," she said,
spreading her wings. "I don't think I need to be concerned
anymore about the acceptance of my species. I mean to generate my own species." She flicked herself with her tail and
took off, and her happiness seemed to spread out in ripples.

A shape appeared in the sky. For a moment Esk thought it
was Chex returning, but instead it was her sire Xap. He
landed before Esk and squawked.

Esk could not understand the winged-monster language,
but he thought he might guess. "You say you have a message
from my grandfather, Crunch Ogre, that I have performed an
act of ogreish destruction, absolutely ruining the Vale, so I
am now considered an adult in the ogreish mode?"

Xap squawked agreement, and took off again. "Tell him I
appreciate his news!" Esk called. "I never would have
guessed, otherwise!"

Xap's final squawk sounded very like laughter. Evidently
the hippogryph's sense of humor was more liberal than his
centaur filly's.

"I shall have to stay here awhile," Esk told Bria. "I promised the demons, and of course I'd like to see the Vale of the
Vole restored to its original beauty, and the Kiss-Mee River
to its former affection. So if you—"

"Speaking of affection," she murmured, "let's go somewhere private and try out that accommodation spell. Now that
your grandfather says you are adult, you should be able to
handle an adult relationship."

"Uh, I meant, if you want half my soul now—"

"That, too," she agreed. Then she hugged him, and he knew that it didn't matter what was done in what order; they would be together.